# A THOUSAND WORDS

UNBROKEN #1

## M. A. FRÉCHETTE

*She's trapped in a nightmare.*
*Unleashing his own could set her free.*

Copyright ©2021 by M. A. Fréchette
ISBN: 978-1-77706-985-8
Hardcover 6 x 9

Cover and formatting by M. A. Fréchette
Stock from iStock
www.istockphoto.com
Editing by D.W. Vogel
www.wendyvogelbooks.com
Blurb by The Blurb Wizard
theblurbwizard.wordpress.com/services-and-rates/

 Created with Vellum

# 1

## ELORA

*T*he alarm rang throughout the house; the first of two set every day of the week at 4:45 and 5:00.

Elora rushed forward and turned it off, her heart racing as she checked on the water inside the pot. It hadn't started to boil yet. There was no way supper would be ready on time.

She grabbed the handles of the cookware, moving it an inch forward, hoping it would suddenly catch more heat and magically bubble within the next few seconds, but all it did was slosh around.

It was the first time in her marriage that her husband's meal wouldn't be ready right as he arrived home, and her stomach tightened at how he'd react.

She glanced at her cellphone as it blinked with a bright blue light, and bit her lower lip.

Another text from her best friend Liana. They'd distracted her for the past few hours; one of the reasons why her meal preparations were delayed. She just hoped Richard wouldn't be too angry with her when he got home.

She glanced at the newest message.

*Liana: Come on. Ask him.*

The second alarm rang, and Elora quickly pushed the button to silence it. She grabbed the spaghettini box, hovering near the pot as tiny bubbles began forming from the heat. If she could just put the pasta inside, at least she'd have something to show for progress.

Three minutes left.

Her pulse sped as the water bubbled higher, and she dumped the spaghettini inside, sweat beading across her forehead.

Two minutes.

Time enough to recheck that everything else was perfect; supper being late was bad enough, but she wouldn't have anything else wrong. She wiped the counter once more, then rushed to the dining room table and placed Richard's chair aligned with the split down the middle.

The sound of the door opening sent butterflies rushing through her stomach. Not the romantic sort; the ones that burned the back of her throat with acid reflux. She swallowed several times, wiping her sweaty palms against the apron. Another click sounded through the house, and she hurried to the entrance.

"How was work?" Elora asked, picking up his briefcase and pushing it between the shoe rack and the small table. When he frowned, she focused on the silver case. It was crooked. She fished between it and the wall and removed a pebble, allowing it to stand straight as usual. The vacuum never picked up everything, and in her rush for time, she'd forgotten to sweep with the broom for good measure. She had already screwed up and hadn't even gotten the chance to ask him permission.

Richard let out a sigh. "Might be another business trip coming up this weekend." He took off his shoes and waited as she placed them with the other footwear. "I'll be gone Friday and back on Sunday." He hung his keys on the third hook from the right.

It was as though the stars aligned for the first time in her life. Maybe she really could go to the author convention with Liana?

She took a deep breath, and forced a bigger smile. "Supper will be ready very, very soon. But do you want a beer in the meantime? It'll give you a chance to relax before eating." She glanced over her shoulder as she strode toward the fridge.

"Sure," he called out.

Her shoulders relaxed a bit as she grabbed a beer and walked into the living room. He sat on the couch, his legs stretched out.

*So far, so good.*

"Here." She handed him the refreshment, and he eyed it.

"And how am I supposed to drink it?" he asked in a sharp tone.

Her pulse sped. "Sorry. I forgot." She dashed into the kitchen and found the opener, then made her way back to him while popping the cap off.

He smiled as he took it, but it didn't reach his green eyes. "Thanks."

She gave a quick nod, then returned to the meal. Three years of marriage, and she still screwed things up.

As she stared at the boiling water, waiting for the pasta to finish, she mentally rehearsed how she'd ask permission.

*There's a convention this week and guess what? No.*

Cringing at her thoughts, she shook her head.

*Liana invited me to… no. My book won an award and… Damn.*

She just had to do it. Glancing at the timer, she wiped her hands. With Liana's phone call, Elora had gotten behind on preparations. She was lucky he didn't comment about it, even if she could tell it annoyed him.

The email came two weeks ago. Elora's book, *My Imaginary Mom*, was named Picture Book of the year by the Canadian Coping for Kids Society. Her face had nearly split from smiling so much.

But she didn't have enough money to her name for a ticket to the convention. Luckily, she lived in the same city, so travel wasn't an issue, but what she earned in royalties became Richard's money, and covered groceries. It wasn't ever hers to spend. There were so many reasons she couldn't go, but Liana pushed, and in truth, Elora really wanted to attend.

But with Richard annoyed, asking was a dreadful idea.

*There's always an excuse. Do it.*

Taking a deep breath, she placed the strainer in the sink. "Richard?"

"Yes?" His tone sounded light, and so she jumped for the chance.

"I've... I'm invited to an author's convention here in town. My picture book won best in its category, and I was wondering if it would be okay if I attended?" She swallowed, trying to get rid of the dryness in her mouth. "Liana is going as well, and offered to pay for the Book Fair ticket." She picked up the pot and moved to the sink.

Richard grabbed the handles with her, and a quiver shot through her; she hadn't felt him approaching. "You want to spend a few nights in a hotel, is that it?" he asked coolly.

She stiffened. "The award is on Saturday, so I'd be there from ten in the morning to three in the afternoon. I wouldn't sleep there," she whispered as he tilted the pot. Boiling water splashed, and she sucked in air as a few droplets burned her arm.

He pulled it and placed it on the oven. "Did it get you?" he asked, running the washcloth under cold spray. He applied it on a few red blotches on her skin. "I guess that's why you cook; I'm so clumsy."

She laughed, but it didn't sound real to her own ears. "You provide for both of us; you do enough work as it is."

When he moved away, she poured the sauce, careful to wipe any drips before they stained. She stirred, keeping her focus on the meal she prepared. "It would only be Saturday... Is it okay?"

She grabbed a plate and spooned a good helping of pasta onto it. When she turned, her breath caught in her throat. He leaned on the large mahogany dining room table, arms crossed.

"And your friend will pay for it? Just like that?" He scoffed. "You'll need money, and once again, it's me who has to pay." He passed his fingers through his straw-blond hair. "Don't you already have enough? A house, nice clothes, everything you desire for your little coloring hobby?" He rolled his eyes.

The last part was another stab, but she pushed down the hurt as usual. "Of course I'm grateful, but——"

"But what?" He straightened, and she tightened her grip on the plate. "You'd have nothing if it wasn't for me. You realize that, right?"

"I know, and I'm so lucky to have you." She took a tentative step, and when he didn't yell, she moved to the table and put his meal at the head. "I just wanted to mention the award comes with prize money. It's something to give back for the times you've spent on me, even though you never need to."

He sat, drumming his fingers on the surface. His gaze was distant, like he thought about it. But she didn't want to get her hopes up. Too many occasions they'd alight only to be smothered.

"Just Saturday."

Part of her didn't seem to process the information correctly for a few seconds. She blinked a few times, her pulse speeding.

She quickly wrapped her arms around him, smiling ear to ear. "Oh, thank you so much."

"And don't make a habit of this." He grabbed his fork. "I'm sure your friend doesn't mind paying this once, but you can't leech off everyone like you do with me. Understand?"

Her shoulders slumped, but she kept the smile in place. "Definitely. I'll join you in a second."

Once back in the kitchen, she served her own plate, but put it down next to her cellphone.

*Elora: I'll be at the convention on Saturday.*

# 2

# ELORA

"*S*top being a baby," Elora muttered to herself. Swallowing hard, she tried getting rid of the lump tightening inside her throat.

She dabbed another layer of toner beneath her eyes, over the redness. On the rare occasions Richard allowed her to go anywhere, he always change his mind and argue.

This time was worse since he threatened to quit his job because of the stress. He said dealing with both his work and her mood swings was too much. That he wouldn't be able to afford the home anymore. She almost let him win and canceled going to the Book Fair with the threat lingering over her. He tugged at the chain binding her to him, and she usually gave up quickly.

But not this time.

Through his yelling, she stood her ground. And here she was in the washrooms of the convention center. There'd be hell to pay when she got back home. Her stomach churned, and she held her breath; the smell of cleaner products not helping her nausea.

Backing away from the large washroom mirror, she squinted. Was it obvious that she cried her eyes out? The sound of dripping water from the faucets ticked into the speckled sinks like a countdown clock. Every second brought her closer to the end of this day. She couldn't figure out if she wanted it to be over quickly or linger forever.

With a sigh, she patted her dress before stepping out.

An authors' convention. A place Elora had dreamed of attending for years. From the earliest character she drew and the short story she wrote, to the first picture book published.

Groups of people walked past, and a few recognized Elora from her photo as a special guest. It was nerve-wracking, yet so exciting. The Book Fair took place in a large hall, separated into a dozen sections, each representing different age categories and genres.

She moved to the children's section where she was most at ease, but stopped when someone called her name.

"Elora!" Liana waved frantically. "Come on. It's about to start." Elora's best friend bounced on her high heels, a feat Elora never understood since she wore flats and managed to fall with those.

*Flats to fall flat on my face… Fitting.*

Elora arched an eyebrow as she approached.

Liana grasped Elora's hands and continued bouncing a bit. Her tight dark red dress fit her like a glove, not leaving anything to the imagination. Elora sometimes envied her friend's self-esteem.

Her outfit was a plain summer dress. Purple lilacs on white, elastic hugging her breasts and waist, and it finished in a flowing design from her hips to her knees. Richard had approved, but insisted she wear a sweater. She had, but once she realized it was warm inside the hall, she took it off. Elora didn't enjoy breaking her word, especially when it was a simple request, but she wasn't about to have a heat stroke.

"What's going on?" Elora asked, staring above Liana's shoulder as a crowd of people gathered closer to the stage of the adult romance section.

Liana gave a devilish smile. "Well, there's a contest, and I… paid for two tickets for us."

Her pulse raced. Liana didn't enter contests unless the reward was worth winning. In other words, something likely to terrify Elora. "You what? What prize?"

She kept a firm grasp on Elora's hand, pulling her toward the stage. They'd announce the winner any minute.

Elora's gaze swept the poster advertising the contest. The chance to win a photoshoot with a male model featured in a charity calendar the prior year.

She let out a groan.

"It's fine. Don't worry. With the amount of people who put their names in, the odds of you winning are——"

The microphone's high-pitched sound echoed across the room, and Elora jumped. She twisted her fingers as the woman who tapped it winced, a sheepish smile accompanying her small blush.

"Sorry about that, ladies. Now, I know everyone here would die for a photoshoot with Mr. July, but only one can win this fabulous prize. And you have to promise once I read the winner's name, there won't be any cat fights," she stated with a wink and a wiggle of her finger.

Elora's heart thumped in her ribcage.

*Just do it already. I want to leave.*

"Before we pick the winner, I should introduce the man who made this contest a possibility." The woman motioned to the side and thunderous screams accompanied the man who walked onto the stage.

Elora breath hitched for reasons she hadn't felt in years.

Vincent Voden.

*He's… handsome. And that's an understatement.*

He wore a suit, giving him the air of sophistication with a hint of darkness. He smiled and waved at the crowd, and she cursed herself for the way her body reacted. A polite gesture should never make her gooey, and yet, there she was, melting on the spot.

People in the crowd gathered closer as a few took out their cell-phones to get shots of him. It took a few seconds for her to realize the women had pushed Elora forward, placing her at the front.

She locked gazes with Vincent. His lips curled in a half-smile, and warmth heated her cheeks as she glanced away.

"I'm honored to see so many wonderful entrants for this contest. Proceeds from the ticket prices are donated to the animal shelter here in the city, and so it's for a good cause." His voice was deep, gentle, but it held a note of command.

They caught one another's stare, and when he grinned at her, she shrank back. His gaze darkened when she did, so she stiffened, trying to hold her ground—oh how she tried—but fear won.

Glancing over her shoulder for Liana, she spotted her at the rear of the crowd. Not that Liana would have noticed; she practically drooled at the male model on stage. Liana, while happily married, often commented there was nothing wrong with looking at attractive people.

The microphone buzzed, and it brought Elora's attention to the large black box next to the podium. "Now, we'll pick the winner—"

Vincent leaned near the woman's ear, and she flushed a deep shade of red. She frowned at first, but when he withdrew, she gave a slow nod.

*Apparently, he's got charm on everyone.*

The woman cleared her voice. "We'll be announcing the winner in a minute."

Most women booed, but the host distracted them with a list of tomorrow's prizes. Part of Elora wanted to bolt in case they picked her. If she wasn't there, they'd pick another name.

Vincent vanished behind the curtains to the side, and Elora pushed through the crowd, aiming for the rear to be with Liana. This was ridiculous. While Elora enjoyed reading romances, there was a good reason she didn't write them. Love was fictional and belonged in fantasy books along with other myths. Besides, people always said to create from experience.

Before she had the chance to get away, Vincent returned on stage to the renewed cheers of the crowd. He took his jacket off slowly, and Elora forgot her escape plan as she gawked. The white dress shirt he wore stretched against hard muscles as he unbuttoned the cuff to his sleeve and rolled it. Tattoos snaked the skin of his forearm, disappearing underneath his clothes. What else was on the rest of his body?

At the thought, she shook her head. She had no business thinking anything like that, being married.

*Why am I fooling myself? He's a man, and they're all the same.*

Vincent pushed his hands into his pockets and waited.

"And here's the moment we've waited for," the woman announced, waving at the male model.

He reached into the black box, rummaging inside for a few seconds before pulling out a folded piece of paper. Elora swallowed hard as he unfolded it, reading the name. He handed it to the announcer who leaned toward the microphone, holding the note higher to read it.

"Elora Reverie!"

The world shrunk. Elora couldn't breathe. A hand grasped her arm, and she yelped.

"Elora? Hey…" Liana's voice cut through Elora's panic, and she blinked several times before her mind caught up with what happened.

The crowd fell silent as they stared at her; a few seemed concerned, but most looked at her as though she had gone mad.

*Maybe I have.*

Elora let out a breath. "Sorry… There was so much noise, and I didn't realize…"

"It's fine." She rubbed Elora's arm. "You won. Go collect your prize." She gave an encouraging smile.

*Right. The contest.*

Heat engulfed Elora's body, but it drained away fast. Her blood seemed to freeze as Vincent took deliberately slow steps down the stairs of the stage, his hands inside his pockets as he approached. His irises were dark brown, and he stared at Elora with an intensity she couldn't describe. Up close, his five o'clock stubble gave him a laid back, yet wild appearance. Without a smile, though, he had a dangerous look, and she wished his mouth curled up.

"Elora Reverie?" he asked, keeping a respectful distance between them. She imagined he didn't want her flying off the handle.

She nodded, wiping her sweaty palms on her dress. "Yes."

He motioned to the side and waited for her to follow. Her eyes widened at the thought of going anywhere with him, but she didn't need to make a bigger scene. So she followed, twirling her fingers together and keeping her head down. They strode up the stairs, and she stiffened to keep from running in the opposite direction. She should've continued walking toward the kids' section when she'd had the chance.

The woman on the stage cleared her throat. "Congratulations!" Her fake enthusiasm didn't match her gaze. "You're quite lucky. Children's book of the year, and now this. Feels like you're holding all the luck to yourself."

Elora stared at her feet, light shining on the small plastic decoration on the flats catching her eye, and keeping her distracted from what was going on.

*Why am I here? I just wanted to stick to my section. This isn't the place for me. Why can't I vanish?*

Vincent moved closer, and Elora pressed her lips tight to keep from gasping at the sudden movement. "I doubt winning an award for writing a book is based on luck, Miss Mervat. Based on talent, I'd say." Although he spoke the words matter-of-factly, his voice had an edge of coldness to it.

The woman shifted on her high heels, a pink hue coloring her ears and face before addressing the crowd. "Of course. Well, enjoy your prize then, *Mrs.* Reverie."

The word hit Elora like a slap.

People applauded, but it was half-hearted, and most of the women had dispersed. Liana gave Elora a thumbs up before leaving with the cluster.

She wanted to tell the announcer to have Vincent pick another name, but the woman was gone. It wasn't fair that Elora won a prize she didn't want.

But Vincent had other plans. He slid in front of her and stared toward the side of the stage. "Let's talk."

"About what?"

He smiled, and warmth bubbled through her. "Winning a photoshoot together."

Before she thought it through, she followed him to the side of the stage and away from prying eyes.

## 3

# VINCENT

*V*incent opened the door to a volunteers' lounge, but stopped halfway through and closed it. The woman already trembled from head to toe, and he guessed it was because she didn't enjoy being alone with him. Going into a smaller room wouldn't help put her at ease. She glanced over her shoulder to the podium for the third time, then at the area as though searching for a way out.

He frowned, hating the fear in her eyes, recognizing it too well. The only individuals he wanted frightened of him were those who fucked with people he cared about.

"Care to sit?" He motioned at the armchairs.

She nodded and walked past him, rubbing along the wall to maintain as much distance as possible. He clenched his jaw to keep from exhaling in frustration.

*This won't be easy.*

Leaning into the cushy seat, he watched her in silence for a few seconds. "Would you like something to eat or drink?" He pointed at the platters lining the counter.

"No, thank you." She shook her head, and he caught a whiff of her scent. Citrus with a hint of peppermint. It was enticing.

He smoothed down his shirt as he sat up straighter. "Mrs. Reverie—"

"Please call me Elora," she blurted, as though her last name was a curse. She swallowed visibly. "I think you should pick another winner."

"Why?"

She played with her fingers, staring at her lap. "My friend entered me in the contest. I didn't. I mean, it's... I can't."

He edged closer, trying to catch her gaze. When he did, a pair of brown eyes pooled in tears met his, and he froze. His instincts told him to reach out and comfort the poor woman, but it would likely scare her even more.

She wiped her cheeks. "Sorry." When she straightened, she plastered a fake smile, and it pissed him off for reasons he didn't care to focus on. "I can't participate in this photoshoot. I'm sorry."

"You can't because your husband won't let you?" Even to his own ears, his emphasis was rougher than he intended.

Her breath came in faster. "I'm not good with physical contact."

"I noticed." He leaned back to give her space. "And why do you have difficulty with that? I've modeled with married women before. It's a shoot, not an affair."

Her cheeks flushed. "I know, but..."

"But what?" He cocked his head, waiting. "Are you trying to come up with another excuse?"

"It's none of your business." Her voice rose.

*Ah. There's still some fight in her. Good.*

He didn't want her afraid of him; he wanted her fierce and proud. Earlier, when he'd arrived at the convention, he watched her read to a group of children in the picture book section as he passed by, mesmerized by her smile and laughter. But most of all, there was an endless joy in her expression.

"You're right. It's none of my business. But you know what is?"

"What?"

"The prize you won." He stood and moved to the table with the snacks. "I have a proposition." He leaned against it and crossed his arms.

She glanced at the exit before returning her attention on him. "I'm listening."

"The photoshoot is scheduled a couple of months away. I suggest working on your physical contact issues in the meantime. We could meet whenever it's possible for you and practice."

He didn't think it possible for her to blush any deeper, but there she was, exceeding his expectations. The woman brought out all his urges to protect.

She bit the side of her finger. "Why?"

"Because I get to do a photoshoot as expected of me, and you try something new. It's a win-win situation, if you let it."

"And how would we practice, exactly?" Her voice was hushed, and he forced his mind to focus on what was happening instead of where it kept taking him. In bed with her. He wasn't above fucking women he didn't know. It was how he preferred it; no attachments.

"We'd start slow. Getting physically closer without you freezing. Small touches and caresses." He took a step forward, but stopped when she bolted to her feet.

*She's so beautiful when she blushes.*

She took a step back, glancing toward the exit. "I can't."

Yet her voice wavered as though unsure.

He grabbed his business card and a pen, not commenting as she jumped at his movement.

There was a slim chance this woman would change her mind, but he was willing to give it a shot. Poor thing was in a bad relationship, if he was making assumptions.

He scribbled his phone number and handed her the card. "In case you change your mind." When she took it, he purposely brushed his thumb over her knuckles. "And I hope you do."

It had been a while since he'd had to chase any woman; most threw themselves at him. But Elora was different. He'd seen the banner with her smiling photo; it showed her as happy, but he saw through the fake smile. The despair was clearer than photos of his own mother. He clenched his jaw. He wouldn't chase too long, though.

"I'll wait a week before calling the contest host and asking for another woman's name if I don't hear from you. But," he closed the gap between them, "I have the feeling you'll call me."

Her eyebrows shot up. "Oh…" As though realizing something, she pointed toward the exit. "I should go. The award is in a few minutes."

"Of course." When she took a few steps back, he didn't comment, but smiled instead. "Congratulations on both your wins. Although," he gave her one of his signature grins, "I believe your best win is the one for your book."

She smiled, and his heart swelled. It wasn't forced. And when she smiled—truly smiled—her face lit up beautifully. "Well, as you said, one was a talent, and the other was luck."

He chuckled as she strode away and glanced over her shoulder at him one last time before vanishing from his sight.

Digging into his pockets, he pulled out the folded piece of paper with the winner's name scribbled on it. Her name. His handwriting.

With a sigh, he put it away, staring where she'd sat just a few minutes ago. He was lucky Elora's friend entered her in the contest. He'd seen her in the crowd and recognized her from the poster.

In that moment, and from then on, he wanted her. At least once—just to get her out of his system. Maybe even help her while they were at it. A part deep within wanted to get rid of whatever had left fear in her eyes. He'd gone to check her poster to spell her name correctly as he scribbled it on the contest's entry. Needing her to be his.

"Luck, indeed."

# 4

## ELORA

*E*lora and Liana stepped inside the café, away from the scorching heat of the prairie's summer. Not that Elora didn't enjoy the sunshine; she rarely had the chance to go outside. But at these temperatures, it was a wonder they didn't melt into the pavement.

They ordered their drinks, and in less than three minutes, the barista had them ready. Elora arched her eyebrow at her friend as Liana held her hot coffee; Elora didn't like any warm beverages, but how did people drink those on summer days?

Liana pointed at their usual spot, and Elora smiled as they took their seats. Favorite table in the place, and they were usually lucky it was free. Elora placed her bag between her leg and the large glass window with the view of the street, pushing it aside so no one would snatch and run. It wasn't a dangerous neighborhood, but there were enough thefts and break-ins she wouldn't chance it. She didn't want to imagine what Richard's reaction would be if she lost her possessions and he needed to buy more.

She stared toward the menu board, part of her regretting her choice at iced chai latte instead of the delicious-sounding triple fudge iced coffee, but she made a mental note to try it next time.

Taking a sip of her drink, she sighed as the cold smoothie cooled her throat. The place wasn't too busy, considering the time they returned from the convention. Elora met up with Liana at this café now and then. But while Richard traveled more lately, she didn't dare leave the house too often, or too long.

Liana leaned her elbows on the table, grinning ear to ear. "So? When is the photoshoot with Mr. Vincent Voden?"

Elora pulled out his business card from her handbag pocket; the one she'd sewn herself so it was hidden when Richard searched through it. "I told him I couldn't do it."

"You what?" Her voice echoed across the cafe and heads spun in their direction like something out of the *Exorcist*. "Are you insane?"

Despite the sounds of grinding coffee beans filling most of the room, Liana was louder.

"Keep it down." Elora flattened on the wooden surface, desperate to make herself small, but Liana didn't pick up on the hint. The woman was a great example of no shame.

Instead, she slammed her fist onto the table and cursed. She surveyed Elora for a few seconds of quiet contemplation before her gaze softened.

"Listen. I'm sorry. Lord knows you already get your fair share of that at home." She let out a breath. "Have you checked out any of the shelters I recommended?"

Elora shook her head. "He's never hit me... he's a good husband."

"There's such a thing as mental and emotional harm, and you know it. He's controlling and abusive." Her black hair fell forward as she leaned even closer. "I can recognize signs of domestic abuse, okay?"

Elora blinked back tears. "He doesn't mean it. Ever. He apologizes. And he's stressed out. He gets long hours at work and then comes home—"

Liana held her hand up and glared. Her gaze seemed to spark with electricity. "Don't waste your bullshit on me. I'm your friend, not a stranger you need to lie to."

Elora's chin trembled, and she clenched her jaw. "I don't want to talk about this." She waved at the room. "Especially not in a public place."

Liana leaned back into her chair and crossed her arms. "Fair enough. Then, in that case, I'll ask why you refused to do the photoshoot. It would be so good for you."

"Are you suggesting I do a photoshoot with a man I don't know?" Her voice shook. Less at the thought of betraying her marriage vows and more at the flicker of fear at the thought of Richard finding out.

"There would be a professional photographer, and he's obviously done shoots with other women. If there had been any complaints about inappropriate behavior, it would have exploded on social media."

Elora sighed. "I can't do it, okay? I don't like being touched, and besides, do you really think Richard would agree to this?"

"He's your spouse, not your boss. You don't need his permission—"

"It's a marriage, so yes, I discuss things with him. And he'll say no, so I won't bother asking. He's stressed out because of the company meetings out of town, and I won't make him worry I'm cheating on him or something." She grabbed her drink and sipped, averting her gaze.

Liana fell silent, and Elora was glad she took the hint. But Elora should've known her friend wouldn't give up on every discussion. "What about the shelters, then?"

"I told you, I—"

"Go talk to a counselor there. If you're so sure it's not an abusive relationship, then what's the harm?" she pointed out.

Elora bit her lower lip. "Fine. If it'll get you off my back, I'll go talk to someone... Which one do you recommend?"

"Best one is the first one on the list I sent you. Do you still have it?"

She nodded, not telling Liana she kept the paper with her at all times. No names or addresses that anyone could read; Elora had a little code her dad and her invented together to play treasure hunts when she was a kid.

At the thought of him, her heart squeezed. She wanted to visit him, but for now, she had to wait. Hopefully, after she gave Richard the check from the award, he'd be in a good mood and she could ask if they could go visit her dad.

❧

The one-story house seemed simple enough, yet everything had its specific spot. Even outside, the garden was arranged by flower type, the grass cut in a perfect lawn manicure. The white picket fence shouted to the world a happy couple lived here, decorated by a few ornaments near the entrance of the residence. Twisted iron poles holding baskets along with small lanterns that lit up at night.

But it was nothing but a beautiful lie.

Elora stepped inside, the air conditioning a relief from the scorching heat. She frowned at the letters discarded on their side table, and when the floorboards creaked from the living room, her heart hammered.

Why was Richard home early?

If he hadn't bothered placing the mail correctly, then he was in one of his moods. She glanced at her bag, debating whether to put it away and change first, or go see him. He didn't care for misplaced items, but ignoring him was a sure way of getting him pissed off.

"Richard," she said with her rehearsed cheery tone, "you're already home? Weren't you supposed to be back on Sunday?"

"We finished earlier," he bit out. "Where were you?"

"The Book Fair, remember?" she said in a quiet voice.

His jaw clenched. "I know that. But the convention ended on time." He glanced at his watch, tapping it a few times. "I checked and made sure it did," he paused, glaring at her, "then I called the taxi company to find out how many minutes it would take in mid-afternoon from the center to here." He dropped his hand. "Now, then. Care to explain what happened to the lost hour and twenty-two minutes you weren't here?"

Heat pooled inside her belly, churning so violently she was sure she'd be sick. She drew a few breaths. "I stopped at a cafe on my way back. With my friend Liana."

"Because you weren't away from me long enough as is?" His smile didn't match his stare.

"I didn't know you'd be here waiting for me. I thought you were returning home tomorrow. I'm so sorry." She took tentative steps, gauging his reaction. "It was so sweet of you to surprise me like this, and I ruined it."

He grasped the back of her neck and pulled her close. "You shouldn't worry me." He kissed her forehead. "Did you get the check?"

She handed it to him, trying to hold her neutral expression. Liana had suggested Elora ask the host of the award ceremony to split the prize money into two separate payments so she could give one to Richard and keep a secret stash for herself. Liana took the second and promised to keep it safe so Richard wouldn't find it on Elora.

"Five thousand dollars?" He slipped it inside his wallet. "It isn't much for us, but it's a wonder baby books get any prize amounts at all," he muttered.

As he put the check away, her heart shrank knowing she'd never use the money to buy anything for herself. He could use their joint bank account for whatever he wanted, but the only things he allowed her to purchase were groceries.

Richard clapped his hands together, and she jumped. He laughed at her reaction, always enjoying when he scared her.

"I have good news," he said, his hair bouncing as he strode into the living room.

She didn't wait for him to call out to her, knowing how much he hated having to point out the obvious.

The convention day was the longest she was away from home since being with Richard, but the house somehow looked different. And yet nothing changed. The coffee table sat over the blue area rug, bathing in natural light coming from the curtain-framed windows. Both couches were a matching set and were the same color as the carpet and curtains. Royal blue for the king of the house.

She approached where her husband stood, near the fireplace. No, something *was* different. She knew every inch of this place, needing to dust and clean often.

On the mantle, an object was added: a small wooden box with a tiny lock. She pointed at it. "What's that?"

"It's a priceless gift I received from my boss," he said with an amused smile.

"How is it priceless?"

He exhaled loudly, and she stiffened. "Why do I always have to explain myself to you?" He threw his arms in the air, and she stayed still. No sudden moves. "You couldn't figure out that if it's from my employer, that's what makes it valuable?"

"It was thoughtless of me. I'm sorry." The words were so rehearsed inside her mind; they came out robotic. "Congratulations on receiving it. Was it related to your latest project?"

"It's a brand new one. Something I did for them they appreciated. This box is my reward."

"Well, that's definitely more important than my award could ever be. I'm so proud of you."

"But it's also for you," he said, taking her hands in his. "This gift came with a lot more money than your silly book thing, and I want to add a sunroom to the living area. A place you can write in." When her eyes widened, he smiled. "I know you have trouble working at the kitchen table because of the lack of sunlight, but with this, it should help."

She wrapped her arms around his neck, half-crying. "Thank you so much!"

"You really are lucky to have a husband like me," he said with a chuckle.

# 5

## VINCENT

$\mathcal{V}$incent stepped out of the taxi and stared at the decrepit building. He hadn't been in this part of the city for a while.

He walked to the back where a police car was parked and was greeted instantly by a familiar woman leaning on the vehicle. Kimberly Grandon. They'd gone on a few dates, and although he made it clear there were no attachments, she always hinted toward becoming a serious couple. Relationships were not something he was willing to try. Especially not with people he worked with on a semi-permanent basis.

She smiled ear to ear, pushing a strand of her short blonde hair. "Well, well. Look what the cat dragged in."

"Speaking of cats; how's Constable Mittens?" He rested his hip against the car door and grinned.

Her face fell for a second. "Cat's got nine lives and kicking. He always returns." She pouted but tried hiding it as she dusted part of her police uniform. "Aren't you going to even ask about how I've been?"

"Priorities, Kimberly." He winked, then waved his hand. "I'm kidding. How are you?"

She let out a sigh. "Running out of good guys to date, that's how. What about you?"

"Can't say I have the same problems with men," he said with a chuckle. He pointed toward the emergency door. "Is Daniel already here?"

She pressed her lips in a thin line, then gave a curt nod. "I hear you've got someone who'll come check the building."

"I have a foreman in mind. Name of Steven. He'd love taking on a job offered by the city."

"That's great." She eyed the building with an annoyed stare. "I don't know who the hell thinks it's funny to vandalize a women's shelter, but if the construction company you recommend can make this place safer, it'll be a step in the right direction."

He nodded, wishing he'd find whoever had broken into this sanctuary to teach them some manners. Kimberly let him in through the door, and he stepped inside the dimly lit room. They'd curtained most windows, and the place seemed vacant, except for the shuffling footsteps above.

Moving toward the lobby, the static of walkie-talkies rang nearby, and he slowed as he approached five officers. Vincent spotted Daniel instantly. His shaven head wasn't the only aspect that stood out in the crowd; the man was so burly he looked like he could snap a tree trunk in half without breaking a sweat.

Daniel slapped his hands together. "Vincent!"

"First, lower your voice. The women here probably get nervous hearing men shouting, even if you sound happy." Vincent put up a finger, then raised another. "And two, don't you think it's a good idea to have Kimberly inside instead of this sausage fest? Seriously, exchange one of your officers with her. If any of the residents have something to say, they'll feel more comfortable telling her."

Daniel opened his mouth as though to argue, but closed it again before nodding. "Chief told us, but it slipped my mind once we were inside and talking to the person who runs the place." He looked at one of his officers, and without a word, the man rushed out.

Vincent motioned his head away from prying ears. "Anything I should know?"

"Whoever broke in also disconnected the alarm. I checked with the city, and there was no power outage, or it would've gone on backup." Daniel started toward the back door. "Nothing was stolen, but they spray-painted messages."

Vincent arched an eyebrow, and Daniel motioned to follow. They stepped inside the living area; none of the furniture matched, and most should have been thrown out years ago. But since the place relied on donations, they couldn't be picky.

The words across the walls dripped in black spray paint.

Whores.

Sluts.

Feminists die.

Any woman seeking shelter here would see these. Vincent's hands curled into fists, but he stayed quiet, not trusting himself to say anything that would get him kicked off this case.

As a consultant with the police, he was privy to some cases, but considering Vincent's past, he understood why Daniel was wary to take him on board this one.

"Do you recognize the gang tag?" Daniel asked, pointing at a spot on the wall.

Vincent approached, staring over a small table, and at the signature left behind. "Looks familiar, but I can't place it right now. I'll ask around." He arched an eyebrow at his friend. "I'm assuming this is as far as you need my help on this?"

Daniel scoffed. "What do you think? Anytime I've allowed you to consult on these types of cases, I've had to get you out of trouble because you attacked the accused. There are only so many times I can do that."

"Fine. In the meantime, I'll contact someone about the tag."

Daniel pulled out his cell and typed. "I'm sending you the photo. Just make sure this doesn't get out to the public."

Vincent's cell dinged. "Will do."

Kimberly walked into the living area, a woman semi-hiding behind her. Vincent tried relaxing his pose, trying his best to look non-threatening, but the woman's gaze darted from him to Daniel constantly.

"She has information you should hear," Kimberly said.

Daniel frowned, but gave a curt nod. "Okay." He glanced at Vincent. "Go have a chat, and I'll check in with the others to see if they've found anything else." He focused on his officer. "I'll want a report from you after."

Once he left, Vincent sat on the sofa, trying to make himself smaller to not frighten the woman further. Both Kimberly and the witness took a seat opposite him.

"This is Amy," Kimberly said, patting the woman on the arm. "Can you tell Mr. Voden what you heard last night?"

Amy's face paled, and Vincent recalled how Elora had reacted similarly to him at the book convention. He almost laughed at himself, thinking of Elora; she hadn't called, and he doubted she'd ever changed her mind.

"Please, call me Vincent." He leaned back on the sofa and smiled.

She swallowed visibly, glancing at Kimberly who gave her an encouraging nod. "A man told someone to leave a tag for the Torren gang because they needed Moe in an organization to recognize it was them. Something like that." She rubbed her hands together, never once making eye contact with Vincent. "I don't understand what any of it meant, but it sounded important."

Vincent tried to keep his expression neutral, relaxing his muscles, and breathing out slowly. Not Moe, but the *MOW organization*. An acronym for *Masters of Women*, and a group that was supposed to be destroyed years ago. A sour taste in his mouth lingered as he heard the name, remembering how everything had ended. Or should've ended.

He smiled. "Thank you for coming forward with this information, Amy."

As soon as he finished speaking, she got up and dashed up the stairs, leaving Vincent and Kimberly alone.

She edged closer to her seat. "Haven't heard the name MOW for years. Aren't they disbanded?"

"They were." He drummed his fingers along the armrest.

"Torren is new, though. If they believe they're working for those twisted fucks, then they're stupid."

Her eyebrows shot up. He didn't bother hiding his smirk, and Kimberly shifted as though uncomfortable. Only Daniel knew of Vincent's past and why he was a great asset as a consultant, so the other officers wouldn't know.

"I'll gather what information I can about this. Hopefully just a gang pretending to be the organization for the sake of getting taken seriously." He got up, staring at the words spray-painted on the wall. "I hope you close this case soon."

He walked out without another word, and the sunshine blasted him with heat. Squinting in the sudden light, he exhaled, leaning against the facade. This shit was so fucked up, he couldn't even find the right emotion to feel. He had lots of contacts in the under-ground world, but if he couldn't discover his answers there, he'd be forced to go see *him*.

Vincent paced around the building and stopped by the side once he found shade from a large tree. Its bright green leaves wavered in the wind, and he stood still, enjoying the cool breeze.

The MOW organization circled his mind, and he gritted his teeth. The gang had taken control of criminal activity in Winnipeg years ago, but that wasn't enough for them. Boss after boss turned on each other until one evil son of a bitch won: Jack Cross. And he had no code or rules for what he allowed. Along with his two subor-dinates in charge, they shifted into human trafficking.

Vincent walked to the street, needing to get his mind off this case for a few minutes. At least until he contacted the people he needed to. As he called up a taxi in front of the women's shelter, he stared at the building. The beige paint peeled off the bricks, and some cracked windows were boarded with wooden planks. Had Elora ever shown up to one of these places, seeking shelter from her abusive husband?

He shook his head, this time scoffing aloud to himself. He had to stop thinking about a woman who would never come around to him.

His phone rang, and he answered when he recognized the name. "Hey, how's it going?"

Larry Georges was a great boss during a home renovation last year. Had even let Vincent show off some development ideas the clients ended up adoring. Although Vincent didn't require a full-time career, he preferred keeping busy; kept him out of trouble. Apart from the occasional police consultation, construction was the only real constant in his life no matter where he traveled.

"Got a job that came at the last minute. Not sure if I'll need an extra man, but in case, thought I'd ask if I can put you on reserve."

Vincent chuckled. "Sign me up."

"I'll text if I need you. Thanks." And with that, Larry ended the call. He was truly a man of few words.

Vincent hoped there'd be a need for him; he wanted a project. Something to keep his hands and mind occupied. Or else this new police case would drive him into the darker parts of his past.

The taxi pulled up next to the sidewalk, and with one last glance at the shelter, he stepped inside.

# 6

## ELORA

The front door opened, and Elora stopped mid-dusting. Lemon pledge filled the air, and she bit her lower lip, worried the house wasn't clean enough. Her stomach dropped, and she dashed to the entrance.

Richard wasn't alone.

A woman beamed at him, laughing about something he'd said. Her smile faded quickly when Elora appeared, the silence heavy.

Richard arched an eyebrow. "Don't you usually do the groceries at this hour?"

Elora swallowed hard. Was she locked up with such a predictable schedule? "Not always. I did extra cleaning in the bathroom, so it got pushed a bit." She stopped her mind from jumping to conclusions. "Aren't you going to introduce us?"

"Of course." He smacked his head and laughed as though this was so amusing. "This is my executive assistant, Stacey Evergreen."

Elora stuck out her hand, forcing a smile as her heart beat hard against her chest. "Hi, I'm Elora. It's nice to meet you."

The woman shook her hand, a pink hue coloring her cheeks. "Same here." Her black hair ended in beautiful waves, piercing gray eyes locking with Elora's. She could easily have been a model. Elora guessed why Richard hired her, and doubted it was Stacey's typing skills.

Elora scoffed at her own train of thought. No. This woman was gorgeous, but it didn't mean she wasn't intelligent.

He turned to Stacey. "Do you need me to call you a taxi?"

"No, it's fine," she said, averting her gaze. "I'll order one up."

"Okay. Well, I'll see you at work tomorrow."

As soon as the door closed, Elora returned to the living room, continuing her dusting. Trying to keep her mind from going to her worst assumption.

"Why are you home early?" she asked, keeping her back turned to him as tears burned her eyes.

He sighed loudly. "You're getting upset as usual?" His footsteps approached, and she stiffened, focusing on a corner of the shelving unit. "For once, it would be nice if I came home early without being interrogated." He grabbed her shoulder and spun her to face him. "This is my home, isn't it?" When she didn't answer, his grip tightened. "Isn't it?"

"Yes, but—"

"But what?" he shouted, and she pressed her back into the bookshelf. "I'm the man of the house. You have no right to ask questions as though you make the rules here."

She averted her gaze, staring at his shoes. "What… what do you expect me to think?" she asked in a small tone. "You expected me to be gone… You looked disappointed you wouldn't be alone with… her."

He shook her, and she gasped, staring up at him.

"I invited her to come see what the living room looked like now so she'd see the differences after the sunroom is added. God, why do you always have to be so negative about everything? Thinking the worst of everyone is telling, you know that?" He gritted his teeth, but let her go. "I came home early because the head contractor will be here in a few minutes and expected you were out doing groceries like you're supposed to be doing. Does that answer your question?"

She bit my lower lip as it trembled. "I… didn't know. I didn't mean to assume, but—"

"But you love to pick fights with me. Yeah, I know already. Despite you'd have nothing without me," he said with a snarl.

Tears blurred her vision. "I'm so sorry. Please…"

He pulled her in for a tight hug and kissed the top of her head. "You just need to stop acting so self-centered all the time."

She nodded, unable to think straight. There was a knock at the door, and he withdrew. He strode to the entrance as she wiped her cheeks. The contractor must have arrived.

She checked herself in the mantelpiece mirror, and once presentable enough, joined her husband.

A larger man stood in the doorway, smiling a toothy grin. Richard had his arms crossed, and she slowed as she approached. His expression didn't show any anger, but she recognized the pose.

"What do you mean during the day? We agreed five to eight in the evenings. You came highly recommended, Larry. Do *not* disappoint me."

Larry shook his head. "City won't approve it. I told you they wouldn't. Not good times for a residential property; too much noise." He shrugged. "Besides, it would cost you more since, with only three hours, it'd take longer to finish."

"I don't care how long it takes or the amount of money." He clenched his jaw, a tick pulsing at his neck. "I'm not here until five in the evening."

Larry stared at Elora. "Is anyone else here during the day?"

Richard shot her a sideways glance, and she forced herself to stay still with the glare. "She is, but I don't like her being home alone when a bunch of men are working here."

For once, the head contractor lost his grin. "Mr. Reverie. My employees are not animals. They'll leave your wife in peace. If this is a problem, I suggest you look for another company, but I guarantee the city will never grant you those hours in this neighborhood."

Richard exhaled through his nose, but a small smile curled his lips. "All right, all right. My apologies; I didn't mean any insult by my comment. But you hear things on the news, and… I worry for my wife, you know?"

Larry nodded. "You have nothing to fear. I check my men

before I hire them. Plus, I only need four workers for this, so it won't be a big group, if it helps."

"I appreciate it, thank you."

"And besides," he patted his beer belly, and winked, "doubt I'll steal your wife away with my good looks."

Richard laughed, and the tension seemed to dissipate from the air. "Just keep your men in check."

"Will do." Although Larry smiled, it didn't reach his eyes.

Once he left, Richard turned to Elora. "I don't like this, but I guess there isn't much of a choice." He took a step closer. "Just don't talk to them. Leave them to their work. Last thing we want is for them to think you're a slut wanting attention."

He walked away into the hallway leading to the bedrooms, leaving her alone in the entrance. She wanted to cry, but bit the inside of her cheek. The whole time a construction team would work on the living room, she'd have to go through his horrible moods thinking she was whoring herself to a group of men.

*I thought he was having an affair with his assistant. I'm not any better.*

Being alone with a bunch of strangers churned her stomach, but she pushed it away. Richard would just use it against her.

# 7

# VINCENT

*V*incent parked in front of a house, then checked his phone to confirm the address once more. Expensive neighborhood, yet it had a family feel to it instead of the modern look he'd seen around. A few abandoned houses remained, soon to be torn down and replaced to match the rest of the builds around them.

Larry had texted him that morning asking if he could come in for a construction job. He warned him the client was an asshole, but paid well. Either way, he wanted the contract done as soon as possible, so he needed four workers for this.

Apart from that, Vincent didn't get much information. But he was used to it; not like he was a regular on their crew.

As Vincent walked up to the door, he stopped on the porch where the other men sat. "Hey."

Ian stood and shook his hand. "Good to see you."

Vincent grinned. From the time he left his old life behind, Ian was the first person he'd befriended. No matter how many years passed, Ian never seemed to age; same dark red hair and light brown eyes.

"Larry wants this done fast?" Vincent asked.

Matt nodded. "Heard this guy thinks we're going to attack his wife."

"Or seduce her," Todd said with a shrug.

Vincent rolled his eyes. Great. A possessive control freak.

*Maybe something happened to her in the past, and he's overprotective.*

"Well, let's give her some room, and get the work done."

"As fast as possible," Matt added. He stood with a huff, a few pounds overweight. Didn't help that he smoked like a chimney either, but the man had an eye for construction. Only normal, since he did this job for a good part of twenty years.

Larry's laughter echoed from inside the house.

Todd grinned. "Well, sounds like the wife is nice. Wonder what she's doing married to a tight-ass." He rubbed his shaven head, but his fingers returned to his beard, and he scratched it.

Vincent stopped himself from making a comment, as they loved to razz Todd about it. He'd stated that because he couldn't grow hair on his head anymore, he'd take it where he could. But the facial hair drove him insane because he sweated so much.

The front door opened, and Larry stood in the entrance. "Come on. I'm not paying your lazy asses to sit around."

"Speaking of tight-asses," Ian muttered with a grin.

They chuckled, but Vincent knew the men liked Larry. He was a fair boss and a good man.

The three walked in, and Vincent grabbed a tool bag left behind. Larry made the introductions inside, and once Ian, Matt, and Todd walked farther into the house, Vincent stepped inside. The place was so clean, it felt wrong not to take his work boots off, even with the long paper mats spread out across the floors. They'd built the entrance in a sunk-in style, with one step going up toward the rest of the household; he couldn't help wondering if the home-owners had ever tripped over it.

His heart skipped several beats, then lodged into his throat as he stared at the woman speaking to Larry.

Elora Reverie.

Everything clicked together instantly. The possessive asshole of a husband.

*Why did it have to be her?*

He'd thought about her here and there during the week, but seeing her again... It was like his pulse had jump-started. When she turned toward him, her eyes widened, and she glanced from him to Larry.

Vincent stuck out his hand quickly. "Hi. My name is Vincent. It's nice to meet you."

She took it, swallowing visibly. "It's... nice to meet you, too."

Larry motioned at her, obviously missing that she jumped back a few inches. "This is Mrs. Reverie. I've assured her we won't be a bother while we construct her sunroom."

Vincent nodded, unable to keep his gaze off her. She wore a plain summer dress that fell flat on her, and he was willing to bet it wasn't her choice. Still, she was beautiful with her brown eyes sparkling in the sunlight. She'd tied her hair in a high ponytail, and all he wanted was to drag the elastic off so he could run his fingers through it.

"Get the bag into the living room, and I'll show you the yard," Larry added, then walked away.

Vincent stared at her, not sure what to say or do for the first time.

"I... Thank you for that," she whispered, glancing toward where Larry had disappeared to.

"He's a good guy, but I don't want him mentioning anything accidentally to your husband." He arched an eyebrow. "I imagine he can find criticism in even the most innocent comment."

She opened and closed her mouth a few times before crossing her arms over her chest. "Aren't you supposed to be working?"

He grinned; he adored her spunk when she allowed herself to let it out. Every little reaction from her when feisty was like a renewed fire in his blood.

With a shrug, he grabbed the tool bag and approached her. When she realized he made a direct path for her, she took a few steps back until she was against the wall.

He didn't get too close in case she wanted to leave. "I haven't called the contest host to pick another name for the photoshoot."

"Oh…" She seemed to lose her defensive stance, but her gaze darted around. "Why not?"

"Because I'm still hoping you'll change your mind."

She inched along the wall, and once she was out in the open, shook her head. "I told you I can't." And without another word, she joined the other workers who had disappeared out into the backyard.

Vincent followed, but slowed when he entered the living room. Everything had its place in an overly organized way. Like the inside was a museum. The throw pillows were placed at the same angles on the couches, lamps on end tables dusted without a trace of fingerprints. Even the area rug under the coffee table didn't show a speck of dirt from the potted plants nearby.

His mother's house had been clean like this, too.

He focused on the job, already figuring out what might work well for the sunroom attachment. Once he stepped outside, he dropped the tool bag near Ian, who gave him a curious look, but Vincent shrugged.

Larry took out plans, going over a few details with Matt as Elora stood at the end of the yard, staring at them.

Todd leaned toward Vincent and Ian, eyeing Elora. "I get why her husband is protective. Sexy piece of ass."

Vincent's jaw clenched. "Don't talk about her like that. She's a person."

Todd laughed. "Oh, come on. I'm not saying it to her face, so—"

"I won't say it again, *Roberts*," Vincent said, hissing out the man's last name.

Ian's eyebrows shot up, and Todd raised his arms as though in defeat. "Hear you loud and clear, man," Todd mumbled.

Once Todd joined their boss, Ian started from Elora to Vincent. "Care to share?"

"I… talked to her. She's nervous with people she doesn't know, and I don't want her to get a negative experience out of this. Let's show her there are decent men, okay?"

Ian nodded. "We'll be on our best behavior."

Vincent turned toward the window looking into the living room. Elora stood in the dining room, staring at them.

Now, all he had to do was be on *his* best behavior.

# 8

## ELORA

The refrigerator's cool air was a blessing on Elora's skin as she put away the vegetables she'd bought. Temperatures had reached an all-time high, especially with the humidity, which was rare in Winnipeg.

As soon as the construction workers left, she caught a bus and made her errands.

She glanced at the case of water bottles and smiled as she grabbed a few to put away. The men needed to keep hydrated in this hot weather, so she'd bought a few. Closing the door and cutting off the cold, she fanned herself. The heat was ridiculous these past few days, and she worried for their health, working in this sun.

Her mind raced to earlier in the day, and a shiver ran through her. Something that shouldn't happen in this warmth, and certainly not to a married woman.

Vincent had worn a tight t-shirt that clung to him, actuating his muscles. More of his tattoos were visible, and it added a rugged look to him. She couldn't help imagining his body pressed up against hers. Guilt filled the pit of her stomach, and she pushed the image out of her head. She finished putting away the groceries and slipped her apron on.

The timer on the stove beeped, and she turned off the element, relieved supper would be ready in time before Richard got home. Pork chops, steamed vegetables, and a side of gratin potatoes.

As she set a plate at his place at the table, Richard walked in. She rushed to greet him at the door, putting on her forced smile as she always seemed to do with him.

*I don't force it when it's Vincent…*

The traitorous thought churned her stomach, and she put an extra bit of effort in her greeting. "Hi. Did you have a good day?"

"Not bad, but my boss told me I'll be working late for the rest of the week." He slipped off his shoes as he handed her his briefcase. "So for a while, have supper ready at nine in the evening instead."

She nodded, placing his case at exactly the right angle where it belonged. "Do you want something to drink with your meal?"

"I'll grab a beer," he said with a smile, patting her hip. "Go sit. You must be tired after your grocery shopping."

She almost laughed at his comment, thinking he was sarcastic as usual, but he seemed serious. Without a word, she trudged to the table, ready to take a seat.

"Elora. Come here." His tone had changed to something… darker.

She rushed into the kitchen, not wanting to turn his mood sour, expecting to fix whatever had annoyed him. He was so happy a few seconds ago, and she'd ruined it.

"Yes?"

He pointed at the water bottles in the refrigerator. "What are those?"

She knew it wasn't the actual question, and she definitely wouldn't test his patience. "I bought them for the construction work-ers. It's so warm lately; I just want to make sure——"

"Watching them work, then? Getting ideas in your head?" He slammed the door shut, and she jumped back. "Where's the grocery list?"

"I… I don't know. It's in my purse."

He marched past her and grabbed the black bag hanging in its proper place. As he opened it and flung it upside down, tears blurred her vision. Everything inside fell in a clatter, and he even shook it for good measure.

"Find it!" he spat.

Her knees hit the floor before her mind caught up. She fumbled for the piece of yellow sheet. When she found it, she got to her feet and handed it to him with a shaky hand.

He read the list, one item at a time, his voice so low, she barely heard him when he reached the end. He shoved the paper in her face, and she winced as his fingers pushed against her forehead.

"I don't see water bottles on this note, do you?"

"I wanted to be nice to them since they're working hard, and it's hot outside," she mumbled, tears rolling down my cheeks.

"Oh sure. You decided. With my money!"

He grabbed her arms, then shoved her. She lost her balance, and her shoulder hit the side of the wall before she landed on the floor. Wincing, she held the throbbing spot, shaking from head to toe.

Richard stared at her for a few seconds before turning away. The front door slammed shut, and she burst into sobs.

❧

Elora stared at the plastic container in a daze as she scrapped the untouched dinner into it. Richard hadn't returned to eat, and the nausea in the pit of her stomach cut her appetite. She filled the sink, hoping to stay numb a little while longer as she focused on the steaming water and soap bubbles; if she didn't think of what happened, then maybe she imagined it all. Maybe it was a bad dream.

But the throbbing in her shoulder was impossible to ignore. The entire area was red and inflamed, but she could roll it with little pain, so at least Richard hadn't dislocated it.

The thought of him sent bile burning along her throat, but she gritted her teeth as she finished cleaning up. When the door opened a few minutes later, she was sure she'd throw up, unsure whether she was terrified or furious.

Richard walked into the kitchen slowly, a bouquet of roses in one hand, and a box of chocolates in the other. His eyes were red, as though he'd cried, and her chest squeezed.

"Elora," he breathed her name, taking a step closer. "I'm so sorry." He extended the gifts and waited, his lips pressed together.

She took the flowers, and she burst into sobs. He gathered her into his arms, but she didn't feel any better. Didn't feel safer.

He pulled away, gliding his finger along the red mark on her shoulder. She winced, clutching the gift closer to her chest. "I'm so stressed out at work lately. My bosses are giving me a rough time, and I'm constantly scared I'll lose my job. We'd be penniless." His gaze locked with hers. "I couldn't afford your father's nursing home."

"I understand. It didn't even cross my mind to ask first. I won't ever do it again. Promise."

He smiled, pulling her in for another hug. "Just so no one asks questions, wear something that covers your shoulder, okay?"

She pulled away. "But it's so hot lately——"

"Please. You know if anyone sees it, they'll jump to conclusions." Tears filled his eyes. "You want me to go to jail? Is that it? How will you afford anything?"

She shook her head. "No. I'll keep covered."

He pulled her against his chest, crying into her neck.

*I made him cry?*

She thought back to when they'd first met. How kind and caring he was. But that was before he'd gotten a stressful job. That was all this was, no? Richard was exhausted from working, and she made it worse.

*Or am I making excuses for him?*

## 9

# VINCENT

*S*unlight beamed down on Vincent and his coworkers as they took their lunch break. Elora had set up their patio furniture at the end of the backyard, and away from the house where they worked on the sunroom. She'd even put up the parasol, but where Vincent stood, the shade didn't reach him.

His cellphone vibrated, and he leaned forward to take it out of the pocket of his jeans.

*Daniel: Come by to see me at my office later.*

He wondered if it was good news with regard to the women's shelter case.

*Vincent: I'll be there around 5:30pm.*

Elora walked out of the large opening where they'd worked all morning, holding a tray of lemonade. Even from afar, the ice cubes were an invitation to heaven and away from this hellish heat.

"I thought... maybe you were thirsty," she said as though unsure, not meeting anyone's gaze.

Ian smiled, getting to his feet. Elora flinched, and Vincent rushed forward, grabbing the drinks as she almost dropped everything on the grass.

"Whoa, sorry." Ian's good mood vanished. He sounded concerned, even.

Vincent took the tray away from her slowly and set it on the patio table. "Thank you for the refreshments. It's appreciated in this heat."

She bit her lower lip as she met his gaze for the first time since he'd started working at her place. "I just… worry you'll pass out in these temperatures."

Larry laughed, grabbing a glass for himself. "We've worked these jobs for years. We'll be fine. But thanks for the concern."

Todd nodded. "Yeah, and speaking of worry," he pointed at the white sweater she wore over her dress, "aren't you going to get a heat stroke if you keep that on?"

"Oh, no… It's okay." She smiled, but it looked forced. "I'm a bit under the weather."

Ian sat on the patio chair. "If you're cold in this hot weather, you might want to go to the doctor."

She shook her head. "I'm… I'll be all right. Excuse me." And without another word, she turned and dashed inside the house.

They remained silent for a few seconds as they took gulps of their lemonade. Finally, Todd broke the tension.

"She's… jumpy, eh?"

Matt shrugged. "Some people are. Let's finish up and get to work."

"The sooner we close up the hole, the better she'll feel." Larry drank the rest of his lemonade and set it back. "As it is, even with air conditioning inside a few of the rooms, she must be warm."

"I'll return the glasses," Vincent said as he grabbed the tray.

Ian smirked. "Sure, go inside and get some cold air, you wimp."

Vincent rolled his eyes as he strode in the house and into the kitchen. Ian had a point; Vincent was getting light-headed because of the heat. Unlike the other men, he didn't take his t-shirt off. Most wouldn't know what the tattoos on his back meant, but he wouldn't risk anyone recognizing them. The ones snaking along his arms and neck looked innocent enough, but the rest…

He rinsed the glasses, and once he found the soap, washed them. If he could guess, Elora didn't need the extra work.

"What are you doing?" Her breathless voice tickled him, and his heart beat faster.

He turned and leaned his hands against the sink. "Cleaning up after me and the guys."

"You… didn't have to." A small smile curled her lips. She wiped the sweat beading her forehead. "But thank you. I'm a bit—"

"Hot?" He pointed at her sweater, arching an eyebrow. "Looks like you're in a sauna. Why not take it off?"

"I'm fine," she said, averting her gaze.

She walked down the corridor, and toward where Vincent guessed was one of the air-conditioned rooms. He followed her, guessing what was going on. When she opened the door to what looked like a guest room, he rested his hand across the frame. Her eyes widened, and she stood frozen in place.

He grasped her sweater slowly, then pulled it to the side, the soft material sliding over a bruised shoulder. His jaw clenched, and he muttered a few curse words as she trembled.

"Is this why you're keeping it on?" he asked. When she stayed quiet, he took a step closer. "Where did you get that bruise?" An unknown feeling tightened in his chest.

*Don't grow attached. She's married. And you know what happens to people like her.*

He kept his gaze locked on her, daring her to not answer him.

"I moved boxes out of the basement and hit myself on the door frame when I lost my balance." She slid the sweater in place and crossed her arms over her abdomen.

"Is that right?" The sarcasm in his voice couldn't be missed.

She narrowed her eyes and held her head higher. "It is."

*There's that fire. Beautiful.*

He ran his fingers through his hair. "I realize I'm a stranger to you, but if you ever need help, let me know."

A flicker of hope seemed to cross her features, but she averted her gaze quickly. "If I have to move boxes again, I'll ask you. Thanks."

He wasn't sure whether to sigh or laugh. "And have you changed your mind about the photoshoot?"

"No."

"But I'm willing to bet you still have my card with my phone number on it," he said with a smile.

Her cheeks turned bright pink, and she pressed her hands on them. "Of course not."

"Is that why you're blushing?" he asked with a purr in his voice.

"It's just warm," she muttered.

He sobered as his gaze focused on her covered shoulder. "Seriously, though. Any time, okay?"

She nodded, and before he could add anything, she darted into the room and closed the door gently behind her.

Vincent stepped inside the police station and smiled at Kimberly, who sat at the reception area.

"Admin work today?" he asked with a grin, knowing she hated that aspect of the job.

She rolled her eyes. "What does it look like?" Pulling out a paper, she scanned it. "So what have you been up to?"

He arched an eyebrow. "You mean since we last saw each other a few days ago?"

"Oh, just wondering what kind of trouble you've gotten into if Daniel called you in and seems to be in a pissy mood," she said innocently, but he heard the curiosity in her tone.

"Just let me in so I can go see him."

She reached under her desk. He strode to the door with the electronic lock and keypad, and when it clicked, he opened it and stepped through.

The hallways brought him to a past he didn't want to focus on too long. Two different worlds had collided in these parts, and as much as he tried pushing the memories away, they always returned when he was there. Vincent could still taste the metal in his mouth as *he* shoved a gun between his teeth.

He counted from ten backwards, took a deep breath, and continued to the break room where he would find his boss. Before he reached it, Daniel strode toward him.

"You're here early. Good." He motioned his head to the side, and they walked in silence, his jingling keys the only sound in the empty hallway.

They arrived at an office with the nameplate Sergeant D. Williams hanging on the door, and they stepped inside. Without beating around the bush, Daniel took a seat and stared at Vincent. "The construction company you recommended accepted to take the job at the women's shelter."

"So why is good news making you look like they handed you shit on a platter?"

Daniel's jaw clenched, the muscles ticking. "There was another break and enter. This time, a woman went missing."

Vincent took a seat on the edge of his chair and frowned. "Any gang tag left behind?"

"Same one as the last."

"Fuck." Vincent slammed his fist on the desk. Before Daniel could comment, Vincent took his cell out and texted a few of his contacts, ordering them to get the word out. He didn't want to do it this way because it meant the most prolific criminal in the capital, Benjamin Karson, would know Vincent was looking for answers.

"I'll let you know once I can get you in to see the newest crime scene. There was more graffiti, and I want you to check them out. We moved most of the women to new locations for now."

Something in the back of Vincent's mind sent warnings. "Monitor places where you didn't transfer women to."

"Why?" Daniel leaned forward. "Gut feeling?"

He shook his head. "If they grabbed one woman, they could've taken as many as they wanted. Obviously, they weren't interested in the others who were there. So next time they'll probably hit a shelter that's not full of women transferred from this one."

"They? So you think it's more than one person? Likely a gang like the tags suggest?"

"They're trying to make it look that way." He leaned back in the chair and crossed his arms. "As soon as I can see the last scene, I'll have a better idea."

Daniel nodded and stood, but Vincent raised his hand, and he sat with a huff.

"I've got work to do. Spill it."

"I'd like to know if there's any kind of file on someone. Her name is Elora Reverie." Vincent curled his hands into fists, his knuckles cracking under the pressure.

Daniel arched an eyebrow, but scribbled on a notepad. He kept his gaze on the page. "By your tone of voice, I'm guessing potential domestic abuse?"

"Yeah."

"I get why you do this, but you can't save them all. They need to want to leave. It's like addicts."

"It's not always about mindset, but lack of choice." He stared at the ceiling and let out a breath. "Some have to stay."

"I'll look into it, but the information I give you is limited." Daniel's voice was grave, but Vincent knew he'd do this for him. Vincent's childhood wasn't a secret from his boss; although he didn't share every detail, what he told him was enough.

"If you get any trouble from the foreman in charge of the construction at the women's shelter, send me a text." Vincent straightened, wanting to change the subject, and fast. "I'll set Steven straight since he owes me."

The ghost of a smile touched Daniel's lips. "Sure thing," he said with a chuckle. "Say hi to Constable Mittens before you head out. He'll smell you and give you the cold shoulder if you don't stop by."

Vincent got to his feet. "I never miss the chance."

The cat had wandered into the police station years ago and won over the entire squad with his mouse-hunting skills. Vincent headed toward the Lost and Found room. Constable Mittens had taken a liking to the place, and it seemed fitting it had become his personal lair.

He grinned at the small sign hanging with the name of the station's cat. The door was always half-opened to allow the feline free roaming privileges, so Vincent stepped inside.

A pair of glowing eyes caught his attention as the light reflected on the cat's yellow irises, and he meowed at the sight of Vincent. He reached a hand out for the cat to smell, then the purring began as the feline rubbed his head on Vincent's palm.

"Hey, Constable Mittens." Vincent glanced down the hallway, and his shoulders relaxed when he found it empty.

No one to overhear.

He leaned on the side of the shelf where the cat rested and let out a breath as he thought of Elora. Her brown eyes filled with fear, terrified of her own shadow. Yet there was a fire within her, despite making excuses for her abusive husband. She must have other reasons for staying with the monster. He assumed it wasn't the same reason his own mother had stayed with his father, since Elora didn't seem to have kids. Vincent himself had used his own body as a shield, trying to protect his little brother.

He let out a bitter laugh. "I failed at that too, didn't I? Failed my family." When the cat's purring got louder, Vincent raised his head and met gazes with the black feline. "I won't fail Elora, though."

One way or another, he'd help her.

## 10

# ELORA

hunder rumbled in the sky, and Elora rubbed her arms at the sound. At least most of the wall was closed off already since the workers were busy focusing on the outside construction.

She slowed as she approached the dining room, her pulse throbbing in her ears. Vincent stood at the window, staring at a familiar paper. She'd doodled on it a few hours ago.

He glanced over his shoulder and gave her a charming smile that sent her heart fluttering. "Sorry. I didn't mean to poke my nose in here." He put the sheet on the table and leaned against the chair. "Did you draw this?"

Heat crept into her cheeks that had nothing to do with the temperature. "Where are the other workers?"

"They left early because of the storm. I told Larry I'd let you know, but when I came inside, I found this, and got distracted." He pointed at the paper. "So did you?"

"Did I what?" she asked, adding an innocent tone to her voice. It sounded... flirty.

He chuckled, taking a step toward her. "Did you draw this?" He grabbed the pad and stopped in front of her.

His scent wrapped around her senses—sweat and the heat of

sunlight—and a sudden flush of warmth spread through her. "I was… doodling."

"It's great. Are you an interior designer on top of a picture book artist?"

She couldn't help the burst of laughter escaping her mouth as she shook her head. "No, no. I just enjoy drawing."

He glanced at the sketch of the sunroom. "Would it be okay if I showed this to Larry? He'd love to use some of these concepts."

"Richard wouldn't want me getting involved—"

"I won't tell him it's yours." He took another step closer, and she caught the hem of her shirt, stopping herself from backing away. "If you don't mind losing the credit for your brilliant ideas?"

She grabbed the drawing from him and frowned at it. "You really think it's good?"

"I do. You've got hidden talents, apparently." His voice turned husky, and she swallowed hard as she stared at him. "I bet you're full of surprises, darling."

Heat engulfed her body at the pet name, and she drew a shuddering breath at the way he stared at her. Not just in interest and lust, but something deeper.

She cleared her throat, putting the paper on the table. "So, are you good at everything?" When his smile turned lewd, she couldn't help grin. "I didn't mean it that way. I meant… you're a construction worker and you model? That's quite the different professions."

"And it's not the only two, either." He pulled a chair and sat, then motioned for her to do the same. Once she took a seat, he leaned his elbow on the table. "They're not so distinct, when you think about it. I mean, I need to stay in shape… This incredible body doesn't happen overnight."

She giggled. Great. She sounded like a fourteen-year-old infatuated teen. With a loud sniff, she tried to get rid of her embarrassment, but it turned into a snort, and they both burst into a fit of laughter.

*When was the last time I laughed like this?*

"Have you modeled a while?"

"A few years. I worked construction on a building in the city when an agent approached me. Thought she was kidding when she offered me a contract, but it turned out legit, so I accepted." He ran his fingers through his dark brown hair. "I don't take on contracts often since it's just a side job for me. I'll usually only say yes if it's for a charity event or something like that. The Book Fair donated the contest ticket price to an animal shelter, and I just couldn't resist helping out."

As she stared into Vincent's brown eyes, the twinkle behind them seemed to hide a darker side. But it wasn't threatening; instead, it cradled her.

*I'll have to thank Liana later for putting my name in the contest.*

She smiled. "So construction is your primary job?"

"No. I take these jobs when a foreman needs an extra man, and since it's quiet at my workplace…" he shrugged. "What about you?"

She didn't mention the sudden shift in his voice; like he wanted to avoid talking about his primary job. Still, she wasn't one to push considering she wouldn't give him much information either.

"Just the children's books, but it's slow. I have several tasks to do each day, but whenever I get a few minutes, I love to put books together. Stories that'll inspire children not to suffer alone, feel loved even if they may not have someone in their lives." She traced a small dent on the wooden table. "But I also enjoy drawing for fun," she said, glancing toward the paper.

Ever since she had imagined a greenhouse attached to the living room, design ideas had filled her imagination.

A flash of light ripped through the sky, followed by a crash of thunder, and she bolted to her feet. Her breath came faster, memories of Richard throwing objects against the walls resonating in her head. The first time she'd showed fear during a storm, he purposely jump-scared her at every opportunity.

Vincent stood and took her hand, squeezing lightly. She froze, his touch so gentle, yet firm, letting her know he had her.

"Elora?" He tried pulling her closer, but she winced, her shoulder still tender. "Can I see?"

She'd kept the sweater on, covering the nasty bruise that had turned a shade of green, purple, and blue. Unable to speak as he held onto her hand, she nodded slowly. He pulled the clothes to the side, his eyes narrowing on the wound, but he said nothing as he pushed her clothes in place.

"It's sore, but nothing too horrible." She tried pulling away, but he took a step closer, closing the gap between them. "I'll have to be more careful with the boxes next time."

"We both know that's a lie."

Before she could reply, thunder echoed, feeling like it shook the house from the ground up. She yelped, instinct pushing her toward Vincent as he wrapped his arms around her. He held her, and they both stood unmoving. As though even the smallest of breaths would break the moment. The safety she felt with him was... indescribable.

Guilt churned her stomach as she thought of Richard. This was unacceptable. She couldn't feel these things for another man. She was married, and through better or worse, she loved her husband.

*Right?*

She pulled away, averting her gaze. "Sorry. Loud noises make me jumpy."

He chuckled, cutting through the heaviness in the air between them. "These big powerful arms are here whenever you need them."

She laughed. "Thanks."

"I should go. I won't be working here tomorrow, but I'll be back next week." He walked to the entrance and opened the door. "Have a good evening."

She hated that not seeing him for a while hurt this much.

# 11

# ELORA

*T*he thought of not seeing Vincent until next week continued leaving a bitter taste in her mouth, and Elora scolded herself.

*Stop acting like a child.*

Richard was busy showering—something she found odd considering his routine was so important to him. Usually, he ate, then cleaned up. Then again, working later into the evening probably exhausted him. He always worked so hard for the both of them. She wished he'd allow her to get a job to help with the bills.

The phone rang, and she jogged into the living room to pick up the cordless.

"Hello?"

"Er, who's this?" a woman asked on the other end.

Elora frowned, the woman's voice sending a creeping feeling deep inside her stomach. "You're the one calling here. Who do you want to speak to?"

"Richard." Her tone pitched higher. "Who the hell are you?"

"I'm Richard's wife." Elora's voice shook. Her heart already knew, but her mind refused to catch up.

"What?" The woman shrieked into the line, forcing Elora to pull it away from her. "He's married? What the fuck? Let me talk to him now!"

Before Elora could think of what to say, someone grabbed the phone from her, and she yelped, jumping back. Richard put it to his ear, glaring at Elora like she was the one who'd done something wrong.

"Hello?" His frown deepened. "I told you not to call here——" More shouting on the other end, and Elora took a step back, her breathing uneven. "Cindy, I'll contact you later. Do not call here again." And with that, he hung up.

"Who was that?" she asked, hating herself for the stupid question. She already knew the answer, but she wanted to hear it from him. From her husband.

He frowned. "What do you mean?"

She curled and uncurled her hands, taking deeper breaths to try staying calm. "I mean, who was that on the phone? What's going on, Richard?"

He rolled his eyes, and crossed his arms. "Really?" he asked in a huff. "You need me to say it out loud so you can make me feel bad about it? Is that it?"

"Tell me what's going on. Her tone grew desperate, and she despised herself for it.

There was no remorse about what he'd done; she could see it in his eyes. "Okay, well, I guess the cat's out of the bag." He clicked the off button to the phone so it would go directly to their answering machine. "I'm seeing other women. Only a few. The late nights, business trips. I mean, I'm working, but also sleeping around."

"But... why?" she asked, tears rolling down her cheeks. After everything, this was it? Just like that? Anger filled her, hotter than the heat from outside. "What the fuck, Richard? You cheated on me? Why? Tell me why."

"If you did things that please me, I wouldn't be forced to," he snarled.

"What the hell do you mean by that?" she shouted.

His hands curled into fists. "I need to experiment in bed, but you never want to do any of it. I found women who do, so what did you expect? This is on you."

"This is *not* on me! You cheated——"

He slammed his fist on the table where the phone was, and it toppled to the floor. She took a few strides back, heart racing.

"Don't you understand how tough my life is?" He screamed, his face turning a shade of pink, the vein on his neck pulsing. "I work hard every day, come home, only to find my wife isn't interested in my needs. These explorations are important as a man. It's psychological. But you only think of yourself. You don't like it after a few times trying, but you never even put any effort into it."

She wiped her cheeks, the lump in her throat making it hard to swallow. "If that's how it is then... I guess we should end this..." Saying the words squeezed her chest, suffocating her beating heart.

"What did you say?" His voice lowered, barely a whisper, the look in his eyes darkening. "You want to leave me?"

He let out a bellow, and kicked the table. It toppled over, sending a notepad and pen holder to the floor in a clatter.

"What choice do I have?" she said between sobs as she backed away farther. "You cheated on me, and you're blaming me for——"

"You're the only one here pointing fingers," he snarled as he grabbed the leg of the table and lifted the piece of furniture.

Elora darted to the side as he threw it toward her, and it smashed up against the wall. Her pulse hammered in her ears. She was unable to think as he marched past her into the living room. If he continued making so much noise, the neighbors would call the police again. It was so much worse when they'd show up.

"Richard, stop," she cried, rushing after him. "You can't destroy everything like this."

He marched to the mantle, and grabbed a photo frame showing a picture of their wedding day. "Why not?" he shouted, rounding on her and brandishing the photo. "Not like any of this actually matters to you right? So ready to just throw it away because you can't have your way." He threw it on the hardwood floor, and it shattered.

"Of course it matters," she said as tears ran down her cheeks. "Why do you think I'm so upset?"

"I can't believe you're being so cruel." His voice cracked. "Why would you threaten something as sacred as our marriage?" His hands curled into fists as he strode toward her. "What the fuck is wrong with you?"

"Sacred?" she repeated louder than planned. "You don't cheat in a marriage, Richard. Or in a relationship. You're the one who's destroyed our marriage."

He grabbed her arms. "Because I can't talk to you without you punishing me all the time! Whenever I suggest an idea you don't care for, you act like a cold bitch with me." He shook her, and she clenched her jaw to stop from accidentally biting her tongue. "Don't you know how much it hurts me when you treat me like that? How much it tears me apart knowing you don't care about my pleasures or wants?"

"Well, if I'm that horrible of a person, then you'll have no issues with us separating," she said through her sobs.

"Why are you so quick to want to leave me? Do you not love me? Is that it?" Tears ran down his cheeks. "Please, don't do this. We can work it out." He grabbed her arms. "We—"

"You slept with other women. How could you do that to me?" Her breath came faster when he dug his fingers into her skin, and he shook her.

"I won't live without you." He gritted his teeth. "I'll kill myself if you leave."

Her eyes widened. "Don't you—"

"Please. You can't leave me, I—"

"You're hurting me! Stop!"

He stopped crying so fast, it was scary. "You... think I'm hurting you?" His jaw clenched tighter. "You consider this pain?"

Her mind didn't react quick enough as he raised his arm and backhanded her against her face. Before she even reached up to cup her throbbing cheek, he did it again, harder, and she fell to the floor. She gasped when his fist came down on her eye and screamed at the second… third. She tried crawling away, but he continued, and she stopped moving, trying to cover her head.

Silence settled, but she stayed frozen on the floor, terrified to move.

"Oh god… Why did you make me do that? What's wrong with you?" he shouted, but her ears rang, and she barely kept up with what he said. "You always instigate me, and now you finally pushed me too hard. See what happens when I lose my temper and snap?" He pulled her to her feet and dragged her to the couch as the room spun. Her skull felt like it weighed too much, and as he sat her on the sofa, his tears started.

He hugged her tightly. "You're my everything, Elora. Why can't you see that? I can't live without you."

She opened an eye; the other too swollen to see through. "But—"

"Who's going to pay for the nursing home then?"

The question, while asked innocently, sent a twisting tug in her stomach. "You… You said you'd—"

"You think I'd pay that much for your father's fancy nursing home if you're not with me? Do you know how much that place costs? He has the best money can buy, and it's *my* money that buys it. If you're determined to hurt me and leave, then he'll have to go somewhere else—"

"What do you mean? Where else?"

"Maybe those first ones we had visited all those years ago."

Her chest squeezed, and she shook her head quickly. She thought of her father.

"No, please." She swallowed hard. "You're… you're right. We can work this out together." She hated herself so much.

He smiled. "We have so much more than sex between us. We have years of love." He took her hand. "We need each other. I just require other things. And that's okay. Lots of couples have open relationships so it's what we'll do."

"You mean… you'll keep sleeping with other women?" She kept her tone as neutral as possible.

"Yes, and I'll continue using protection so you don't need to worry. It's an excellent arrangement, and you know it." He grasped her chin. "I'm sorry I lost my temper. I couldn't seem to think straight when you threatened to leave me." He leaned closer. "That's how much I love you."

"It's... okay. I didn't want to upset you."

"Don't go out this weekend, and stay in our room when the workers come on Monday."

At that moment, she didn't know who she hated more—Richard, or herself.

## 12

## ELORA

The weekend came and went, then Monday arrived. Vincent hadn't shown up for the day. A part of Elora hurt at not seeing him, but another was relieved. There was only so far makeup could hide the bruising on the side of her face. She was lucky she healed fast, but the bruise around her eye and cheek had turned the colors of the rainbow.

At least she could open both eyes again.

Richard stayed home that day as the other workers came inside the house. He didn't want any of them to see her.

As Elora sat in the bedroom, a strange relief washed over her at the fact that her husband was having sex with other women. Maybe he wouldn't bother her with it anymore. Or at least, considerably less. It was the only silver lining in this nightmare.

Richard walked inside the room, scowling as though displeased with the way she looked. He slumped in the armchair facing the bed. "You couldn't have covered up better? Are you trying to remind me how much you hurt me when you threatened to leave?"

"I… did my best."

He scoffed and leaned into the chair as he drummed his fingers on the armrests. "The foreman informed me they encountered a problem."

She tensed. Bad moods usually ended up with a new bruise lately, but if she stayed still, perhaps he'd forget she existed. Her pulse sped as every second ticked by, waiting for his hands to rise before striking down.

"Apparently, when they tore off the south side of the living room, they discovered asbestos." He glared at her. "I'm regretting this gift to you more and more."

She wanted to tell him she was sorry, but knowing it would likely make him angrier, she tried coming up with a solution instead. "They... can remove it though, right?"

His fingers tightened on the wood until his knuckles turned white. "So you're a construction worker now? Or are they teaching you the tools of the trade while you spread your legs for them like a slut?" he spat.

"I'm not the one sleeping around," she snapped, then pressed her lips together. Her heart hammered. "I didn't mean..." She swallowed several times to get her dry mouth to work as he gave her a deadly stare. "I understand we're in an open relationship now, and although I haven't slept with anyone, I thought—"

"Oh, I'm sorry," he leaned forward and grabbed her knees, squeezing hard. "I wasn't aware you lacked sex. Do you need me to fuck you more often?"

"That's not what I meant," she said, her voice shaking. "But why would you call me a slut if—?"

"Because this isn't an open relationship for you," he shouted, his fingers digging into her. "You don't have the same needs as a man. I give you enough, and looking for more makes you a selfish bitch."

Tears burned her eyes, but she blinked them away as she nodded. "Has the foreman said what he'll do about the *assbeestosy*?"

"God, you're so stupid. It's called uhs-beh-stuhs." He pronounced the word slowly and loudly.

"Oh, sorry," she mumbled.

"And don't try changing the subject." he said through gritted teeth. "Are you fucking the construction guys? Is that it?"

"No, I'm not," she said, but her voice shook at the thought of Vincent. At the way he made her feel.

The vein in his neck pulsed. "Bullshit. This house needs to be empty for the next week while they remove the material. Did they tell you ahead of time so you could stay with one of them?" His grip on her knee tightened, and she winced. "I should've known you wanted an open relationship the whole time. Wanted an excuse to whore yourself, but made me out to be the bad guy, as usual." He bolted to his feet, and she scooted back on the mattress.

For a second, he stared at her in silence, his expression stony. Without a word, he left the room, slamming the door behind him. Elora trembled, continuing to draw in small gasps, unable to take a deep breath. Was the construction team still here, and it was why he hadn't hurt her this time? Or had he managed to regain control of himself?

Richard's muffled voice sounded from his office next to the bedroom, but she didn't catch much of what he said. She frowned when his tone switched to something like surprise or confusion, and she wondered who he spoke to on the phone.

A few seconds later, Richard returned to their bedroom, but left the door open. She stiffened, waiting for him to say or do something bad since they were obviously alone.

"I wanted to speak to my religious advisor before reacting harshly," he said through his teeth.

Her eyebrows shot up. "I… Since when are you religious?"

"Since you've been testing my patience more and more," he spat, and she recoiled at his tone. He let out a sigh, and shook his head. "Father Brian is a priest I speak to whenever I'm at a loss for what to do about how you treat me. I often feel hurt and alone with everything you put me through, and he helps me through those difficult times, and also provides advice."

Her stomach churned, but she nodded. "Oh." She wasn't sure what else to say; as long as she'd known her husband, he had never been religious nor had an interest in any of it.

"I don't always agree with what the Father recommends, but he hasn't led me astray so far." He grabbed her arm, and yanked her to her feet as she gasped. "We need to be out of the house for a week while they remove the asbestos from the walls. During this time, you're free to do as you wish. Go ride every cock you can find, and when you return to me, you'll apologize for it."

"What?" she mumbled, growing cold.

"You won't ever learn to appreciate what you have until you're used and thrown away like the trash that you are. I'm the only one who'll ever love you, but you really believe you can do better." He shoved her out of the bedroom, and continued down the hallway as she hurried farther.

He grabbed her purse, and shoved it into her arms.

Her pulse sped so fast, her vision darkened. "Wait, Richard. I—"

"Why are you making this harder for me?" he bellowed. "Now, get out, and sin like you've always wanted. Once it's out of your system, you'll come back home, and we'll discuss what you've learned." He smiled, but it was icy. "When you realize no one wants you except for sex, you'll come crawling back to me and beg for my forgiveness."

Her eyes widened, and she took a few steps back as her heart hammered. He pushed past her, and opened the front door. Without a word, she stepped out into the heat, the sun setting in the horizon painting the sky in golden colors.

With a trembling hand, she pulled out her cell from her purse and texted Liana. Her throat tightened. This wasn't over. Richard expected her to come back. But she was free to do what she wanted for a week. A priest suggested this?

*Elora: Hi. It's last minute, but can I stay at your place until Monday?*

She lowered her cell, staring as the three little dots floated as her friend typed.

*Liana: Of course.*

Her fingers shook as she replied.

*Elora: Thank you. Talk to you soon.*

The idea of having a whole week away from him seemed like a miracle... even if it was temporary.

Staying at Liana and Brad's house came with a freedom Elora hadn't felt in years. The kids, despite their young ages, were angels, and she found calm within herself being there.

When Liana had seen Elora when she arrived, her friend had wept, holding her in her arms so tight Elora thought she'd cracked a rib. But Elora didn't mind because it had given her the chance to feel safe. She hadn't cried, though. She couldn't. Not anymore. She'd made her choice, and that was it.

A few times during the day, Elora sat in the guest room, holding her phone as she stared at the phone number for the nursing home. She wanted to see her dad so much, but the only way was in person since he was deaf. And while he often didn't recognize her when Richard brought her for visits, sometimes when they'd be about to leave, her dad would smile at her as though suddenly recalling who she was.

But if she called, Richard would find out, and she didn't want to imagine how he'd react now that he'd become physically violent.

As the end of the first day rolled around, Elora and Liana sat in their favorite little coffee shop, enjoying drinks while Brad stayed home with the kids. Brad was lucky with his flexible hours as a university professor, although Elora never understood how he graded papers with two toddlers and an infant to take care of. The man was some magician.

"I can't believe Vincent Voden is working construction at your house," Liana muttered for the hundredth time once Elora had told her.

"He's got three jobs, so I guess he keeps pretty busy," she said with a shrug. She hated how much she missed him.

Liana crossed her arms. "You should call him."

"Who?"

"Mr. Voden." She leaned forward. "You need to get out there and live a little. You're twenty-seven, but you act like your life is already over."

*It could be at any second.*

"I... don't know. I mean, maybe doing the photoshoot is still an option if he hasn't called for another woman yet." The thought twisted her stomachs into knots.

Liana nodded quickly, "Do you have the business card he gave you?"

Elora's face heated as she pulled it out of her purse, tracing her fingers along the blue ink. Liana motioned to the card, and Elora handed it to her without thinking.

Liana whipped out her phone as though by magic and typed the number in.

Elora's eyes widened as her pulse sped, and she tried grabbing for her friend's cell. "What... what are you doing? Stop!"

Liana kept it out of reach and smiled. "Hello Mr. Voden. This is Elora's friend, Liana."

Her heart thumped inside her chest, half-hating, half-adoring Liana. Before she thought of protesting, Liana told Vincent she was passing the phone to Elora, then pressed the device on her ear.

"Elora?" he whispered, and goose bumps crawled along her skin as she held the phone without Liana's forceful help.

Vincent's voice caressed Elora. If she thought her pulse beat frantically before, it was nothing compared to hearing him.

She swallowed. "Yes. It's me."

He chuckled. "I'm glad you called. Well, technically, it was your friend, but we'll count it as a step in the right direction." He breathed out, and a tingling sensation ran across her ear as though he was with her. "Is everything okay?"

"I was wondering... if it's too late to take you up on the offer you made me."

"No, of course not. Can I ask what changed your mind? Did you miss me working outside your house?" he asked with amusement.

"Yes. I mean, it's... er, complicated. But I'm... on my own until Monday," she whispered.

"Is that so?" His tone grew huskier. "I imagine we'll have a few things we need to work out to make sure everything goes smoothly."

*Damn his sexy voice.*

"I… Yes."

"What's your number?"

"He… checks my cell," she mumbled as Liana glared at the wall opposite from where they sat.

It wasn't like she couldn't listen to what was happening in front of her, and Elora was positive she guessed what they talked about.

"I'll block it before I call, then."

"If it's too repetitive…"

He sighed impatiently, and Elora flinched, gripping the table. Liana arched an eyebrow and motioned to give the device to her.

She brought the phone to her ear, a poisonous smile lacing her voice. "Be gentle with her and keep your temper in check, Mr. Voden, or we'll have a problem."

A swell of pride and love formed a lump in Elora's throat.

Vincent's muffled laugh echoed from the other line, and he muttered something Elora didn't hear, but caused Liana to blush.

"Very funny. Now, then. How can I help?"

Elora tightened her ponytail and twirled it between her fingers, trying to catch anything he said.

"Tomorrow at one o'clock. I'll text you, yes." After a quick thanks and goodbye, Liana hung up. "Let's go back to my place and rescue Brad."

## 13

# VINCENT

*V*incent settled into his condo, his mind focused on two opposite things. Three more women had disappeared from shelters. And while his contacts confirmed Torren gang members were active, the infamous MOW organization remained silent and disbanded.

He dropped his bag near the sofa and stared around his residence. It was a nice place, but if he was honest, he missed his home in Ottawa. A cozy house nestled outside the city, surrounded by maple trees. It was heaven. In autumn, the leaves changed to bright red, mixed with yellows and oranges, setting the forest aflame.

He dusted a few of the surfaces, but his attention turned to the large window taking up most of the brick wall. The sun set, and tomorrow, he'd see Elora. He wondered how she was since they last saw each other. She had let him hold her, scared of the thunder; it had made him so happy she was willing to seek safety in his arms.

Leaning his forearm on the glass, he gritted his teeth at his own reflection.

*Why do I care?*

The same question plagued his mind since he met her. From the time he watched her read to kids at the book fair. Her award photo hiding despair behind a fake smile that called to him for help.

He shifted from the view, and grabbed the remote, clicking on the television to add background noise. Being a studio apartment, the only private space was the bathroom, but the design was interesting to him when he'd seen it. To this day, he adored it. Large windows allowed plenty of sunlight into the area, and at night, it looked like a scene out of a Sci-Fi movie with the city lights sparkling. Most of the walls were made of red brick, and the hardwood floors were polished. They designed it in a rectangular shape with the kitchen on one end with its marble counters and state-of-the-art appliances. Then it changed into a living room with a study area, and a bedroom near the door leading into the bathroom. He had purchased dividers for privacy, hiding the king-size bed. Foldable stairs hung on the side of the wall that opened to a loft overhead where he sat and looked out of the highest window. It was also where he kept bookshelves and velvety throw pillows, so he read in comfort.

He sat on the sofa and opened his laptop sitting atop the coffee table, checking his emails. One from Daniel. His chest tightened as he studied the information Vincent had requested from his boss.

Neighbors had called the police for years, saying they heard yelling, screaming, and shattering noises. But whenever the cops showed up, Elora assured them everything was fine, and they had a crazy cat.

He closed the laptop with a sharp snap and stared at the wall. How many times had his mom made the same excuses? The police weren't a great help then. Different cities and different times. He remembered sitting at the kitchen table, biting the inside of his cheek so hard it bled as he cradled his little brother. The cops had asked his mother what she did to provoke her husband to hit her, and Vincent's blood had boiled.

But he hadn't defended her. What could he have said at nine? Who would listen?

Years of regret weighed on him. He wouldn't let Elora become another statistic. Pulling out his phone, he texted Daniel, thanking him for the information.

*Vincent: You need me to come in later today?*

Anything to distract him while waiting for tomorrow.

It buzzed, and he frowned at the reply.

*Daniel: Not a good idea for you to check in right now.*

*Vincent: Why not?*

Three dots hopped on the screen as Daniel typed.

*Daniel: Domestic abuse case. Husband is being interviewed.*

Vincent dialed Daniel's number, each ringtone gritting on his nerves.

"You don't take no for an answer, do you?" came Daniel's voice on the other line.

"Only with the ladies." Muttering in the background caught his attention. "You sure you don't want me there?"

Daniel huffed. "We both know it wouldn't be a good idea."

Vincent let out a snort. He couldn't help remembering how Elora had done the same, then had burst into laughter. She had such a beautiful laugh and smile when the fear melted away from her.

"By the way, I'm taking a few days off this week unless it's an emergency. Just text and I'm there, okay?"

"Sure thing, boss," Daniel said with amusement in his tone.

Vincent chuckled, then hung up. He wouldn't sleep much tonight, being so tense. And seeing Elora tomorrow set his blood on fire. He glanced toward the partition hiding his bed, and pictured her lying there, naked, underneath him.

With a groan, he rubbed his hand over his face and laughed.

Right. She could barely be approached. And on top of it, she constantly reminded him, and herself, she was a married woman. She just needed to work on getting comfortable. That was it.

But he wished to have her laugh. See what she looked like when she was relaxed for a while. When she felt safe. He wanted her body to respond to his; burn for his touch.

His lips twisted in a bitter smile. Sex was perhaps on her mind, but the question was, would she be able to?

"I guess we'll find out soon enough, darling," he whispered.

꙳

One benefit of living in an expensive condo was the perk found on the first floor of the building. A private gym for residents. And Vincent needed to burn off his pent-up frustrations if he wanted a chance at sleep tonight.

The place was lit better than the last time he was here, the mirrored panels on the wall creating the illusion it was bigger than it was. Music played on the speakers—a good beat, and nothing annoying like he'd heard in other gyms.

Men and women worked out on the equipment, and Vincent swept his gaze along the faces. No one he recognized. He grabbed the antibacterial wipes and walked to the first machine on his list for the evening.

His thoughts alternated between the burning in his muscles and Elora. Her face kept flashing through his mind, every grunt sending images of sheathing himself inside her. Thrusting until she moaned his name. He gritted his teeth, inhaling deep with his nose, trying to focus. His workout was supposed to unwind him, but instead, was running his sexual fantasies with an untouchable woman.

*Talk about frustrating.*

With a sigh, he moved to the next machine, and focused on her issues. That put a quick damper on his excitement as the thought of her pain pissed him off. They'd have to work on her reactions, but it would be easier said than done. Instincts learned from fear weren't suppressed in a month, let alone a few days. It would take a while. And yet, the prospect of helping her through it lifted a weight off his shoulders. He'd spend time with her, get to know the woman who had a passion for writing children's books. For once, he didn't want to learn about someone so he could just take her in bed, but also because he was interested in her as a person.

He scoffed, knowing if he said it out loud it would make him sound like a real asshole. Maybe he was, but he couldn't help his disinterest in the women he'd dated. Most desired him for his looks or money. Or both. A few, like Kimberly, craved a deeper connection to him, but he had problems getting close to people. No one came without issues nowadays.

The metallic clang of a barbell bouncing on the floor brought him to reality for a few seconds. He wiped the equipment he finished with, the antibacterial cleaner burning his nose. Sweat slid down his back. He took a gulp from his bottle, the water cooling his throat.

His muscles ached by the time he returned to his loft. He looked forward to reading before getting to sleep, his heart lightening at seeing Elora soon. No matter what he did, the woman kept coming to his mind. Dangerous, considering her situation.

What would happen when they got to know each other better? Would his attraction for her grow? If it was the case, he'd become even more protective; a recipe for disaster since she was married to an abuser.

The bruise on her shoulder…

He stood in front of his door and kicked it open. It took a second for him to regret it. Not only for his throbbing toes, but for the old instincts he kept from years of living with violence in one form or another. He'd need to watch his reactions when he was with her. The last thing he wanted was for her to fear him.

He wanted her to feel safe with him. No matter how long it took.

# 14

# ELORA

*G*lancing in the selfie-mode of her cell camera, Elora checked the bruise on the side of her face, and sighed. She'd done her best to cover it, and at least it was healing. But it was a constant reminder of the pain and terror at the hands of Richard. For years, he was verbally abusive, but these last few weeks had pushed him to become physically violent. She wasn't sure how long she could live with it.

Liana beckoned to her, standing at the door of a small coffee shop. They'd driven into downtown Winnipeg.

They stepped into the cafe, Elora's attention focusing on the chalkboard with specials written in bright colors. An employee had even drawn their latest new drink: a mint Frappuccino. Knowing she'd talk to Vincent soon, her sweet tooth vanished, and the smell of the ground beans churned her stomach.

*What am I doing?*

They sat at a small table at the back, and Elora set her handbag on the extra chair between them.

"Did you get any writing done this morning?" Elora asked.

Elora had spent time with Liana and Brad's kids to give her friend a break, but hadn't kept them calm. Sarah was a noisy big sister, and she encouraged her little brother, Philippe, to be as bad. At least Marc was quiet, despite only being one.

"Actually more than I expected," Liana said with a grin. "How's your newest picture book coming?"

Without a house to clean every few minutes, Elora had used her free time to write and draw that morning before the kids woke up.

"I have an idea for a new character, so it's a start. I thought maybe a teacher who's a sheep, teaching different animal children to live together in harmony. Accept differences."

"Is that how you see yourself?" Liana arched an eyebrow. "A lamb for the slaughter?"

"I… No. It's just fiction."

"What about Vincent? What kind of creature would he be?" Liana asked with a teasing expression.

At the mention of his name, heat crept into her cheeks. Closing her eyes for a few seconds, she pictured him in his suit when she'd first met him at the book fair. All black with his dark brown irises and hair. Then she remembered when he held her in his arms as she trembled under the sound of thunder. The way his stubble had rubbed on her head.

A small smile curled Elora's lips as she stared at her friend. "A wolf. A fierce protector, but dangerous if crossed."

Someone set a coffee cup on the table in front of Liana.

"I'll take it as a compliment," Vincent whispered in Elora's ear.

Elora spun, heart pounding so hard against her ribs, she was sure it would burst. Vincent took Elora's handbag and placed it on the floor next to her chair before taking a seat. He wore black jeans with a charcoal-colored t-shirt stretching over his muscular torso, but more than just complimenting his physique, it made his dark irises stand out deeper.

Liana clapped her hands together, and Elora jumped. "Well, I've got to get home. Talk to you later." She grabbed her coffee and winked at Vincent.

"What? Hey! Wait." Elora gaped at her. "You're leaving?"

She had thought Liana was staying with them.

*Idiot.*

Liana grinned. "I am. Have fun." And without looking back, she left.

Elora couldn't look at Vincent. She compared him to a wolf, and he took it as a compliment. Of course he would, but he'd heard the way she spoke the words. She pressed her lips together, muffling a groan.

Butterflies fluttered in her stomach at the potential of freedom with Vincent. So many days they'd have together. But panic flooded her at those same thoughts.

"Are you working with Larry at my place this week?"

He shook his head. "He and Matt are the experts in disposing of that toxic stuff, and I took time off from my primary job today. The rest of my days are free unless my boss calls me in for… assistance."

She smiled as her shoulders relaxed. It would be okay. They were out in public. No danger there.

Vincent arched an eyebrow as his gaze searched Elora. "Why did you change your mind?"

Elora stared at a spot on the table. "My husband… cheated on me. He said he… Well, he made our relationship open, so it's not cheating anymore, and he can keep… doing what he wants with other women." She swallowed hard. "He specified the open relationship was only for him, but… Now he said it's okay for me as well." Heat filled her cheeks at what her words suggested. "It's not why I called you, though," she added quickly, staring at him. "I just… I feel it's okay for me to practice for a photoshoot now. That's all."

*Of course he wouldn't want to do anything more with me; he's a hot model, and I'm nothing.*

"Well, we can start slow and keep it in public," he said with a gentle smile.

*What if it's all a joke to him? Will he tell the other construction guys so they can laugh at me?*

"And you're sure you… still want to do this with me?" she asked in a hushed tone.

"I thought I'd made it painfully obvious," he said with a chuckle as he leaned closer, "I very much want to help you, Elora. Whether that's practicing for a photoshoot together, or… *more*, I'm all in."

She swallowed hard at his emphasis on more, but the thought that he was being genuine relaxed her a bit.

He glanced at his watch. "There's a good ice cream parlor if you enjoy frozen treats," he suggested with a dashing grin. How he melted her on the spot faster than the heat wave outside, she'd never know.

"I don't have the money to—"

He raised his hand, and her palm shot up to cover her cheek as she turned away. When she realized what she'd done, her arm dropped to her side. She closed her eyes, unable to face him after her traitorous reaction.

Silence hung heavy between them, the sound of ice grating in a blender muffled in her ears.

His chair gritted on the floor as he got closer, the heat of his body searing her. "Please look at me."

She couldn't ignore his voice. Fury sparked behind his gaze as he lifted his palm slowly this time.

"I raised my hand as a gesture for silence. I'll never strike you. Ever. I promise that to you, and I never go back on my word."

"I… I understand."

"Mean those words. Don't just repeat them. Mean them." Although his voice was hard, it wrapped around her to keep her safe.

She raised her head. "I understand."

He took a deep breath, and smiled. "Ready to go?"

"I am," she said, smiling. It was nice to do it without feeling forced.

He leaned closer. "I'm pleased you changed your mind, darling."

*So am I. But I'm also terrified.*

## 15

## VINCENT

*I*n normal circumstances, Vincent would use his natural charm to make his date laugh and blush, but with Elora, he treaded carefully. He wanted to act himself, but his personality was on the rougher side and would likely frighten her. Not to mention, this wasn't a date.

*Do I want it to be?*

They stood in line at the ice cream shop, not talking to one another. The colorfully painted walls gave the place a cheery look, and he hoped it would help put Elora at ease. People ahead of them ordered, taking their time, figuring out which to pick. He couldn't blame them with all the choices; two hundred and fifty flavors would take a while deciding on.

Thankfully, it would give him the occasion to watch Elora; see how she reacted to him. Physical touching scared her, but proximity... he'd try it again.

Leaning close to her ear, he smiled as a small shudder ran through her. "Do you know which flavor you want?"

"I enjoy chocolate." Her skin turned pink, heat radiating off her. As soon as he withdrew, she let out a breath.

As their turn came, he pointed at the glass. "They have a bunch of different chocolate flavors. Which kind would you like?"

She shifted her attention to the dessert. "Oh wow... I have no idea. There're so many."

"Do you prefer fudge, fruity? What about mint?" he asked, pointing at the black and green tray.

"I love mint." Her body tensed, and she bit her lower lip. "Are you sure you want to buy this for me?"

He assured her it wasn't a problem, and once he picked his own flavor—cookies and cream—he paid the cashier. As they were about to choose a place to sit, Vincent glanced over his shoulder, and stared at a child standing behind him. He held a few quarters in his half-opened hand as he approached the glass and peered inside.

The kid looked no older than eight, and Vincent frowned. Although, he reminded himself, some kids were alone at an early age; not always the parents' fault.

The boy cleared his throat, and the employee smiled at him. "Excuse me? How much is an ice cream cone?"

"Two dollars for regular."

The boy's face fell as he stared at the money in his palm. Vincent counted what he saw; the kid had enough for one. Fishing inside his jeans pockets, Vincent pulled out a toonie, and placed it in the boy's hand.

The boy looked at him, wide-eyed. "For me?"

"Buying for a friend?" Vincent asked.

"My little brother. He's waiting for me at home." He glanced at the coin, then at Vincent. "Thank you, mister."

Part of Vincent cringed at being called that. He and his brother had referred to old people with the same word once upon a time. When had he turned thirty-seven?

Elora smiled at him. "That was sweet of you."

He'd given the kid money because he knew what it was to scrounge; knew what it was like to afford one thing and choosing to give it to his brother. No reason both couldn't enjoy a treat together.

They picked a table in the far back of the room, and she hovered between the chair in the corner, and the one out in the open. Finally, she settled on the corner chair. He sat, and for a few seconds, they ate in silence. Elora pushed her spoon into her ice cream, then out again, staring at the movement in a daze. Vincent chuckled, and she met his gaze.

"Is that an innuendo for something?"

She dropped her plastic utensil, her eyes widening as though realizing what she was doing. A flush crept in her face, but instead of looking away, she stared at him straight on.

"Oops?" She giggled, and it was the most delightful sound he'd heard.

She was teasing him? Oh, she had no idea what game she was playing. But she'd learn soon enough.

*Gentle.*

"Anywhere you'd like to go next?" he inquired with a husky voice. He dropped his hand from her cheek and waited as he took another bite of his dessert.

"Can... we visit a mall? I haven't been in years."

Music to his ears. She was comfortable enough to tell him where, even if she asked it as a question. He smiled. "Sure. We're not too far from Polo Park."

Her eyebrows rose, and she grinned. "Really?"

He was tempted to tease her and say he wanted to buy condoms—better have them and not use them than need them and not have them—but he didn't want to scare her. Instead, he settled for gentlemanly. "Of course. It's fun to look around. Plus, time in public might be a good idea."

"Okay, sounds like a plan." A flicker of excitement crossed her features, and Vincent couldn't help smiling. She was beautiful; whenever a positive emotion ran through her, she wore it on her sleeve, and she radiated in a light that made him swell with pride.

❧

The mall was quiet since most people were at work, and Vincent's concern diminished. It seemed less crowded places were better for Elora, and he was glad it put her at ease. Still, every time he spoke to her, she flinched as though he'd pounce. The thought of her afraid of him didn't sit well in the pit of his stomach, but he'd be patient with her. Show her he wasn't a threat.

"Want to stop here?" he asked, pointing at a shop with large glass windows selling dresses. Most were summer themed like the one she'd worn at the book fair.

She clutched at the hem of her long-sleeved shirt. "No thank you."

"I know you don't have money to spend." He turned to face her and smiled. "I'm offering to buy a few to give you the chance to wear clothes *you* want."

She stiffened. "But why?"

"Ever heard of a gift?" he asked with a grin.

She stared at the dresses and took a deep breath. "It usually comes at a price."

Her voice sounded so sad, tugging at his heartstrings. Gently, he put his hands on her shoulders, trying his best not to react to the way she trembled.

"I'm not asking for anything in return. This is my treat to say thank you for agreeing to do the photoshoot with me." He pushed his finger beneath her chin. "And you can change your mind about it and keep the gift. It's not an exchange."

Her gaze seemed to search him for a second before she nodded. "Well… Okay. But just one." She stepped into the store, then spun toward him. "Thank you." Her face glowed as she smiled, and Vincent couldn't help the way his pulse sped.

"We'll stop by the underwear shop after if you're feeling adventurous."

A slow blush crept along her skin, but this time, she didn't lose her smile. She focused on the clothes, running her fingers along the material. "I suppose if we'll be doing a photoshoot, I should get used to being outside my comfort zone."

After picking out two dresses and insisting she didn't need more, they continued walking.

She lingered in front of the video game store for a second. "I used to play these when I was a kid. My dad…" She swallowed visibly. "We couldn't afford much, but one Christmas, when I was ten, he got me a Nintendo 64." She glanced at him, her smile radiant. "It was from Santa, so for the longest time, I didn't even realize it was him. He never took credit until I was older. Let me believe in magic for as long as possible, you know?"

There was never any Christmas or gifts when Vincent was a child, but he remembered hearing other kids talk about it once school opened again. He didn't want material things, but the celebrations and food people talked about always made him envious back then. Once they'd started living with his grandmother, money was often tight, and by then, he didn't care anymore to even try.

"Vincent?" she breathed his name with concern.

"Sorry. Lost in memories a bit," he said with a grin. "We never celebrated holidays when I was a kid. Too poor, and it…" He paused, trying to find the words. "Home wasn't a place with any joy."

"I'm sorry." She held his gaze. "If I can, I'll buy you a Christmas gift this year, then." As the words left her mouth, she seemed to realize what it meant, and her breath hitched. "I… mean, if we're still in contact by then."

She looked sad at the thought they wouldn't be, so he took her hand in his, and gave it a small squeeze. "Unless you're the one to cut our ties, I'll be here."

Her smile returned, and she pointed at the store. "Can we go in and look? Do you like video games?"

"I do. I have a PlayStation at my place."

"Lucky!" she said, walking to the section for his console. "Which games do you have?"

Vincent forgot he wasn't on a date—he even forgot how delicate Elora usually was as they discussed games, and she shared her favorite childhood ones. She took an interest in what genre he enjoyed and asked if she could watch him play since she was out of practice.

"Isn't that boring?" They stepped out of the shop with a new horror game he'd wanted for some time.

She shook her head. "It'll be like watching a movie." She

glanced at the plastic bag he held. "I don't go for anything with violence, but a story with ghosts and haunted houses? Definitely."

They walked by a shop selling lingerie, bras, and panties. Amongst other delightful little outfits Vincent would kill to see her wear. Elora froze as she stared at a poster showing a woman in her underwear. He frowned when he noticed how wide her eyes had become, her chest heaving as she struggled to breathe.

"Elora?"

She shook her head, and took a few steps back. "I…"

He took her hand, stopping her from backing away too far. "Please tell me what's going on in that lovely mind of yours."

She scoffed, and the sound broke the tension. "Lovely? The way I think is messed up. There's nothing lovely about my mind."

"I read the picture book you won the award for; your mind *is* lovely. Now," he motioned his head toward the poster she panicked over, "will you tell me what's wrong?"

She glanced at the photo. "I… what happens with the photos from the shoot? Will they end up anywhere public?" A shudder ran through her.

"They might be, but I requested a photoshoot without head shots. The photographer is an old friend, and she reluctantly agreed. Not that she had a choice since it was that or cancel, and she enjoys her work too much to refuse," he finished with a chuckle.

"You…" Her gaze seemed to glaze over for a few seconds before the sweetest smile curled her lips. "You had already thought of that for me?"

"I figured you don't want others finding out you're doing this, so it's best not plaster your face all over."

"Thank you."

He pulled out his wallet and took out cash. "Here. Go buy yourself whatever you'd like."

"What? Why?" she asked, glancing so fast between the shop to Vincent he was sure her head might snap off.

"You'll likely be wearing these types of clothes during the shoot. If you wear these in front of a mirror by yourself, it may help make you more comfortable about wearing them." He handed her the money. "I'll be sitting on the benches across the shop when you're done."

Her eyes widened at the amount, but then a slow smile curled her lips. "What's your favorite color?"

He arched an eyebrow. "Navy blue."

A tiny giggle left her lips, and she grinned at him. "Maybe this will be a gift for you, then." And without waiting for him to reply, she walked into the store.

Taking a deep breath, and readjusting his jeans so his erection would stop pressing into his zipper, he sat on the benches and sighed.

*A present for me, eh?*

# 16

## ELORA

*A*fter Elora stepped out of the lingerie shop, they headed to the bookstore. The scent of dry paper put her mind at ease, and she inhaled deeper as her shoulders relaxed. These were the places she loved. Being anywhere near books was a treat.

Vincent pointed to the section on the upper level. "We can browse a bit, then get a coffee. How does that sound?"

"Sure."

It was strange to be at a bookstore with someone other than Liana. With a date... Elora slowed her steps and frowned. Did Vincent consider this a date? Why was she considering it? Yet, it sounded so natural in her mind.

She stared at the back of his dark brown hair, trailing her gaze along his broad shoulders. Did he want to be here?

He slowed, and when she was next to him, he placed his hand on her lower back, the heat from his palm sending a jolt through her. Whenever he placed his hands on her, she felt safe and cherished.

He guided her to the Fantasy section and grinned. "One of my favorite genres." He glided his finger along the spines. "I was a troubled kid and teenager… and adult," he said with a scoff, "and novels helped me cope."

"Books let us escape to a world outside our own. It's why I love to read."

He shifted to her, a slow lecherous smile curling his lips. "Is that why you enjoy erotica?"

Heat engulfed her as she spun on him. "How——?"

"I saw you checking out the risqué stories at the book fair," he said with a sly grin.

She turned toward a series with colorful spines. "I… yes. Fine."

His soft chuckling sent goose bumps over her skin. "Maybe we could read one together sometime."

They continued browsing, and the entire time, she couldn't help smiling like an idiot. Vincent made her at ease—an emotion she'd long ago forgotten existed.

The coffee shop inside the bookstore was bare, so they walked up to the counter. Once the drinks were ordered, they picked a table in the corner near shelves, and sat.

He eyed her for a few seconds before putting his hand on hers. "Are you still planning on coming to my place?"

"Oh… Well, I already agreed to it, and——"

"You can always change your mind."

Her chest tightened, and she lowered her head. "Do you want me to?"

"No, but I don't want you to feel you don't have a choice." His thumb traced along her hand. "Right now, you're doing better with touching, but it's also because we're out in public. Going to my place where you'll be alone with me terrifies you, as it should."

Her eyes widened, and she tried pulling away, but his grip tightened.

"I didn't say that to scare you. You'd be a fool to go to a stranger's home without planning for it, and I know you took precautions, because I did too."

She froze. "You did?"

"I called your friend, Liana, and told her I would remind you to send texts to her so she knows you're okay. That's when I also suggested she call from time to time so she can make sure you're the one responding." He smiled. "I'd never hurt you, but until you know for certain, you need to feel safe."

He pulled out his phone, scrolled a few times, then handed it to her. She frowned, staring at the message thread between Vincent and her best friend. He wasn't kidding when he said he'd taken precautions for her.

Elora returned his cell. "And what about you? Did you call someone to make sure I'm not a threat?"

He chuckled, his gaze gentle. "I'll be fine. I trust you."

"I guess you don't need to since I wouldn't be able to hold you down if my life depended on it," she said with a laugh.

Desire pooled in his eyes, and her pulse quickened. "If you asked, I'd let you *think* you're holding me down, but…" He leaned forward, and her fingers curled on the edge of her chair. "I'd much rather pin *you*."

She stayed quiet. The usual fear she felt when Richard got into her personal space faded. Without commenting further, he checked his phone, then stared at her.

"Do you want to head to my place soon?"

She uncurled her fingers from the chair. "What's for supper?"

"Lasagna." He stood. "I have one more store I need to stop by before we leave." He put out his hand, and she took it without thinking twice.

While they were at the pharmacy, Elora ambled down the aisles, not looking at anything in particular.

"I'll be right back," he said, then headed into another aisle by himself.

Elora lingered, staring as she walked back and forth with nothing in mind. Richard's sudden change of mind still lingered; why was he suddenly confiding in a priest? Had she really pushed him over the edge, and it was the only way he felt he could get help? It wasn't the first time he took up an interest out of the blue, but this was different. Agreeing to let her sleep around was so out of character for him, let alone when it wasn't even his idea.

With a sigh, she trudged to the next aisle without thinking, but slowed when she spotted Vincent. She froze as he picked a small box from the shelf.

He was buying condoms.

Her instincts shouted to run, but a larger part urged her it was okay. If she didn't want sex, or even intimacy, he wouldn't force her.

She paced the aisle next to him. Was she insane to do this? With a loud sigh, she ran her hand across her face. She focused on thoughts of Vincent. The way he smiled and laughed, and how he took everything slow because he cared.

"Are you good to go?" His voice made her flinch, but she nodded fast, hoping it covered her reaction a bit.

She eyed the plastic bag he held in his hand, the thought of teasing him too great to pass. "Did you buy me a present?"

She should've known not to play a master of flirt. His gaze darkened past desire.

"Oh yes. A gift I'm certain could please both of us." He took a step closer, and she parted her lips. "And it's not a one-time gift; plenty to use again and again... and again."

Her fear of going to his place vanished, replaced by lust. And the trust she felt in her heart when he was close.

# 17

# VINCENT

The door to the condo swung open, and Vincent leaned on the wall, waiting for Elora to step inside. With the way she glanced around every few seconds, he was sure she fought herself on running off. He was proud of her; making it this far took bravery on her part.

"I can stay out here while you search the place on your own."

She twisted her fingers together. "It's okay." Without looking at him, she walked inside.

He followed, putting the shopping bags by the entrance, and moved to the kitchen counter. Giving her space was important, but they'd have to lay out ground rules.

"Elora," he breathed as to not frighten her.

When she turned to stare at him, her gaze shifted to the door of his condo, and she frowned. "You don't close and lock it?"

"Yes, but I'm keeping it open for a reason at the moment." He crossed his arms, and she swallowed visibly. He couldn't help smiling as she focused on his chest. "I want to make a few things clear before anything goes further."

She grabbed the hem of her loose t-shirt and met his stare. "Okay."

"Whatever happens from now on, all I ask for is honesty." When her eyes widened, he shook his head. "I don't mean you spill everything about yourself. You share what you're comfortable with, but when you do, it has to be the truth. In return, I promise the same."

"I promise I'll be honest."

He pointed at the exit. "Once it's locked, you're always free to go. I ask that you please don't run off or I'll worry. If you want to leave, tell me, and I'll make sure you get to Liana's safely."

"Thank you." Her expression changed, and she strode to the entrance.

He gripped the edges of the cool marble counter to stop himself from wrapping his arms around her to hold her back from leaving. But she closed the door and spun the lock. For a few seconds, she kept her fingers there, unmoving as though she fought not to cry.

"Do you want me to show you around?" he asked, and as she turned to face him, he pointed to the only other door in the condo. "Once you see the bath I have, you'll want to try it out. Especially if you need time alone to relax and unwind."

Her cheeks turned pink, but she nodded. "That sounds nice."

She followed him into the enormous bathroom, and her mouth fell open. Because of the design of the residence and where the door stood, it gave the impression the room would be small. He remembered the first moment he'd stepped inside, his reaction similar to hers.

They'd built it in the same rectangular shape as the condo itself, most of it made of tan marble. The initial part of the bathroom was for storage. Towels, oils, shampoos—everything of necessity.

Once past the area, he showed her another section with a toilet and sink. "You can put your necessities in here if you'd like."

She nodded, still looking at the space as though mesmerized by it.

With a light heart, he opened the French doors ahead, and they ambled down the three steps into the other part of the bathroom. A large bath took an entire corner of the sunk-in section, while glass encased the shower near a long counter.

"This is huge, but it doesn't look like it from the outside." She stared from the tub to the door leading into the room. "It's bigger on the inside," she said with a grin. "Like the TARDIS."

He chuckled, the same thought about *Doctor Who* having crossed his mind when he'd seen the place. "I told the same to the real estate agent. Although the Doctor's ship is a little more impressive than a bunch of marble."

Her smile widened. "Which is your Doctor?"

"I'm fond of Ten... David Tennant was born to be the Doctor. But there's something about Nine I always admired. He wanted everyone to live, but also understood death is part of life."

"They were all *fantastic*," she said with a teasing laugh, referencing how the Ninth Doctor often used the word.

He chuckled, motioning his head to follow, and they left the bathroom. "I'll get supper ready. If you'd like, you can watch TV or even play video games."

"What?" Her eyes widened. "I can help with the cooking or cleaning in the meantime. I'm useful if you let me know what you want me to do."

The desperation in her voice was a vice around his heart. "No one needs to be useful all the time. Everyone deserves breaks, and you've certainly earned several." When she opened her mouth as though to protest, he shook his head. "Chores don't define you. You're so much more than that. If you wish to help, that's fine, but it should be because you want to. Not because you believe your worth is tied to it."

Before she answered, Elora's cell rang, and she fumbled in her jeans' pocket to pull it out. She paled as she pressed the screen, then brought the device to her ear, her body tensing like an iron bar.

Vincent guessed who it was on the other side.

He did his best to stay quiet so as to not arouse suspicion.

"Why?" she asked, then quickly pressed her lips together as her gaze darted in a panic. "No, no. It's not... I'm staying at Liana's place. But you said——"

She winced as her husband's tone rose to the point Vincent could hear. He gritted his teeth, hoping he had enough self-control not to grab the phone from her to tell this bastard to leave her the fuck alone.

"Yes. As soon as she gets home, I'll call you. Okay." She nodded quickly. "I'm sorry."

She stared at the cell as her chin trembled. He waited in silence, not wanting to push her into sharing something she wasn't willing to, but after a few seconds ticked by, he broke the unanswered question hanging in the air.

"He wants you to prove you're at your friend's place, doesn't he?"

She slipped the phone into her pocket as she gave a quick nod, then strode to the door. "I have to get back to Liana's. She won't be home until later since she works until six today." She put on her sandals.

"Didn't he tell you it was an open relationship for you as well?"

She muttered to herself as though her mind spiraled her into a panic, but her head snapped up at his question. "What?"

"If your husband turned your marriage into an open one, why does he need to make sure you're with Liana?"

"He wants to make sure I'm... safe." She shook her head. "Even though he gave me permission, he still needs some control." Her breathing accelerated, and he wanted to hold her.

Instead, he settled for taking a step closer to her. "Deep breaths, darling," he whispered.

She met his gaze and did her best to calm down.

He smiled. "Let's get in the car and drive to Liana's place, okay?"

"I'm sorry," she breathed with a trembling voice. "I really—"

"One step at a time." He slipped on his shoes and grabbed his keys. "Start by getting to your friend's house, then take it from there."

Once he opened the door, she walked out, head down. It was like he could see the weight of her situation crushing her from all sides. Not for the first time since meeting her did he consider reconnecting to his old life to make Richard disappear. But he left that life once. If he went back, he'd never leave again.

Vincent remained silent while Elora held her cellphone so tight, her hands shook. He wanted to comfort her, but whenever he spoke, her panic seemed to heighten.

Leaning in the patio swing chair, he let out a breath, thinking of how they could work on her issues while being stuck with that monster. Maybe if he showed her what it was like to be with a decent man, she'd know what she was missing?

He almost snorted out loud at his own thoughts. Decent man? Him?

*No, but I'd never hurt her in a million years.*

He focused on the swing set and matching slide in the backyard. As a kid, he was jealous of families who had the money to buy these. But what he'd envied was how they could play so carefree, without a worry in the world.

Liana joined them in the yard and sat on the outdoor sofa nearby. "He hasn't called yet?" she asked, an edge of annoyance in her tone.

Elora shook her head, her gaze fixated on her screen. "No. I'm so sorry about this."

Vincent gritted his teeth as he glanced at her cell. As soon as Liana had returned from work, Elora had called her husband, but he blew up at her because he was busy. After hanging up, Richard texted he'd call when *he* was ready. Ever since, Elora stared at the phone as though, if she looked away, it might attack her.

A few minutes ticked by in heavy tension before the device rang, and Elora yelped before pressing on the screen, and bringing it to her ear. She paled as the voice echoed from the other side of the line.

"Okay, one second," she mumbled, handing the phone to Liana with an apologetic expression.

Liana took it, and crossed her legs as she leaned back, her head held high as fire burned behind her gaze. "Richard. So nice to hear from you," she said in an icy tone.

Vincent grinned; the woman could easily win a contest for the most sarcastic voice when she truly hated someone.

"Yes, everything here is fine, but we unfortunately have a problem now," Liana continued in a deadly smooth expression.

Elora stiffened, her eyes widening as though her friend was about to throw her under the bus. Vincent took Elora's hand, rubbing his thumb along her knuckles. She stared up at him, and when he smiled, she relaxed a bit.

"You see, both my husband and I work, and I've got my three young kids, which means, when I get home, *they* are my priority." Her voice had turned to a honeyed poison. "If you want to check in with Elora, I won't stop you, but I have other things to do besides wait for your phone call. In the future, I won't be checking in with you, and if that's a problem, then Elora can't stay here for the rest of the week."

Elora's grip tightened on Vincent's hand as her breath sped up, but he knew exactly where Liana was going with her little speech. Slowly, he wrapped his arm around Elora and held her as Liana continued.

"I suppose you'd have to pay for a hotel room if it's not to your liking, but like I said, I don't need to check in with anyone, and don't intend to start now." Her lips curled into a wintry smile. "I hope we understand each other?"

With a smirk, she handed the phone to Elora, who took it with an awed stare in her eyes.

"Hello?"

This time, Richard didn't shout, but it didn't stop Elora from paling with every word spoken on the other line. She opened her mouth a few times, but then snapped it shut as though knowing better than to try.

"Okay," she said before finally hanging up.

"So?" Liana asked as she crossed her arms. "I'm sure he had pleasant things to say about me after that."

Elora nodded, but didn't share what he'd told her, and Vincent couldn't help thinking it was probably for the best. He rested his hand above Elora's, hiding the phone from view so she'd look at him.

"He'll call and speak with you from now on?"

"Yes." She turned her focus to Liana, and a small smile appeared on her lips. "He mentioned he prefers I stay at the house of a woman who should have her husband put her in her place than pay for several nights at a hotel for me."

Liana winked. "I'll tell Brad he can spank me tonight. He'll be so pleased," she said with a laugh.

Elora let out a giggle, her cheeks turning a dark shade of red. "Tell Brad, 'You're welcome'."

Vincent grinned, enjoying how the two women smiled and laughed together. It was music to his ears when Elora was fearless and full of life. And he wanted to make her feel that way all the time.

Liana shifted her attention to a potted plant near her and played with the leaves. "So, am I preparing the guest room for you, or are you heading back out?" she asked in an innocent tone.

Vincent grinned, not missing Liana's quick glance toward Elora.

"Oh... er, well, I..." Elora fidgeted as her cheeks turned a lovely pink shade. "I mean... I don't want to... impose last minute or—"

"You're welcome to stay at my condo," he said with a smile. "But I won't mind if you prefer sleeping here instead. I can always pick you up tomorrow morning if you'd like to meet up again." His pulse sped as he stared at her, waiting for her answer.

She swallowed visibly, but nodded. "I'd like to... go back to your place tonight. If that's okay."

Liana stood. "I'll get your bag, then," she said with a sly smirk, wiggling her eyebrows at Elora before returning inside the house.

Slowly, Vincent placed his hand over Elora's, and she turned to him. They didn't say anything to one another, but her gentle squeeze on his fingers caused his heart to flutter.

# 18

# ELORA

*T*he second time Elora stepped into Vincent's place was easier than the first. Her pulse sped as she glanced at the shopping bags she left behind. Deep down, she always intended to return. Even if Richard had set her up in a hotel instead.

Vincent threw his keys into a bowl near the door, slipped off his shoes, and walked to the kitchen. She stared from him to the discarded key chain, her stomach clenching. A part of her urged to put them away properly, as she always had, but this wasn't home. And Vincent wasn't her husband. He was the total opposite.

Vincent leaned his hands on the marble island, actuating his muscular biceps. "This must've been a hard day for you." He glanced at the oven's clock. "Since it's late to start supper, do you mind eating takeout?"

"Do I mind...?" she repeated the words with a frown. What if it was a trick question? Was this his way of telling her to cook dinner instead? Her head swirled with hundreds of scenarios, each ending in her screwing up.

Vincent's voice brought her out of her panic, and she blinked a few times as he approached her.

"Is there a place you prefer ordering from?" he asked as he took his phone out.

"I... No. Not really. I haven't ordered in years, and apart from the coffee shop I sometimes go to with Liana, I don't eat out."

Vincent seemed to search for the words, then smiled. "What kind of food do you enjoy eating?"

"I'm pretty easy," she said. When she realized the innuendo, she muffled a laugh. "I mean, I'm not picky, but I haven't had a burger for a long time," she whispered.

"Then we'll order from Mrs. Mike's. Best burgers in the city."

Her stomach growled loudly, and she let out a small laugh. "I guess I'm hungrier than I thought."

He chuckled. "Let's get you fed."

She took a few tentative steps farther into the condo as he called the restaurant. She'd noticed how expensive the place looked when she first arrived, but as she stared around, she realized almost everything in here was luxurious. His seventy-inch flat screen television sat on a console holding gaming systems, and on most of the walls, he'd anchored speakers into the brick.

Construction likely paid well, but not to this extent. Not in downtown Winnipeg. And not for the first time, she wondered what his other job was.

❧

While they ate, Elora felt a kind of joy she hadn't realized she missed. Richard insisted on her cooking, and refused to eat anything that had the potential to make her gain weight. As soon as the hamburgers from Mrs. Mike's arrived, the smell brought back memories of when her dad used to return home late after working his second job.

Elora and Vincent sat at the dining table, and as soon as she bit into the hamburger, she had to hold back from devouring the food. The chili mixed in with the usual burger toppings brought out the best taste, and she couldn't help smiling as she ate.

For the first few seconds, she did her best not to spill too much, and wipe her hands on the napkins.

Vincent grinned at her. "It's a sacrilege to waste such delicious taste." He licked the sauce from his fingers, and she laughed, following his lead.

She couldn't remember the last time she had greasy fingers. Or how her skin got sticky.

It was such a small thing she'd missed.

Once they finished eating, Elora gathered her courage to ask Vincent if he'd play the horror game he bought. It had been years since she had fun like this. She held on to a cushion as he played, squeezing it tight and gasping whenever a ghost appeared and chased the main character down a creepy hallway.

He often chuckled at her reactions, but unlike Richard, it was never to mock.

As the hours passed, Vincent saved the game, and turned off the television, rolling his shoulders as though to get a kink out.

He glanced at her and smiled. "I hope I didn't drag it out for too long."

"Not at all." She grinned. "I'm not even sure why you stopped."

With a laugh, he got to his feet, grabbing a remote on the side table as he walked toward the area with a partition. A few button presses later, and lights switched on at different places within his home.

"It's getting late, and I thought watching horror games before you sleep won't help you relax."

Her stomach clenched. "Right."

Would he insist on sleeping next to her? Could she take the couch?

As though reading her train of thoughts, he motioned over his shoulder. "You'll have my bed, and I'll bunker down on the sofa."

"But it's your bed. Shouldn't I——?"

"It's sweet of you to offer, but you're my guest," he said as he leaned against the love seat nearby. "Besides, this is a sofa bed, so it's not like I'll be uncomfortable. But I want you to have privacy."

"Well, if you're sure…"

"I am."

A cellphone noise dinged, and she jumped, fishing inside her pocket to retrieve her device, but then stopped when she realized it wasn't the same sound as usual. Vincent swiped the screen to his cell and rolled his eyes.

"I have a report I need to get in before the end of the night. Time mishap, apparently." He spoke absent mindedly as he smoothed the back of his head.

Her pulse sped. "Report?" She doubted construction came with that kind of task. Likely this was for his primary job.

He nodded as he walked to the coffee table and reached underneath to pull out a silver laptop. "I won't be long. You can use the bathroom to change into pajamas if you want, and then I'll show you something I'm certain you'll like."

Her curiosity peaked as an icy chill ran through her. This was their first night together, and so far, everything had gone so well. He was patient, and kind; she hadn't been so relaxed in years. But they'd stopped playing the video game. His work texted him, and it was as though reality fell once more.

This wasn't a fantasy that would last a lifetime. She'd eventually need to go home. Back to Richard and the way he treated her. It was dreadful for so long—and she knew it—but getting a taste of what Vincent offered made living her normal life somehow worse.

"Are you all right?" Vincent's tone cut through her panic, and she looked at him.

He hadn't moved from where he sat, and yet his gaze embraced her like a protective cocoon. This was why she was here; so when days at home were difficult, she'd have Vincent's image—his voice, his powerful arms, his eyes—to get her through whatever happened.

She smiled. "Just a bit tired."

Without waiting, she walked to the entrance where she left her bags, and grabbed the one she originally brought to Liana's place. As she reached the bathroom, she glanced at him. Warmth filled her chest as he typed on his keyboard, focused on what he wrote; he looked so cute when he concentrated on a task.

With a gentle click of the door so she wouldn't disturb him during his work, Elora put the bag on the floor, then opened it. Her stomach churned when she found clothes that weren't hers inside, and a folded note on the top.

*Elora, since you obviously packed your great-grandmother's pajamas, I took the liberty of replacing them both with a few better choices for your age and the year we're living in. I washed them (although some I've never worn), so pick which you want to wear, but feel free to go nude instead. Have fun! Liana.*

Was Liana insane? Elora needed to shake sense into her best friend. Her pajamas weren't that atrocious.

With a sigh, she pulled out a few of the choices, her eyes widening with every piece she discovered being skimpier than the one before. She was tempted to ask Vincent to borrow his clothes to wear instead. At the thought, she pictured herself wearing one of his dress shirts after they'd slept together; a wild night of sex fresh in both their minds.

She shook her head to get her mind out of the gutter, but the pulse throbbing between her legs didn't vanish as easily. After pulling out every item of clothing in her bag, Elora settled on a pair of baby pink pajamas shorts with a matching tank top—both of which had white lace along the hems.

Shaking sense into Liana wouldn't be good enough. Elora needed to get back at her friend. Maybe forcing Elora's supposed great-grandmother's sleepwear on Liana.

Elora couldn't help laughing at the thought; Liana would rather die than put on something so drab.

She paced near the door, twisting her fingers together. Could she really wear clothing that didn't cover much of her? The shorts ended a few inches above her knees, and the spaghetti straps of the tank top left her so bare. At least it wasn't see-through since it was cotton—and it was comfortable. But did she dare?

*I'm being stupid. The photoshoot will likely have me wearing even skimpier outfits. That's why I bought what I did at the lingerie store.*

At the thought of her purchase, Elora groaned, still not

believing she actually went through with picking that set. What had she been thinking?

She knew the longer she stalled, the harder it would be to leave the bathroom, and so, after taking deep breaths, she walked out.

Vincent typed away on his keyboard, occasionally glancing at his cellphone as though using it as a reference for something.

When she closed the door behind her, it clicked, and Vincent smiled at his screen.

"I've got a few details I need to finish up, but I'll…" he trailed off once he looked at her, the smile slowly vanishing from his lips. Instead, something in his gaze darkened to hunger as it swept along her body.

She averted her gaze. "Liana switched out my pajamas, and it was the only one that's not see-through," she mumbled. Part of her needed him to know she rarely dressed like this, but she wasn't sure why. He wouldn't care, so why did she?

"Remind me to thank her," he said with a grin as he closed the laptop.

Heat burned her cheeks at his comment, and the way he continued staring at her. As though he pictured what was running through her mind for the past few minutes.

He motioned for her to follow, and she did without a second thought, her feet cooling on the hardwood floor. As he approached one of the large windows looking out to the city, he pulled on a rail attached to the side of the wall, unfolding a small set of stairs.

Her pulse sped as she stared up toward the loft, unable to see what was on the small platform. "What's up there?"

He chuckled. "And spoil the surprise?"

She bit her lower lip, her breathing speeding up. "I… Maybe just… a hint?"

"You don't care for the unknown, do you?" There was no annoyance in his tone; only understanding.

"Not really. It… makes me nervous."

"It's a small sitting area with a thin mattress on the floor, blankets, and pillows. I put bookshelves up there and use it as a reading nook. At night, you get a wonderful view of the city. It's a place I like to relax in."

Excitement flooded her as soon as he'd mentioned a reading alcove, and without waiting, she climbed the stairs. Once at the top, she quickly sat on the small pile of blankets, and ran her fingers along the book spines on the shelf in front of her. There were so many genres of books, ranging from thrillers to romances, poetry to fantasy, and even a few non-fictions.

When she finally tore her gaze from the selection, her heart hammered. Vincent leaned against the side of the wall at the top of the stairs, smiling. It was the only exit out, and he was in the way. What if she had to run? She glanced around, realizing that with the walls, window, and railing surrounding her, she'd boxed herself in.

*Deep breaths. Calm down.*

"Having known *reading* is your magic word, I would've started with that." His voice was gentle, and she relaxed a bit.

She focused on the bookshelf. "There aren't any novels at my place. No books… nothing. Not even the picture books I write." She was about to make excuses for her husband, but it didn't feel right. Not with Vincent. "Richard says they're a distraction from my job as a wife. The only time I ever get to see or read books is when I go to Liana's house or if we visit shops."

His hand curled on the railing until his knuckles turned white, making the tattoos on his fingers stand out. He stared out as though lost in his own thoughts—or trying to calm himself—then took a couple of steps down as he looked at her.

"While you're here, please read to your heart's content." Despite the hush in his voice, anger blazed behind his eyes. "I'll finish up with work, then join you as soon as I'm done. If you'd like?"

Her stomach churned at being in a small space with him, but she reminded herself for the hundredth time she was safe with him. "I'd like that."

"Then I won't keep you waiting long," he said as he stepped down the stairs, vanishing from her sight.

As she tried choosing a book to read, her mind wandered to the typing noise nearby. She had to stop being so fearful of him when all he did was be kind. He'd brought her here so she could work on her physical contact issues, and she was certain it also meant working on trust.

In that moment, before she tugged on the spine of a romance book, she decided to make a bigger effort by being comfortable with him. Trust him to take the lead, and if she fell, he'd catch her.

# 19

# ELORA

*E*lora blinked a few times to get the stinging out of her eyes as she continued reading. The story was interesting, but she was so tired, she barely understood the words in front of her. Yet she wasn't ready for sleep; she was too restless, and she didn't even know why.

The lights in the living room below switched off, leaving only the small table lamp next to her as a source of illumination. Her heart hammered as the stairs creaked, and she slowly closed the book, trembling as Vincent climbed the steps.

As soon as she saw him, she forgot about being tired. He wore baggy sweatpants with a white muscle shirt showing off the sleeves of tattoos on his arms, and even the ones on his neck were better visible.

She swallowed hard, her gaze sweeping along each line and curve, wondering what they meant; did they have a story or did he just like the designs?

"May I join you?" he asked with a smile. There was nothing expectant of him; as though if she said she preferred being alone, he'd be on his way without a second thought.

She moved closer to the shelf and nodded. "Sure." Her voice

sounded so small and unsure, and she hated herself for it.

He took a seat next to where she'd sat, and she decided not to overthink as she scooted between his legs and leaned against his chest. His muscles tensed so much, she was certain he'd turned harder than the brick walls surrounding them. For a second, she thought she'd gone too far; he always asked permission before doing things with her, and she'd done whatever she wanted without asking.

Just as she was about to apologize and get up, he wrapped his arms around her, and they seemed to melt into each other in silence. Lights sparkled outside, the city creating beautiful stars.

"Thank you for today," she whispered, unsure she said anything aloud.

He kissed the top of her head, and she slid her hands along his arms, holding him a little tighter.

"And thank *you*," he breathed. "Have you already read my entire library?" There was amusement in his tone, as though trying his best not to make the moment between them too serious.

Had she pushed too far? Was he only interested in flirting and sex? Maybe affection made him uncomfortable.

She forced herself to stop questioning everything. "My eyes burn a bit. I guess I'm more tired than I thought, but…"

"But you're not ready to go to sleep yet," he finished for her with a chuckle.

They sat in silence a little longer as the night sky darkened from a deep blue to a pure black. He shifted, reaching to the side for a small red book near the lamp.

"Do you enjoy poetry?"

She pondered on his question for a few seconds. "I'm not sure. I've never read any."

He leaned his cheek on her head and breathed out, his breath tickling her hair. "Would you like me to read one to you?"

Her heart sped. No one had ever offered to do that for her. It was surreal; like something out of a fairy tale or movies of old.

"Please."

He brought the small book in front of them, and she smiled as he opened it to page seventeen. "Hope" by Joseph Addison. She

closed her eyes, leaning even more into his chest until she was sure
she'd become one with him.

> Our lives, discolored with our present woes,
> May still grow white and shine with happier hours.
> So the pure limped stream, when foul with stains
> Of rushing torrents and descending rains,
> Works itself clear, and as it runs refines,
> till by degrees the floating mirror shines;
> Reflects each flower that on the border grows,
> And a new heaven in its fair bosom shows.

His voice was low and rumbly, sending tingling sensations
throughout her body. As though her brain received a gentle
massage, numbing from her scalp to her spine. Her breathing
slowed, and she wished she could bottle this moment for eternity.
The peacefulness swallowing her was like nothing she'd ever felt
before, and part of her never wanted it to end.

"Time for bed," Vincent whispered in her ear.

Goosebumps ran across her skin, and she nodded slowly,
squinting even though their surroundings were dim. She was
suddenly so tired. So relaxed, she was sure she could sleep for hours.

He helped her down the steps as she held his hand, and only
once she had slipped into his bed did she let go. She buried her face
into a pillow; it smelled like him.

"Good night," she said with a yawn as she pulled the blanket
under her chin.

His lips brushed against her cheek, and she smiled as he wished
her sweet dreams.

❧

The sound of a door opening woke Elora, and she frowned, trying
to understand what was going on. Had Richard left? Was she safe to
sleep soundly without waking to him touching her?

She opened an eye; her surroundings plunged in dark blue shadows. These walls weren't hers. Slowly, her memories filled her mind, pushing away her sleepiness. Turning to her side, she breathed in deep. Everything was all right. She was at Vincent's place.

Motion caught her gaze, and she sat up, staring into the living room. Vincent put a duffle bag near the television, his muscle shirt drenched in sweat. He stretched, moving his arms as his shoulders rolled.

She recalled how he'd said there was a gym in the condo's basement. Had he gone to work out? In the middle of the night? He must have left not long after she'd fallen asleep.

He walked by, then vanished into the bathroom. Water ran as she lay back, staring at the ceiling. She was so tired, but falling asleep again would take time. She was tempted to ask him to read her a few other poems to help her relax. Maybe if she didn't sleep, the night would never end.

She shook her head at her ridiculous thought. Even if her circumstances were different, and she could leave her husband, it didn't mean Vincent was interested. He wanted intimacy between them—that she could tell for sure—but dating? He could've been in an open relationship for all she knew.

At the idea, it was like a hand squeezed around her heart.

Vincent left the bathroom, and she flinched at the sudden movement. The condominium was well designed to help reduce noises, and so it was as though he'd appeared out of nowhere.

She rolled to the other side of the bed, able to see where he stood from that angle without having to sit. Her pulse sped as he pulled the shirt off, revealing his bare back. She never believed drooling over someone was possible, but she was nearly doing it.

Tattoos covered every inch of his skin in black lines, forming different images and patterns. There seemed to be color, but from where she lay, she couldn't tell what any of them were. There was something so sexy and… dangerous about them.

Her gut tightened as she bit her lower lip. She really didn't know the man standing in the dark nearby. What was his other job? His age, birthday, where he grew up, family or friends—he was a stranger. Had she made a mistake coming here?

And she slept in his bed.

Vincent lay on the sofa, and as a few minutes ticked by, Elora's eyebrows rose when quiet snoring reached her ears.

He was already asleep? What kind of sorcery was that? It took her hours of tossing and turning before being able to sleep, but he'd done it with record time.

She rubbed her hand over her face, mumbling how it was unfair some people were lucky like that. Her doubts returned, reminding her constantly he was a stranger and being here was dangerous.

*Stop. It's not true.*

With a huff, she slid out of bed and paced along the partition, trying to calm down. She just had to get to know him. He wanted to help her open up, and to do that, they'd need to trust one another and share.

She wasn't looking forward to certain subjects that may arise, but if it meant finding out more about the man who made her feel cherished and safe, she was willing to try her best.

After using the washroom, she stepped out into the living room. His hair stuck up in a few strands, and she grinned at how different he looked; there was a wildness to him when he slept.

She approached, her focus drawn to his muscular chest where more tattoos were visible. There were so many, but in the dim lighting, she couldn't tell what they were. Yet, even without knowing, they were beautiful.

Beautiful because they were on him.

She sat on the edge of the sofa bed, her finger hovering over a tattoo near his heart. It curled into what looked like a flame, and as her pulse sped, she traced his skin as though wanting to memorize every line and curve.

His hand shot up, and she screamed when he grabbed her wrist. In a matter of seconds, she was on her back as he pinned her beneath him, his forearm pressing against her chest. Her heart hammered so hard, she was sure he felt it.

"Vincent...?" she whispered in a shaky voice.

# 20

# ELORA

*E*lora trembled as Vincent's gaze searched hers; dangerous and almost animalistic. His jaw clenched tight. A few seconds ticked by, her vision blurring as tears rolled down her cheeks. Something in his expression switched, his eyes widening as he seemed to realize what had just happened.

He took a deep breath, pulling away while keeping a grasp on her wrist, forcing her to sit up. She wiped her face with her free hand, unable to breathe properly as he continued staring at her.

She tried tugging from his grip, but he didn't loosen his hold. "Please let go," she whispered between choked breaths.

"Will you run if I do?" he asked in a quiet tone.

His features had turned to the gentle person she'd gotten to know earlier that day, but she kept recalling the way he'd looked so murderous a few seconds ago.

Was he pretending like Richard had? Wearing a mask of kindness when, in fact, a monster lay beneath?

The thought of that hurt worse than it should have, and she muffled a sob by pressing her lips together.

"I… promise I won't… run."

He shifted position so his thumb brushed along the back of her hand. "And why wouldn't you?"

"Because you'll get mad, and I don't—"

"No." He shook his head as he let go of her. "We discussed this before, remember? You don't run because I'd worry. Walking in the city at this time of night is dangerous."

"I promise I won't."

"Elora, I…" He stopped, staring at the wall as though lost in thought or trying to find the words. Finally, he looked at her, his gaze boring into hers. "I'm sorry. Normally, I never invite people here. It's a sanctuary of sorts to me, so I'm usually the one to crash at someone else's place." He passed his fingers through his hair a few times. "I'm not used to having a person here, so when I woke up with you hovering over me, my mind jumped into a fight or fight mode."

Her pulse continued speeding, but she tried her best to listen. "Don't you mean… fight or flight?" she muttered.

A sad smile curled his lips. "I never flee."

"Oh. Sorry. I didn't…" She slipped off from the sofa bed, her urge to run for the door so strong she gripped the armrest to stop herself. "I didn't mean to question or correct you—"

"Elora," he spoke her name so gently, and the lump in her throat threatened to choke her.

Why did it have to be this way? Someone had shown her patience and affection only to turn around and seem like he was about to kill her.

She recalled the last time Richard had punched her in the face repeatedly; she'd been sure she would die.

"Do you want me to drive you to Liana's place now?" he asked, his tone cutting through her memories. "Or do you prefer to wait until morning?"

She swallowed hard, willing her voice to work. "In… the morning is fine."

And, without a second look, she rushed to his bed, needing to be alone. She wrapped the blanket around her shoulders and sobbed into the pillow, doing her best to muffle any sound. They usually annoyed Richard, and the last thing she wanted was to make Vincent angry like that.

She never wanted to see that expression on his face again.

Time passed—although, she had no idea how much since there was no alarm clock nearby, and she didn't dare get up to retrieve her phone. As she calmed, she rested her chin on her hand, focused on the pattern of the pillowcase. His reaction had scared her. But how would she have reacted if it was the other way around?

She frowned, picturing herself waking up to Vincent sitting on the side of the bed, and tracing her skin as she slept. Her stomach churned; she would've screamed for sure, and if she were any good at fighting, she'd have punched him.

*So why am I reacting like this to what he did? I was in the wrong. Not him.*

She pushed the cover off her so quickly while jumping to her feet she almost tangled herself and fell to the floor. Luckily, she caught onto the side of the mattress last minute, then strode to the living room.

Yet her steps slowed as she approached where he lay. His head leaned on his arm as he scrolled on his phone. What if he wouldn't forgive her? Had she already undone everything? He had offered to drive her to Liana's without even asking if she wanted to go back. Was she too late?

She marched to the side of the sofa bed, stiffening her muscles to keep from trembling. Vincent's eyebrows rose as he put his phone next to him.

"I don't want to leave tomorrow morning," she said, hating that her voice shook.

He rubbed at the stubble on his cheek and nodded. "I understand." Sliding to the edge of the mattress, he felt around as though looking for something. "I'll drive you back now. Have you texted Liana to let her know?"

It took a few seconds to process what he assumed she meant, and when she did, panic overtook her at the prospect of leaving. She placed herself in front of him, waving her hands quickly.

"No, no. I don't want to go." She swallowed hard as she stepped forward so she stood between his legs. The heat of his body was searing.

His expression was unreadable, and she wasn't sure whether she'd pushed boundaries again. Had he already decided she needed to leave, and now she was being pushy? Or maybe he had enough of her, and she didn't take the hint. She was troublesome, as Richard often reminded her; she was lucky he loved her.

She blinked fast as the corner of her eyes burned, biting the inside of her cheek to stop from crying.

He leaned his forehead on her abdomen, and she froze as he gripped her hips. "Are you sure?" he asked in a hushed voice. "I know I scared you" He looked up at her. "I'm so, so sorry, Elora. Considering why you're here… what you go through every day…." He let out a breath. "I'm sorry."

She shook her head. "I'm the one who snuck up on you like a pervert."

His mouth curled into a grin. "Are you saying you had naughty thoughts about me?"

She was relieved it was dark so he couldn't see how heated her cheeks had gotten. "I… Well, it's just that you have so many tattoos and they're so interesting, and——"

He stood, and despite a tiny flinch, she stayed put as he wrapped his arms around her. "My past isn't all good. There were moments when I slept with a weapon under my pillow because people wanted to hurt me." His expression changed to something dark, as though he recalled those times. "It's an old habit to attack on instincts, but I am truly sorry I reacted that way with you."

She slid her hands along his bare chest, the beating of his heart under her palm comforting. "If you'd done what I did, I would've called the police. It's my fault. I didn't ask if you wanted to be touched or anything. And worse, I did it while you slept. While you're vulnerable. I'm the one who's sorry."

Nothing in his smirk said he was ever weak, but she smiled at his renewed good mood.

"All is forgiven if you accept my apology as well."

"Done," she answered quickly, then laughed at how urgently she had responded. "I'm still tired." She glanced at the partition. "Bed?"

He nodded, then tried to sit, but she gripped his biceps, and he stopped. They stared at one another as her breath came faster.

"Would it be okay...? I mean, would you sleep next to me for the rest of the night?"

Even in the dimness, his eyes seemed to turn a deeper shade of brown, turning almost black. Like two pools of desire swallowing her whole.

"Are you sure?" He grasped her chin, keeping his gaze locked on her. "You don't owe me anything."

"I don't want to be alone right now." Her mind continued to repeat the same doubts. But when he stood close to her, they slowly faded to whispers she barely heard. He gave her peace.

His thumb traced along her bottom lip. "You're a surprising woman, Elora. Behind the wall you've built to protect yourself, I see a fierce person with so much fire. You just have to break free," he breathed.

"And you'll help me?"

"Yes." He glanced at her mouth. "I'd like to kiss you. If that's all right?"

Her pulse seemed to jump into her ears, muffling every sound, while at the same time, it throbbed between her legs in need. She parted her lips, closing her eyes as he brushed his mouth along hers.

He kissed her, slowly at first. She melted into him, kissing back as she slowly relaxed against him.

# 21

# VINCENT

*T*he oven beeped to alert Vincent it reached the required temperature, and he turned it off quickly. He'd never noticed how loud it was until he struggled not to wake someone.

Elora still slept; cocooned under the blankets like she had tried protecting herself from nightmares during the night. She had stayed on her side of the bed, but as they laid there in silence, her fingers slowly intertwined between his. A few minutes later, she was fast asleep, and he hadn't had the heart to let go of her hand. So small, yet stronger than she realized.

And today, he hoped to show her that.

He slid the breakfast casserole on the oven grill, then closed the door. It was past noon when he'd woken, so he thought it best to make a hearty brunch for the both of them. Bacon, sausages, ham, eggs, cheese, hash browns, and broccoli.

Elora stepped out from behind the partition, playing with the hem of her tank top. "Good morning."

She was so beautiful; her hair was disheveled, falling past her shoulders in brown wisps. Last night was the first time he hadn't seen her wearing a ponytail, and he'd stopped himself from running his fingers through her hair at the sight.

"Good afternoon," he replied with a grin. "Do you want to practice for the photoshoot while we wait for brunch to finish cooking?"

She swallowed visibly. "You... made brunch?"

"I don't know about you, but I enjoy eating when I'm hungry." He tried his best to keep the mood light, hoping if she wanted to talk about something, she'd take the initiative.

She smiled. "Okay, but I'm still not sure what this *practice* even is."

"One step at a time, darling." He enjoyed the pet name for her; it suited the woman he got to know. And he loved how she blushed whenever he spoke it.

"I should get dressed." She rubbed her hand across her face. "I must look like a mess."

Her eyes were red and swollen, her hair tangled, and the bruising on the side of her cheek turned to a faded green. Yet she was striking to him; a flame of life glowing within her, clearer than anything else in the world. How did she have this kind of effect on him? He had kept deeper feelings like these at bay for years—a weakness he never wanted his enemies to use against him.

He pushed his emotions down and gave her a sly smile. "You look like someone who had a good night's rest."

She laughed, trying to run her fingers through her hair, but grimacing when she caught a knot. "I slept well."

"Maybe a nice shower before we eat instead? It'll help you relax." He strode to the door and picked up the shopping bags. "Did you want to wear one of your new dresses?"

She stood next to him, and he hid a smile at how comfortable she already became by approaching him on her own.

"The navy blue with white flowers. Please."

He rummaged inside, and found the one she spoke about, then handed it to her. "I'll show you how the shower works."

Once in the bathroom, she hung her dress on a hook as he ran the water, then joined him by the glass shower. Her cheeks turned pink, and he couldn't help wondering what was going through her mind.

He showed her how to run the taps, the multiple sprays, and even the heater for the pipes running beneath the tile floor. She looked so excited to try everything, and he smiled at how adorable she was when enthusiastic.

He grinned. "Take your time."

As he was about to leave, she placed her hand on his arm, and he froze.

"Thank you, Vincent," she breathed his name, and his pulse sped.

He swallowed hard as her scent reached him. A citrus and mint smell reminding him of autumn in his home in Ottawa. Once again, his heart swelled bigger than he thought possible at her mere presence.

# 22

# ELORA

*W*ith the soft towel wrapped around her, Elora stretched, her muscles relaxed from the warm water spraying from every direction. It was like a massage just standing in the shower.

She ran a cloth over the steamed mirror, and her stomach churned. With no foundation, the bruise on her face was visible. Green hues and disgusting. How could Vincent stand to look at her?

*He's not that way.*

She slipped on her panties and clipped her bra into place. Nothing special; plain like how she often felt. Part of her wished she had cuter ones to wear. She frowned, wondering why it even mattered.

*I want Vincent to see them. To undress me.*

At the traitorous feelings of lust, she grabbed the dress from the hanger harder than planned. Luckily, nothing tore, and she let out a breath. She'd never had such a visceral reaction of desire; as though she wanted to tear his clothes off and ride him like a wild animal.

Heat pooled within, and she groaned. What was wrong with her? She turned the tap, and splashed the cold water on her face, the sudden shock bringing her to reality.

*It's just stress.*

Calming down, she undid the buttons to the navy blue dress, but stiffened when she caught movement in the mirror. The door opened, and Vincent froze.

She faced him, clutching the dress to her chest, but heat burned her face knowing he could see her in the reflection.

He turned his back, leaning against the doorframe. "Sorry, I thought you were finished since the door was unlocked." His voice was gravelly.

She raised her eyebrows. "I can... You don't mind if I lock the door?"

He tensed and took a deep intake of breath. "You have the right to privacy."

She slipped on her dress, then spun to look at herself in the mirror. It was a cute dress, and it hugged her curves perfectly. The clothes she had at home had to be approved by Richard, although it hadn't started out like that.

At first, he'd comment that other men leered at her, making him uncomfortable—under the pretense he wanted to shield her from sleazy people. Slowly, he controlled what she could wear by commenting that she was doing on purpose to get attention. That married women shouldn't dress inappropriately. She vividly recalled the first time she went to a store to return a top she purchased. The shame of what he'd said stung as she waited for the employee to refund the money.

*"You look like you're asking to be raped with that kind of cleavage showing off."*

After that, he declared it would be easier to accompany her when she bought clothes instead of having to reimburse his card every time. Then slowly, he stopped going with her, and without his approval, she wasn't allowed to use his money.

During one of his vacations at home, she'd return from buying groceries to find he donated the clothing he objected to. All she had left were the ones he had given her permission to buy. Even outfits from before they'd dated were gone.

He'd stripped away at her piece by piece, so gradually that by the time she noticed, it was too late. She had lost herself to his abuse, and her spirit for life extinguished.

And then she met Vincent.

Elora glanced at the mirror. "It's okay now."

Her pulse filled her ears as he walked toward her, and she shifted to face him. Standing so close, she could smell his cologne; masculine and earthy. He took her chin between his finger and thumb, leaning forward so his mouth brushed along her cheek. Goosebumps covered her skin. She turned her head, and their lips connected, her breath cutting when they kissed. Every time was a passionate experience; like they were both starving for it.

His arms slid around her, holding her. She moved her hands to his chest, caressing along the soft material of his dress shirt, the hard ridges of his muscles warm beneath her fingers.

He slipped his hand lower, grasping her ass, and squeezing. She let out a small gasp, and he thrust his tongue between her lips, ripping a moan from her throat.

A flicker of fear ignited at what she was doing, but she smothered it quickly. She wanted this. Maybe not all the way, but kissing like this was heaven.

She circled her tongue around his, playing and teasing. A mixture between a sigh and a growl vibrated from his chest, and her mind blanked on everything except the safety she felt with him.

A beeping sound rang from outside the bathroom, and he pulled away. His eyes were hooded, and his smile turned lecherous as he breathed hard.

"At this point, I wouldn't care about letting our meal burn, but I don't want the fire alarms to go off." He laughed.

Lust awoke within her at his mischievous grin.

Last night, it was easier to show affection in the dark, but with him seeing her in a clear light, this time was real—it wasn't a dream. With a trembling hand, she cupped his cheek. He closed his eyes and leaned against her palm.

The beeping noise in the kitchen rang a second time, and she shot away from him as though a current ran through her arm. He locked gazes with her as his pupils dilated.

"Let's eat."

❧

The brunch was delicious, but even better than the food was Vincent's company. From time to time, Elora flinched at his sudden movements, but she was making progress.

They finished eating, and he pushed his plate to the side. "I wanted to apologize for what happened in the bathroom. I should've knocked whether or not the door was locked. I'm sorry."

She touched a finger to her lips and smiled, remembering their kiss. "It's okay. It… didn't bother me."

His eyebrows rose as though not expecting her response, but he didn't comment. He got to his feet and brought the dishes to the kitchen. She stood, but stayed near the table, a bit at odds with not cleaning up after a meal; this was usually her job.

As he busied himself with the dishwasher, she focused her attention on the area. The appliances were black stainless steel, matching the dark marble counters. Her kitchen was pretty, but nothing compared to Vincent's place. She was willing to bet a service cleaned here every few days. Even the rack of metal pots and pans dangling overhead sparkled.

"I have a question I need an open response to," he called out after pressing the button for the dishwasher.

Fear of him asking for details of her personal life crept into the back of her mind. "I'll do my best."

He straightened, and the lewd grin on his lips sent her pulse throbbing farther south.

"If you choose to press through your fears and discomforts for the photoshoot, I have a few ideas. But if you're doing this because you want to work on yourself as well, then we can push further depending on what your limits are." He leaned on the island. "In short, how far deep do you want to go with me?"

She didn't think her answer through before she answered, "As far as you'll take me."

# 23

## ELORA

*V*incent's gaze seemed to penetrate through Elora's core as he straightened, a lustful expression turning his eyes darker. "Would you like to practice with what you purchased at the underwear shop?"

She wished her body wouldn't betray her so swiftly with the way her face heated. Did she want to wear what she bought? Did she dare?

After some mental debating, she nodded, and trudged to the front door to retrieve the shopping bag in question. A warm hand slid along her back, and she yelped, spinning so fast, she lost her footing.

Vincent let out a breath. "I just wanted to mention you don't have to wear it if you prefer not to. If you never use it, I don't consider it a waste." He grasped her chin. "If you put it on, make sure it's because you choose to, not because you feel forced."

She clasped the shopping bag against her chest. "I… I'll freshen up and decide then. If it's okay?"

"You don't need my permission." He smiled. "It's your choice, and yours alone."

As she walked to the bathroom, she couldn't get rid of her

frown. Her decision. It seemed like a strange notion after having lost it for so long. She had choices when she was with him, and knowing that lifted a weight from her shoulders. One she never realized she carried.

Once she closed the French doors, she eyed the latch for a few seconds. Her finger hovered over it, unsure if she could really lock it. She wouldn't mind if Vincent walked in on her.

*That's not the point.*

With a shaky hand, she locked the door and backed away, waiting. Her back was so stiff from trembling that her muscles ached with every passing second. Would he test it? She clenched her jaw as she rummaged inside the bag.

*Vincent isn't like that.*

After calming down, she placed the lingerie on the counter, and stared at it.

"What was I thinking?" she whispered.

She lifted it so it reflected in the mirror, and bit her lower lip. The navy blue lingerie came in two pieces. The panties were almost useless. Small and low riding; they were see-through in what looked like a thin mesh. The top was the sexier part of the outfit, and the one causing Elora to sweat profusely at the thought of wearing it.

As she undressed, Elora couldn't help wondering what had possessed her to pick this. There were modest choices, so why had she gone with this piece?

After slipping on the panties, she checked herself in the long mirror next to the counter. Despite the see-through material, she was pleasantly surprised the mesh was thicker in the front area. Her ass, on the other hand, was only partially covered.

"Why, why, why?" she mumbled as she slipped on the top.

She spun, her pulse speeding so fast, she was sure she'd pass out. A few deeper breaths later, she tried imagining she was inside the store, and it was a mannequin who wore the outfit.

The lingerie had a cute skirt ending past her ass and a plunge neckline reaching above her navel. Despite the lace material, it hid enough, so she had to focus hard to see her nipples, but the rest was visible. With the halter design, it left an open back, so she let her hair fall loose, helping her feel a little less naked, but not by much.

She reached back and grabbed hold of the silky tie closures. With a smile, she tugged on them, which tightened the elastic waist and secured it in a bow. She faced the mirror, glancing at the straps hanging loosely at the bottom of the skirt part. It was too hot to wear any nylon, but she wasn't sure if they looked weird just being there.

"Okay. I can do this. Don't think. Just unlock the door, walk outside into the living room, and stand there."

She rubbed her sweaty hands against her thighs and grimaced at the reminder she barely wore anything. Her stomach clenched, and she rushed to the mirror again, turning to the side. Pushing her hands on her stomach, she sucked in a breath, but sighed when her image didn't shift.

It was still just her.

Nothing. A no one.

She straightened, and held her head higher, determined to crush the negative thoughts away. Or at least ignore them.

Her legs trembled as she approached the door. She lingered near the door, glancing around at the towels and washcloths put away in built-in shelves. A few clothes hung on a bar, and she caught sight of a robe. The idea of taking something without permission lingered over her like a looming threat, but as she slid her fingers along the soft material, she reminded herself that Vincent didn't react the same way as her husband did.

She took a deep breath, and grabbed the gray robe, then slipped it on. There was no cord, so she closed it up and held it instead, staring at the door once again.

The longer she put off, the harder it was to leave, and so she did as she continued repeating inside her mind. Every step closer was an unfamiliar experience in heart jolts, but she ignored them as best she could.

Once out, she took several deep breaths. Vincent had his back turned to her, rummaging in a kitchen shelf. At the other end of the condo, she was less nervous, but the bathroom door was too close behind her. It wouldn't take much for her to bolt, so she forced her leg muscles forward until she stood next to the dining table. Her grip tightened on the clothing, and she stiffened to keep from shaking like a leaf.

"I… hope it's okay, but I borrowed a robe that was inside your bathroom," she said in a quivering voice.

He glanced over his shoulder at her, and grinned. "No problem at all."

She dropped her hand, and the robe fell open. "Do the garter belts look weird with no stockings?"

His expression changed to something past desire; a need had lit up within him, and burned so fiercely, he'd melt her by just staring.

She fumbled with the straps hanging on her thighs and averted her gaze. "I didn't want to buy any since they weren't included, and it's too hot to—"

"It certainly is," he said in a husky tone as he approached her, "extremely hot." His breathing deepened, like he had difficulty catching his breath.

Slowly, he slid his finger along the lace near her collarbone, and she quivered at his touch. His nostrils flared, but he dropped his hand.

"Is it… okay?" she asked in a small voice, unsure if she'd displeased him with her choice. "I'm sorry." She shook her head, staring at the floor. "I should've picked something modest. I mean, I'm sure the photoshoot won't have me wearing anything like this, but I—"

She froze when he wrapped his arms around her. "It's magnificent, as you are. I had told you that the photoshoot wasn't an affair, but I'm regretting those words." He kissed her, and she sucked in a breath at the tingling sensation. "I'm regretting that I'm supposed to be a professional, because I don't want to stop touching you like this."

Her cheeks heated. "Oh… so you like it?"

"That's an understatement. I'm trying hard not to act on my urges because I *like* it so much, darling."

She giggled at the way he sounded so desperate. "I don't think I'll apologize for that."

His smirk reached his gaze, his brown eyes turning almost black. "Teasing me?"

A part of herself came back to life as though a chain around her vanished. As though she could let go and fall, knowing Vincent would be there to catch her no matter what.

She slipped her hand under his t-shirt, her fingers brushing along what seemed like old scars and muscles—lots of muscles. "Is it working?" she breathed.

He chuckled; a mix of lust and playfulness laced in his voice. "It is. Do you want to practice with a game?"

Her pulse sped as she nodded before thinking his proposal through. She didn't even know what it entailed, and yet, the trust she felt with him was unlike anything she'd ever experienced.

He walked to the refrigerator, and opened the freezer door, pulling out a fruit ice pop.

She wanted to laugh at the idea he could use it in any game, but when he faced her, she stiffened. He looked playful, but darkness lurked behind his gaze. He ambled toward her, taking slow steps as though cautious, and put the treat on the table next to her.

He smiled. "At any time, you say stop, and it stops."

"Okay."

"I want you to believe it. Not just rehearse it." He slid his hand to the back of her neck and gripped.

Flashbacks of Richard grabbing her at the same spot when he was pissed off ran through her mind. Tears blurred her vision, and she took a shuddering breath. Vincent came into focus, and he waited, unmoving. When she said nothing, he squeezed harder, and she gasped.

"Please stop."

He let go, and she gaped at him. "You… knew I wouldn't like that, didn't you?"

"Yes. And now you know what happens. You want it to end, you say so, and it's over. No questions asked. Okay?"

She nodded, not fully trusting the idea. "I understand."

"Good. Now, we can start."

She glanced at the frozen treat next to her hand. "Eating is going to help me with my physical issues?"

"Indeed."

"Can I know what the rule of the game is before we play?" she asked with a grin.

He placed his finger under her chin, locking gazes with her. "If you don't want to do this after I tell you, promise you'll say so."

"I promise."

He gave her a curt nod. "I'm going to feed you, but you're not allowed to bite the treat, and you can't use your hands. For every drop you lose, I'll have to…" he leaned forward and licked the bottom of her lip, "clean you."

She was certain her body had turned red at those words, but she couldn't help but lick the place where his tongue had touched her. A slow groan vibrated through his chest, but he didn't move, allowing her to decide first.

"I want to… play."

"If you're sure, then I won't object," he said with a chuckle. He stared down at himself and grinned. "Wouldn't want to get dirty," he muttered before pulling off his shirt.

Her mouth dried, staring at his muscular torso covered in tattoos. So far, she'd seen them at night when the lighting was dim but in full sunlight, he was breathtaking. She pictured him hovering over her as he sheathed himself inside, and she pressed her legs together.

"I think…" she held his gaze, and smiled, "I like this game even more now." Slowly, she slid the robe off, and draped it over a dining chair.

His gaze swept across her body as he grabbed the ice pop. He took her hand, and led her to the sofa, then took a seat. After placing the dessert next to him, he patted his thigh with a grin. "Let's start."

Taking a deep breath, she took a seat on his lap, instantly feeling something hard pressing against her ass. She blinked a few times at him, and he grinned.

"I'm a professional, but I'm also human," he said with a laugh.

He slipped his hand behind her and trailed along her skin. Her breathing came faster, but she did her best to relax under his touch. His fingers were so warm and sitting on him was like he wrapped her in safety.

The air conditioning of the condo sent goose bumps along her exposed skin, but not as much as the way he looked at her. Like she was a treasure to cherish. She grasped his free arm to keep from trembling, and he stopped.

"We can slow down," he said.

She let out a breath. "I'm... okay." When he arched an eyebrow, she smiled. "I promised I'd let you know if I need to stop, and I keep my promises, too."

He nodded as he slid his finger between her breasts, his breath quickening with each stroke. He grabbed the frozen treat next to him and undid the wrapper.

"What flavor is it?" she asked in a hushed voice.

He placed the ice pop along her bottom lip. "You tell me."

# 24

# VINCENT

*V*incent fought for his self-control when Elora opened her mouth and darted her tongue out to lick the tip of the frozen treat. His pants grew so tight, he was sure he'd burst through. But this was for her pleasure, not his. Not now.

"It's peach," she whispered.

He trailed the ice pop on her lower lip and smiled. "Do you like it?"

"Yes." When a small drop dripped down her chin, she laughed. "Hey! You're cheating."

It rolled along her neck, and he eyed it with a smirk as it descended. "Careful now, or you'll lose."

He licked at the sticky juice, and she let out a shuddering gasp. "I don't know if I want to win," she said in a soft tone that seemed to vibrate through him.

"Then you won't mind a bit of cheating?"

She gasped when he placed the tip of the ice pop between her breasts. "Not fair," she said as a shiver ran through her.

"Can I taste?" he asked in a hushed tone.

Her pupils dilated. "It dripped, didn't it?"

He slid the frozen treat along her skin, watching as a trail of melted peach juice streamed down.

Leaning forward, he lapped at the syrup, and she panted. "Ah…"

"Delicious."

When he withdrew and brought the ice pop to her mouth, her face was flush. But a spark of playfulness also shone behind her gaze.

She opened her mouth and sucked the frozen treat. Her lips parted enough to let him see her swirl her tongue around it, and he jerked as he pictured her doing the same to his cock. She met his gaze as she gave him a smirk, and he chuckled at her teasing.

He pulled away the ice pop and slipped it into the wrapper, laughing at her pout.

"Don't worry. I've got a freezer full." His palm slid lower along her hip, then slipped between her inner thighs. He kissed along her jaw, then slanted his mouth over hers, plunging his tongue between her lips.

She moaned as their tongues intertwined, sliding her arms around his neck.

A knock at the door shattered their intimacy, and Elora jumped off him, staggering back. Her eyes widened, glancing from Vincent to the door like it had materialized as some sort of monster. Without a word, she rushed into the bathroom.

He frowned, wondering who visited him since he rarely had anyone over. Clenching his jaw, he got to his feet, then repositioned his jeans to take some strain off his erection.

His old instincts kicked in as he reached the entrance, his hand resting on a fake telephone book on the side table. He hadn't used a gun in a while, but for him, it was like riding a bicycle; he never forgot, even if he wanted to.

After checking through the peephole, he opened the door, arching an eyebrow as Officer Kimberly Grandon walked inside.

She fished in her purse and pulled out a folder. "Look, I get you asked for a few days off, but you still need to check your phone from time to time," she said in a huff.

"Sure, come in," Vincent muttered.

He glanced at the bathroom door, but Elora hadn't stepped out; likely for the best, considering the situation.

Kimberly finally looked at him. "Well, I'm not exactly thrilled about being sent out like an errand boy to bring you this." She shoved the folder toward him, and he grabbed it. "Maybe you don't care anymore, but I want this case——"

"Kimberly." He hissed her name through his teeth, and she narrowed her eyes at him. "I don't discuss work at my place."

"What's up with you…?"

"I make a point of not mixing my personal life with my job."

She scoffed. "Oh, sure. That's why you ask Daniel to send you files you're not even assigned to, right?"

"The difference is, I choose what I bring into my home and what I don't," he said through gritted teeth.

The bathroom door clicked, and Vincent rubbed his hand against his face. He wished Elora would've stayed hidden, but he guessed since she heard a woman's voice, she assumed it was safe to come out.

He stepped aside so Kimberly could see her, his pulse speeding at what Elora might have overheard. Being a consultant wasn't anything he usually hid, but with Elora, he was scared she wouldn't trust him because he was with law enforcement. That she would assume he worked a case on her husband or something.

Elora had put on her blue dress again. She swallowed visibly, but smiled. "Hello."

Kimberly glanced from Elora to Vincent, her jaw clenching. When she settled her gaze on him, a poisonous smile twisted her features.

"I thought you never brought women to your place? Or was it a lie when I asked to come over after one of our dates?"

"You're being unprofessional." He crossed his arms. "And petty. It doesn't suit you."

She laughed, not with any humor, but instead, anger. "Sure." She reached in the side pocket of her purse and pulled out a USB key. "*Sarge* also wanted you to have this since there's some extra information that isn't in the folder. In case you're still interested in your job, you know?"

He grabbed it from her, wishing he'd never opened the door.

Footsteps sounded behind him, and he turned as Elora approached. "What's going on?"

Kimberly stared at Elora for a few seconds, then she pressed her hand against her chest. "Oh, now I get it," she said as she let out a breath—as though relieved. "Another abuse victim project you're working on, Vince?"

Elora took a few steps back as Vincent grabbed Kimberly's arm and led her out of his condo. "What the fuck is wrong with you?" he spat as they approached the elevators.

"What's wrong with *me*?" she repeated as she blinked quickly. "Is this why you never wanted an actual relationship with me? We had fun during our dates and have a lot in common. Now I know you're only interested in being with people you need to help. You can't stand being with a strong woman like me." She shook her head.

He pressed the button for the elevator so hard, the plastic cracked. "I'll be reporting this to Daniel. You're out of your fucking mind."

The door slid open, and she stepped inside. "I wonder who he'll believe between one of his cops, or the man who has a weird obsession with rescuing broken women. Drop the hero complex, and maybe you'll finally move on from whatever is drawing you to these people."

She disappeared from view as his muscles tensed so hard, he was sure he'd explode if he didn't punch the living hell out of something. He closed his eyes, pushing away at the words Kimberly had cut him with. Since working with the police, he'd done his best to help women out of abuse situations, but nothing like what he was doing with Elora. She was different, and now she likely thought she was one in many. That he did this with others when it was far from the truth.

He leaned against the brick wall, taking deep breaths as he

rubbed his hand across his face. How would he fix this rift between them? Had this already done too much damage? He'd planned on telling her what he mainly did for a living, but not like this. Not now.

His jaw throbbed from how hard he clenched his teeth. He needed to find a solution, but first, he had to call Daniel to let him know what happened.

He brought his phone to his ear and waited as it dialed.

Motion caught his eye, and he slowly lowered the device as Elora dashed from his condominium and left by the stairwell.

*Well, shit.*

She took her bag, so obviously planned on leaving for good. Part of him was pissed she ran off instead of talking, but he couldn't blame her for reacting this way.

He ran to his condo, grabbed his car keys while dumping the folder and USB at their place, then slammed the door as he headed to the elevators. Pressing the button to the elevator, he ignored the sharp pang as the broken plastic sliced his thumb; he didn't have time for such an unimportant thing as pain. Luckily, the cab was a floor below, and less than five seconds later, he stepped inside. The whole way down, he kept wondering what he'd say to her. What he would do.

As soon as the elevator reached the ground level, he strode to the stairwell exit, and wrenched the door open. He had to calm down, but the idea of losing her hurt more than he could put into words. The emotions running through his heart didn't make sense to him, but he knew he had to clear the misunderstanding between them.

He leaned against the wall, waiting. His pulse sped faster than the steps on the stairs overhead. She was slower than he'd imagined she'd be in the circumstances, like she had second thoughts about going.

When she reached the last flight, she froze, her eyes widening as she spotted him. She backed away, tears running down her face, her breathing so fast, he was sure she'd hyperventilate.

He raised his hands in the air in surrender, and she stopped backing up.

"I'll drive you, okay?" he said, his throat tight. She looked so scared of him again, and it broke his heart to know he'd done that. "Please?"

She tightened her grip on her bag and purse, trembling from head to toe, but nodded. He opened the door and stood aside so she'd have enough space to walk through; he hoped she wouldn't bolt from there. Catching her wasn't an issue, but if he ran after her, she'd likely break down in panic.

She stayed silent as they walked to his car—save for the occasional shuddering breaths and tiny sobs escaping through her lips. She never once looked at him as she slid into his vehicle, keeping her head down as he got in, and started up the engine. For the first time in a long time, he had no idea what to do. He was usually good at problem solving, but it was so much deeper with Elora. He needed to make her feel safe again; a way for her to trust him, despite the damage Kimberly had done.

*It's my fault for not being honest.*

His fingers tightened on the steering wheel, and she flinched, holding onto the seat belt like her life depended on it. She wouldn't agree to go back to his condo to talk, and in public wouldn't be any better. He recalled how he'd arranged nightly meetings in Kings Park. The place was quiet, but not to the point of seclusion either.

He could use the same route he would to get to Liana's house, but would keep driving instead for an extra ten minutes. His stomach hardened at tricking Elora; she didn't deserve the anxiety she'd feel when she realized what was going on.

No. Hiding the truth had to stop.

"Elora," he muttered her name, and this time, she didn't flinch away from him. "I'd like a chance to explain, if you'll let me." When she stayed silent, he took it as permission to continue. "I understand you don't want to go to my place, but would you consider going to Kings Park so we can talk there?"

"I've... never been there," she said in a small whisper.

"It's near the University of Manitoba. Lots of people use the trails." He glanced at her; certain his heart stopped beating as he waited for her answer.

If she said no, he'd respect her decision no matter how much it hurt him. No matter how much he'd want to wrap his arms around her and never let go.

She took a shuddering breath, but gave a quick nod. "Okay."

## 25

## ELORA

*a*s soon as Vincent put the car in park, Elora unbuckled her seatbelt and slipped out of the vehicle. She needed air. Space. Anything away from feeling boxed in.

She nearly tripped into a pothole in her haste to get elsewhere, but she didn't care. Her chest squeezed, trying to wrap her head around what had happened at Vincent's place.

After he'd escorted the woman out of his condo, Elora couldn't stop shaking. It was like everything had shattered. The only goal she fixated on was leaving. Escaping this nightmare—the lies.

She had grabbed her bag and purse, crying so hard, she barely saw where she was going. But it hadn't mattered. Vincent had caught up to her.

Nausea took over as she walked ahead with nowhere in particular in mind. Sunlight beamed on the few cars and trucks parked in the remote lot. The beep of a car lock echoed, and she jumped.

Vincent leaned against his vehicle, staring at her. She curled her hands into fists, her fingernails digging into her skin. Her emotions changed from hurt to anger, feeling so betrayed she wanted to scream. Richard's betrayals had stung, but Vincent ripping her trust away tore her heart to pieces.

*It's my fault. I should've known better. The men who show any interest end up betraying me every time.*

It felt like every limb was too heavy. She hated herself so much. How could she be so naïve? What had she expected? A happily ever after? Even without this betrayal, she was always going back to her husband. But as she'd gotten to know Vincent, her walls had slowly lowered, and her emotions had taken over.

*I'm so stupid.*

Vincent approached her, and more than anything, she wished he'd leave her alone. Couldn't he understand how much her heart ached?

"Elora—"

"How could you?" The words spilled out with a whimper.

He looked like she'd slapped him in the face. There was a sudden unnaturally stillness to him, and she backed away, her steps uneven under the gravel ground.

"It's not what you think," he muttered, his voice tight.

"No?" She took several deep breaths, but nothing worked. "So what that woman said wasn't true? Can you really stand there and lie to me even more?" she shouted the last part, her chest tightening.

His gaze darkened. "I never lied to you."

When he walked toward her, she raised her hand, and he stopped in his tracks. "Leave me alone."

The pained look in his eyes sent a jolt of anguish inside her, but she wasn't sure what to believe anymore.

He let out a breath. "I brought you here so I can explain." His voice was low. "Will you please let me?"

She gripped the material of her dress, staring at it. Could he truly fix this with an explanation? And even if it was a misunderstanding, wasn't it too late after telling him to leave her alone?

"Yes." She scanned the woods surrounding them and spotted a meandering stone path nearby. A signpost with images showed benches up ahead, and so she pointed toward it. "Can we sit? I'm not feeling well," she mumbled.

He glanced at his car as though about to offer sitting in there, but looked at her and nodded. "There's a section of this place with a garden. Plenty of seating."

She followed him in silence, the lump in her throat threatening to choke her. Birds chirped as they walked along the hiking trail, and despite the cooling breeze among the swaying tree leaves, sweat trickled down her back.

A few hikers and joggers passed them, often making a point of putting a good distance between them and Vincent. She wasn't sure why, but her mind was too preoccupied to care too much.

They reached a fork, and after a few minutes, her heart hammered at how secluded they were. No one had walked by them for a while, and even the path grew uneven with roots sticking out at some places. She jumped at the crack of a branch in the distance, swallowing several times at her drying mouth.

Vincent glanced over his shoulder at her. "We're almost there." He frowned at her, then stopped walking.

"Why did we stop?" She took a step back, pebbles bouncing behind her.

"Are you scared of me?" he asked. When she didn't answer, he sighed. "So it's already too late, isn't it?" he muttered.

At the defeat in his voice, her stomach churned. "I… am scared. Not of you, but about what I realized after that woman left."

"And what did you realize?"

"That I don't know you. You had plans for me all along, and I was an idiot as usual, blindly following like an obedient twit because I… believed you were… different." She pushed her hands against her face and sobbed. "I hoped I could… trust you, and for the first time… I finally thought I had some… worth. But I'm just another abused woman to you. I'm nothing more than—"

She gasped as he folded his arms around her and held her tight. No fight was left in her, and even if there was, she didn't want to move. Why did a part of her trust him?

*I didn't give him a chance to explain.*

The ticking tap of a woodpecker echoed like a hammer in the forest, and as the smell of sun-heated earth reached her, she calmed her breathing. She pulled away, and looked up at him, her vision blurry from having cried.

"I never lied to you, but I hid things I thought would scare you away. But I swear to you, Elora, you are not just another woman to me." He glided his finger across her cheek, and wiped a few tears. "You are worth so much. Every part of you is mesmerizing. Your passion for books. Your love of creating children's stories so they can better cope with difficulties in their lives. The design ideas you doodle. There's a way about you in everything you do." He leaned his forehead on hers, and her breath hitched at the intensity in his gaze. "You have such a beautiful soul; there's a fire inside you that's stronger than you realize."

She did her best to stop her tears, but it was useless. They trickled down her face, and he hugged her, letting her cry as he murmured comforting words in her ear.

❧

They sat on a bench near a bed of flowers, and although Elora had calmed down, she wasn't sure how Vincent's explanation would fix things.

The hum of insects filled the air as he looked out toward a few small animals moving in the underbrush nearby. He reached in his pocket and pulled out a black wallet, his hand curling around it tightly for a few seconds before handing it to her.

She glanced from it to him as she took it, unsure what to do next.

"I'm not a cop," he said as he motioned to the leather.

Holding her breath, she opened it, and the first card behind the plastic cover showed a photo of him. Police consultant. Her pulse sped as she snapped it shut.

"Close enough." She handed it to him, averting her gaze. "So what Kimberly was talking about… A case? And you mentioned you had to write a report. Why keep it from me?"

He shrugged. "Honestly, when it was finally brought up in conversation, you were so nervous with me, I assumed telling you I have a connection to the police would make it worse." He rubbed the back of his neck where the collar had dampened with sweat. "I know your neighbors have called the cops about noise disturbances and potential domestic violence. Knowing I have access to that information would have pushed you away." He turned to the side and locked gazes with her. "Am I wrong?"

She opened her mouth to tell him he was, but then closed it. "No. You're right."

"As for her comment about not bringing other women to my place, you already knew that." He slid his arm along the wooden backrest. "I went on a few dates with Kimberly a couple of years ago, but it never clicked for me." He shook his head and chuckled. "Well, that's not entirely true. I wasn't looking for a serious relationship, but I made sure it was clear. Kimberly didn't accept I wasn't interested in more."

Elora got to her feet, and walked toward the farther end of the garden, focusing on the bees fluttering between the flowers. Vincent joined her, and she wasn't sure what to say to break the heavy silence between them.

Thankfully, he took the lead.

"I've hurt the trust between us, and no matter how many times I apologize, it won't repair the damage I've done. I promised you honesty, and I keep my promises. I shouldn't have hidden things from you, but as a first step, I want to rectify this."

He squeezed his wallet, then unzipped a section, and he pulled out a familiar piece of paper. She frowned when she realized it was the photoshoot contest ticket from the book fair.

With trembling fingers, she took it from his outstretched hand. She stared at the ticket, her breathing faster. "This isn't Liana's handwriting…" Her eyes widened. "You didn't pull my name out of the box. You held this when you pretended to pick one at random."

"When I saw your photo on the award poster at the convention, I wanted to destroy whoever gave you the despair in the depths of your gaze. You were smiling, but it didn't reach your eyes." He took her hand, and she looked up at him. "I want to help you. That was never a lie."

"So what Kimberly said is true. I'm just another abuse victim project. But you can't fix me, and——"

He grabbed her shoulders, and she gasped, gripping his biceps to keep steady. "You're not broken. There's nothing for me to fix. But accepting help isn't a weakness."

"It is if you trust the wrong person," she whispered. "So you assist other abuse victims?"

He dropped his hands. "Yes. Never directly, but I made sure they had the resources to escape."

"So why did you change your tactic with me?"

He averted his gaze, his jaw clenched as he seemed to find the answer. Instead, he let out a breath and shook his head.

"It's a good question, but I don't have the answer." He stared at her. "Why do you stay with him when he hurts you?" His voice was harsh, the desperation to understand tearing her apart.

She wanted to tell him the truth. How it was her fault she had to stay with Richard. That there was more than just paying for her dad's nursing home on the line. But she couldn't. Telling him meant he'd realize what a selfish and horrible person she was.

She twisted her fingers. "I... I don't have a choice."

"There's always a choice," he stated between his teeth. "People in your situation end up leaving their abusers one way or another. Alive or in a body bag." His tone was laced with anger. He pressed his lips together and closed his eyes for a second. "I'm sorry. I didn't mean——"

"I get it," she said with a trembling voice. His words hurt deeply, but as an advisor with the police, he must've seen a lot of death.

"Elora——"

"This can't last forever. You know that, right?" she whispered. "I'll go home on Sunday. You'll eventually finish up the construction project on the house. We'll do the photoshoot, and then..." The lump in her throat ached so much.

"Then?" When she didn't answer, he pushed his finger under her chin and tilted her head. "Then what?"

"What good does it do to keep seeing me? Doesn't it only upset you?"

"Because as long as you want me, I'm here for you." His voice was raw, as though his emotions fought for release.

Never being with him again was too painful to consider, and she gave in. For what time they had, she'd take comfort in what he offered. No matter how much her heart longed to have more with him.

## 26

# VINCENT

*R*eturning to his place felt wrong—there was still tension between them. Deep down inside, he knew it was too late. They'd passed the playful, getting to know each other, part of things, and had jumped into something he wasn't sure how to describe.

He needed time to figure things out and give Elora the same courtesy.

"Do you want to go see a movie?" he asked, keeping his focus on the road. He'd driven for a while with no destination in mind, but he couldn't stall forever.

"I'd like that. Haven't gone there in years..." She stared out of the passenger window and leaned on the headrest. "I wonder if there are any ghost movies playing."

He chuckled, recalling how she'd enjoyed watching him play the horror video game he'd bought. "You really like ghost stories, don't you?"

She nodded, a smile curling her lips. "I used to love watching *Goosebumps* and *Are you Afraid of the Dark?* as a kid. My dad tried to discourage me because he thought I'd have nightmares, but eventually he gave in when he caught me reading the *Goosebumps* books."

"Ah, so you were a little rebel?" he asked, laughing at the image of a young Elora, reading under the covers with a flashlight.

A memory of hiding beneath his covers as a child flashed through his mind, and he gripped the steering wheel tighter. Vincent's brother had wet the bed again, and was crying, terrified their father would kill him for it. Vincent had spent many nights washing out accidents in the basement sink as quietly as possible. A few times, he hadn't caught it fast enough, so he'd take the blame for it, needing to protect his little brother.

"Vincent?" Elora's voice drew him out of his mind, and he glanced at her.

"Sorry." He gave her a sheepish smile. "I guess I'm a bit tired."

"Me too," she said. "Well, it makes things easier, right?" When he arched an eyebrow, she grinned. "We can pick a movie at random since we'll both fall asleep."

He laughed, his mood picking up at the sight of her smile.

The movie theater in question wasn't far from where they were, and within minutes, Vincent parked, and they stepped into the lobby.

Crowds were definitely an issue for Elora as she kept glancing around. She jumped at every little sound like they were monsters waiting to attack her.

He led her to the area showing off framed movie posters. As her gaze swept the posters, she bit her lower lip.

"What if someone recognizes me?" she asked quietly, glancing over her shoulder for the hundredth time.

He tapped her sunglasses and grinned. "That's why you've got these. And with your hair loose and almost covering your face, I'd say it would be hard to identify you even if you robbed the place."

"Who would rob a movie theater?"

"Anyone with a brain would. With what they charge for the food alone, you'd make out of here with millions." He pointed at the posters. "Anything you'd like to watch? Or fall asleep to?"

She nudged him with her elbow and threw him a smile. "Not really. I guess something quiet if we plan on napping."

They stepped up to the concession counter where neon lighting and pricing boards flashed overhead. She clutched at her dress, glancing from him to the sign. "You've spent a lot on me..."

He leaned forward and kissed the tip of her nose. "And it's my pleasure to keep doing so."

Once he paid for the tickets, the rattle of popcorn popping caught his attention, and he motioned to the line-up for the food. She followed in silence, and he took her hand in his, giving it a quick squeeze. This time, her grip tightened, and she didn't let go. Why was his heart beating so fast? It was such a small act—something he did on first dates and even hook-ups. But with Elora, it meant so much more to him.

As they stood in line, Elora's phone dinged with a text notification, and she stiffened. He wanted to take it from her and smash it against the wall, but instead, settled on throwing a few popcorn bites into his mouth.

She took a step back, bumping into him. His stomach hardened at how much she trembled, but before he asked what happened, she strode away from the line. A few people in line shot her curious looks, but Vincent ignored them, rushing after her.

He wanted to give her room, but when she stepped outside, he grabbed her arm and spun her. A tiny cry escaped her, and she moved her hand to her mouth.

"What is it?" he asked quietly, already guessing who it was from.

Her panic tore at his core, so he led her to a bench as far away from the entrance, and sat.

Without a word, he wrapped his arms around her waist, and stared at the cellphone she held in her hand.

Of course, it was a message from her husband.

*Richard: The foreman called. They removed the asbestos. There was less than he assumed. I want you home tomorrow. I'll be there around 5:00pm. See you later.*

Tears fell on her screen. "I thought... we had more time," she said, her voice thick. "It was supposed to be until... Sunday."

"We will. Don't worry." He pushed her hair to the side and nuzzled her neck. "We have today, and a bit of tomorrow. You said he goes on a lot of business trips and dates with other women, so when he leaves, we'll arrange something." He clenched his jaw. "Besides, construction continues on Monday, and I'll be there."

Her phone buzzed.

*Richard: There are workers coming by early tomorrow to finish sealing something. Just be careful when you go into the house.*

Vincent grabbed his own phone and texted Larry, asking if he needed any help tomorrow. Sure enough, the foreman could use a hand for about an hour to bring the materials from the truck into the yard.

"Tomorrow, I'll drive you to Liana's place, then I'm heading to your house to help Larry." He tightened his hold on her waist. "If you'd like, I'll linger after they leave, and we'll have a bit of time before I have to go."

She nodded, putting her phone into her purse. "Can you get a refund for the tickets? I... just want to go to your place. If that's okay?"

He forced a smile. "You read my mind."

Vincent wished the day had gone differently. It had started off so well, but ended in a nightmare for Elora. They walked into his condo, and she immediately marched to the window, staring out for a second before heading toward the sofa, but just stood near it.

He was tempted to drive her to Liana's house, but decided against it; the last thing he wished was for Elora to think he didn't want to be with her. On the contrary, time ran too quickly, and every second they were together was a countdown to an end he wasn't ready for.

She rubbed her arms as though cold, trembling so violently he thought she'd be sick. He rushed to her and held her from behind.

"How about a bath? It'll help warm you up, and will help you relax," he murmured in her ear. "I've got bubbles."

Teardrops fell onto his hand, and he leaned his cheek on the top of her head, closing his eyes. Her pain hurt him, but he couldn't let her go. He couldn't stop trying to reach her, despite knowing she'd likely never leave her husband.

*Unless he's no longer breathing.*

The dark thought circled in his mind for a few times before he extinguished it. If he turned back to his old life, only one person could bail him out, and then there would be no leaving it a second time.

"A... bath would be nice," she said in a small voice.

He helped her to the bathroom; she seemed so dazed, he wasn't sure she'd know what to do once she arrived at the tub. Not bothering to show her how the taps worked, he busied himself with running the taps, and turning on the jets. Continued warm water sprayed inside, the overflow drain ensuring it didn't reach a flooding limit. He squeezed bubble bath soap under the flow, and once it reached a satisfactory height, turned off the main tap.

"Take your time." When she nodded, he moved to the door, then slowed his steps, leaning on the frame. "Was it... too much for you today?" he asked quietly.

"It was a lot... but this morning, before everything... it was good."

"I didn't go too fast?"

"No... But right now, it's easy for me to say that. If we were ever... you know, in the middle of *that*, then would it matter if I wanted to slow things?"

He gripped the framing harder to keep from reacting too harshly to her words. But heat filled him, and he spun on her, closing the gap between them in two steps. She staggered back, hitting the glass door, and covering her face with her arms.

Her reaction was like a bucket of cold water splashed over him, and he swallowed the lump constricting his throat. He couldn't breathe. Despite everything——the good and the bad——she was terrified. Years of abuse wouldn't disappear in a few days.

*I'm an idiot.*

She lowered her arms slowly, her gaze fixed on nothing in particular, as though she processed what had just happened, her breathing uneven. To hear her think he wouldn't stop if they were in the middle of sex hurt like hell. Her trust for him was likely more than she'd trusted anyone for a long time, but it was not much.

She lifted her hands and blinked a few times. "I... I *am* broken." As large tears rolled down her cheeks, it felt like he was stabbed in the gut—again.

*This is what happens when you care about someone. It hurts.*

"Elora, look at me," he said. "There are a few things I need to make clear." When she stared up at him, he ran his fingers through her long brown hair. "You're not broken, remember? I told you the truth when I said you're not a project, but you *are* special. I can't explain it to you because I don't understand it myself, but I do care for you."

"It changes nothing, does it? My life is what it is."

He cleared his throat, desperate to stop it from choking him. "It doesn't need to be that way. I know how most abusive relationships end. I wasn't making a crack at dark humor when I said people in your situation either leave alive or in a body bag."

She straightened, glaring at him as her lips trembled. "I know!" Her voice rose. "But I don't need to hear it from someone who——"

He leaned forward so fast, she froze. "From someone who had an abusive father?"

His lips twisted in a bitter smile when her eyes widened. He didn't want to feel victorious at her stunned silence, at the pity in her gaze, but a part of him did.

Her expression softened. "I'm sorry."

He looked aside, sitting on the edge of the tub. "My father hit my mother every day. I remember her screams, the bruises... the fear in her eyes." The ceiling seemed to descend as though wanting to crush and suffocate him. "I was playing inside a crawl-space connecting my bedroom to my parents' room one day, as I often did, away from him and his rages. But he was drunk and more violent than usual. He pulled her into their room, and I saw him beat and rape her." He leaned his elbows on his knees, squeezing his hands together so tight, he was sure his bones would shatter. "And I watched. I let her cry and scream for him to stop, beg for help...

and I did nothing." He laughed, and it sounded eerie to his own ears. "I was five when it happened."

"What were you supposed to do?" Her voice shook so much, he turned to her. Tears fell, but these were different. They weren't for herself or her situation, they were for him. For his pain.

Years of anger and regret flooded through him. "I was supposed to do something. Anything." He scrubbed the back of his neck. "She gave birth to my little brother nine months later. My father despised him because he wasn't planned. And my mother barely looked at him without breaking into tears because he was the reminder of what happened. So I took care of him. I hid him in closets and took the beatings meant for him."

"I'm so sorry," she whispered. She sat next to him and placed her hand over his as she leaned on his shoulder.

Her willing touch filled him with a joy he couldn't describe and hated himself for feeling it while remembering the horrible memories of his childhood.

"It was a long time ago," he muttered.

"I shouldn't have assumed you didn't know what it's like in my situation."

The urge to tell her the rest of the story bubbled beneath the surface, but he motioned to the tub. "Do you still want the bath? I'll have one after you're finished."

She withdrew, getting to her feet. "Actually, I'll take a nap… If you don't mind?"

Before he answered, she walked away, her head down. His heart seemed to stop as his stomach churned. Had telling her about his past been a mistake? Was she repulsed by him not having done anything to protect his mother?

He dipped his hand into the warm water, staring at the bubbles. He hadn't confided in many people the story of his childhood. Maybe he should've kept it to himself.

# 27

# ELORA

*E*lora focused on the empty spot next to her as Vincent's childhood replayed inside her mind.

*Is he trying to save his mother through people like me?*

But there was more between them than that. The way he looked at her, and how she felt with him. The idea of going back to her life after the photoshoot lingered, but every hour that passed with Vincent seemed less and less possible to return to it.

She'd gone to bed with her dress on, but as the minutes ticked by, she slipped off her panties and bra, unable to get comfortable while wearing something so constrictive. With just her dress, it was better, almost like a nightgown.

Turning on her side, she stared off at the partition. The sun lowered in the sky, casting pink and orange hues against it, creating beautiful shapes as it touched the paper material.

Vincent had stayed in the bathroom, and unease crept inside her. With a frown, she sat up in bed, bringing her knees to her chest. He'd shared a traumatic event in his life—his childhood, no less—and she left him alone. She wanted to comfort him, but was scared he'd see her care as pity. He learned what it was to grow up with domestic abuse, and told her about leaving by choice or in a body bag. Which had his mother ended up in?

She swung her legs out of bed and approached the bathroom door, the sound of the sprays reaching her ears. He was likely in the bath. Alone with his thoughts after he'd been vulnerable and opened up to her. Her shoulders slumped, realizing how cruel her actions were. If she'd confided in him about something so personal, and he'd left her after, she would've felt horrible.

At that moment, she needed to hold him. Not necessarily say anything, but be there for him, as he was for her several times. She swallowed hard as she stepped inside. The French doors were ajar, and she approached slowly.

He sat in the tub, his cheek leaning on his fist as he stared off into nothingness. His muscles were tense, and he didn't look like the bath relaxed him. Without a second thought, she pushed the door open, and walked down the steps. He stared at her, an unreadable expression on his face. Still, she followed her instincts of what he'd do if the roles were reversed. Followed what her heart told her he needed.

She slid the dress over her head, and let it drop to the floor, standing naked in front of him. His gaze threatened to melt her on the spot, and despite the heat pooling in the pit of her stomach, she approached.

"Can I join you?" she asked. When he nodded, she motioned to the side and smiled. "Scoot."

He arched an eyebrow, but slid forward. She dipped a foot into the water, the warmth relaxing her muscles.

Her breath caught as she stared at his back; a tattoo piece covered it. The ones on his arms and chest reached toward it. They were black and gray, but the bright red touches made it stand out, impossible to look away.

A phoenix bursting through blood. Reborn.

Feeling awkward standing there, she sat, then slid her hands along his shoulders and pulled him back. He leaned against her chest, stiff at first, but gradually relaxed with time. The jets continued adding water, the bubbles floating at the top. Silence hung between them, and as his torso grew cold, she grabbed a sponge resting on the side of the tub, and submerged it underneath the water. Slowly, she brought it up to his collarbone, and squeezed the warm water.

He took her hand, then drew it to his lips. "You didn't need to——"

"I want to," she said, leaning her mouth close to his ear. "Unless you don't?"

A half-chuckle, half-grown left his throat. "There's nothing more in the entire world I want."

She ran her fingers below his navel and brushed his pubic hairs. "Nothing?"

"I'd like to remind you torture is illegal in this country," he said in a strained voice.

She grinned. "Can we... go lie in bed?"

He nodded as though not trusting himself to speak and slid forward so she could stand.

Once out of the tub, she grabbed a towel hanging on the metal bar near the shower, and wrapped it around her waist. She averted her gaze, swallowing hard as nerves took a hold of her.

"I'm going to use the washroom. I'll join you in a minute," she said, quickly making her way to the separate room with the toilet and sink.

She leaned on the door. Sex wasn't something she was afraid of; she wasn't overly fond of it with Richard as the years passed, but she had the feeling with Vincent, it would be different. And that's what she was nervous about. If they shared that kind of intimacy, saying goodbye would be harder. Yet the idea of him embracing him sent flutters in her chest; she wanted him so much, it was painful.

Among her friends in high school, she had been the first to lose her virginity. Not something she ever boasted about or was proud of, but it made her popular with the guys, and she enjoyed the attention at the time. But it wasn't like she slept around a lot; on the contrary, she always dated the person for a while before getting intimate, and all her relationships had been monogamous. A value her dad had taught her. As Elora got older, she understood it wasn't the only way, but for her, anything else didn't work out. She didn't care for the one-night stands or open relationships.

Elora thought back to when she had met Richard in university. He was completing his bachelor's degree at the same time as her, but in computer science. Lots of young women were all over him, but he only had eyes for Elora, and continued pursuing her even though she had a boyfriend. As soon as her boyfriend left her, Richard seemed to magically appear wherever she went. It was romantic to her then, but as she remembered the details without the rose-colored lenses of love, it seemed like he was stalking her. Memorizing her schedule, where she ate breakfast and lunch.

With a sigh, she finished drying herself off, her mind going back and forth between wanting to have sex with Vincent and being too scared of the feelings it would likely bring to the surface.

As she freshened up, she hung the towel on a hook behind the door, and stepped up. The air was cool on her naked body, but she continued forward, only stopping when she reached the foot of his bed.

Vincent sat on the mattress, leaning on the headboard, his legs stretched out. The blanket covered his pelvic area, leaving the rest of him on display like a marble statue of rippling muscles. His gaze was hooded as he stared at her, but he waited patiently for her to make the first move.

She pushed her uncertainties from her mind, and walked to his side of the bed, pulse speeding with every step. He took her hand, his thumb brushing over her knuckles, as if he needed to touch her even if it was only a few inches. Before she lost her nerve, she kneeled onto the mattress, then straddled him, wrapping her arms around his neck.

Their gazes locked, and her breath hitched as he glided his fingernails gently along her back. Goosebumps crawled on her skin, and she closed her eyes at the feel of him.

He kissed her, his hands exploring her curves as she slid her fingers through his hair. A gentleness surrounded her, and she opened herself to him, allowing the walls of defense surrounding her for so long to lower.

She shifted her hand along his abdomen and grabbed the blanket as she lifted herself a bit to pull it away. With the barrier between them gone, she withdrew, panting as she stared at him. Her gaze searched his as his erection pressed against her mound, the heat of his cock threatening to sear her.

"I want you…" she whispered.

He buried his face in her neck and muttered a few curses. "I crave you too. So much, it's breaking me into pieces. But today was difficult for so many different reasons." He grasped her chin. "You're vulnerable and hurting."

"The way I feel with you is… I don't know how to put it into words," she breathed, grasping his wrist. "When you hold me, nothing can hurt me. The world could end, and as long as you had your arms around me, I'd never notice because I'm safe. But it also feels like no matter how close we are, I want more." She guided his hand between her legs, and a small gasp left her as his fingers slid between her swollen lips. "I want to feel you inside, too."

He let out a shallow breath, leaning his forehead on her shoulder as his muscles tensed.

## 28

### ELORA

*S*ilence hung heavy between them, and Elora was sure she'd asked for too much.

"I need to… get a condom," Vincent said, his voice rough.

She kissed along his jaw, his stubble rough on her lips. "Okay."

He reached toward his nightstand, and opened the drawer, his breathing heavy. Once he grabbed a condom, he tore the small packaging with his teeth. She raised herself off of him a bit, butter-flies fluttering in her stomach as he slipped the protection onto his erection.

He crossed his legs beneath her, then leaned forward, and she yelped as she wrapped her thighs around his hips.

Straightening, she tried catching her breath; the position they were in was intimate in a way she didn't know how to describe. Their bodies intertwined together, the heat radiating from them creating a fire of desire.

He lifted his knees a bit as he reached between them, then pressed the head of his cock against her wet opening. A throbbing need pushed her on the edge to beg him to take her.

"Are you sure?" he asked in near desperation, as though suffer-ing. His gaze was dark, swimming in hunger as he stared at her.

"Yes."

She gripped his shoulders, bracing herself as he gently lowered his knees. His hot flesh slid into her, and she fought for air as he guided himself slowly, inch by incredible inch. He kept his arms wrapped around her, his hand grasping her shoulder until he filled her to the hilt.

Their bodies' joining was beyond pleasure; it was like an erotic dream she never wanted to stop. The harsh rush of his breath warmed her cheek as she dug her fingers into him, trembling at the fullness.

His palm slid along her hip, higher and higher until he cupped her breast and gently squeezed. She gasped, brushing her cheek on his jaw, his stubble rough against her. He captured her lips and ravaged them as though starving, his tongue stroking her mouth to ecstasy.

He rocked them, each stroke slow, yet relentless. She lifted her knees, leaning back to meet each possessive thrust, the pleasure building within like molten heat. His throbbing shaft moved hard into her, and she twisted in his arms, desperate for more.

"Vincent..." she moaned, the smell of sex turning her lust into an animalistic need. She gripped his shoulders tighter, lifting herself to take all of him inside.

He hissed through his teeth, his gaze like a brand as he slowed his thrusts. Leaning forward, he pulled out before laying her on her back. A rush of heat flashed through her as he licked his lips with untamed sexuality. He pressed his shaft at her center and entered her fully in one deep thrust. She cried out, and spread her legs wider. He sank himself into her, again and again, then captured her lips in another kiss.

She panted into his mouth, unable to catch her breath, his rhythm increasing until she was on the edge of an orgasm. He slowed, and she whimpered at the sudden loss of thrusting.

"Please... don't stop," she begged, grasping at his shoulders.

He smirked, running his hand along her body until he reached her chest. Pleasure flashed through her as he tugged gently at her nipple, then he leaned to her other breast and whisked her aching peak with his tongue. He captured it between his lips, then suckled, his index and thumb rolling her other engorged tip. She shuddered as he brushed his mouth on skin, lower and lower until he dipped his head between her thighs.

Bringing her legs over his shoulder, he slid his fingers inside her wet opening, and she whimpered. He lapped at her clit, so slowly she thought she would die of need. She writhed, and he grasped her thighs before capturing her sensitive nub between his lips and sucking. Waves crashed against her and she cried out, running her fingers through his hair, and muttering his name as a curse.

His tongue delved inside her heat, his thumb rubbing along the side of her clit, faster and faster until her grip in his hair tightened. Pressure built in the pit of her stomach, her muscles stiffening as her breaths came in quick gasps. He moved his mouth to her pink flesh, suckling as his fingers pumped into her center in firm thrusts. Overwhelming spasms shook through her body, and she screamed in ecstasy.

Her gasps were shallow and fast, her legs jerking as he gently removed them off his shoulders. She rode the waves of her orgasm as he loomed over her. He buried his cock to the hilt in one thrust, and she sucked in a startled breath, her toes curling at the fullness. She brought her knees up to accommodate him, and he slammed into her, forcing a cry past her lips. The sound of their skin slapping together sent goosebumps all over her body as he pumped wildly inside her. She couldn't breathe, but it didn't seem to matter at that moment. Every thrust pulled her closer to the edge, but whenever she was close, he slowed, taking his time to touch her. As though he needed this to last a lifetime.

Pressure built within her, and she arched her body into his. Sweat coated his forehead as he lost the rhythm of his pounding and they turned frantic.

Overwhelming spasms reached their peaks, and she screamed, convulsing under an incredible orgasm. He groaned long and low, the last slamming thrusts of climax pumping into her.

He laid his body over her, leaning against his forearm so she wouldn't take his full weight. Slowly, he brushed his lips along her neck and kissed her. His shallow pants tickled her skin as she drew ragged gasps, her mind in a fog of after-pleasure she didn't know was possible.

He raised himself and smiled. "How are you feeling?"

"I'm sure if I tried walking, I'd fail." She grinned. "I feel *fantastic*," she said, putting emphasis on his favorite doctor's catchphrase.

"Using a *Doctor Who* reference after sex?" He rolled them to the side, spooning her. "A woman after my heart."

His words caressed her, yet at the same time, pained her. She couldn't think of anything to say, so she slid her fingers into his hand in a silent show of affection. He nuzzled her neck, and soon, his breathing evened and slowed.

She closed her eyes, truly safe.

❧

Elora woke, blinking a few times to get her vision to adjust to the night plunging the condo in darkness. She had no idea what hour it was, but knowing their time together would shortly end left a bitter taste in her mouth.

Turning to her side, she smiled as Vincent's gaze locked with hers. He kept his arm around her, bringing her closer to him. He rolled onto his back, stretching out to reach the nightstand. A small click echoed, and a multitude of miniature lights flicked to light; like a tiny universe circling the ceiling above them in a soft, orangey glow. She stared as he shifted to his side, facing her.

"It's beautiful," she breathed.

His fingers glided along her shoulder where her bruise was barely visible anymore. "This one was the first time, wasn't it?"

She nodded. "It was…" Averting her gaze, she focused on his chest, tracing the lines of his tattoos. "It wasn't always like this, though. At the start, it was perfect. He was friendly, gentle, and thoughtful." She bit her lower lip, glancing at him.

He stroked her cheek with his knuckles. "It rarely begins with the monster showing their true face." He slid his thumb below her eye where her bruise had faded. "But it also doesn't mean everyone who is kind turns out to be evil."

She nodded. "Once I told him what was happening in my life, and he offered to support me, things changed. It was so gradual, too. By the time I realized what was going on, it was too late. His help came at a price; I just didn't know yet."

"What do you mean?"

"It started after I got my master's. He said I assumed I was better than him because he only had a bachelor's degree. I told him he was being ridiculous, and I was allowed to be proud of my achievement. That's the first time he yelled at me. I was so scared, but I thought he was right... that it was my fault. He was always quick to apologize, and I forgave him every time without really thinking about it. We were already married by then, and I guess, in my mind, I thought marriages were something that involved a lot of effort. But everything he'd say to me brought me down. Even when he acted nice, he always made me feel so... wrong."

"There's nothing wrong about you, Elora. You're so much stronger than you realize." He smiled, but it seemed forced, like he tried his best not to keep her mind on the negatives of her past. "You mentioned you finished school and got a degree. Was it in visual arts?"

"A bachelor's in teaching. Then a master's with a specialization in development of kindergarten-aged children."

"Is it your dream to be a teacher?" he asked, a strange tone of awe in his voice.

"It was. I always wanted to write picture books as well. My dad used to say I have a natural talent for drawing and coloring, so I put it together. Though, for me, it would be a part-time job."

"Your father sounds wise."

She couldn't tell him the rest. He'd offer to help, and the last time someone offered, she had married the man. No. It wouldn't happen again. It couldn't. Even if she was willing to take the chance, her hands were tied. And Vincent deserved to be with a better person. Someone who wasn't selfish and earned the consequences.

She needed to change the subject, fast. "Did you enjoy modeling for the calendar last year?"

He chuckled. "To an extent, yes. Working with photographers and other models is fun. I got to meet people... It opened my world."

"Is there a 'but' in there?"

"There is." He slid his hand to her and squeezed. "Right here."

She giggled. "Gutter-mind."

"I wonder why," he said, his smile widening. "I prefer building. The aspect of designing is nice, but to build from scratch? Watch something grow into what you imagined? It's what I love the most." He brushed his lips across her forehead, and her heart beat faster.

"Have you considered starting your own company?" She smiled, recalling him working hard on her greenhouse, muscles straining with his skin covered in sweat. She inhaled deeply, trying to get herself to focus on the conversation.

"Yes, but I used to be in charge of people, and I don't want to do that anymore." He pulled away, his gaze locking on her. "One thing's for sure. If I started a company, it would be in Ottawa. I've got a home there as well, and it's my favorite."

Her heart sank at the idea of him never returning to Winnipeg. Never seeing him again. But maybe it was for the best. It wouldn't be as difficult to move on if she knew he was miles away. She swallowed against the lump in her throat. "I hear it's a great place to live."

"It is. But for now, I have a good reason to stay here," he breathed.

His eyes were so striking; she swore when she looked into them long enough, pools of darkness showed the way to golden ambers glimmering deep inside. It was like she could see his soul, and it was nothing short of radiant.

Her vision blurred, her chest tightening at saying goodbye. She had to do it, but it hurt so much.

"What is it, darling?" he asked gently. "What's wrong?"

She took a shuddering breath, but it choked her, and she grasped his arm for support. Nothing was all right. It would never be all right. Not after meeting Vincent and getting to know him like this. There was no going back in time to erase his memory, but remembering his touch, his care, his voice, and never being able to feel the way she did with him—it shattered her heart into a million pieces.

In that moment, she was sure she'd suffocate from the anguish of letting him go. She needed him so much more than she ever believed possible. But keeping a hold on him would be another one of her selfish acts, and she didn't want to hurt him more than she already had… and would.

## 29

# VINCENT

*T*he next morning seemed to roll by in a blur. They watched television together, cuddled on the sofa, but as time passed, Elora slowly grew distant. As though she needed to prepare herself to return to her normal life.

To her nightmare.

As three-thirty rolled around, they left his condo, and a part of him wanted to get on his knees and beg her to stay with him. That whatever Richard had as a grip on her, he'd fix.

He mentally scoffed at himself; he didn't even know what the monster's hold was. And no matter how many times he brought it up, Elora made it clear she wouldn't leave her husband.

Vincent dropped Elora not too far from Liana's place—a precaution she insisted on, fearing someone would see them together. Then he drove to Elora's place and started work immediately.

Thankfully, the house was built like the older ones; with a back lane to park vehicles. It took a while, even with Vincent, Larry, and Todd hauling the materials.

When they finished up, Elora walked inside the house, carrying the overnight bag she'd brought to Liana's place. She'd also changed, and Vincent imagined she left whatever he'd bought her at her friend's home.

With a quick wave at Larry and Todd, she rushed down the corridor, and the door slammed behind her. Vincent's stomach tightened; it was as though he already lost the woman he helped break out of her shell during the past few days. Just returning here sent her into the state of fear he first saw when they met.

Todd placed a glass panel on the side and frowned. "Well, fuck. We're missing two of these."

Larry marched to the upside-down bucket where all the receipts were held down with a rock, muttering curses under his breath. After scanning the sheet with his finger, his jaw clenched. "Idiots missed them. It's not an error on our part." He glanced at his watch. "Almost four. They'll be closing up pickups soon. Don't have time to get them to bring it over." He shot Vincent a smirk. "Since you were late today, how about taking the truck out for a drive and picking up those puppies?"

Vincent rolled his eyes, but knew better than to argue. Fair was fair—he was late—but he hated how Larry asked when it was rhetorical. With one last glance at the living room window, hoping to get a glimpse of Elora, he left, shoulders tense.

As he drove toward the store, he tried thinking of ways he could make things work with her. Maybe he could convince her to make her open relationship with him known to Richard.

*Relationship?*

He frowned. This was never supposed to become anything more than helping someone in need. Yet Elora had entered his heart, settling in a place he didn't know existed within him. Why did she have to be so perfect to him?

Pulling up into the parking lot, his stomach tightened when he noticed the hour. Her husband had likely returned, and the prospect of meeting the man who terrorized Elora was too much to bear. He didn't have it in him to look into Richard's eyes and not snap his neck without hesitation.

It wouldn't be the first time he murdered someone.

He curved his hands into fists, drawing deep breaths before stepping out of the truck. He had to calm down; killing Richard in front of witnesses guaranteed prison without question. But if he did it alone, when the monster was secluded and vulnerable... All Vincent had to do was make a phone call, and he'd get away with it. But going back to his old life meant putting Elora in another kind of danger. He'd have to leave her behind for her own safety.

They seemed cursed to be separated no matter what.

After getting the missing order sorted, he grabbed the first glass pane, relieved at the strain of carrying the thing by himself. The effort took his mind off the pain of what choices they had, because there didn't seem to be any.

As Vincent finished tying the panel, his cell buzzed, and he noticed Daniel's name pop up. He'd sent him an email with what had happened with Kimberly, and although Daniel had replied he would contact Vincent for further details, it had taken longer than he expected.

"Thought you forgot about me," Vincent said with a touch of humor.

"You're too much of a boil on my ass to forget, Voden," he muttered, but there was a note of amusement in his voice. "I got your email about what happened with Officer Grandon after she spoke to me. Normally, I'd make you two to patch things up while I moderate, but she wants to file an official complaint saying you were inappropriate with her."

"That's not—"

"I already read your side. No need to explain it to me," he said in a huff. "Because this will become formal, the best defense for you is to bring the woman present during the altercation to write a statement of what transpired. Of course, I'm aware there'll be bias, but it's something—"

"No." Vincent's voice was harder than intended. "If I ask, she'll do it, but I don't want her to. She's the one I asked you to look into. The domestic abuse victim." He rubbed his hand across his face. "Talking to the police is too risky for her. She'd be terrified her name would appear somewhere public where she admitted to being at someone else's home."

"Oh sure, but fucking another man isn't risky?" Daniel shot.

"That would never become public information, unlike a formal complaint which includes a committee." Vincent was relieved they weren't face to face, or he'd be tempted to punch Daniel in the face for his comment.

Daniel let out a breath. "Yeah. I know, I know. It's just gotten messier than I would've liked it. They'd rather lose a consultant over a cop."

"If it happens, I'll deal with it then. But I won't put Elora in that situation no matter what."

"I respect that, Vince." The sound of shuffling paper caused static on the line. "Now, I wasn't calling about just that mess. We found the first victim of the women's shelter case."

"I was really hoping this wouldn't turn into a homicide," Vincent said through his teeth, wondering what happened to the poor woman.

"And how do you know we didn't find her alive?"

"Because you would've texted me the info. A call means it's bad news."

He scoffed. "I'm that predictable?" He didn't wait for an answer. "And yes, she was murdered. They left her body hanging in front of the women's shelter they took her from. There were words carved into her skin…" He let out a sigh. "A message of terror if I've ever seen one."

Vincent stared into nothingness, thinking of Elora. If she'd gone to a refuge to get away from Richard, she could've been the victim. They were supposed to be safe places for victims to find sanctuary, and whoever was behind these crimes was turning them into Hell. He curled his hands into fists and closed his eyes tightly, pushing away the thought of Elora being taken and murdered from his mind. It was more than he could bear; like a knife twisted inside him.

"What can I do?" Vincent asked quietly, trying his best to control the rage surging through him.

"I'm assigning Officer Hall as your liaison until we settle things with Grandon. I'll need you two to go to the morgue and grab the coroner's report on the victim. Note as many details as you can pick up. The sooner we arrest these sickos, the better." And without waiting, Daniel hung up.

Vincent put his phone away as he strode to the store's entrance to pick up the final panel. It wasn't often Daniel sent him to the morgue with an officer; the only time it happened was when Sarge knew Vincent would likely catch minor details because of the life he used to lead.

Death wasn't new. It always followed him. Like a shadow to remind him of the first person he'd killed before reaching the age of thirteen. The list had grown since then, and it would take a lifetime to clean the blood from his hands.

*Even if she gave herself to me completely, I don't deserve her.*

# 30

# ELORA

he front door opened, and Elora's pulse sped. Richard was home early, and despite being ready for his arrival, she was jumpy.

She rushed to the entrance, forcing her usual smile, but it faded quickly when he sneered.

"Well?"

She opened and closed her mouth, unsure what to say. It was never her plan to tell him about Vincent; she didn't trust Richard not to fly off the handle even if he'd given her permission to sleep with other people.

She swallowed hard. "I stayed at Liana's for the week. It was nice. I got some writing done."

He arched an eyebrow. "What? No fuckboy with you? No boyfriend?" He laughed. "Are you seriously saying you couldn't find anyone who wanted to fuck you?"

"I—"

"Father Brian was right," he breathed. "He said you'd realize your mistakes while on your own like that. Now do you understand I'm the only one for you? Other men would take advantage of your naivety and ignorance." He pulled out his cell, and tapped the screen. "I know and love you despite your problems. How many other people can say that when it comes to you?"

Every moment she'd spent with Vincent seemed to fade into dust as though it was nothing but a dream. How could it have been real? Yet, she could still feel his warmth and words of comfort; and they were real.

Richard stared at her, his jaw clenched. "Do you understand or not?"

"I do. I understand," she said with a nod.

"And you've finally got the idea of sinning out of your mind? You'll stop being a pain about my open relationship?"

"Yes."

A knock sounded on the door, and Richard opened it. A young woman walked in and stood next to Richard, grinning ear to ear at him like she was in awe of his presence.

"I'm relieved to hear that." Richard said. "Now then, this is Sophie. We've been seeing each other the past few months, and I wanted you two to finally meet." He turned to the woman. "This is Elora, my wife."

Sophie smiled, her lips pinched tightly together as though looking at Elora left a sour taste in her mouth. "Hi. It's good to meet you," she said, her overenthusiasm so fake Elora was sure Richard would comment.

But he didn't. "Sophie and I met at the pub near our work buildings. She's an accountant with the City of Winnipeg."

Sophie nodded. "That's right. And you're a housewife? It must be nice to lounge all day while your husband works so hard." She placed her palm on his arm. "He's so kind."

Elora stiffened, grabbing the hem of the loose top she'd slipped in once she got home. Compared to the woman standing in front of her, Elora felt like she was a sack of potatoes; something to shut away in a dark place. Sophie, on the other hand, seemed to glow with her platinum blonde hair and baby blue eyes. Wearing short jeans and a cute blouse, she looked barely out of her teens.

"Working as an accountant sounds interesting," Elora said. "Did you start right after high school? Sometime recently?"

Sophie's cheeks flushed, and Richard narrowed his eyes. Elora swallowed hard, hating that she sunk to Sophie's level.

For a second, Elora swept her gaze across Sophie, and she breathed a sigh of relief when she didn't see any visible bruising. The last thing Elora wanted was for anyone else to suffer needlessly at the hands of her husband. No one deserved that.

Sophie shrugged. "If you're ever interested in learning about my career, feel free to ask. Even a woman of your advanced age can learn. Never too late to teach an old dog new tricks," she said with a wink.

Richard laughed, and Sophie joined in, but Elora could barely hear them anymore. She'd gotten used to his hurtful words throughout the years, but hearing them from someone else churned her stomach. Two people thought the same thing of Elora; were they the ones who were right about her? Was Vincent the one who was blind, and she was truly a stupid mess of a person?

Elora wiped her sweaty hands on her pants, waiting for them to stop laughing. Richard shook his head, chuckling like what Sophie had said was the funniest thing in the world.

When his gaze settled on Elora, he sobered. "It's warm. Why haven't you offered our guest a drink?"

Sophie giggled. "You're always so thoughtful," she cooed, hanging onto him like she was a crushing teen.

Elora hoped this woman was of age. And that she'd escape as fast as she could at the first sign of who her husband truly was. With a quick apology, Elora rushed into the kitchen and got two glasses out. Richard hadn't mentioned any for himself, but she learned to be ready in case.

She grabbed the filtered water from the refrigerator and poured it into both cups, the cold air refreshing through her heavier clothes. The air conditioner ran, but with part of the house dismantled, the place was warm.

Someone cleared their throat behind Elora, and she spun. Sophie stood in the kitchen, arms crossed as she looked around.

"You know, it's bad to keep a refrigerator door open too long. Usually breaks them quicker. Maybe you don't care, but Richard will have to pay for a new one if the other goes out." She cocked her head, each word more condescending than the next. "Don't think he'd appreciate that much."

Elora closed the door, her chest tightening at being told what to do in her own home. It had never felt safe here, but it was the only home she'd ever known after moving out of her childhood house.

*I feel safer at Vincent's place. Anywhere with him.*

"I'll keep it in mind," Elora said with forced politeness. "Thank you for the suggestion."

Elora grabbed the water glasses and walked toward the entrance. Sophie stuck out her foot, and Elora caught her ankle against it, watching in slow motion as she lost her footing and both glasses slipped out of her grip.

She hit the floor with such force, she was sure her knees had shattered. The pain flashed through her legs, and she cried out, her voice drowned out by the shattering glass.

Her eyes widened as the water spilled near her, the sharp fragments glistening in the sunlight. She tried catching her breath through the agony, her stomach clenching at the mess.

Sophie walked past her, tears running down her cheeks. "What's wrong with you?" she screamed with a sob.

Elora opened and closed her mouth, her hands shaking as they hovered over the glass and water, unable to react.

*What's… happening?*

Richard strode into the kitchen, staring from Elora on the floor to Sophie, then wrapped his arms around the woman. "What happened?" he asked gently.

Elora hadn't heard that tone of voice from him in years. When was the last time?

"Your wife is crazy," she said in an exaggerated whine. "She threw the glasses at me when I talked about how lucky she is to have a wonderful husband like you. I was sure she'd kill me."

Before Richard could say anything, Larry walked in, frowning as he stared at the scene. "Heard glass shatter. Is everything okay?"

Richard smiled, and Elora had forgotten how good he was at charming people. She'd seen him as a monster for so long, it was all she saw.

"Just an accident." He rubbed Sophie's back. "Thank you for checking in, though."

Larry nodded and gave a low grunt. "Anytime, Mr. Reverie."

"Oh, and before I forget," Richard continued with the pleasantries, "I'll be leaving, and my wife will be working on her book, so please make sure no one comes inside for the rest of the day."

"Not a problem. We're finishing up with the panels." And without another word, he left.

She wanted to call out to him for help, so she wouldn't be alone, but her voice didn't work.

Richard kissed Sophie on the forehead, then handed her his keys. "Go wait for me in the car. I'll be there shortly."

"But——"

"Now." He bit out the word, and she lowered her head, quickly leaving the kitchen.

Elora trembled as she picked up a couple of shards. "I'm sorry. I'll clean it."

He crouched in front of her, and she froze. "I thought we'd finally dealt with your jealousy. Attacking Sophie because I brought her here so you two could meet is nuts." He grasped her face, his fingers digging into her cheek. "You're more and more unstable every day. I'm thinking you're doing this on purpose to hurt me."

"I didn't——"

"Is that it?" he asked through his teeth. "Are you punishing me for something?"

He pushed her aside, and she winced as her knees pressed harder on the floor.

"I'm sorry," she repeated, her voice raw. "It was... an accident." Even if she told the truth, he wouldn't care. He likely already knew Sophie had lied and accepting it was the only way Elora would survive the next few minutes.

He grasped her and wrenched her head back. She gasped, grabbing hold of his wrists to keep pressure off her scalp, but at the angle, it was impossible.

"I swear, you're just so... worthless." He spat in her face, and she squinted as the saliva hit part of her eye. "And it's why you're trying to hurt me. I work, I have a house and car to my name, a gorgeous young girl who's head over heels in love with me, and who does what I say." He yanked harder, and she cried out. "Shut up," he hissed.

She pressed her lips together, snot trickling down her nose until she could barely breathe.

"I give you everything, but it's not enough for you, is it? You know why?" He shook his fist so her head moved from side to side. "Because you've earned nothing of value in your life. You spend your time with your little doodles for kids because that's what you are. A brat."

He let her go, and she sobbed, pressing her hand on her mouth to keep from making too much noise. A sharp pain in her back knocked the air out of her lungs as he kicked her, and she shrieked as her upper body landed on the broken glass. She'd raised her arms up for protection; the shards impaling her skin.

"I said shut up!" He pushed his foot against her shoulder blades, pushing the fragments deeper.

She sobbed, closing her eyes tight.

*Stop. Making. Noise. Stop.*

She blew out small shallow gasps, trying to concentrate on anything but the slicing pain. Grabbing hold of her collar, he shoved her upright and slapped her. Her vision blurred, his face out of focus as he glowered at her.

"If you're determined to hurt me, then I'll do the same to you. But don't you ever try hurting my girlfriend again. It's not my problem you couldn't find anyone else who wants you."

"I'm... sorry," she said in a croak.

"Good. I hope you'll think about what you did today, and change your bitchy attitude, but knowing you, I won't hold my breath."

He left the door slamming a few seconds later. Elora blinked a few times, not sure if she was breathing or if this was a nightmare she hadn't woken from yet. She looked down, a cold chill washing over her as she watched the blood streaming on her arms, and mixing with the spilled water.

*I have to clean this before Richard comes back.*

# 31

# VINCENT

*D*ark clouds rolled in the sky, creating an eerie green hue to the surroundings. Vincent crossed his fingers it wouldn't rain before they installed the two last panels, or it would take a few days waiting for things to dry.

He took the back lane to get to the parking, breathing a sigh of relief when he noticed Richard's car wasn't there. He hoped it was because the bastard already left again, because if Vincent had to meet him, he may not care too much about witnesses at this point.

Larry joined him at the truck, and Vincent frowned when no one else showed up.

"Was it something I said?" Vincent asked with a grin.

"Sent the rest of the boys home for the day. It rained a bit here and there a few minutes ago, so I installed a tarp for now. Just need to get these near the house and wait out the incoming downpour." He shrugged. "Once it dries, we'll install the last two panels, and then I'll give everything a double check before calling this job done."

Vincent's chest squeezed. With the contract completed, only the photoshoot remained to keep Elora and him connected. What would happen after? Would she still want to see him or spend time with him?

Thunder crashed through the sky, and he turned to the house, pulse speeding at the thought of Elora jumping at the noise. He wished he could go inside her house and hold her as it passed, but he had to finish up with Larry.

They grabbed the first piece as a few drops fell.

"So did the client return home yet?" Vincent asked, trying to keep his tone casual.

Larry grunted as they leaned the panel along the siding. "Yeah. He asked us not to enter the house for the rest of the day because he left, and he didn't want us to bother his wife while she worked on her book." He walked toward the truck. "I didn't know she was an author."

Vincent's heart seemed to miss several beats as he caught up with his boss. Richard didn't consider Elora's writing a career, and he'd never care to not have her disturbed. He tried his best not to rush to Elora or sound hysteric, but with the nausea building in the pit of his stomach, it was almost impossible.

"When did he say that?" Vincent kept his voice neutral, but his shaking hands would be a dead giveaway if he ended up dropping the last panel.

"Heard a crash inside the place not long after you'd left and went to check." Larry panted as they leaned the material near the greenhouse. "I have to stop smoking," he said with a huff.

"And?" Vincent pressed, glancing at the window. "Was everything all right?"

Larry arched an eyebrow, but nodded. "Yeah. Wife slipped and dropped glasses of water. There was another woman hanging onto the husband, though. Don't know what that's about, but it takes all kinds in this world. Maybe one of those poly relationships or something?" he muttered. "Anyway, it was all fine, but I think they might've had a fight. Not too long afterward, he left."

Vincent's stomach churned with every second, his hands curling and uncurling as he tried bringing his panic and rage to controlled levels.

Larry strode to the truck. "I'll text you when the panels can be installed." He gave a wave as he hopped into the vehicle, and Vincent watched as he drove away.

With the coast clear, he rushed to the back door, but they'd locked it. He knocked on it, but when no one answered, he smashed his fist against it, hoping she'd hear this time.

Nothing.

He couldn't think or breathe properly as he ran to the greenhouse and pushed the tarp aside. With part of the panels installed, walking in was impossible, so he grabbed the edges and hopped inside.

An unsettling silence wrapped around him, broken by an occasional small noise he couldn't place.

"Elora?" he called out as he hurried to the kitchen.

The scene in front of him seemed to register in his mind one piece at a time.

Spilled water stained in red.

Shattered glass on the floor.

Elora kneeling, repeatedly wiping the same spot as blood dripped down her arms.

Shards sticking out of her skin.

She barely blinked, focused on what was in front of her. The rag was soaked, but she continued to clean. A flash of memory filled his mind: his mother washing blood off the living room floor as she held her hand to her broken nose.

"Elora?" he repeated as quietly as he could so he wouldn't scare her.

"I need to tidy," she said, her tone emotionless. "I don't understand what I'm doing wrong. I keep cleaning, but there's always more." She gripped the rag harder until her knuckles turned white, and blood streamed from between her fingers. "Why can't I do anything right?" she muttered.

Vincent recognized this reaction. He walked over the glass, the shards crunching beneath his work boots, then crouched in front of her. Thunder echoed, and she didn't react.

"You're in shock, Elora." He grasped her chin and lifted her head. One side of her face was swollen and red, a minor cut splitting her bottom lip. "Deep breaths, okay?"

She nodded, but her eyes didn't seem to see him. "Sorry." Turning away from him, she continued cleaning.

He hated to be so rough with her, but in her state, reasoning wouldn't work. Clenching his jaw, he took a heavy breath, pretending she was one of his men back in the day. He didn't care for how easily it came to him.

"Look. At. Me." He bit out every word, his voice deeper.

Her head snapped up, and her gaze filled with something he didn't want to see: fear. Not of the situation, but of him.

"I need to clean this," she blurted. "Before he sees it."

He took her face between his hands. "Listen to me. Richard isn't here."

She swallowed visibly, tears filling her eyes. "But he always comes back. I don't—"

"Stop." The word came out in a hiss, and she flinched. "What happened?"

*Talk to me so I can snap you out of this daze.*

She lifted her bloody palms, staring at them with a frown. "I… There was an accident?"

"Describe it to me." He grasped her elbows and straightened, pulling her to her feet.

Her legs shook violently, and she gasped. He wrapped an arm around her waist, holding her steady as they walked to the dining room table and he sat her down.

Blood stained her top and leggings.

"Richard introduced me to his girlfriend," she said, blinking fast, but not staring at anything in particular. "Sophie. They laughed about… old dogs?" Her breathing sped, and he was sure she would hyperventilate.

He wanted to smash something. Preferably, Richard.

"Do you have a first aid kit? Tweezers?" he asked, trying to gentle his tone, but keeping a note of command that would keep her as focused as possible.

"Is someone hurt?" She looked at her arms. "Oh. I am. It's me," she mumbled. "It's always me. But it's because I upset him."

He leaned forward a few inches from her face, jaw clenched tight, and not hiding his anger. Her eyes widened, but she froze, her rambling ceasing quickly.

"I won't ask again," he said in a growl, despising himself with every second. "Do you have an aid kit and tweezers?"

She sucked in a shuddering breath and nodded. "Bathroom. Under the sink."

He strode to the room and found what he required in record time. Everything was placed so precisely, and it pissed him off knowing it wasn't by Elora's choice. He returned with the container which had tweezers inside, grabbing a chair, and drawing it in front of Elora.

He grabbed the tool he needed and locked gazes with her. "Give me your arm."

She didn't hesitate. He leaned it on his thigh, gently pulling out the shards. Not once did she wince or make a single noise.

"You haven't told me what happened," he said, glancing up at her with a look of warning. "Start talking, Elora."

She stiffened, her fingers flexing as though in reflex to grab hold of something, but she stopped when the glass cut deeper into her. Her words were jumbled at first, but he didn't interrupt her, focusing on getting the shards out. As he cleaned the wounds and cuts with the peroxide, her shock seemed to ebb as she described what had happened.

Vincent was glad he was too busy with her arm to stare at her while she explained because he was sure he likely had a deadly glare in his eyes. As she reached the part where Richard spat in her face after what he'd done, her voice shook, but she continued. She pushed through the sobbing and the trembling as he placed bandages on the cuts. Thankfully, nothing was deep or large enough to require stitching, but it would take time to heal.

Elora fell silent, having finished explaining what happened, and Vincent couldn't seem to find his voice. He couldn't even figure out what emotions ran through him as he rose and put away what he hadn't used from the first aid kit.

She continued to tremble, her arms laid out in front of her as though she was scared to move them.

"Can you stand?" he asked.

With a grimace, she grasped the side of the table and stood. Her legs trembled, but she took a few steps. "Yes. Just sore."

"You should change. Your pants are wet, and with the air conditioner on, you're freezing."

He wished she would look at him.

"I should clean the kitchen. I don't want to dirty more clothes since—"

"Never mind that." Why couldn't he get the sharpness out of his voice anymore?

She opened her mouth, but then closed it, and limped past him toward the corridor. He gripped the first aid so tight, he was sure the plastic casing would crack under the force as he marched to the bathroom and put it back.

Lightning flashed from the window, and the sound of rain faded for a second as thunder crashed. Vincent listened for any sign of distress from Elora, but when silence greeted him, he strode to the kitchen.

There was no way she'd clean her own blood. He'd never allow it.

*Allow it?*

He gritted his teeth. His past seemed to latch onto him whenever he brought it forward. Or was the mask he'd slipped on when he left it behind couldn't withstand what kind of person he truly was?

A monster in his own right.

He picked up the mess in the kitchen with paper towels, throwing it in a plastic bag. The water and blood weren't as easy to get rid of, but after many times of wiping and squeezing off the rag, it was gone. He rummaged under the sink and found a disinfectant, then washed the floor.

As he finished, the sound of a door opening reached his ears, and he stood. Elora approached, her eyes widening.

"You... cleaned everything? Even the broken glass?" She rushed to him, and grabbed his hands, running her thumbs on his skin as though trying to find wounds. "You shouldn't have done that. You could've cut yourself!"

She burst into tears, backing up quickly as she shook her head.

"Hey, it's——"

"It's not okay," she shouted. "None of this is."

Heat filled him. "You're right, but you knew that when you made your choice to stay with him. Just like I knew the same when I decided I wanted to help you."

He wished he could take his words back, but it had slipped out faster than he could stop himself. She ran her fingers under her eyes to wipe her tears and winced as she caught the reddened side of her face. Her breathing slowed, and something in her expression changed. His stomach churned, a part of him already realizing what was happening.

"I can't do this anymore." Her voice had stopped shaking, but it was so quiet. Like she didn't dare breathe.

He knew she wasn't talking about leaving her husband, but for a split second, he hoped he was wrong. That he hadn't stepped over a line and had pushed her to stop wanting to be with him.

He took a step closer. "Can we talk about this? Please?"

She clutched at her shirt collar, averting her gaze. "No. This isn't right. We're hurting one another. I just... I can't. I need you to leave."

"So that's it?" Even to his own ears, his tone sounded menacing. But it was that or plunge into a despair he had never felt before. He had no idea how to deal with any of this.

She let the tears fall, not bothering to wipe them away. "I'm sorry."

He stopped in front of her. "Elora——"

"Please don't," she cried, backing up so far she nearly hit the wall. "Just go. I need you to leave. Don't come back. Don't talk to me again. Live your life and forget about me."

An icy chill seemed to spread from his core. The same feeling he used to turn to whenever he had to shut his emotions to survive. "I told you as long as you want me, I'm here for you." Why was his heart hammering against his ribs like it fought to break out? "If you can look me in the eye, and say you don't need me anymore, I'll disappear from your life." He stiffened his muscles to keep himself from shaking. "But you can't tell me it's over without even looking at me. After everything, we owe each other that much."

*Please say you need me.*

Her cheek hollowed to one side as though she bit the inside, then met his gaze as large tears rolled down her face. "I... don't want... you anymore. Now please... get out."

His heart stopped trying to break out, and instead, he was sure it had broken. He took in a shallow breath, but nodded. As he walked to the door and unlocked it, his emotions shattered as Elora let out a sob.

## 32

## ELORA

*R*ichard sat at the table, finishing his supper, looking pensive about something. He hadn't commented about her swollen, puffy red eyes, likely assuming she'd cried about his latest anger toward her.

Every day since she'd told Vincent to leave, she'd broken into tears.

But nothing hurt more than her lie to Vincent. She wanted him, but she couldn't ignore the pain in his gaze after what happened. He tried so hard to help her, but it was useless. There was no leaving this place, and if she hadn't ended it with him, it would've gotten worse with time.

"I spoke to a coworker this morning," Richard started, pulling Elora out of her regrets. "He told me how his wife used to be like you. She was unhappy and bitter, always instigating fights. The usual imbalance of hormones, you know?"

She frowned, pushing at her green beans with her fork. "Hormones?" she repeated.

He nodded as he pushed his plate away. "Exactly." Standing, he pulled his chair next to hers, and she stiffened as he sat. "I hadn't realized what I was doing. I'm sorry for being so cruel in my thoughtlessness toward you."

Slowly, she put down her utensil, her mind racing as she tried preparing for whatever hurtful words he'd say. A brutal comment usually followed anything sounding like an apology or a compliment.

"It's…" She looked at him. "I don't know what you mean."

He smiled, and her guard rose. "You're not getting any younger, and the whole time I'm living my life to the fullest as a man, I've denied your purpose as a woman." He placed his hand on her abdomen. "I'm going to put a baby inside you."

Her pulse sped and her breath caught. Of all the things she expected, this wasn't one of them, and it was worse than any of the possibilities combined. Chills ran through her, but she did her best not to throw up as she opened her mouth to say something.

"You… already work so hard for the two of us." She forced a smile, despite her trembling chin. "Is adding a child a good idea? I mean, I don't want you to have to stress out."

He waved his hand dismissively, and she flinched, expecting him to strike her. He chuckled and shook his head. "Nonsense. This is important. You've been worthless your whole life. Think about it. You'd finally have a reason to live. No more being selfish and acting like a brat, because you'd have a baby to take care of." His palm slid lower until he reached her thigh. "Women are supposed to bear children. It's what you were born to do. When you married me, you made a vow to God to serve me as a wife. That includes giving me kids."

She wasn't certain how much longer she'd keep from being sick. Her body kept going from hot to cold chills so fast, she thought she had a fever from the shock. Luckily, she was on birth control since meeting him. He didn't know about it, and she'd kept it that way for years. She wasn't able to buy any without him discovering it, and so she visited the health clinic once every four months to get half a the shot for free.

But they'd always used condoms on top of her pills. What if they failed? What if every time she took a pregnancy test, and it was negative, he'd hurt her for failing? Her heart beat faster as fear coursed through her veins; the condoms they used were lubricated. He didn't know she faked her pleasure because he never did any foreplay. How would he react when he'd realized her body didn't respond to him the way he was used to?

Richard took his phone and swiped his finger along his screen. "When was the last time you had your period?" he asked without looking at her.

Her mind didn't catch up with his question as she continued her inner panic. "Why?"

"Obviously because I need to track when you're fertile," he said in annoyance. "Hopefully having a child will help you become a little smarter. Or at least logical," he muttered. "Now. When was it?"

"About two weeks ago," she answered quickly.

"So we have a couple of days of you ready to breed." He nodded as though satisfied with her answer as he tapped his screen a few times. "Perfect."

It wasn't the first time she wished she'd die, but in that moment, it was the strongest she'd ever felt. She couldn't bring a child into this nightmare.

He glided his finger over the cheek he'd slapped, and she winced. "I'm sorry about what happened the day I brought Sophie here. You just hurt me so much; I needed you to understand what it did to me. I tried so hard to show you I love you by not keeping her a secret, but instead, you attacked her." His thumb traced along the split in her lip. "Once we have a child together, it'll never happen again, okay? You'll be too busy to act out, and your mood will probably change for the better. We can be happy."

She couldn't speak. If her heart could beat this fast, why couldn't it stop instead? Why couldn't she escape this Hell?

He took her hands in his and stood, pulling her to her feet. "I've missed you lately." He nuzzled her neck. "I'm not lacking for sexual satisfaction, but making love to you differs from the others." His palms slid lower, and she squeezed her eyes shut. "Lying with you is a unique pleasure for me as a man. The only kind that is holy because it's a right I have as your husband."

He trailed kisses along her skin, and she focused on her breathing. She'd practiced for years to keep her body's genuine reactions to him hidden—at first, to avoid confrontation, but eventually, it turned into a matter of survival.

She closed her eyes, and a vision of Vincent floated in her mind. A part of her wanted to cry after what had happened, but she drew comfort in his smile. In that moment, she needed his memory more than ever.

He pulled away and took her hand, leading her toward their bedroom.

❧

Elora sat in the tub as water ran from the showerhead above. The trickling sound kept her mind numb as she stared at the shower curtain. It was one of the few accessories in the house he allowed her to pick; a forest with a brook and waterfall. She almost heard the sounds of nature when she closed her eyes, picturing herself there. Away from here. Was it like this at Vincent's place in Ottawa?

She ran the washcloth between her fingers, squeezing the water out every few minutes. As long as she didn't think too much, she was all right. But anything beyond that, and she wanted to vanish down the drain along with the other filth. That's what she was. Dirty and dysfunctional, as Richard had called her.

The throbbing between her legs didn't stop, so she pressed the cloth between her thighs, wincing at the sting. When she pulled it away to rinse it, her eyes widened at the blood smear.

*I started my period earlier. A bit of spotting is normal.*

But deep down, she knew it was a lie. And no matter how many times she tried convincing herself of it, the lump in her throat squeezed tighter. A few of the bandages on her arm had slipped off, and she stared at the cuts. Would they leave scars?

She gasped at the loud pounding on the door and stiffened when it opened. A shadow appeared on the other side of the curtain; a monster looming over her. Richard pulled it back, then sat on the toilet in front of her.

"I didn't want to hurt you." His tone was gentle. "But can you imagine what it's like for me to think you don't want me anymore? My own wife? How would you feel?" He cried, his chin trembling. "We need to start over, but it has to be together. We'll keep our relationship open, but we can create a family, and things will work themselves out, okay?"

She nodded, keeping the washcloth hidden, despite knowing he wouldn't care. "Okay."

He reached out toward her, and she closed her eyes, expecting another slap. Instead, he slid his fingers along her hair.

"I love you," he said, sounding like he was about to sob.

She ignored her churning stomach and forced her eyelids open. "I love you too."

He stood, and her heart skipped a beat, wondering if she could use his sudden gentler mood to her advantage.

"Richard?"

He stopped, and for once, didn't look annoyed with her. "What is it?"

"Have you heard any news from... the nursing home?" she asked quietly, as though lowering her voice would help.

Instead of his usual impatience, he smiled. "I called a few days ago. Your father is doing well, the attendant told——"

"Can we visit him?"

"Do. Not." He took a step forward. "Interrupt me."

A chill shot through her despite the scorching water. "I'm sorry."

"He's doing nicely, but just got over a case of bronchitis, and the nurse recommended we don't see him until he's better."

Her heart deflated at being denied to see her dad. It had been months. But as Richard often reminded her, he was the one paying for the long-term nursing home. And he'd picked a location too far away to get to by bus, and too expensive by taxi.

More than once, she considered calling the nursing home to explain her situation to them. To explain how, because of her selfishness years ago, she'd given up her father's guardianship to her husband. How Richard controlled where her dad ended up, and that, if Elora left Richard, he'd make sure to place her father somewhere horrible. Even if she called, they'd only be able to provide her general information. Having given up the title of guardian, she wasn't on file as someone the staff could divulge any specifics to. And worse, they'd leave a note in his file to advise Richard she'd called. The thought sent her stomach churning.

She wanted to beg for her dad's guardianship back; it was on the tip of her tongue. But he'd likely assume it was so she could leave him. And it would be true. Elora still recalled how he'd beaten her when she told him they should end their relationship after he cheated. This time, Richard would kill her for sure.

Richard pointed toward the door. "I'm going to work a bit in the office before coming to bed. There are contracts I need to finish up before leaving for my next business trip."

He was gone so often, and yet the few times he was home, he hurt and terrified her more each time. How long would it be before he killed her? Or until she died in an accident?

A few minutes after he left the bathroom, she stood, holding her breath as pain shot through her. She turned off the water, her legs shaking as she got out of the tub, and wrapped a towel around herself. What would she do if she became pregnant? The thought made her want to vomit.

If she left Richard, then went to court to become her father's guardian again, it could take months. Not just that, but while they'd be waiting for court dates, where would Richard move her dad to? The province might take over his care, but Richard's company had expensive lawyers who probably had a few judges in their pockets. He'd even mentioned a few times how they had buried an ex-employee under so much legal paperwork that it would be years before anything was settled. And what would happen to Elora's father if they did the same to her?

*No. I have to stay. For dad. I won't abandon you. I swear. No matter what.*

She stared at the outline of where the old doorknob used to fit. Richard had changed them when they'd moved in... ones without locks. For fire safety, he'd explained. All lies.

She closed her eyes, wrapping her arms around herself, and picturing Vincent behind her. He'd hold her tight, and murmur words of comfort in her ears, reminding her she was strong. For a second, she felt his heat. Her heart hammered as she spun, but the shower curtain was the only thing that greeted her.

She swallowed against the sting in her throat, her head lowering. At least she wouldn't hurt him anymore, no matter how much anguish she felt at having to let him go.

# 33

# VINCENT

*T*he bright lights reflected in the room, a cold place in feel and temperature. The morgue wasn't where Vincent wanted to be, but it came with the job.

He stood over a dead body lying on the metal table in front of him, the smell of bleach too familiar. Officer Hall paced, not staring too long at what had once been a person. Daniel had sent them to gather the report on the first victim. But between the call and the next morning, officers had located three more bodies.

Vincent was used to death, but the last of the victims hit him hard.

It was Amy. The woman at the initial shelter who'd given the police information about the gang names she'd heard. She was the last to disappear, and several bodies followed afterward. What started as serial abductions had turned into murder.

Officer Hall—Charles—was a new officer who transferred to the homicide department recently and hadn't seen death like this before.

Vincent gritted his teeth while waiting for the doctor. Ever since Elora had told him to leave her life, everything grated on his nerves. It wasn't the first time a woman ended an affair with him, but it had never hurt before. He cared about her more than he wanted to admit and didn't know how to process any of it. The worst part was she cut him off because she didn't want to hurt him.

He pictured holding her as she rested her head against his chest, the scent of her speeding his pulse. But until she decided to leave, he couldn't decide for her.

He let out a breath, wondering if she was all right. How many times had Richard hurt her since he'd seen her? Vincent had quit Larry's crew under the excuse that the case took up too much of his hours. It wasn't a lie. This was the third time he'd had to show up to this place in the past few weeks.

A woman marched inside, and Vincent arched an eyebrow. "Rose?"

She halted in her steps and smiled as she recognized him. "Well, well, well. Vincent Voden. It's been a while."

"Do you two know each other, then?" Charles asked, coming closer, then as soon as he stared at the body, backing away.

Vincent nodded. "This is Rose Marcelle. We met when I worked a construction job at her apartment building."

The woman was interesting. He hadn't expected to see her in a place like this, but then, what made her personality so particular was her unpredictability. Styled in rockabilly fashion, she managed to look both tough and innocent at the same time. There was never any sexual attraction between them—although they enjoyed teasing each other while the crew renovated parts of the loft she lived in, and they'd become friends.

Vincent turned to her. "This is Officer Charles Hall. So is this where you work?" He frowned. "This is the first time I've seen you here."

"I've worked as an assistant to a forensic pathologist for three years, but I was at another location before. This place offered better hours and money, so I transferred a few days ago."

Charles leaned on the wall and crossed his arms. "I'll be glad never to return here. Pretty sick and tired of hearing about mutilated women, let alone seeing one."

Rose narrowed her eyes. "I'm sure they're not pleased about it either."

"I didn't mean it like that…" Charles said, rubbing the back of his neck. "I just… I saw the report. She helped the police from the start of this total mess, and we couldn't even protect her."

Vincent stared at the face of the woman on the table. Or what they left of her. Cuts and bruises twisted her features, and from the reports on the previous victims he'd studied, the rest of her was probably worse. "Is the report ready?"

Rose nodded, grabbing a file on the desk and handing it to him. "I've studied the past findings of the other bodies, and it was unpleasant enough to read, let alone write this one."

He opened the folder and frowned as he scanned the report. "They're different, aren't they?"

"So you noticed, too?" She grabbed a page from the desk. "I've noted what I've found strange about these bodies. They're severely disfigured, and although they have the same type of pre-mortem wounds, none are identical."

"Well," Charles chimed in, his voice quiet, "it's not like someone could repeat the exact same damages on different people, right?"

Vincent shook his head. "No, but there would be similarities or patterns." He handed one of the report pages to the officer. "They stabbed her multiple times, but the wounds are shallow. Whoever did this hesitated."

"Yes," Rose continued, rummaging through papers on the desk. "But the two earliest victims had wounds caused by distinctive pointed objects, and they weren't the cause of death. The first even had cigarette burn marks. It's too different, but it follows a pattern…" She trailed off, blinking as she stared off into noth-ingness.

"Pattern?" Vincent repeated.

Rose lifted her head and looked at him. "Torture these women as much as possible before butchering them."

Vincent's jaw clenched. He immediately thought of the MOW organization, and considering their name was passed around for this case, it wasn't likely a coincidence. The freezer room inside the organization's warehouse flashed in his mind, and he took a deep breath to keep from being sick. There had been so many mutilated bodies.

His heart pounded as he grabbed a pair of surgical gloves and slipped them on.

"Thought of something?" she asked.

He pushed the victim's matted hair to the side, checking her ear, and froze. "Fuck."

Charles took out a pen and pad. "What is it?"

"Did any of the other victims have a hole near here?"

She blinked quickly, her face turning paler. "Oh. Yes, they had what looks like a large barbell piercing, close to the superior crus."

He frowned. "And that doesn't count as a pattern?"

She stiffened. "It's… not uncommon, nowadays. A bit like finding pierced ears." She swallowed visibly as her voice shook. "Although, I suppose that with a hole this big, it would be notice-able…" she trailed off staring at the wall like something trapped her inside her mind. Gently, he placed a hand on hers, and she jumped.

"Are you okay?" he asked quietly.

She cleared her throat and nodded. It was as though she was back to normal and nothing had ever happened. Just when he was about to make sure she was all right, she covered the body as though unable to look at her anymore. "I'll inform Dr. Bedard there may be a pattern after all."

Vincent continued watching Rose, but seeing her differently. Her reaction told him she knew what those holes meant, but the only ones who'd know were the people in the monstrous organization, or the ones there the night they dismantled them. And Rose definitely wasn't in his business then or now.

Charles opened the door, ready to dart out. "Thank Dr. Bedard for us, please." He gave a small wave, then left.

Vincent decided not to linger too much on Rose's possible knowledge of the infamous organization; he was likely overthinking her reaction.

He sighed as he headed to the exit. "This is the first time Charles has seen a body. It takes getting used to."

"And you are?" Rose asked. It was dismissive, like a side note, but her tone made him pause.

"Comes with the job."

She grabbed the disinfectant and placed it on the instrument tray. "You work as a consultant in Winnipeg, but nowhere else in Canada?" When he nodded, she gave him a small smile. "So you have, at best, a few years of experience since you'd mentioned you often live in Ottawa. And being a specialist, you'd rarely get sent to these kinds of places. That tells me you were used to death before you got to your job."

"Are you a detective and a morgue assistant?" He asked, his tone light, but there was a definite edge to it. They had chatted before, but the fact she retained a lot of the small information he'd given about himself didn't sit too well with him.

"Like you, Mr. Voden, I had a different life before becoming a member of society," she said with a shrug, yet a haunting look settled in her gaze.

Before he could comment, she grabbed the rest of the files and left by the personnel door.

# 34

## ELORA

*E*lora finished vacuuming Richard's office, then put away her cleaning supplies. He had left for another business trip, but she doubted the truth of that. It made little sense that his workplace would send him on all these trips, but she also couldn't come up with a logical reason for why he'd lie about it either. If he spent the weekend with a woman, why not just tell her?

With him gone, she had taken a walk to the nearest health clinic, needing to clear her head at the same time. Knowing her husband slept with other women, she wanted to ensure she hadn't gotten an STI, and so she got tested. The nurse spoke to her about domestic violence, but Elora had repeated her usual lies. Finally, she ended up leaving with a few pamphlets, but threw them out.

Tomorrow would be over two weeks since they checked her. If she didn't receive a phone call, she was okay. Luckily, Richard didn't touch her when he was home, saying he would only lie with her when her body was ready to be impregnated. But the time would come again in a little over a week, and she didn't know what she'd do during those days. There was only so long she could feign ignorance about why she wasn't getting pregnant. Eventually, he'd insist on fertility tests, and he'd find out she had the birth control shot every four months.

Her stomach churned. Would it be better to stop taking it, and give him the child he suddenly wanted so much? She bit her lower lip at the thought. Maybe it would bring out paternal instincts in him, and he'd become gentler?

She almost scoffed at the thought; there was no kindness in Richard unless there was something he wanted. What if he took out his rage on their child like Vincent's father used to do? The last thing she wanted was to bring a baby into this violent situation.

The dryer dinged from the linen closet, and she pushed away the panic circling her mind, trying to focus on her chores for the day. She let out a breath, finishing the last of the folding, and grabbed the dishrags. The pitter-patter of rain fell against the greenhouse windows, and every time she heard it, her chest squeezed. Construction was finished and Vincent had never returned.

The more she thought of Richard's sudden obsession with getting her pregnant, the less she knew what to do about it.

Movement caught her eye as she walked across the living room toward the kitchen, and she gasped, dropping her laundry to the floor when she spotted a man inside her house. He leaned on her front door, and didn't react to her, scrolling on his phone as though bored. Her stomach churned as she backed away, unsure what to do. If she turned her back, would he come after her?

He glanced up at her and smiled, sending a chill down her spine.

Deciding not to linger, trying to figure out who he was, she dashed for the rear door, but skidded to a halt when another man waved at her from the spot. Her throat squeezed so tight, she thought she'd be sick.

He wore the same type of suit, but looked older than the one at the front. With a smile, he pointed behind her, and she spun. The room tilted, and she took a few steps forward to lean on the back of the sofa, trying to catch her breath.

The man sitting in the armchair turned the page of a book he held, and she stiffened when she realized it was one of her children's books.

"This is a heart-warming story," the man said, not looking up.

She swallowed hard, debating whether to stay still or make a run for it to Richard's office since it was the only room with a lock. He lifted his head, his light brown hair falling above his brown eyes. His white dress shirt was unbuttoned at the top, revealing several tattoos, but one stuck out in particular: a red blood drop below his neck.

He smiled and the hairs on her neck rose; like an unmoving spider in its web, he waited for an unsuspecting victim to fall into his trap, and strike. Break and enters weren't uncommon here, but something told her this wasn't what was going on.

"You need to leave," she said with as much force as she could muster. "My husband will be home soon, and he'll—"

"Out of everyone here, he's the one who'd cause you the most harm." He closed the book and placed it on the side table next to him. "We'll have a problem if you don't comply, but nothing like what I imagine he does to you."

She glanced at her phone near the landline, her heart hammering. The man at the front took a few steps forward, and she stiffened, glancing at the man obviously in charge.

"What do you want?" she asked in a cracking voice.

He motioned to the sofa facing him. "Have a seat."

Her breath came in small gasps as her vision blurred.

*Don't pass out. Don't pass out.*

The man waved toward the front door. "You can leave, or use your phone to call someone." He leaned his chin on his tattooed knuckles. "Although, if you do, I guess it means you don't care what happens to Vincent Voden."

Her stomach tightened, and heat filled her. They were here for Vincent. Why?

"I... don't know who you're talking about." Her voice didn't shake. "My husband's name is Richard Reverie, so you must have the wrong house." If she got them to leave, she could call Vincent and warn him.

"Is that why you're suddenly so pale?" he asked with a half-smile.

"I'd be concerned for anyone you're looking for, whether or not I know them," she said louder than she planned. Her fear faded, instead replaced by anger at the thought of these men searching for Vincent. She wouldn't let them hurt him.

He pointed at the sofa. "Sit, Elora. If I may call you, Elora?" He glanced at the book next to him. "You used your maiden name as an author. Interesting."

She walked around and slumped on the cushion. "Who are you?"

He grinned, pulling out a card, and leaning forward so she would take it. She eyed it for a second, then grabbed it.

*Benjamin Karson. Business management.*

She slipped it into her pocket. "What do you want with Vincent?"

"I was told he works here."

"He used to. For construction. But they're done. If you want to get in touch with him, I suggest calling." She stared toward her cellphone.

"He's not answering my calls or texts." There was an edge of resentment in his tone that sounded like more than annoyance.

She grasped the hem of her top. "Look, I've already told you he doesn't work here anymore. I don't know what else I can help you with."

He reached into his jacket pocket and pulled out a cellphone this time. As he scrolled through it, his smile widened. "This contract wasn't the only thing connecting you two together, though, now is it? Vincent isn't known for bringing people to his place, and the women he dates aren't usually the same too many times in a row." He put his phone away. "My information tells me considering you break both those rules, you're someone *special* to him."

Her throat tightened as she looked at her hands. "Not anymore. I… I broke things off."

"Decided to fuck Vincent for a thrill to escape your husband for a while, then smash his heart in tiny pieces?" He asked so matter-of-factly it felt like he'd punched her in the gut.

She raised her head, narrowing her eyes at him. "Not that it's any of your business, but I care too much for Vincent to continue hurting him because of my circumstances."

Curling her hands into fists, she did her best to remain calm despite having blurted out an obvious leverage for them.

*Keep. Your. Mouth. Shut.*

His expression was unreadable, but the longer he stared, the more something about him seemed... familiar. "Is that so?"

She stood. "Please leave. He's not here. We're not together anymore, so you'll need to find another way to reach him." She motioned toward where he'd put away his cell. "Besides, you obviously have information about us, so you know where he lives. Why not go there? Or why didn't you come here while he'd been working?"

He got to his feet and buttoned his jacket. "He chose his condo because of its high security system. Not to mention, the arsenal in his house would create a war zone if I stepped in there with my men." He grabbed the children's book as she blinked several times, trying to wrap her mind around what he said. He wasn't making any sense. "And as for coming here while he was working, the answer is simple." He locked gazes with her, and she held her breath. "I don't care for witnesses."

"So what do you want with me?" she inquired in a small voice.

"The easiest way to catch a predator is by luring him with something he cares for." He took a few steps closer, and she stiffened.

*Luring? Into a trap?*

Her eyes burned. "Please don't hurt him."

"If you don't make a fuss, I promise I won't," he said with a smile.

She nodded. "Okay."

Benjamin motioned to the man at the front door, and he approached, grabbing her cellphone on the way. As he handed it to Benjamin, Elora bit her lower lip, wondering what would happen next. She had no idea how to react in this insane scenario. Could she warn him?

Her eyes widened when he gave her the phone. "Call him."

The grip on her cell tightened. "Anything specific I'm supposed to say?"

"Tell him Benjamin is here with you."

Her finger hovered over the button for Vincent's number. She had listed it under Liana's husband's name in case. With a slight shudder, she pushed the dial button and brought it to her ear.

The line picked up after two rings. "Hello?"

Tears rolled down her cheeks at the sound of his voice. She never thought she'd hear it again. She drew in a deep breath, but it turned into a cry. "Vincent… I'm sorry. I don't know what's going on, but there are three men at my house. One of them said his name is Benjamin. I don't know what to do, but they want to lure—"

Benjamin took the phone from her hand with a chuckle as several curses flew on the other side of the line. He held the device to his ear. "Ignoring me was a bad idea."

The two men who'd stood by the door approached and grabbed her arms. She screamed, trying to squirm away as the cuts stung. "Let go!"

Benjamin continued, "Meet me at the usual spot. No harm will come to her as long as you show up."

He pushed the end call button and walked to the rear door as the two men led her forward. When they stepped into the backyard, she spotted a black SUV with tinted windows, and dug her feet into the ground.

*This isn't happening.*

"We're going for a little ride." Benjamin opened the vehicle door, and before she could say anything, they pushed her inside.

She tried sliding out, but Benjamin stepped in after her and closed the door. She reached for the latch on the other side, but they'd locked it. Her pulse sped as the front doors snapped shut, and the engine roared to life.

Pushing herself into the corner, she trembled so violently, she was sure her bones would shatter.

"No need to be so scared," Benjamin said, leaning so close to her she was sure he'd hear her heartbeat, "you're just the bait." He grabbed the seatbelt and buckled it for her before sliding to his side.

The SUV rolled forward, and silence filled the vehicle. She wrapped her arms around her waist, focusing on her breathing.

*What have I gotten myself into?*

# 35

# ELORA

he SUV drove into an underground garage, but despite the empty spaces, they continued driving. As they approached a large gate, Benjamin pulled out his cellphone, and tapped his fingers on the screen a few times. Elora jumped when the metal slid opened, the noise like a thunderous mechanical monster coming to life.

She tightened her grip on the seatbelt as they parked near what she assumed was a private entrance. Men in suits guarded a single door, and her eyes widened as they pulled out guns. The driver stepped out of the vehicle, and barked something at them, and they quickly holstered their weapons, but Elora's heart continued beating hard against her chest.

Benjamin undid her seatbelt, and she jumped as the sudden movement. When she didn't let go of the belt, he tapped a finger on the back of her hand. "Don't you want to come upstairs and see Vincent?"

His charming tone could manipulate anyone into getting what he wished for, but he was about to find out it wouldn't work as efficiently on her. Still, she released her grip, and he smiled.

The man in the passenger seat opened her door, and she

flinched, but slid out. She wanted this to be over with as fast as possible and make sure Vincent was all right. Had he gotten into trouble with the wrong people? Could she help?

*Do as they say, and maybe they'll be in a better mood to let us both go unharmed.*

And so, she followed, keeping silent, and doing her best not to jump every time they came across more individuals who looked like they would shoot on command without a second thought.

As they walked into a narrow corridor, she slowed her steps. Glass replaced one wall and showed a casino room on the other side.

Flashing lights of machines reflected in mirrored walls as people gambled. Could they see her? A sudden urge to catch someone's attention to call the police crawled into her mind.

Benjamin leaned next to her, and she held her breath. His smirk gave her the feeling he knew exactly what she'd thought of, and she didn't like it one bit. Was she so easy to read?

"Two-way mirror," he stated with amusement. "Gives the casino a bigger feel, and lights up the place too." He looked out onto the floor. "You're not the first person to get the idea of calling for help."

"I considered it, but I don't want to cause any problems for Vincent," she said, walking around him to continue.

The corridor turned, and she stopped in her tracks. Up ahead, the silver doors of an elevator looked like the most ominous thing in the world. It didn't look big, and the idea of being stuck in there with these men sent her pulse speeding.

Benjamin strode ahead, hands in his pockets, and the doors opened as though by magic. He glanced over his shoulder at her. "Going up?" he said with a wink.

She forced her legs forward until she stepped inside with him. To her partial relief, the rest of the men didn't join them. Although, she wasn't sure how she felt about being alone with Benjamin either.

The lift slid up so rapidly, her stomach rose a good foot into her body, and she pressed her hand against her abdomen.

"Take a deep breath," Benjamin said with a grin. "It'll help."

"Going up this fast should be a crime." She breathed hard through her nose as her legs shook.

The doors opened, and he gave her a side glance. "Just be happy we weren't heading down instead."

"Why? Is it worse?" She followed him.

"Not really," he answered with a shrug. "But the destination is."

Her heart pounded. What was in the basement? She clutched the hem of her top, pushing the question from her mind; actually, she didn't want to know.

They walked in through double oak doors, and she gawked at the room. They'd built the ceiling with glass, giving a perfect few of the black clouds rolling in the sky. Lightning flashed, and she jumped when thunder echoed.

Benjamin stood at a wooden circular table and pulled out a chair. "Have a seat."

She twisted her fingers together as she approached, pretending she was with Richard. Staying on guard while complying was the best course of action.

He sat next to her, and she glanced around; large plants filled the room, and with the dark red carpet, it gave the place a cozy ambience. Despite the situation.

"Is… Vincent in trouble?" she asked, gripping the edges of her seat. "Is there anything I can do to help him?"

He observed her for a second, his expression filling with an amused cruelty. "What are you offering?"

"Well, I guess it depends on why you're after him. If it's money, I don't have any, but I can work it off. I'm good at cleaning, so if you have anywhere you need a cleaner or something, I could do my part." Even as she spoke the words, she knew it sounded ridiculous, but she didn't know what else she could do.

He leaned closer to her, and she stiffened. "You have no idea who Vincent truly is, do you? What his old job used to be?

"No, and I'm not interested in hearing it from you. If he ever wants to share, he'll tell me when he's ready."

"I'm glad to hear he had a taste of what it is to have someone who cares." He leaned in his chair, his smile genuine as though he meant it. "No need to worry, though. He doesn't owe a debt, so there's nothing for you to work off. I just want to have a little *chat.*"

The elevator doors opened, and her heart skipped several beats as Vincent strode into the place. It seemed a lifetime ago since she'd seen him, yet there was something different about the way he looked. Like he'd turned into a predator who focused on calculating how to destroy everyone in the room who stood in his path.

His gaze locked on her, fury and relief flooding behind his eyes. Before she could think of what to say or do, four men rushed out of a side door, and one kicked him in the leg, and Vincent fell to his knees. Her stomach churned as she jumped to her feet, heart hammering. All four pulled their pistols out, pointing them at his head.

She couldn't breathe as she dashed past the table, but didn't make it far. Benjamin wrapped an arm around her waist, keeping her back.

Vincent scowled. "Get your hands off her."

"And put her in the line of fire?" Benjamin asked sarcastically. "Seriously?"

"Line of fire?" she repeated, her tone high-pitched as she struggled harder. "You promised you wouldn't hurt him."

Benjamin arched an eyebrow. "As you can see, I'm not doing anything."

The sound of a gun's hammer being pulled sent more bile into her mouth, and she swallowed hard as she rounded in Benjamin's grip.

"You're the one in charge here!" She tried punching him, but he caught her wrists.

He drew her close, and she struggled to get some distance. "That's a cute effort, but don't try it again."

She gritted her teeth. "Then let him go."

"If he managed to get up here without an escort, it means I've got some pretty beat up guys downstairs," he said as he shot a glare at Vincent. "I want him patted down before letting him go." When she opened her mouth, he shook his head. "And no, I'm not having it done without the weapons. Last time, he put two of my men in a coma."

Her eyebrows shot up as she turned to look at Vincent. His knuckles were bloody; was Benjamin telling the truth?

Vincent slowly raised his hands, his eyes darting from side to side. But there was no fear in his gaze; instead, he looked annoyed. They patted him while the others kept their weapons aimed at him.

Her chin trembled at the sight. "They don't need to point them at his head," she whispered. "Please don't kill him. Please. Whatever he's done, I'll help make it right. Anything you want." Tears rolled down her cheeks as her throat tightened.

"Never offer just anything," Benjamin said quietly. "You have no idea what people will request." He motioned toward Vincent with a grin. "Besides, they're rubber bullets. I wouldn't aim to kill, but if he attacks, it'll hurt like hell, and I'm fine with that."

Vincent scoffed. "And you wonder why I don't come see you?"

"He's clean," one of the men said as they backed away. None of them holstered their guns as though there was still a chance Vincent would attack them.

As soon as Vincent got to his feet, Benjamin let go of Elora, and she ran to him. She was sure she cracked her bones as she threw herself into his arms, holding him tight like she could somehow shield him from everyone in the room.

# 36

# ELORA

*V*incent wrapped his arms around Elora as she trembled against him. "Are you all right?" he asked in a gentle voice.

She nodded, unable to pull away from him. "I'm sorry. I tried to get you out of trouble, but he wouldn't tell me what was going on and—"

"Deep breaths." He kissed the top of her head. "Everything will be okay. Just breathe."

Benjamin chuckled, and she turned to stare at the man. "No need to look so pissed off, Vincent. Come sit." He returned to the table and took a seat, waiting with a grin.

Vincent withdrew and smiled. But the rage she'd seen a few seconds ago lingered in his gaze. "Don't worry."

She nodded, and they both joined Benjamin. Once Elora sat, Vincent pulled her chair next to his so he could keep her closer, and while Benjamin smirked, he didn't comment.

Vincent let out a breath, but nothing about him seemed to relax even a bit. "So tell me what's so urgent you'd go to the lengths of kidnapping someone to talk to me?"

Benjamin raised his eyebrows. "Kidnap? I have no idea what

you mean. Elora willingly agreed to comply." He leaned to the side and caught her gaze. "Isn't that right?"

She narrowed her eyes. "I agreed on the condition he wouldn't hurt you."

"And did I harm you?" Benjamin asked Vincent in a baby voice.

"Get to the point," Vincent snapped. "Why am I here?"

"You've asked around about the Torren gang and another infamous organization I won't mention out loud. But you didn't come to me, despite knowing I'd have the most information. I'm hurt. We were family once."

"You terrorized the person I care for the most in the world because you were upset at not being asked for help?" Vincent chuckled, an edge of darkness behind it. "When did you become a sensitive little flower?"

Elora's breath hitched. And not just because he taunted the man who had the power to have several people shoot them, but also because of what he'd said about her.

*I'm the person he cares the most about?*

Benjamin laughed, then waved his hand dismissively. The men left the room, closing the double oak doors behind them.

"First you ignore my calls, and now you insult me." He blew out a breath. "Hell of a big brother you are."

Elora gaped from Benjamin to Vincent several times as she tried to process the information.

*They're… brothers?*

Another lightning bolt flashed across the sky, and she flinched. Vincent wrapped an arm around her as thunder echoed.

Slowly, she stood, pushing her chair away as both men watched her. "Just going… to walk in the room. You two talk," she muttered, unsure where she even aimed toward or why.

Brothers. What siblings acted this way with one another? She frowned, stopping in front of a window looking out onto a roof. Chairs, tables, and parasols wavered and wobbled in the wind as rain streamed along the glass. Vincent had told her how he'd protected his brother from his father's abuse.

Benjamin glowered at Vincent, then turned his attention on

Elora. She backed away at the anger in his gaze. Had Vincent told him how much she had hurt him? Or how she was a coward for not leaving Richard?

"You need to tell her," he said through gritted teeth. "There's always a chance she'll head to a shelter. You want the next time you see her to be laying on the morgue's metal table, so disfigured—"

"Keep talking and I'll disfigure *you*." Vincent's hands were curled into fists, looking like he was ready to attack him.

Elora approached, her heart beating fast, and stared at Benjamin. "I... I don't know if it's me you're speaking about, but I swear, I never meant to hurt Vincent. It was the last thing I wanted to do, but I did." Her voice cracked as she blinked away tears. "I care about him so much, and it's why I ended things. Because I'm a coward and I was selfish, and now I'm paying the price, so I can't leave—"

"Whoa," Vincent stood from his chair and wrapped his arms around her, "it's nothing like that, darling." He rubbed her back.

Benjamin leaned his chin on his knuckles. "I'm not angry with you, Elora. I'm pissed at him," he said, pointing a finger at Vincent. "Now tell her before I do."

Vincent's jaw clenched. "Fine."

He pulled away, holding her hands as he sat. She took a seat, trying to control her breathing at his somber expression.

"Tell me what?" she whispered.

"The case I'm working on as a consultant. Women's shelters are targeted, and so far, they took six women." He slid his thumbs over her knuckles as she trembled. "We've found three bodies, all of them..." He let out a hollow breath. "It's violent, Elora. The messages they're leaving when they kidnap someone are vile."

"Do... do you know who's behind it?" she asked in a shaky voice, then glanced at Benjamin.

Benjamin shot her an icy smile. "If you're thinking of me, I hate to disappoint, but I don't murder innocents."

*But you do kill.*

She shook her head. "I don't think you did. I'm just wondering if it has anything to do about the Torren gang and organization you mentioned before."

He grinned. "Smart cookie."

"And you have… information about these people because…?" She left the question lingering.

"You've heard of the Crimson organization?" he asked.

Vincent tightened his grip on Elora's hands for a second before letting go. He looked like he resigned himself to something, no matter how angry it made him.

She nodded. "Well… yes. I mean, everyone who lives in this city knows about them. They apparently run the criminal underground." She arched an eyebrow. "Wait. You think they're involved in this?"

Benjamin chuckled. "I already told you I have nothing to do with this."

Her heart pounded in her ears. "You're… in the Crimson organization?" She recalled what Benjamin had said about what job Vincent used to have, and she spun toward him. "Did you work for them as well?"

Vincent's smile didn't reach his eyes. "No. I was in charge of it. When I left, I handed it to Benjamin. He's the boss now."

"You… were the head of the Crimson Organization." Her mind tried coming to terms with the information as she glanced at Benjamin. "And you're the… current…" She'd guessed correctly he was in charge, but she hadn't thought it was of the entire group.

Vincent averted his gaze. "I promised you honesty, remember?"

Slowly, she placed her hand over his, careful to not touch the cuts on his knuckles. "It's part of your past, and I'm sure it's not something you share with many people." She smiled. "Thank you for trusting me."

His eyebrows shot up, and without a word, he wrapped an arm around her, then pulled her onto his lap. He held her against him as she buried her face into the crook of his neck. His pulse throbbed frantically like he was running, and she slid her hand along his chest.

Benjamin grinned. "This is lovey dovey, but I have another

meeting in a few minutes." He stood, and Vincent did the same, putting Elora on her feet gently. "I have information you'll need for the case. If you want it, you'll set up a date with me, and we'll talk then."

Vincent grasped Elora's hand. "Text me the time and place, and I'll be there."

Benjamin grinned. "Oh, you better be, or I'm coming after her again," he said with a wink at Elora.

She smiled back.

# 37

# VINCENT

*V*incent brought Elora to his place without even asking if she was okay with it. They needed to talk, or he'd go mad.

As soon as they walked in, he slammed the door and counted backwards from ten, trying to compose himself. Nothing worked. He marched toward her, and she backed away until her knees hit the sofa, and she toppled over.

He kneeled in front of her, trailing his fingers along her thighs. "Did anyone hurt you when you were with Benjamin?" he asked quietly, the strain in his voice tearing at him.

She shook her head. "No. I… I was so scared for you today. I thought they were luring you into a trap to kill you. It's why I made him promise not to hurt you if I didn't cause trouble." Tears rolled down her cheeks, and his chest tightened. "I'm so stupid. I knew they probably wouldn't keep their word, but I just… I needed to do something. When they pointed their weapons at you like that, I wanted to throw myself on you to make sure none of them hit. I couldn't stand it if anything happened to you."

His eyes burned. "So willing to give up your life for me, but you're also fine with staying with your husband until he kills you."

He stood. "Forgive me if your sacrifice doesn't mean much." He despised his words, but he couldn't keep his rage bottled up anymore. It poured out of him in waves of pain.

"You're right," she said, her voice barely a whisper. She got to her feet, averting her gaze as she walked past him. "Thank you for coming today. I understand there wasn't an actual threat, so I guess it doesn't matter. If it had been, you wouldn't have shown up since I mean so little."

His hands curled into fists as she approached the door and slipped on her sandals. "That's not what I said," he said through his teeth.

"I know." She grabbed the doorknob and turned to him, smiling through her tears. "But there's no point in risking your life for someone who'll end up in a body bag, right?"

He wasn't sure which hurt more between the fury boiling his blood or the agony as her words ripped through his heart.

He closed the gap between them in a few steps, leaning his arms on either side of her as she pressed her back against the door. "Do you have any idea how many times I've considered returning to my old life so I could see the fear on your husband's face before I put a bullet through his fucking head?" He grasped her chin, his throat burning. "I'd do it with no remorse, but it would mean I'd never be able to be with you. People in crime organizations have to constantly watch our backs, and I'd be putting you in danger if we were together. And it's the only reason I haven't killed him." When her eyes widened, he forced a smile. "I'm a monster, too, darling. Just a different kind."

"I'm not any better." She swallowed visibly. "I've wished people I love would die because I used to think it might change my situation." Tears rolled on his hand, and his chest tightened, threatening to stop air from entering his lungs. "But it wouldn't. Now he wants a baby with me, and he's become obsessed about it. Even if things changed, he wouldn't let me go. He'd hurt anyone who stands in his way."

Her words were like a punch to the gut. "Has he..." He took a shallow breath, unable to ask the question.

Her gaze darted from one side to another as though looking for an escape. "I'm… fine. It's okay."

"Elora—"

"I said it's fine. It's already done anyway and…" She took a shuddering breath, then sobbed into her hands.

He gathered her in his arms as tears burned his eyes. Screams and cries echoed in his memories, and he couldn't breathe. He wanted to locate her husband and beat him to death. Watch as blood streamed down his face, and his skin split open, screaming in pain before he'd put the monster out of his misery.

"Tell me what's his hold on you. Let me help you."

"I can't. He'll hurt you, I know it. He'll find a way." She tried pushing him away, but he held her tighter. "It's why I ended things. I have to leave."

"I'm not letting you go. Not again," he said through his teeth, not caring that she stiffened in his arms. "I'll take any time with you. No matter the pain I have to bear." He withdrew and looked at her, his heart beating fast. "Let me keep you. For however long we have. For the few seconds outside a coffee shop. Or the minutes in a bookstore. An hour playing video games. The days and nights we can spend together." His gaze searched hers as his vision blurred. "Please say yes."

She ran her thumb along his cheek, and he held his breath when he realized it was wet with tears. When was the last time he'd cried?

"I want to protect you—"

"Let me protect us both. I know you can't tell me why you have to stay with him, but maybe later…" He took a shallow gasp. "Things can change, Elora. And if I have to die just to have you with me for a little while longer, I'll choose death in a heartbeat."

A calm expression gentled her features as she searched his gaze. "It would be easier to leave you if I…" She trailed off and traced a finger along his jaw. "Why can't I find the words to explain how much I love you, Vincent?"

The air seemed to turn into lead in his lungs as he stared into her eyes. The brown irises sparkled in the light, creating glowing stardust in their depths.

Tears rolled down his cheeks as he smiled. "For the same reason I can't describe how much I love you, darling."

❦

Vincent watched as Elora slept, holding her in his arms. Relief flooded him, knowing he could have her stay with him like this. But he also thought of fresh ideas so she could get away from Richard once and for all. Perhaps seeing a therapist would help her with whatever hold he had on her.

She stretched, her eyelids fluttering open, then frowned.

"Not a good nap?" he asked with a chuckle.

Pressing her hand below her abdomen, she groaned, sliding her legs over the edge of the mattress. "I need to... One second."

She got to her feet, and their gazes both turned to the spot of blood on his sheets. Her eyes widened, and she quickly tugged at the blankets. "I'm sorry. I'm so sorry! I can clean it out. I know how. It won't leave a stain and——"

"Elora?" When she froze and stared at him, he grinned. "It's me, remember? No worries."

She glanced from the stain to him, biting her lower lip. "I... It's okay..." Taking a deep breath, she nodded. "Can I please wash it, though? I have a trick to get stains out."

He rolled off the bed and undid the fitted sheet. "I'll show you the washer and dryer machines. Feel free to work your magic," he said with a wink.

"Do you have any baking soda and vinegar?" she asked as she curled the blanket up in her arms, grimacing at the stain that soaked through to the mattress.

"No, but there's a convenience store next to the condo." He walked to the bathroom, and she followed closely behind. "I'll go buy some. Do you need any pads or tampons?"

Her face flushed. "What? I... It's not... I mean...." She averted her gaze as though it was the most embarrassing situation of her life.

He couldn't help laughing, and when she narrowed her eyes on him, he lifted his hands in surrender. "Sorry, sorry. You're just so adorable when you're shy."

"It's not a subject I've... discussed with others," she said in a small voice, her cheeks red. "My father raised me alone, and he gave me books about it. Whenever I needed... stuff, I'd tell him I was going to the pharmacy, and he'd give me money without asking questions. And it's not something I talk about with Richard."

He wondered why her mother hadn't been in the picture while growing up, but decided not to prod at the moment.

"I understand. But there's no need to be embarrassed about it with me, okay? It's not like blood makes me uncomfortable." He reminded himself she knew about his past, but wasn't sure how accepting she was of the knowledge yet. "I imagine it leaked through your panties, though. Do you want me to get you some at the store? They have a section with socks, underwear, and nylons."

She blushed a deeper shade of red. "Oh. It... Yes, please." She twisted her fingers together. "And I need... pads," she whispered the last word as though it was better to say it quietly. "I didn't realize I'd be away from my house today."

"I'll let Benjamin know he owes you a pair, then."

Her eyes looked like they were about to pop out of her skull. "What? No!" Her voice was shrill, as though she might die at the thought, but when he burst into laughter, her lips quirked up in a smile. "You're horrible," she said with a grin.

Her phone dinged, and she rushed to it, grabbing it quickly. Her muscles relaxed a bit, so he approached her, assuming it wasn't Richard texting her.

"Everything okay?" he asked.

"It's a text from Liana... she wants me to come over for supper at her place tomorrow since Richard is out of town." She swallowed visibly. "She said to invite you."

"You hadn't mentioned what happened?"

She shook her head. "I haven't talked to her in a while, except for the occasional quick texts to check in. I guess... part of me tried to detach from everyone when things got worse with Richard."

He rubbed her back, picturing her alone and hurting. "You're

not getting rid of us. We're here to help in whatever way you need."
He leaned forward and kissed her cheek. "Tell her thank you for the
invitation, and we'll both be there. It'll be good for you to hang out
with a healthy couple. Experience a fun double date."

Her smile lit her eyes. "I'd like that." She typed away on her
cellphone, answering her friend.

"Now then, before I leave, what pads do you use?"

She stiffened, but gave him the details of what she needed while
focusing on her device, even though she wasn't typing anymore.

"I'll be right back." He grabbed his keys, and with a small wave,
left.

It had finally stopped raining, but the smell of ozone lingered in
the air, so Vincent hurried to the building next door, and stepped
inside the store. He was so proud at how Elora had calmed down
quickly after her initial panic about the blood; she slowly got better,
and he intended on keeping her feeling as safe as possible.

His phone buzzed as he grabbed the baking soda, and he pulled
out the device. "Hey, Daniel. What's going on?"

"Bad news. There's been another disappearance, but it's so
different we're not even sure it's linked to our case."

Vincent stiffened as he trudged through the aisle; looking for the
items he needed while not registering anything he saw. "There must
be something related to them if you're calling me, right?"

"A woman was supposed to meet up with her boyfriend at a
motel near the airport during the week, and then she never showed
up for work." Daniel's voice was strained, as though he'd talked for
too long. "No history of visiting a women's shelter or any kind of
past abuse. She has a job, friends, family, a support system. Basically,
she's not high risk like the others."

"It sounds different." Vincent put the vinegar into the store
basket. "Has the boyfriend been located? Do we know who he is?"

"No. The motel employee said he paid cash and looked older
than the missing woman. The reason I feel there's a connection is
because of the security footage. As usual, crap resolution, and of
course, we can't see his face, but he brought a large tarp into the
room."

Vincent's stomach clenched. "Never a good sign."

"Exactly. I'm just wondering if this is related, and if so, how," he said with a sigh. "This one is going to hit the media hard because she's an employee with the city of Winnipeg."

"Well, maybe it's not a bad thing. Might get lucky and someone will recognize her."

"I sure hope so because I'm getting sick of sending you to the morgue. The last victims were… Why kidnap and murder women who likely won't be reported as missing if they're going to leave them for everyone to see?"

Vincent clenched his jaw. "To send a message to the others seeking shelter. But this newest one… It's the complete opposite." He grabbed a few last items he needed. "Look, I'm at the store, and I've got a guest waiting for me at home, but I'll come in as soon as I've spoken to my latest contact. He apparently has information about the gang and organization that are likely related to this."

"Fine, but make the meeting with Benjamin Karson fast, because I can't keep sitting on my ass here."

Vincent's eyebrows rose, but he grinned. "I should've known you're keeping tabs on him."

"And yet he slips away every time I think I've got something on him," Daniel said in a huff. "Get that information."

Daniel hung up, and Vincent rolled his eyes. Benjamin was good at hiding his activity—even better than Vincent had ever been—so he wasn't too worried about his brother getting caught.

Too many cops, lawyers, and judges in the Crimson organization's pockets.

Vincent paused at the frozen aisle, and smiled as he picked up a gallon of mint chocolate ice cream, recalling how Elora had chosen the flavor when they'd gone to the parlor together. It seemed like forever ago when all they were doing was practicing for the photoshoot.

He grabbed a few candy bars and a heating pad, then stepped up to the cashier to pay.

# 38

# ELORA

The red summer dress Elora slipped on was shorter than she was used to wearing, but she loved the way it flowed when she spun in front of the mirror. She had left the two dresses and underwear Vincent had bought at Liana's house. It seemed like a good time to put on the second one she hadn't worn yet.

Elora stepped into the kitchen, helping Liana with the plates.

"That dress is hot as hell," Liana said with a grin.

One of the kids yelled from a bedroom, and Liana rolled her eyes.

"I'll get the roast out, no worries." Elora shooed her friend away.

Elora opened the oven, the heat blasting on her face as she bent to grab the platter. A growl sounded from behind her, and she giggled as she placed the meal on top of the stove.

"I know you're hungry, but it's bad manners to grunt like a beast. Even if you are a wolf." She faced him, and warmth burned through her.

His gaze raked across her body, his pupils dilating. "You look gorgeous."

"Thank you." She stared at his black jeans and white dress shirt. "And you're handsome," she said.

He pulled her closer, nuzzling her neck. "I have arrangements for this upcoming weekend. Is that okay?"

Her heart felt like it shrank, but she kept her expression as relaxed as possible. It wasn't like they had any concrete plans to spend the weekend together, but she had assumed that since Richard was out of town again, they'd see each other.

"Of course. You have a life of your own. I'll use the time to——"

"I meant plans for us." He kissed her shoulder, pushing the strap along the way.

She leaned back to stare at him. "Oh, well, then that's even better." She could barely think straight as he slid his hand under her breast, his thumb sliding over her skin.

How could she have feared him a short time ago?

The front door opened, and she pushed her strap in place as Brad came in. The kids dashed to their father, shouting and talking all at once, but not once did he look annoyed in the slightest.

Vincent motioned his head toward Brad. "I'll go introduce myself."

Just as he left, Liana entered the kitchen and grinned at Elora.

"What?" Elora asked.

"You've got quite the blush," Liana said with a wink.

"Oh shut up." Elora couldn't help grin.

As the evening progressed, Elora noticed little things she never had despite having hung out with her friend and husband. The way Brad leaned in toward Liana, and how they beamed at each other, never losing eye contact when they spoke to one another. A few times, Elora even caught secret small touches; Brad brushing his fingers along Liana's wrist, Liana giving Brad's arm a quick squeeze. There were no expectations from one another; just love.

Vincent placed his hand on Elora's thigh as they ate the chocolate cake he'd bought from a bakery and drank coffee. His touch sent butterflies fluttering inside her stomach, and she smiled at him.

Brad put his fork down and turned serious. "Elora, I want you to know if you ever need anything from us, we're just a call away."

Elora started from Brad to Liana, her pulse speeding.

Liana straightened, but her gaze had gentled. "Anything at all, okay?"

"Oh..." Elora shifted in her seat. "You're aware of... my situation?"

"Liana told me, but please don't be upset with her. She was coming home in tears, and..." He took a deep breath, and Liana shifted her body closer to his. "I just started worrying so much when she wouldn't tell me why. And then I found our browser history filled with women's shelter locations. I was sick to my stomach thinking I did something dreadful without knowing." He slid his fingers into Liana's hand. "Finally, she explained. And I want you to know, you're family to us. We're here for you no matter what. You say the word, and we'll help, no questions asked."

Vincent gave a curt nod. "I'm glad to hear Elora has such good friends."

"Thank you," Elora said, her voice thick. A few plans formed in her mind, and for once, they didn't vanish under despair. No. This time, they became stronger under the support of friends. And family.

❦

Back at Vincent's condo, they hung out on the couch, laughing at stories they told one another about adventures with alcohol. For what seemed like several hours, she forgot this wasn't her normal life.

"Do you want to watch a movie?" he asked.

She grabbed his shirt and looked up at him with a smile. "Yes please."

She couldn't help her good mood when she'd wrapped her mind around what having her periods meant; she wasn't pregnant. And since it was past two weeks, and the clinic hadn't called her, her STI tests were negative.

They cuddled against one another, watching a haunted house movie. She barely paid attention to the story, though; the whole time, she came up with ideas on how she could convince Richard of leaving her while also making sure she wasn't abandoning her father's fate in his hands.

"You seem preoccupied," Vincent said as he slipped off his shirt.

She focused on his chest longer than she intended, and when he grinned, she averted her gaze. "Oh… It's nothing. Just thinking of things."

As he unbuttoned his jeans, she cursed the fact she had her period, a renewed need for him to be inside her, heating her core. Her usual unease of being partially naked vanished as she took off her dress and unclipped her bra, pulling it off.

Vincent grabbed her from behind, and she yelped as he picked her up in his arms. Her eyes widened for a second before she grinned, realizing he carried her to his bed.

She giggled. "You should've told me you were this tired."

"Tired of waiting, yes," he replied in a husky tone.

He placed her gently on his mattress, his gaze hooded as he lay next to her.

Despite being horny, she had never cared much for having sex while having her periods; always too messy in her opinion. She just hoped he didn't mind that they wouldn't be doing anything much.

Her stomach clenched at the thought of saying no for a few seconds, but she relaxed as she glided her fingers along his neck and gave him a sad smile. "You remember I have my… time of the month, right?" Needing to hide her embarrassment, she rolled away from him a bit, and pointed at the sheet. "By the way, did you see? No stain. I told you I had a trick."

He chuckled, scooting closer to her. "I have to say, I'm impressed. Where were you when I needed to get rid of evidence?"

She gawked at him, but let out a laugh. "I can't believe you said that."

"Sorry. Dark humor." He gave her a sheepish smile. "And as for your periods, unless you're not in the mood, I don't mind it."

His mouth brushed along hers, and he thrust his tongue between her lips, his kiss filled with lust. He pushed her legs apart, repositioning himself so his erection rested against her mound. Even through both their underwear, she felt the heat of his hard shaft. Slowly, he moved his hips forward, rubbing himself on her.

She moaned, his mouth swallowing her whimpers as he rolled her nipple between his finger and thumb. He straightened, then tugged on her panties until they were halfway down her thighs. When he took off his briefs, his erection sprung out, and a shiver of anticipation ran through her as he lowered himself.

"Wait..." she breathed. "I mean..." She averted her gaze for a second. "It's just so... messy, isn't it? Your sheets—"

"If it's something you're not comfortable with, I won't push, but just know that I have no issues with it, okay?"

She bit her lower lip. "I'm sorry..."

"There's nothing to apologize about." He gave her a playful smile filled with promise. "Besides, there will be plenty of other times, darling."

He grasped the head of his cock and slipped it between her labia, and she let out a shuddering breath as she rubbed herself along his shaft as though she was in heat.

He closed his eyes for a second. "You make me so hard."

Thrusting forward, his cock slid between her lips, rubbing against her sensitive nub. He moved back and forth, and she groaned in frustration, needing more.

Kissing along her neck, he reached her ear. "You sound like you're enjoying this, darling."

"Yes," she breathed. "Please don't stop."

He took her nipple in his mouth, sucking hard until a shuddering breath escaped her throat. His free hand tugged on her other hard peak as he continued rubbing his cock faster between her legs. Heat pooled within her core, spreading out as her clit throbbed harder. He licked his thumb, then circled it around her sensitive peak.

"Ah... ah... Vincent... yes."

Sparks exploded in her vision, and she cried out, her fingers digging into his shoulders as he thrust faster and rougher.

He clenched his jaw and groaned between his teeth as hot cum spread across her belly and breasts. He leaned on his forearms, resting his forehead on hers as they both panted. His hair stuck to him with sweat, and she grinned, pushing the strands away.

He smirked. "Nothing like a good quickie before sleep."

She giggled, lifting her head to kiss his cheek. He rolled off the bed and disappeared into the bathroom for a few seconds, then returned with a wet washcloth. After helping her with cleaning up, he threw the cloth into the laundry basket, and cuddled up next to her.

They stared at each other in silence, his hand resting on her hip as she took comfort in the pulse of his beating heart beneath her palm. She had to find a means out of her marriage, because there was no leaving Vincent anymore.

# 39

# VINCENT

Three days had passed since Vincent had seen Elora, but she had continued texting him from time to time with keywords they'd planned in advance in case Richard checked her messages. So far, everything was all right.

He'd sent a prepaid credit card to Liana so she could take Elora shopping for a cocktail dress. At the same time, he invited Liana and Brad to attend an event she'd feel safe to attend since it was closed to the public and press.

On his way to the hotel next to the convention center, Vincent glanced out of the car window. "Stop here."

The driver, one of Benjamin's men his brother had sent him, pulled to the side. He shot him an amused glance through the rear-view mirror, and Vincent scoffed.

"Don't say a word," Vincent said as he stepped out into the summer warmth. He was glad he hadn't changed into a suit yet or he might have suffered a heat stroke.

He walked into the flower shop, relieved the air conditioning worked. Tonight he'd see Elora, and as always, he wanted it to be special. And with her husband busy, they'd stay at the hotel for the night.

The woman at the counter beamed. "Hi, how can I help you?"

"I'd like a bouquet in an arrangement of white roses and lilies of the valley." It was an easy pick since Elora had mentioned she loved those when they were at Kings Park together.

After he paid and thanked the florist, then slid into the private car. "Let's go."

The driver grinned as he put the vehicle in drive. "Those are lovely flowers, Mr. Voden."

"Know what else is lovely, Derik?" Vincent asked with a smirk. "Shutting up."

Traffic wasn't too heavy, and they arrived about twenty minutes later. Vincent thanked Derik for the ride and walked into the five-star hotel. Once checked in, he explored the room, his mind stuck in the gutter. So many places he wanted to take Elora.

But more than anything else, he needed to make her his. Because she already was.

The space featured a living area with a Jacuzzi, and a private bedroom with a king-sized bed. He caught sight of a glass vase near the balcony, and placed the bouquet inside, then walked into the bathroom to fill it with water.

He hoped the room would smell lovely by the time the evening ended, and couldn't wait to give them to her. His heart thundered thinking of Elora.

He returned the pot to its place and stepped outside, looking out onto the city.

*I'm in love with her completely.*

Gripping the railing, he gritted his teeth as the hot metal burned his palms. The only way she'd ever leave was if her husband weren't in the picture. And if it's what it took, then he'd give her the way out she needed.

Even if it meant stepping into his old life and bringing her with him.

The event was in full swing.

Vincent smiled as he stared at the crystal chandelier hanging from the vaulted ceiling above the glossy hardwood dance floor. Perfume and cologne hung in the air as waiting staff circulated the crowd to exchange empty glasses for fresh ones.

Vincent stayed toward the back near a decorative mirror hanging on the wall, glancing at Benjamin as he conversed with associates. Everyone was dressed in their best attire, matching with the high-end feel of the event.

It was the right decision to leave his brother in charge when Vincent left the organization. There was too much blood on his hands, and he needed peace. But Benjamin would never quit; it was what he loved.

Benjamin approached, his shirt collar open wide enough to show off the blood drop tattoo below his neck. A message to the rest of the gang members attending the party to watch themselves because they'd be fucking with the wrong person. Vincent had the same design once, but had an artist cover it up after he left.

"Hiding?" Benjamin asked with a grin.

Vincent scoffed as people called out to one another, the murmur of many voices surrounding them. "I'm waiting for certain people to arrive."

"Speaking of which, you haven't told me what you're planning with Elora."

Vincent arched an eyebrow, keeping his annoyance in check. "Didn't know I had to explain myself." After a few tense seconds, Vincent sighed. "I'm trying to get her out of the situation she's stuck in."

"You don't need to keep seeking forgiveness for what happened to our mother."

If they were alone, Vincent would have punched Benjamin in the face for the comment. He curled and uncurled his fists, taking deep breaths. "How do you feel about being thrown out a window?"

Benjamin scoffed. "Shutting me up won't change what you already know. She won't leave her husband. If she wanted to, she would have. Showing her a light at the end of a tunnel she can't reach is cruel." He shook his head, staring at the guests speaking amongst each other. "Whatever he has on her, she seems trapped."

Vincent's stomach clenched, knowing Benjamin wasn't lying. Statistics didn't lie. Vincent and Benjamin's childhoods were proof.

*You leave alive or in a body bag.*

Before they could continue the conversation, Vincent spotted a familiar face. Elora's friends, Liana and Brad, walked toward them.

Brad wore a tuxedo; his hair gelled, giving him the air of sophistication. Vincent didn't get close to people easily. Sure, he had charm to pretend pleasantries, but he felt a true growing friendship with the university professor. Liana's dark purple cocktail dress stole a few glances as she walked past. She was a wonderful woman. Strong and fiercely loyal to Elora, which he adored about her. With one double-date, Vincent gained new friends. Two individuals who might know what Elora's secrets were.

*If she won't tell me willingly…*

He hated the thought of going behind her back after she'd refused to hear about Vincent's past, wanting him to tell her when he was ready. But he wasn't in her position; in danger every day of being beaten to death by a monster.

"I can see the wheels turning." Benjamin cocked his head.

He shrugged. "I'm thinking."

"Back then, it meant you had a plan… a deadly one." He chuckled, crossing his arms. "I remember the first time I saw that look…"

Vincent shot him a dark stare, and Benjamin lost his smile.

Benjamin glanced around, then looked at his brother. "I wasn't going to tell you, but I've had my suspicions relating to your case, and plan on testing my theory tonight. The only reason I'm saying anything now is because I don't want your hasty decisions to clash with mine."

"You planned something involving Elora without telling me?" he asked through gritted teeth.

Benjamin turned to him and drew a step into Vincent's personal space. "If I left this alone, you'd eventually kill the bastard, and I'd bail you out. But it would mean returning to the organization." He gripped Vincent's jacket, his gaze burning in anger. "Some members want you to return as boss. If you come back, people will side with you, and it'll create a fucking war within our midst." His jaw clenched tight. "I won't have that happen, so yes, I took action, and tonight, I'll see if I'm right. If I am, she may be able to leave safely with no one dying."

Vincent grasped Benjamin's wrist, but a few of his brother's men shot glares toward him, and he slowly dropped his hand. One wrong move, and they wouldn't hesitate to bring Vincent down.

"What do you need from me?" Vincent asked in a sigh.

"I'd prefer knowing what his hold on Elora is before I take any actions."

Vincent turned toward the crowd of people. "I need to speak with Elora's friend. Alone."

"Consider it done. But get the information, or I'll use my own methods to find out."

Liana glanced over her shoulder. Vincent's breath caught inside his chest as he stared where Liana was looking.

The dress fitted Elora like a glove. It hugged her curves in the perfect places. Vincent wanted to run his hands over her body, relearning each part of her. The clothing was black, but covered in beautiful blue flower patterns made of lace, some with tiny pearls in the middle. She let her honey-brown hair down, the bottom ending in waves at her lower back.

But something was wrong; she looked... sick. And when he glanced at their friends, they seemed nervous.

When he caught sight of Richard strolling next to Elora, Vincent nearly rushed toward the man to flatten him permanently.

*What. The. Fuck?*

Benjamin grabbed Vincent's arm and squeezed. "Don't do anything stupid."

"Tell me this wasn't part of your plan," Vincent spat.

Vincent's hands curled into fists, locking onto Richard like he was an insect needing to be exterminated. Benjamin dragged Vincent away until a large column hid them. Benjamin rammed his brother against it, and it worked in snapping Vincent out of his rage.

"Focus. If you can't control yourself, then leave, but I won't have this event turn into a bloodbath."

Vincent took a deep breath. "Fucking hell. You could've at least given me a heads up."

Benjamin backed off. "As far as Richard is concerned, I invited him to network for his job, and Elora is here because her friend had an extra ticket."

Benjamin's gaze glanced upward, and Vincent followed his brother's gaze. He couldn't help grin as he spotted a sniper on the upper level of the curved observation balcony. "Security?"

"Can never be too careful," Benjamin said in a growl. "Once I have confirmation, I'll let you in on it. Until then, remember anything you do to piss off Richard hurts Elora. Turn on your charm, and reel in the killer in you."

"Your suspicions better be right," Vincent muttered.

Benjamin slapped Vincent on the back, hard, then motioned his head. "Let's greet our guests."

Vincent wanted to punch his fist through Richard's face, but instead, smiled. He had to keep Elora safe, and if it meant being nice to her fucking husband, then so be it.

For now.

# 40

# VINCENT

*V*incent and Benjamin approached the newest arrivals, and it took everything in Vincent not to squeeze the life out of Richard. He was so close... so easy to kill. One twist of his neck and it would be done.

Instead, Vincent smiled at Brad.

"Good to see you again. And this must be your wife?" Vincent shook his friend's hand, hoping they'd play along.

Liana grinned, a sassy expression flashing in her gaze. "You're Vincent Voden, aren't you?"

"I am, yes." He hated the need to pretend.

But he'd keep his woman safe at all costs. When he turned his smile on Elora, it felt like a stab in his heart. She had tears in her eyes.

Brad waved toward Elora. "This is my wife's friend, Elora Reverie. She's our extra for this evening."

Liana nodded. "Yes, and it turns out someone gave her husband a ticket during a business meeting. I guess it worked out for the best." Even Liana's smile was twisted in fury.

Richard smirked. "Indeed, it has." He put out his hand. "I'm Richard Reverie."

Vincent shook it, counting inside his mind, repeating Elora's name between each as a reminder not to crush the bastard's bones. "It's nice to meet you."

Benjamin covered a snort with a cough, and Vincent clenched his jaw.

"Ah, where are my manners?" Vincent said. This evening would kill him. "This is Benjamin Karson, the man who organized the Safer Sanctuaries charity event.

Benjamin's charisma outshined everyone as he shook hands with Brad and Richard, then grasped Liana and Elora's fingers, and bowed. Elora paled, and Richard's stony gaze followed Benjamin as he straightened.

Brad laughed. "Oh, I'll have to keep my eye on you."

That seemed to calm Richard a bit, and he gave a hearty chuckle.

The microphone on the podium echoed in the room, and Benjamin glanced toward the stage. "If you'll excuse me, I have to make an announcement."

As Benjamin walked away, he grabbed his phone and spoke to someone. Vincent sat at the dinner table with Elora, Liana, Brad, and Richard, and a few seconds later, his cell buzzed.

*Benjamin: I'm sending Krystal in your direction.*

Vincent couldn't help grin. That woman could easily catch a priest's eye; she'd distract Richard in less than a minute.

Sure enough, Krystal ambled toward them, hips swaying from side to side in a dress barely covering her panties—if she wore any. Long golden blonde hair curled without a single frizz in sight, her smile beaming with straight white teeth.

"Mr. Voden. How good to see you." She put out her hand, manicured fingernails painted in gold, matching her attire. "Will you introduce me to your lovely friends?"

Vincent made the introduction, his chest squeezing when Elora glanced from him to Krystal, and he could see the doubt in her eyes. When Vincent introduced Elora's husband, Krystal's smile widened, and he mentally thanked Benjamin for his quick thinking.

"Oh, are you a model?" she asked, batting her eyelashes as she took the empty seat next to Richard.

Richard lapped the attention. "No. My career stems in computer science and code development with Hitech."

"I bet you're the *top*, too…" she said, the innuendo so obviously Vincent almost cringed.

Benjamin began his announcement, speaking about keynote speakers and opportunities to donate to the charity.

Vincent glanced toward Richard and Krystal as they flirted with one another, oblivious that Elora had her gaze set on Vincent.

Once finished, Benjamin joined them.

The evening passed by fast. Wait staff, dressed in black and white, carried trays of gourmet food. Scallops, shrimp, salmon, prime rib, and filet mignon laid out on the tables covered in white cloth. Vincent stared as Elora sipped on Champagne flutes, the flickering candles casting shadows along her delicate skin. Chatter and laughter filled the room, mixing with the silverware clinking against plates.

Benjamin pushed his plate aside. "Richard, I hear you're also a talented salesman for your company's coding development."

"I am." Although he seemed annoyed at being taken away from Krystal's attention.

Benjamin smiled and waved toward Vincent. "Mr. Voden here is a consultant. Deep pockets and many connections. I'm sure you two would have lots to discuss if you set up a meeting."

Vincent wanted to punch his brother, but gave him the benefit of the doubt, seeing where he took this. When the live orchestra played, and people rushed to the dance floor, Richard's eyes lit up like a cartoon character getting a brilliant idea.

"It would honor me to discuss business with you, Mr. Voden." When Vincent gave a curt nod, Richard turned his attention on Elora. "My wife loves to dance. Please, I insist you accompany her."

Vincent smiled at Elora. "Would you care to dance?"

Richard leaned in toward Elora, muttering something in her ear, and she flinched. She nodded quickly, then got to her feet.

"I'd love to." She slipped her hand in his, following him beneath the chandelier.

>

They intertwined their fingers together, and Vincent slid his fingers over Elora's lower back, pulling her close. She locked gazes with him as they moved across the dance floor to the music playing. She looked worried, but when they both glanced toward the table, it was obvious her husband was too busy talking with Krystal to care.

Soon he forgot they were in a room full of people. The orchestra vanished, and all he could see was her.

Elora. His Elora.

"Are you okay?" he asked, his voice quiet.

"We arrived, and Richard... He was here, and he spotted us. Liana and Brad were with me, so he didn't seem too angry, but..." She took a shuddering breath. "I don't understand why he's here."

The guilt pressing on him lifted. Benjamin had a plan, and Vincent was willing to follow through; he refused she lived in fear any longer. But first, he needed to find out what chain tied her to the monster.

Elora stared at their table for a second, then frowned. "I never asked, but why does Benjamin have a different last name than yours?"

His mind wandered to his choice when he was younger. After child services sent them to live with their grandmother. "Benjamin chose our grandmother's maiden name. Despite being a hell of a rebel, he did his best to help her with anything she needed. She was old and sickly when we started living with her, so she wasn't able to take care of us, but he did what he could for her." He brought her closer. "I picked my mother's maiden name. A sort of..." Letting out a breath, he shook his head. "No one in the organization knows we're related, and we've kept it like that. Gangs would likely target the other for leverage."

She nodded, averting her gaze. "That can't be easy."

He leaned forward, brushing his lips on her ear. "By the way, you look breathtaking, darling."

A tiny gasp escaped her. "Thank you."

When the music stopped, he led her to their table.

Richard got to his feet and pulled Krystal with him. "I'll take the next one." He winked at Elora, and even Benjamin looked like he wanted to off the asshole.

Benjamin stood, and before Elora could sit, he grasped her wrist so fast, she gasped. He bowed his head, but didn't let go of her. "Would you honor me with this dance?"

Vincent clenched his jaw, but when Benjamin caught his gaze, he realized what his brother was doing.

She visibly swallowed before nodding. "Okay."

Benjamin led her into the crowd, and Vincent's shoulders relaxed. Deciding to use the opportunity, Vincent turned to Brad.

"Can I borrow your wife? I promise to bring her back."

Brad laughed. "Hey, don't look at me."

"I can decide for myself, thank you." Liana got to her feet and winked. "But yes, I'd like to dance."

Liana held her head high as she pulled Vincent forward.

"I need to ask you something," Vincent said.

"If it's about Elora, I suggest you talk to her."

He grinned. Oh, she was quick. "Problem is, by the time she tells me, it'll be too late for her." He gave a pointed stare toward where Richard and Krystal danced, so close they could be dry humping.

Liana's face fell, tears shining in her eyes until she blinked them away. "What do you want to know?"

"Why does she stay with him?" His voice came out in a growl, and Liana's grip tightened on his hand for a second.

She stared at Elora, biting her lower lip. "She never told me why, but it has something to do with her father."

"Her father?" He frowned, trying to figure out the link.

"He's in a nursing home. It's all I know." And it sounded like it was. "I wish I could shake sense into her, but that isn't the problem.

Whatever hold the bastard has on her, it's a tight leash, and she won't leave until… well, I don't know," she finished with a sigh.

"It'll be cut soon. One way or another."

"What do you mean?" Her eyes had widened, and she leaned closer. "Look, I've thought of threatening the fucker for a while, but don't do it. If you go to prison, it would crush Elora."

Vincent smiled, but he knew it wasn't reaching his gaze as fear flushed her face. "I don't bother with threats."

# 41

# ELORA

*R*ichard showing up was a nightmare. Elora caught sight of him dancing with the woman named Krystal; she couldn't care less.

Elora glanced at the glossy hardwood floor, the classical music filling the room as she danced with Benjamin.

"There's something you should know about Vincent." Benjamin spoke so matter of fact, he could've been discussing the weather.

"Please stop trying to constantly tell me his secrets."

He glared at her, and for the first time, she saw the resemblance to Vincent. They were so different, yet so alike. Especially when they were angry.

"Did he tell you he's murdered people?" he asked quietly.

Her pulse throbbed inside her ears. "We didn't discuss it, but considering who he used to be, I assumed. I imagine you have blood on your hands, too. Why are you bringing it up?"

"Because it'll help you understand what kind of position you've put him in." He pulled her closer. "And keep dancing or Vincent will get suspicious and beat the living shit out of me if he thinks I upset you."

"You *did* upset me," she said, glaring at him. She surprised herself with how pissed off she sounded.

He smirked. "Oh, is there fight left in you?"

She gritted her teeth. "Look, I know he wants to kill my husband. He told me himself. But he also said it would mean having to join your organization, and I won't have that."

"I'm glad to hear we're on the same side about that." His eyes flashed with sorrow, and his smile twisted into something cold. "There were two murders that changed Vincent, and both of them were to protect me. He gave up everything in more ways than you can imagine. He had to make impossible decisions no one should ever have to."

"Like what?"

"I'll tell you about the second time, because the first is his to tell." He spun her faster to the edge of the dance floor where they were secluded. "After he left me in charge of the organization, my best friend, Tristan, was shot and killed during a police raid. The cop who shot Tristan was a friend of Vincent and his boss. It pissed me off, and I wasn't thinking straight." He grinned, staring over her shoulder as though remembering. "I stormed into the cop station with a few dozen men, planning to murder the pig who took the life of Tristan."

She frowned. "Since you're here, I don't have to ask if you made it out alive. But I don't get how."

"Vincent placed himself in front of Daniel, and I lost it. I assumed my brother chose his boss over me, and the idea of losing him… I stuck the gun into Vincent's mouth, intending to pull the trigger."

She tightened her grip on his hand, wanting to crush his bones. Benjamin winced, but laughed.

"You can relax, sweetie. I obviously didn't go through with it."

She let up, but hoped her glare sent the message she was angry. "So what happened?"

"Vincent pulled me into Daniel's office and showed me evidence. Tristan had written a statement ratting me out. Threw me under the bus to get out of being charged with drug trafficking.

They would've sentenced me to life with the details my supposed best friend swore to." He glanced toward Vincent, who continued dancing with Liana. "Vincent sent the cops on Tristan a second time, busting him for firearms dealings."

"But I thought Daniel killed your friend. How does it make Vincent a murderer?"

"He didn't die from the wound. While the police arrested other members, Vincent found Tristan with a bullet in his gut. Could have made it if they brought him to the hospital, but Vincent shot him a few times for good measure. Wanted to ensure the betrayal died with him. Burned the confession in front of me inside the office."

An icy chill settled over her at the visual of Vincent murdering someone, but she couldn't blame him. Having grown up surrounded by violence, becoming protective was second nature to him. What wouldn't he have done to look after his brother?

Her stomach churned as she stared at Benjamin. "The first time he killed to protect you... what happened?" she asked quietly, deep down, already having a few ideas.

The same icy smile curled his lips. "Ask him. I'm sure, for an exchange, he'd tell you his darkest secret."

"Exchange?"

"Why do you think he's dancing with your friend?" He motioned toward the pair. "He needs to know what's holding you hostage to your husband."

She gaped at Benjamin, wanting to tell him he was wrong; Vincent wouldn't go behind her back. But she pressed her lips together. What lengths wouldn't he take to save her?

*He's killed to protect his brother.*

"Does he plan... on killing Richard?" she whispered, her heart hammering. "Is that why my husband is here?"

The music ended, and Benjamin bowed. "He abandoned that life. But I don't doubt for a second that if he becomes desperate enough, he'll return to it." He tightened his grip on her hand when she tried to pull away. "Tell him the truth. Let him help you. Don't force him down that road."

Without another word, he stalked off, leaving her rooted to the spot. The next piece began, and she held her breath as Richard approached.

He grabbed her wrist and pulled her closer as they danced.

"I hope you're not about to cause a scene about me dancing with Krystal? Let's refrain from having one of our *discussions* in public," he said with a smirk.

"I don't want to ruin this evening for you. I promise to be on my best behavior." She forced a smile.

"Once the night is done, I plan on talking business with her. Turns out, her father is CEO of a financial corporation, and she has a lot of pull with him. If I get in her good graces, it'll help me."

"Sounds like a great opportunity for networking," she said with a nod.

His eyebrows shot up. "Didn't expect you'd understand, but I guess I was wrong. You're more intelligent than I thought." He laughed, and she did her best not to glare at him.

"Will you be back tonight, or…?" She left the question hanging in the air between them.

He sighed, rolling his eyes. "What did you think I meant by getting into her good graces?"

"I guessed it meant fucking her," she said, snappier than planned. He tightened his grasp on her, and she winced. "I didn't mean it like that. I realize you're going to sleep with her, and I'm fine with it. But I wanted to know whether to have a late dinner ready, or breakfast, or go straight to making lunch."

He kissed her cheek, and she had to fight the urge to flinch away from him. "You're the best. Late lunch for tomorrow."

"I'll make grilled cheese sandwiches for you when you get back, then."

"Ask Liana and Brad for a ride home. Be home tonight before midnight and I'll forget all about how you didn't tell me you were attending this event."

She swallowed hard. "Thank you. I'll be on time."

"I hope this leniency on my part won't spoil you too much." And with a small squeeze of her hand, Richard walked away toward

Krystal. Once together, they left, his hand giving her ass a playful pat.

Elora's mind seemed to jam. She didn't care what had just happened with her husband, but was instead focused on what Benjamin had told her. Vincent would kill Richard if he couldn't find another way for her to leave. And she'd have to tell him her secret.

*That my father is in a horrible situation because of my selfishness.*

Vincent's gaze was fixated on Richard and Krystal, and as soon as they vanished around a corner, he turned to Elora and came closer.

His smile didn't reach his eyes. "We need to talk."

Something in his tone hid a hint of darkness, and she tensed.

"Yes…we do."

## 42

# ELORA

*E*lora twisted her fingers, standing in the hallway. Part of her felt guilty about leaving Liana and Brad at the event. They'd seemed worried, but both relaxed once they found out Richard had left.

Vincent swiped the key card to his room and opened the door, waiting for her to step inside. She did, but her fight or flight was on high alert after what Benjamin had told her. She didn't blame Vincent, but she also couldn't pretend it didn't make her nervous. To assume he'd killed was one matter, but to hear details made it too real.

The place was gorgeous and smelled like fresh flowers; a living room with a Jacuzzi and a large balcony overlooking the city. When she stepped in farther, she noticed two doors down a short corridor. Probably a bedroom and bathroom.

The door closed with a snap, and she spun to face Vincent. He leaned on it and crossed his arms. His dress shirt strained along his muscles, and she tried keeping her focus off his body. This wasn't the time.

But the way he stared at her… both with hunger and anger, she couldn't hold his gaze. Instead, she kicked off her high heels and walked into the living room. Everything looked so interesting when avoiding someone.

She caught sight of the flower bouquet and approached it, her heart speeding. White roses and lilies of the valley.

He remembered.

Her vision blurred, and she blinked the tears away as the lump in her throat squeezed. She swallowed hard and leaned forward to inhale their scent. Never in the time she'd even dated Richard had he bought her favorite flowers. They were always red roses because he didn't care to ask or remember.

"They smell delightful. Thank you." She froze when she caught his gaze.

His eyes had darkened; two black pools staring into her.

"What did my brother tell you?" He didn't sound angry, but his eyes betrayed him.

She focused on the couch facing the plasma screen television, then glanced over his shoulder at the exit.

"Elora," he hissed her name, and she backed away.

"I... We talked. I mean, he... Please don't..." She couldn't breathe, and the closer he got to her, the more black spots appeared in her vision.

Strong arms wrapped around her, and she took a deep breath. Once her pulse slowed to normal, he put his finger under her chin, and pushed up so she'd look at him. Anger flashed behind his glare, but there was pain, too.

"Do you really believe I'd hurt you?"

"I... No. But it's... when Richard gets angry, he hits now. When I hear someone who's furious, I react."

His gaze softened. "You never need to fear me. Couples can have arguments, and get heated, but most people won't hit each other. I guarantee we'll argue, but I'll never raise a hand to hurt you."

"You're... a good man. You're patient and understanding." She buried her face into his chest, closing her eyes. "I know you've killed people, but it's... I'm sorry you had to, but I understand."

He stiffened. "Benjamin's next."

"That's not funny." She withdrew. "You two love each other. Despite that, you both act like ex-business associates more than brothers. But you care for each other."

"You're a kindhearted woman."

Tears sprang to her eyes. "No, I'm not." She pulled away from him and sat on the edge of the couch. "If I was, I wouldn't be in the mess I'm in."

"Will you tell me?" He took a seat by her side and placed his hand on her knee.

She locked gazes with him. "Are you sure you want to understand why there's no way out for me? Not without that body bag."

He bolted to his feet, and she flinched as he paced the room. It took him a few seconds of hard breathing to calm down, but when he did, his shoulders slumped. He pulled off his jacket and threw it on an armchair. "Tell me."

She swallowed a few times. "My mother died of cancer a year after I was born. It was always my dad and me. I… love him so much. He did everything for me. Sacrificed working multiple shitty jobs to keep a roof over our heads."

Getting up from the couch, she walked to the patio door, staring out the glass. "He helped me pay for university, but not long after I started, he… there were signs. I ignored them because I didn't want to deal with it. Didn't have time. He gave me every moment of his life, and when he needed me the most, I thought of myself." The lump in her throat stung. "Dementia."

"I'm sorry." His voice was gentle, and she pressed her lips together to keep from sobbing.

*I don't deserve his sympathy.*

"It got so bad by the end of my second year in my Master's. He burned a good part of our house trying to make me soup in a plastic bowl inside the oven. I knew I had to put him in a nursing home, but couldn't afford it."

Vincent sat on the sofa, his elbows leaning on his knees. "Is your father still in the nursing home?"

She nodded. "I told you I met Richard during university?"

"Yes."

"I was so... determined to complete my teacher's degree. I wanted it more than anything else in the world. Richard proposed to me while I was doing my Master's, and offered to have me move in with him so he'd pay the rent on the apartment. He was always taking care of everything... taking care of me. I suggested having my dad move in with us, but Richard insisted that a good care home was the best option so I could concentrate on my studies." She took a shuddering breath. "He suggested I sign my father's guardianship to him so I wouldn't need to worry about taking care of him. Just focus on university." She let out a bitter laugh, wrapping her arms around her waist, staring at the flowers. "Whenever things went wrong between Richard and me, he'd remind me how he wouldn't pay for the home anymore. Or how, if I refused him anything, he'd stress out and talk about how he'd lose his job, and we'd be penniless. When I threatened to leave Richard when I found out he cheated on me, he lost it. Said if I left, he'd transfer him to a cheap nursing home with a poor reputation. Richard can do that—can make those decisions."

Vincent stood. "I can pay—"

"It doesn't matter. If Richard says my dad goes elsewhere, no money will help. He's my father's guardian and decides. The company he works for has expensive lawyers, and it wouldn't take much for Richard to tie this up in legal tape. And all the while, my father could be stuck somewhere dreadful. I've seen those places. The ones with bedbugs, where they just leave people sitting in their own filth, covered in sores. The staff were so rough with them... They're shut down eventually, but how long would my dad have to suffer? All because I just thought of myself." She let her tears go, no longer trying to blink them away. "When Richard became more controlling and violent, I'd..." she burst into sobs, "I used to hope my dad would die so I could be free. What kind of daughter thinks that? I'm not a good person. And I deserve what's happened to me. I deserve the beatings, and I'll deserve to leave in a body bag—"

He closed the distance between them so fast, she didn't have time to react when he grabbed her arms. "You. Don't." He glowered, his jaw clenched. "You put your father's care in the hands of someone you loved and trusted. A person who used it against you. That isn't your fault. Don't blame yourself for what monsters do."

"But don't you see?" She tried wrenching away, but his grip tightened. "Now you know. Richard has the power to hurt my dad. He made sure we visited the terrible homes, so I knew they existed. I won't let him end up somewhere horrible, but I can't stay with Richard anymore. I... just don't know what to do."

He hugged her tight, squeezing the air out of her, but she didn't care.

## 43

# VINCENT

*V*incent texted Benjamin the information about Elora's father and the legalities. A few minutes later, he received his brother's response: a simple—and frustrating—'thanks'. That's it.

*Would it kill him to share?*

Without knowing much about Benjamin's plan, Vincent decided not to share anything with Elora until he knew more.

He lay next to her over the comforter and pulled her into his arms. The silk sheets were cool on his skin, and he was glad they'd moved to the bedroom. It felt private and intimate.

"If you were free of Richard, what would you do?" he asked.

She was silent for a few seconds. "I'd continue writing picture books, but I'd also try getting a job as a kindergarten teacher. It would be... so freeing to finally do what I want." She stared at the ceiling. "I'd move from this place. Not just the house, but the city. Go somewhere else. I think... I'm not sure."

He thought of the courage it took her to share with him her secrets and recalled how they'd promised one another honesty.

It was his turn.

"Did Benjamin give you any details about the people I've

killed?" he asked. In the dim light of a bedside lamp, he could see her, but it gave him the privacy not to be careful with his facial expressions. He never revealed this story to anyone. Not even his brother or grandmother.

She shook her head. "He mentioned two changed who you are, but he just told me about the one. Benjamin's supposed friend, Tristan. He said the other was your story to tell."

Vincent wanted to both laugh at his brother and punch him. "I came home from school, and found my mother unconscious at the bottom of the stairs. I couldn't really think. Just ran upstairs to find my brother. My father had beaten Benjamin so bad, he was passed out. He was six years old at the time and had never been hit by my father before. I always hid him and received the punishment for him. There was blood on his clothes... he looked so small at that moment."

Elora rolled to her side and grabbed his hand.

"I heard the garage door slam downstairs, and my father shouting about how his little boy was making him so proud. That he had the instincts of a real man. He was beyond drunk, and not making much sense. But finding Benjamin unconscious like that... something inside me just snapped." He took a deep breath, but his chest tightened so hard, it was painful. "I... I ran downstairs into the kitchen, and grabbed a knife. My father staggered toward me, laughing as he took his belt off. He was going to whip me again—a new way of beating me he enjoyed. But I guess he never expected his twelve-year-old son to stab him in the throat."

She held her breath, waiting. He rubbed her back and nuzzled her hair. "Keep breathing, darling. He can't hurt us here." When she nodded, he continued. "I'd never seen so much blood, and when I pulled out the knife, it pooled at his feet like something out of a gore movie."

"It was self-defense, not murder."

He closed his eyes. "No one ever said I killed him. You're right—it was self-defense in his case. But I made sure he was dead and wouldn't ever hurt us again."

She shifted. "What did Benjamin mean when he said you murdered him, then?"

He locked gazes with her, the pain of telling the truth out loud ripping away at him with every word. Years of regrets and what ifs piling on top of him; a weight he barely held. "The story isn't quite over yet," he said quietly as his throat burned. "I checked on my mother. She was still at the bottom of the stairs, breathing. I wasn't sure what to do to help. She could barely speak, but she kept saying we could take off together, and how she loved me so much. How, if the two of us left, my father would likely not chase us since he'd have Benjamin." He straightened. "She said she didn't care what happened to my brother because she never loved him." He looked at his palm, the memory fresh despite the number of years that had passed. "She grabbed me, begging me to call for aid, and promised we'd take care of one another like we used to before Benjamin was born."

Elora pressed her hand to her mouth.

"I realized she was as much of a threat to my brother as my father was. So I made a decision. I told her I'd... call, and then pretended to." His stomach clenched, remembering his mother's relieved expression when he came back a few seconds later. "I laid next to her, and told her the ambulance was on its way. The whole time, I kept repeating that... I loved her so much." His eyes burned, and tears rolled down his cheeks. "She stopped breathing not long after. I'm not sure how much longer I stayed curled up next to her body afterward, but eventually, I called the ambulance. I just...I couldn't let her hurt Benjamin. When my mother had returned from the hospital with my baby brother, I promised I'd protect him no matter what. And I've kept that promise ever since."

Elora took a shuddering breath, and it came out as a half-sob. Slowly, she placed her hand on his chest, the pain in her eyes for his sake squeezing his chest.

"The police assumed my mother died because of my father's actions. They brought Benjamin and me to the hospital, and it became obvious I'd suffered years of violence, and so, they ruled his death as self-defense."

"I'm..." Her voice cracked, and she swallowed visibly. "I don't know what to say. I'm just so sorry you had to live through that."

He forced a smile. "And now you understand I'm a monster, too. Not the same kind as Richard or my father, but one nonetheless." Tears continued blurring his vision, and no matter how much he tried, he couldn't gulp enough air. "I'd always known my mother would leave in a body bag, but I didn't realize it would be because of me."

She leaned her forehead on his. He stilled, nervous she'd realize what he was and recoil.

"Listen to me." Tears rolled down, and his heart ached. "You did what you did to save Benjamin and yourself. You both had to escape the situation, and I can't see you being able to live with yourself if you'd left with your mom without your brother."

"I don't regret my choice, but it still hurts. Especially when I look at you. What if I'd convinced her to take Benjamin with us? Could I have saved her? Did I rip away her chance to become strong?"

She shook her head. "You were a kid. It wasn't your responsibility to make those kinds of decisions. Too many what ifs."

"And what if you left Richard? Couldn't you go into court to prove your husband doesn't have your father's best interests? As his natural daughter, you'd likely have more rights."

She sat back, staring at the wall. "He once told me, if I ever escaped him, he'd find me, and make sure I would regret it for the rest of my life."

He got to his feet, needing to burn away at the horrible memories, but nothing worked. Never having spoken the story before, it was like the recollection had ripped open the wound he'd kept closed for so long.

Elora stood and approached him. "Have you ever told Benjamin about this? Or your grandmother?"

"No. Benjamin already has enough guilt as it is without adding this to the mix. And my grandmother... it would've killed her to find out I was the one to end her only child's life."

She took his hand. "Your secret will die with me. Thank you for trusting me with it." She stepped closer to him. "You look like you need a change of ideas."

He grinned, but he wasn't sure if it was genuine. Everything hurt inside him. "That would be great, but I'm not sure how."

She pushed the button on the small stereo, and a radio station playing classical music filled the room. He arched an eyebrow, and she smiled.

"Will you dance with me?"

He wrapped his arms around her, bringing her close while they turned on the spot. His fingers traced her arm, then moved to her hip. "The moment I touch you, it's like the world melts away."

She stayed quiet as they continued dancing. He slid his hand to the zipper of her dress and pulled a few inches at a time. It opened, and he breathed out, running his palm along her smooth skin.

She withdrew to meet his gaze. "I need you."

He slanted his mouth over hers, hands sliding to her shoulders, and pushing her clothing down. It fell at her feet while she unbuttoned his dress shirt. He plunged his tongue between her lips, squeezing her ass, and ground his erection against her. She shuddered, pulling his top off, then moved to his belt.

He pulled and grasped her hand. "I crave you, but right now... I'm hurting and angry at everything. The last thing I want is to be too rough with you, but it's where I'm stuck. I don't—"

She pushed her finger on his lips and smiled. "I'm here for you in any way you need me to be. If it means we fuck like animals so you can get rid of those negative emotions, then I'll do that with you." She undid his belt as his erection hardened. "I trust you with all my heart. Let me be here for you the way you're always there for me."

"I don't deserve you," he breathed.

"You're a good man. You just don't know it yet."

His pants dropped to the floor, quickly followed by his briefs and socks. She smiled, placing her hand on his chest. He unclipped her bra and tossed it aside, muffling a growl when she barely waited to pull off her panties. She seemed in as much need as he was.

He picked her up in his arms, and she wrapped her legs around him as he pinned her on the wall. He'd gone past wanting and needing her to a burning obsession; like he'd die if he wasn't inside her in the next second.

She arched as he grasped his cock, pushing it against her wetness. With one hard thrust, he sheathed himself deep, and she moaned his name. He usually wanted to go slow with her, but it was impossible this time. Even Elora seemed to be impatient with him as she ran her fingers through his hair and gripped them tight.

He hissed, grabbing her hips and pumping into her hard. She lifted her knee to give him easier access as she wrenched his head back, licking at his mouth. His muscles tensed, and he angled himself in a different position so he entered her balls-deep with every thrust. She cried out, holding onto his neck for support. The smell of sex pushed his urge for her higher, and he moaned.

Leaning forward, he licked her jaw, nipping and kissing until he reached her mouth. Their tongues intertwined, her scream muffled as she milked his cock with her orgasm, her body trembling against his. He let out a guttural cry, pumping his shaft into her so fast he wasn't sure when he'd emptied himself.

He pulled out, panting hard as he carried her to the bed. She smiled as he laid her flat on her stomach, and she glanced over her shoulder.

"That was… amazing," she panted, trying to catch her breath.

He hovered above her, trailing kisses on her back, fingers tracing every curve of her body.

"Again?" he inquired in an almost desperate tone.

"I'm glad you asked because I was about to beg for more," she said with a giggle.

He hummed, imagining her begging him. As her muscles relaxed under his touch, he teased her ass, grinning when she squirmed. He continued lower until he reached her heat and pushed his finger inside.

She lifted herself, exhaling and making the noises he loved to hear from her. He thrust a second finger, pumping in and out as she whimpered. She was so wet from their last fucking. Once he coated his fingers with her juices, he rubbed them along her tight hole, and she froze.

"Do you want me to stop? You control this."

She shook her head as her muscles relaxed, and he smiled. He grabbed a pillow and placed it under her pelvis, then strode to the overnight bag he'd brought. It didn't take any time finding the lubricant, and when he returned to Elora, his breath caught.

She touched herself, moaning as she rubbed against the pillow. The sight was so erotic, he was sure he would cum then and there. She slowed, and looked over her shoulder at him, a deeper flush on her face. "Please come back," she breathed.

He kneeled on the bed behind her, pushing his fingers inside her wet opening as she continued rubbing the cushion, and shuddering.

"You are truly breathtaking," he whispered.

Placing his erection against her heat, he thrust in slowly. When she moaned in frustration, trying to back into him, he pushed his hand between her shoulder blades, keeping her still. He withdrew slowly, and in again. His rhythm was gentle, deliberate, and he adored hearing her cry out.

"Please…" She cried at being kept on the edge, and he clenched his jaw at his own denial. But getting her to plead and seeing her body's reaction to his torture was worth every second.

He pumped harder into her, and she threw her head back with a moan. Oh, how he loved undoing her. He grabbed the lube, not slowing his thrust as he lathered his finger, and moved to her ass. She stiffened, but relaxed as he pushed into her tightness, still slamming into her, and slowly matching the speed. He clenched his jaw as he plunged all the way to his knuckles, his cock pumping into her faster.

"Ah… Vincent, yes. Yes." She buried her face into the pillow, and he growled.

Pulling his finger out, he grabbed her arms and pulled her up so she kneeled. He never stopped thrusting into her as he grasped her breasts, fondling and squeezing. In this position, he pushed deeper into her than he thought possible, and she sucked in a breath when he tugged at her hard peaks.

"Fuck… I'm gonna…" He slid one hand to her sex and rubbed along her clit as she bucked against him. She tightened around his cock, crying out his name as she rode her orgasm. He pressed his face into her neck, groaning as he spilled his seed inside her, shuddering at how good she felt.

He lay on his side, pulling her with him so he could hold her close. She squirmed out of his grip and turned to look at him.

She cupped his cheek. "I love you."

"I love you too. So much."

## 44

# ELORA

*E*lora returned home early next morning despite Vincent's attempts at keeping her away. He kept telling her he had a plan, but she told him that until it was safe to escape Richard, she had to continue pretending.

She finished cleaning the walls of the corridor to remove the residue dust from the construction of the sunroom. Her mind wandered, her heart growing heavier with every minute.

*I have to leave Richard.*

But she couldn't. It was impossible to escape, but impossible to stay. If she divorced him, she'd be in for long months—or even years—ahead of legal fights for her dad's guardianship. The company he worked for had prominent lawyers, and she wouldn't put it past him to use them to make her look unstable.

She stepped into his office and ran the washcloth as best she could behind the desk. He rarely checked those spots, but she knew the one time she'd decide not to do it would be the day he checked. Nearly losing her balance, she caught herself on a plug sticking out of the electrical outlet, and gasped when it unplugged.

Her stomach churned as she pulled gently on the cord, but thankfully, the pins weren't bent. With a sigh of relief, she plugged it in, but yelped when the printer roared to life. She quickly rushed to the front of the desk, biting her lip as paper slid a few inches at a time through the device, unsure what to do. Should she let it print and explain? She wasn't sure if he'd see something had printed.

The sheet fell into the tray, and she picked it up without thinking, sweeping her gaze across the information. It was a reservation for a motel near the airport with a queen size bed. She frowned at the date from a few weeks ago, recalling how he was supposed to be in the middle of a business trip at that point. Why was he lying to her about it anymore when she already knew he slept with other women?

She rubbed the back of her neck as she stepped out of the office and approached the front door. She shook her head as she folded the paper a few times before slipping it into her purse in the pocket where she kept her pads.

As she strode to the kitchen, set on cleaning the top of the refrigerator, the front door slammed, and she jumped as Richard walked inside. He was home much sooner than planned, and she shook with relief that she left the hotel earlier.

As she approached him, her blood froze when he gave her an icy grin. She glanced from him to the floor, trying to figure out what she'd done wrong to make him angry so quickly, but couldn't find a single thing out of place.

She forced a smile. "Hi. Did you have a nice evening with Krystal?"

He pulled Elora in his arms and hugged her tight. "Dancing with you last night was better than anything else."

Being held by him felt so wrong for a long time, but when he didn't let go, she did her best to keep her breathing steady, wondering what was amiss.

"Is… everything all right?" she asked quietly.

"Yes, now that I'm holding you it is," he said in an amused tone that sounded… unbalanced. "Did you have a good morning?"

"I cleaned the walls, and did some organization," she responded as her pulse sped. "I was about to clear the fridge."

He chuckled, and red flags flashed in the back of her mind. Something was definitely wrong.

"I'm such a lucky husband to have a wife like you. Getting up early in the morning to clean for me." He held her tighter, and she forced her lips together to keep from gasping at the pressure.

She swallowed hard, stiffening her muscles so she could breathe easier. "Just doing my part," she said with forced enthusiasm.

His mouth brushed along her ear. "I got home earlier this morning, Elora. Very early. And you weren't here."

She didn't think it was possible to feel the blood drain from her face. Her heart seemed to halt as he pulled away, and she took a few strides back, her mind racing to come up with an excuse.

Before she pulled out of his reach, he wrapped his hands around her throat and slammed her on the wall.

"Stop...!" she gasped, clawing at his arms, trying to breathe.

"I told you to be home by midnight." He squeezed tighter, and black spots filled her vision. "Where were you this morning?"

She opened and closed her mouth, trying to survive. An image of Vincent floated in her mind. Of Liana and her family. Elora's father. She threw herself to the side, wrenching from Richard's grip. For a second, she thought she'd escape, but her toes caught the step going up, and she fell. Agony shot through her body, and she gasped for air as she tried crawling away.

"Where were you?" He yelled as he kicked her in the leg.

When he lifted his foot as though to smash it against her, she raised her hands.

"I spent the night at the hotel... with Liana. Brad left earlier, and she ended up drinking too much, so she rented a room because it was late," she said in small gasps.

"Liar," he spat. "You lied about being up early to clean. What else are you lying about, you fucking whore?" He kicked her in the stomach, and she curled into a ball, unable to breathe through the pain.

He marched away, and she did her best to crawl forward, unsure where she'd even go to save herself. Something hard hit her in the head, and she whimpered, blinking at the cellphone next to her.

*My phone?*

"Call the bitch and put her on speaker," he hissed.

Her fingers trembled as she tapped on her friend's name. On the third ring, Liana answered, and Elora almost sobbed.

"Hello?"

Richard glowered at Elora in a warning that was clear; he wouldn't fall for her tricks.

"Hey. Is Brad feeling better?" She sucked in a shuddering breath as her body ached.

The question was a code Elora used to let Liana know Richard listened to their conversation. It was her friend's idea a while ago when Elora had caught him listening in on the other landline phone.

There was silence on the other end for a few seconds. "He is, thanks for asking. Sorry, but the kids are in the bath so I'm a bit busy. Call me later, okay?"

Before Elora had the chance to reply, the line disconnected.

He squatted in front of her, the anger in his gaze burning behind his eyes. "What else have you lied about?"

She curled into a tighter ball. "Nothing, I swear, I—"

"Your begging won't save you, so shut it," he snarled. "You're lucky I've got better ways to vent, but God help you if I ever found out you slept around during that week and didn't tell me. I'll make you regret it for an extremely long time." He straightened and turned to the front door.

Her eyes widened as he reached at the top and bolted a lock.

*When did he install that?*

He stared at his hands with a grimace, then approached her, wiping the grease off his fingers on her clothes. "Now that you're finally home, we need to get ready. I parked the car out back. We'll take necessities," he muttered as though talking to himself. "I don't know who sent that fucking bitch on me. But it's okay, they'll make sure we're safe." He focused on Elora, and she froze. "I have to take care of a few things in my office before we leave. In the meantime, make lunch. I'm hungry."

She didn't dare ask what he rambled about, but one thing was clear; he'd lost his mind. Pressing her lips together, she got to her feet. Her body throbbed, and she winced as she stepped into the kitchen.

*I need to hide. Or get out. Now.*

Fishing in the fridge, she grabbed what she needed for a sandwich, and placed it on the counter. She ripped a few pieces of lettuce that had turned brown and threw it into the garbage. Her stomach clenched as she clutched the matchbook she'd discarded a few days ago, an idea forming in her mind. She could barely breathe, terrified he'd catch her. If it didn't work, he'd kill her for sure.

As quickly as she could, she rushed into the living room and grasped a chair. She placed it at an angle against the back door so it was jammed under the doorknob, then returned to the kitchen. The typing sound from Richard's office continued, and she opened the cupboard beneath the sink. With trembling hands, she placed the garbage bin back, and set off the matches at once before throwing it inside. Once closed, she backed away, her pulse speeding at the amount of cleaners and chemical products she knew were under there.

She grabbed her purse and put her phone in as she slipped her sandals on. Sweat covered her hands, but she did her best to act normal as she walked into Richard's office.

"We're out of bread," she said, keeping her voice as steady as possible. "I'll buy some before we leave."

He frowned, his jaw clenching. "You must've missed it. Did you check the refrigerator with your eyes opened? Check again."

"Okay, but I'm a bit worried since there's smoke coming out from beneath the sink. I'm not sure what's going on or——"

"What?" He jumped to his feet and pushed past her. After counting to three, she closed the door and locked it. The only room in the entire house Richard hadn't changed the doorknobs.

She dashed to the window and opened it wide. Richard pounded on the door, screaming at her to unlock it. Her hands shook as she got the screen out, bile threatening to burn her throat as his footsteps rushed away.

Without hesitating, she jumped out, thankful it was a one-story house so there wasn't much danger. Richard's bellows echoed from their residence, and she ran, not slowing for a second. She couldn't if she wanted to; her legs seemed to have decided for her.

For as long as she had lived here, Elora had noticed little things other people may not have paid attention to. She dashed for one of those spots in particular, her lungs aching as though they were flooded with water as she drowned.

The old, condemned house under renovation came into her line of sight, and she dashed to the back. A fence circled the property, but behind the garbage bins, the chain link bent on the interior. She crouched, slipping through the gap, and wincing as the metal sliced through her skin. Forcing herself to her feet, she continued to the window well, and jumped inside. Her heart pounded as she sat, bringing her knees up to her chest, shaking violently.

There was no sound around her, so with a trembling hand, she pulled out her phone and dialed the last number on her history.

"Elora?" Liana's voice sounded strained, and Elora burst into tears.

"I… ran away," Elora said, taking deep breaths to stop herself from crying. If Richard was close, he'd hear her. "I left Richard. He… wanted to take me somewhere. Or kill me. I don't know. Can you… pick me up?"

Liana sobbed on the other end of the line. "Yes, of course. Where are you? Are you safe?"

"He might be looking for me." She stopped talking; listening for any noise nearby, but it was quiet. "There's an abandoned house near the bridge for the train. I'm hiding there."

"I'll be right there, Elora. Stay put."

They hung up, and Elora tapped on her house's landline, holding her breath.

"Are you fucking insane?" Richard shouted on the other end. "You tried to burn our home with me inside. Where the fuck are you?"

Elora took a shuddering gasp; he was at home. She was safe for now.

"You don't get to speak to me like that anymore. It's over. We're over," her voice shook, but she didn't care.

There was silence for a few seconds. "What did you say to me?"

"I'm going to a lawyer and filing for divorce. If you know what's good for you, you won't fight me on this, and you'll give my father's guardianship back to me. If not, I'll file a report with the police for the times you hurt me. Did you understand *that*?" Her voice rose with every word.

"You're a fucking idiot, Elora," he said with an icy laugh that sent a chill down her spine. "You have no idea what's happened the past few months. Well, surprise, surprise, but I've had a new job for a while. These people, they accept me. They recognize the way things should be. You believe you can escape from our marriage? Only death can separate us. They have connections everywhere. Go to the cops and see what happens. They'll bring you to me within a few hours." His tone was poisonous. "But don't worry. Like God, I'll forgive you. It's not your fault society brainwashed you into thinking you have independence. Once they return you by my side where you belong, we're going to live in a unique community. You'll be re-educated, and things will be better."

Bile burned her throat. "You're crazy. I'm never coming back. Do you hear me? Never."

She ended the call, and turned off her phone, too scared he'd track her location with it. Was he telling the truth about the police? Who had Richard been working for?

She grasped her knees and let out a breath. Was she finally free?

A strange sort of panic settled inside her as she stared at the pebbles surrounding her feet, barely feeling the sharp points on her skin anymore. Every sound sent her pulse racing, and a few times, at the sound of footsteps, she thought for sure she'd throw up. Vehicles rolled by in front of the abandoned house, and she'd close her eyes each time, holding her breath; what if Richard had guessed where she hid? Would he drag her away or just kill her?

The window-well borders heated on her back, but from time to time, a cooler breeze fluttered along the top of her head. How long had she sat in this hole? It felt like forever.

Car tires slowed nearby, and she tightened her hold on her cellphone. Her stomach tightened when a door snapped shut, and she stiffened her muscles to keep from trembling so hard, she'd alert everyone where she was.

"Elora?" Liana's voice whispered as her footsteps crunched on the dried grass.

Elora almost let out a cry of relief as she sucked in a deep breath, unable to actually move.

*Why can't I move?*

She wanted to wave and shout at her friend, but no sound came out, and her limbs ignored her commands to get up. Her heart hammered against her ribs as she opened and closed her mouth. Black spots obscured her vision and the world seemed to tilt beneath her for a second.

"Li...ana..." she croaked, her mouth so dry, she was sure her tongue had cracked.

Her best friend rushed to the edge of the windowsill, her eyes widening. "I'm here," she said, her voice thick as she crouched and reached out toward Elora. "I've got you."

Elora's arm finally obeyed, and she grasped Liana's hand.

She was safe for now.

## 45

# VINCENT

*V*incent hated that Elora had returned home, but with no word from Benjamin, he couldn't convince her to stay. He hoped Richard would be busy with Krystal, and that Benjamin's people were still watching Elora's house.

A call from Daniel came in not long after she'd left, and although he wanted to decline, Daniel's tone didn't encourage argument.

As Vincent approached the station, his cell vibrated, and he rolled his eyes before checking the screen. He slowed his steps, the incoming call showing the name of the photographer for the photo-shoot with Elora. He'd forgotten about the whole thing. It seemed like so long ago that he'd set out to help her get through the shoot with him. Everything had changed so much since then.

"Catherine, good to hear from you. You get my email?"

Her usual gum-chewing habit sounded from the other end. "Yeah, but I'm still not too pleased to hear I wouldn't be able to use any shot of the female model that shows her face. Publishers want—"

"Don't even try that on me. We both know they love cutting our heads off if we don't perfectly fit. They're mostly looking for bodies." He chuckled at her huff. "Come on. I'll only ask this favor one time."

"Yeah, fine. One time, and that's it."

"Thanks. I'm glad I could convince you." He leaned on the wall near the doors. "Look, I have to go soon, but did you get the photos I attached, too?"

"The ones with the navy-blue corsets and matching panties?" Something clattered on her end, and she muttered a curse. "Yes, I got those in a few sizes. Have to say, you've got good style."

He grinned. "You know it. I'll talk to you later before the photo-shoot to check in."

"All right. Take care." And with that, she hung up.

As soon as Vincent stepped through the personnel-only door, Daniel marched toward him. "Perfect, you're here." His boss beckoned him to follow. "Shit hit the fan early this morning. We caught the Torren gang smuggling drugs, and it went bad. Found a human trafficking ring too. Kids involved… it's a fucking nightmare. We didn't find any of the missing women from the shelters, so they're either already dead, or they had nothing to do with it."

Sirens sounded from outside the back of the building as officers dashed out of the gear room, talking loudly amongst each other.

Vincent curled his hands. "I'll meet with the Torren members if you allow it. Get information. They won't want murder attached to their rap sheets, so if they know anything, they'll talk."

*I'll have to tell Benjamin about this.*

His brother controlled crimes in the city, and if there was one thing they never tolerated as an organization, it was selling people. Especially children.

Daniel nodded. "When we bring them in, you can talk to them. For now, I need you at the morgue. We found the missing woman who didn't match the usual patterns of the other victims from the shelter. She was murdered."

"Fuck," Vincent muttered. "I hoped she'd turn up after having taken a sporadic vacation."

"Same here." Daniel spoke through his teeth. "The assistant to the forensic pathologist called and said their report is ready. I hate that this monster is good at hiding his tracks, and that the pattern is never quite the same. Hopefully, Dr. Bedard found something." He motioned his head toward the exit. "You go to the morgue and bring me back good news that'll lock this murderer up."

Vincent excused himself to use the washroom, but sent a text to Benjamin, telling him what happened with the Torren gang. Even if the law didn't get these bastards, Benjamin and his men would serve their own justice.

⸘

The elevator slid open into the second basement, and Vincent stepped out. An employee rolled a body into the corridor, the gurney wheels squeaking as he pushed it into a room, the door closing behind him with a swishing sound.

His cell rang, and he pulled out his phone. "Hello?"

"What the hell did you do?" Daniel shouted.

Vincent arched an eyebrow. "I've done a lot of shit. Be specific."

"There are lines you don't—"

"Seriously, Daniel, what's going on?"

"Did you let any of your contacts know about the Torren gang's dealings?"

Vincent kept his expression relaxed despite his pulse speeding. "I'm a consultant here because of my connections. I already told you I'd contacted people to find out more about this gang."

"Don't play smart ass with me," Daniel spat. "I'm talking about the human trafficking part. That's new information, and I never told you to share any of that."

"What did you think would happen once I asked around to start with?" Vincent asked in a dark tone. "Others would not only look into their activity, but also keep an eye on them. Someone likely found out. It's the way it works."

Daniel let out a few curses. "Well, we showed up, and most of the Torren members are dead, while the others are missing. Any chance the Crimson boss, Karson, took care of this matter?" Daniel asked.

Vincent leaned on the wall, the stone bricks cold on his back. "He'd likely know the police were on their way so it wouldn't make sense for him to show up now."

"Sure, because Karson always thinks with a clear head when emotions are involved?" Daniel scoffed. "Well, never mind anyway. I need to fix this shit, so if you speak to your brother, tell him not to kill the remaining members if he hasn't already done so."

Vincent gaped, ready to deny the relationship, but he sighed. He'd never disclosed it to Daniel; he hadn't even told him he used to be head of the Crimson organization. The only thing Daniel knew for sure was Vincent had been part of it. "Nothing gets past you."

Daniel laughed. "Hopefully not too much. And before you ask, I've known since he stuck a gun in your mouth. Had a friend open sealed juvenile files on him and you, and found a bunch of shit I wished I hadn't."

Vincent stayed quiet for a second, worried about asking his question. "Why didn't you kick me out when you realized who I was?"

"Exactly. *Was*. It wasn't you anymore, and you were here to work on the right side of the law. When it's convenient for you," Daniel added with a scoff.

"Sometimes the law doesn't carry out justice. You know that."

"True, but I had a hell of a time explaining how we showed up to a massacre. Higher ups were convinced there was a mole in my team. I had to explain how it was likely one of your sources, but now, we need to meet with human resources to see what your rights are as a consultant. This mess hasn't helped your case against Officer Grandon's either, so they'll throw that at you."

Vincent stiffened; he'd forgotten Kimberly filed an official complaint. It seemed so insignificant now.

"When?" Vincent asked with a sigh.

"After you're done at the morgue, I want you at the station. Meeting with human resources is in an hour. Then we meet with the board of ethics by the end of today, so get ready for a long night."

Vincent clenched his jaw. "I don't have time——"

"This is your job. You make time. If you don't show up, they'll slap charges on you for non-compliance. Play nice and jump through their hoops, and then you'll be done with it." He let out a breath, sounding exhausted. "Don't forget, as your boss, your actions reflect directly on me. Just get here."

They ended the call, and Vincent turned his phone off, not wanting to be disrespectful while hearing what Rose and the doctor had to say about the latest victim. He'd have to find a free minute to check in on Elora, and let her know he'd be busy for the rest of the night, so she couldn't reach him.

He glanced from side to side as he walked down the corridor, trying to locate Rose. When he spotted her, he entered the room, the smell of blood strong in the air.

Fresh victim.

"How long ago was she found?" he asked.

Rose gasped, holding the clipboard against her chest. "Don't sneak up on me like that. I'm surrounded by the dead, and you think sneaking is a good idea? If I had a knife, I would've stabbed you."

"If you reached me first."

She rolled her eyes, flipping through the pages. "They found her yesterday. Sophie Wilson. Age twenty-two, died of multiple stab wounds."

He frowned, coming closer to the autopsy table. Rose handed the file to Vincent. As he skimmed through the report, his jaw clenched at what they did to the victim pre-mortem; the anguish she had endured for it to end in a painful death.

"Similar to the other victims, but not quite…" he muttered, closing the folder.

Rose stared at the white sheet covering the body. "There are strangulation marks on her neck, but there are multiple in various positions. Some more bruised than others. The murderer likely choked her long enough for her to pass out, then would wake her to start over. One thing is divergent, though. Unlike the other victims, she didn't have a large hole in her ear."

Dr. Bedard walked into the room holding a clipboard. "I've finished my collective report on the victims discovered so far. It's my medical conclusion that different individuals killed the women." Her gaze focused on the body. "She's the first victim to be stabbed to death, but the torture done to the others before dying is too similar to be a coincidence. What their connection is will be for the police to find out."

"Multiple murderers. Fucking great." He shifted to the doctor and sighed. "Sorry for the language."

"Tell your Sergeant about this." Dr. Bedard turned to leave, but glanced over her shoulder. "Oh, and Mr. Voden? Catch these fuckers, please."

He grinned and gave a curt nod.

He would, but he'd send the Crimson members on them. They deserved pain, and a lot of it.

# 46

# ELORA

That day, after Liana brought Elora to her house, Elora passed out and slept until the next morning. Elora had left a voicemail on Vincent's cell asking him to call her back, but she didn't go into too many details. Part of her couldn't believe she escaped Richard. She hadn't gone to the police, too paranoid what Richard had rambled about was true. Before doing anything, she wanted to see a lawyer and have them serve her ex-husband divorce papers; if he signed them, she'd keep her word, and not file a report on him.

She checked her cell when she woke, her chest squeezing when she saw a missed call from Vincent late last night—she'd finally changed the contact information to his name instead of Brad's. No message or texts since he didn't know Richard wouldn't have access to her phone anymore. She hoped everything was okay.

Considering the hour Vincent called, she imagined he'd had a long night, so she decided to wait until later in the day to call him. Besides, they'd have plenty of time together now that she was free.

Liana strode into the living room where Elora sat, her mind wandering at the uncertainties she faced. She had left a message on the answering machine of the nursing home where her father was;

the first few times, she hung up, too scared they'd let Richard know she called. But with Liana's encouragement, Elora finally let it ring.

"I have to do some grocery shopping," Liana said as she grabbed her purse. "I'll also be buying clothes for the kids since they've managed to outgrow them, so I'm heading to Superstore." She rummaged inside her bag. "There's a bank, so I can grab some applications for a card so you can deposit the other half of your check from your book award."

Elora stood. "I'd rather come with you if it's okay? I feel like I'm going insane waiting for people to return my calls."

Liana grinned. "Are you sure? It's an absolute zoo when all three are together."

"All the better reason for me to help." The idea of having her own bankcard and depositing a check that would be hers was such a strange feeling, but she was excited; it would be her first genuine act of freedom.

After getting the kids ready, they got into the minivan, and drove to the store. It wasn't a place Elora usually shopped at since it was too far by bus, and so she looked forward to seeing what was inside. Liana had often talked about how they sold food, clothing, and even furniture within one building. For the entire ride there, Elora kept glancing in the mirror to make sure the summer scarf her friend had leant her held; the last thing she wanted was for people to stare at the swollen marks on her neck.

As they stepped inside the massive store, Elora gawked; it was bigger than she'd imagined. Liana grabbed a shopping cart with a built-in car for the two eldest, Sarah and Philippe, to sit in while Elora buckled in the youngest, Marc, at the back.

Eagerness filled Elora when she spotted the bank, her pulse speeding. Liana stepped inside with Elora, the kids pretending to drive loudly as they approached an available representative.

Some explaining later, along with Liana's address as a temporary residence for Elora, she opened an account and deposited her check. With a card in her purse, Elora smiled ear to ear as they walked through the store.

Liana was right; it wasn't easy shopping with three young kids, but Elora enjoyed every second. Even the part when they both struggled to try shorts on Marc.

Liana smiled at her daughter. "Can you get the cereal with the raisins like a big girl?"

Sarah nodded quickly, her black hair bouncing up and down before she rushed forward, searching through the boxes.

Marc fussed a bit. The plastic toys Liana had attached to the cart were not distracting the one-year-old enough. Elora tickled her finger under his chin, and he giggled.

"There's a smile."

Yesterday seemed like a strange dream. Ending her marriage on the phone was surreal, and yet, she was relieved it was finally done. Now all she could do was wait to find out what next steps she had to take to make it official.

As the cashier scanned the items, Marc became agitated, and with a full cart, Elora wondered how they'd do this.

"Want to get the van and park it in the loading zone at the front while I stay with the kids?" Elora offered.

Philippe threw a box of granolas at her sister, and Sarah cried, trying to retaliate. Liana gave a death stare at her middle kid, and Philippe stopped moving right away.

"Great idea. Although, I hate leaving you with these little terrors," she said, distracted as she pulled her keys out of her purse. "Sarah, you're okay. Your brother didn't mean it." She turned her attention to her oldest boy. "Say sorry."

"Sorry…" Philippe muttered, but then stuck out his tongue at his big sister.

"Mom!"

Before Liana could keep scolding them, Elora stepped in, talking to them about the importance of being kind to one another. Liana gave a quick pat on Elora's arm and rushed away to get the vehicle.

After calming the kids, and getting them distracted by playing *I Spy*, Elora pushed the cart outside, squinting at the sunlight beaming on them. Apparently, everyone had the same idea about parking in the loading zones, and with no spaces left, Elora tried to find Liana.

Liana waved from the side of the building, jumping up and

down to get Elora's attention, and Elora grinned as she picked up a bit of speed to meet up with her friend.

"Not a bad spot," Elora said as she stopped near the opened doors. The blast of air conditioning was a welcome to the sweat already covering a good part of her clothes.

Liana grimaced. "Yeah, well it's illegal parking, so let's hurry."

As they got the kids inside, then started loading the groceries, Elora's phone buzzed, and she pulled it out of her bag.

The nursing home's number displayed across the cracked screen.

"It's the nursing home," she blurted.

"I'll park where we were before and wait there, okay?" Liana waved Elora away so she could take the call in private.

Elora walked farther along the side of the building, leaning on the wall. She was glad she wore a dress in this heat, but it didn't help protect against hot concrete. And despite the thin material of the scarf around her neck, she was boiling.

"Hello?"

"Hello, this is Paul from the Saint-Tache's Quality Living. May I speak to Elora Letan, please?" the male voice on the other line was friendly, but the pit of her stomach roiled.

It was strange to hear her maiden name, but not in a bad way. "Speaking."

"You left a voicemail to call you back. How may I help you?"

"Can I talk to someone about my father? He's a resident there with you. George Letan."

There were a few keyboard taps, and then a few seconds of silence. "I'll transfer you to Violet Mosser. Will you please hold?" His tone had changed, but before she could put her finger on it, there were a few beeps, and then music as she waited.

She paced, glancing toward where Liana had parked to load the van, but it was gone.

The other line picked up again. "Hello?"

Elora swallowed hard. "Yes, hello. I'm calling about my father, George Letan."

"And what is your full name and date of birth please?" Violet asked gently.

Once Elora answered the questions, the woman on the other side's tone gentled even more. "My name is Violet. I was the nurse in charge of the care of your father."

"Was?" Elora grabbed the hem of her dress and squeezed. "There's someone else looking after him, then?"

"I'm sorry, but your father passed away."

Her heart seemed to stop for a few seconds, and she clutched her purse closer to her chest. "No, there has to be a mistake…"

"We informed your husband of his passing since he was the legal guardian on file…" Her question was left lingering in the airwaves between them.

Tears rolled down her cheeks, and she took a shuddering breath. "He… didn't tell me. When? When did my father…?"

Another few seconds of silence that felt like an eternity. Violet gave her the date of death, and it was as though the world fell from under her.

*That was… several weeks before the book fair.*

Black spots blurred her vision as she tried to get air into her lungs. Her hands shook, her stomach churning.

"I… There has to be… a mistake." Her chin trembled as the lump in her throat tightened.

Her father was dead. She never got to see him again. Never said goodbye or held his hand as he died.

Violet used her softest tone yet. "I am truly sorry about this. Mr. Reverie picked up your father's ashes and said he'd bring them home to you. If it's any comfort to you, in the last few days before his death, your husband visited him often. He was with your father the day he passed—"

Elora didn't hear the rest as something sharp pressed against her side, and the phone was yanked away from her. Someone pushed their hand on her mouth, and her eyes widened, trying not to black out from panic.

"If you scream or make a scene," Richard whispered in her ear, and she almost threw up between his fingers, "I'll hurt Liana, and her little kiddies. You wouldn't want that, would you?"

She shook her head. Her mind numbed as he dragged her toward the dumpsters where his car was parked. He threw her cell on the ground and stomped on it until the screen cracked and turned black. Once inside the vehicle, he locked the doors, and her heart hammered, noticing the lock on the passenger side was broken off.

He grabbed her purse, and threw it in the back before driving off, going in the opposite direction to where Liana was. Her chest tightened, the phone call fresh in her mind. But she couldn't process anything that happened. "My father... The nursing home... they told me he was dead. That you knew about it..."

"You found out sooner than I would've liked, but I suppose it's better, all things considered," he said with a shrug.

"Why didn't you tell me he died?" She screamed the words as they poured out of her.

He raised his hand as though to hit her, and she closed her eyes, bracing. Instead, he laughed, turning his attention on the road.

"No need to worry. We'll go to the pickup location, and once we arrive at our new home, this won't matter anymore." He had a determined look in his gaze, his hands tightening on the steering wheel. "We'll stay married as God intended, and I'll keep an eye on you in our new home."

Her eyes widened. He'd lost his fucking mind. "Richard, it doesn't have to be this way. I don't—"

"Stop arguing," he yelled, and the car jerked to the left for a second. "No, no. It's not your fault. I have to remember you don't know any better yet, but you will soon. You will soon," he muttered.

As they passed the Perimeter Highway, Richard pulled over onto a gravel road to the side. Dust rose into the air, the leaves in the trees swaying in the hot summer breeze nearby.

He drew out his cell and scrolled along the screen. She stayed quiet, but kept glancing around the vehicle, trying to find anything to use as a weapon. Her purse didn't have anything useful, and since it was in the back seat, she wouldn't reach it in time anyway. But there had to be something somewhere.

He reached toward her, and she flinched as he opened the glove compartment, pulling out a coarse rope. Her pulse sped, and she yanked on the door latch, desperate to get out.

"You're not getting out," he said in a dark tone as he grabbed the knife he'd threatened her with before. "You either obey, or I hurt you just enough so you don't have a choice."

Sunlight reflected on the serrated blade, and she held her breath. Tears flooded her eyes, but she blinked them back, refusing to show him any fear.

She put out her hands and held his gaze, jaw set.

His eyebrows shot up, but a slow smile curled his lips. "There we go," he breathed as he wrapped the rope around her wrists. "See? You're already learning. Your re-education won't be too brutal if you take steps starting now."

The material dug into her skin, scrapping roughly with every little movement. Still, she kept quiet. The best way for her to escape this situation was remaining calm, no matter how much she screamed for help within.

# 47

# ELORA

*E*lora staggered as Richard led her through the tall double doors of an old barn. It stood in the middle of nowhere surrounded by a small, wooded area, making it impossible to see from the road.

He pushed her on a partially cracked chair, clenching the knife in his hand. She stared at him, chest tightening. "My father… What happened after he passed?"

"Not that it matters, since he's a sinner, but I returned him home." He checked his phone and glanced up when the boards overhead creaked.

She looked at her hands, her heart squeezing. Richard had brought a box the day Elora had returned from the convention. This whole time, her dad's ashes sat on the mantle in their living room. She couldn't breathe, her anger boiling. "The box you mentioned was priceless and was given to you by your boss?"

"That wasn't a lie," he said with a sneer. "Although I changed a bit of the wording to avoid confusing you, since it happens regularly."

Mice skittering across the floorboards, and Elora pulled her feet higher as she yelped. Richard burst into laughter, shaking his head.

"You get scared so easily. Pathetic." He tapped the point of his weapon on his chin, staring at her as though trying to think of something. "My boss… He's the Savior. He leads our flock and ensures we follow the righteous path God has planned for us. Society has twisted his words, and has turned an entire generation into feminists who actually believe they are equal to men." He pointed the knife at her, and she recoiled. "Men require animals to eat, water to drink, work to keep busy, and women to serve and bear children. Those who turn away from their use are branded as *meat* and are used accordingly."

Her eyes widened as her breathing sped. She didn't dare say a word as her stomach churned.

"I remember when the Savior came to me. He wanted a website designed to sell specific types of orders. When he finally told me what they were, I have to admit, it disgusted me." He leaned his hand on the armrest and pushed the blade's end against her chest. "But he understood. He was patient and explained. Helped me discover what I lacked in life—what every true born male lacks—is a way to unleash our natural power."

She recalled how he'd said something about finding a fresh approach to vent his frustration, and her pulse raced at the look in his eyes. "Vent?" she repeated in barely a whisper.

He nodded so fast, she thought he'd break his own neck. "Yes, yes! Exactly! And all I had to do to prove I believe and will follow in his teachings was take a life." He pushed the point harder, and she winced as the spot stung.

Wind blew from the broken boards, and the smell of dirty straw reached her nose. She had no idea how she'd get out of this. He talked about murder like it was nothing. Her mind caught up quickly, and her throat tightened so hard, it burned more than the blade pushing into her skin.

"Did you… kill my father?" she asked in a small cry.

He pulled and paced. "Don't look so devastated," he said with a scoff. "It was painless. Just pressed a pillow on his face, and poof! All done!"

"How could you?" she whispered.

He shrugged. "He was old and useless to us."

"He was only seventy-seven," she yelled. "And you don't get to decide who's useful. Who are you to judge, you murderer?"

He raised the weapon, and she lifted her bound arms, trying her best to protect herself. A slicing pain ripped across her skin, and she screamed. She pushed her wounded arm against her thigh, keeping pressure as she stared at Richard, gasping for air.

"Sorry, sorry," he said with an amused smile as he grabbed an old, discarded cloth, and wiped the blood from the blade. "I recently made a mistake, and until I repent with the gift they requested, I'm being punished for what I did." He peered at the ceiling above, and let out a deep breath. "It's been a while since I vented. I don't know how long I'll last. Maybe they'll show mercy once you arrive…"

She tried her best to keep calm through the pain shooting down her arm. "Is there anything I can give to help with the mistake?"

She hated even pretending to care, but the only way she had any hope of escaping this was to play the part of the loving wife as she used to.

He approached her and crouched. "Yes, and it's already planned, so you don't need to worry about the details."

"What's the mistake they think you did?"

He narrowed his eyes on her. "They don't *think* I did it, Elora," he said through gritted teeth. "They know I did. But I couldn't wait for the next order of meat, so I made do with my own. Without permission from the Savior. That was my sin."

"What exactly do you mean by meat?" she asked in a trembling voice.

He straightened and paced. "Whores who don't understand their place," he spat. "They get a last use and then are disposed of." He scratched at his head, the blade wobbling quickly. "But the waiting times are… I couldn't wait, so I brought Sophie to a motel. Rented the farthest one out. Barely anyone there during that time of the week. I had privacy for what I needed to do. Usually there are specific places to go, and without the correct instruments, it was difficult to subdue her."

Elora gawked at him, her chest heaving. Sophie? The girl he'd brought home the day he pushed her into the smashed glass. He had murdered her? And all that about women being called meat and sold on the internet. What was this nightmare?

He slid his finger along the blade, a cruel smile twisting his features. "It was a mess... but it felt so... good. The best I'd ever vented." He let out a deep, gratifying sigh as he closed his eyes. "She was so beautiful when she took those last breaths."

Richard's phone rang, and he turned his back as he answered it.

Elora pressed her lips together, trying not to throw up. She slowly got to her feet and inched away from the chair. She spotted a ladder leading up to a loft, her heart beating fast as she tried figuring out if she'd make it. But once up there, could she stop him from using it? It seemed bolted to the wooden beam.

A few of the empty stalls were left open, but two were latched shut. There were so many places that looked perfect to hide, but they weren't enough. A small place with discarded water buckets and scattered hay caught her eye, and as quickly—and quietly—as possible, she dashed for it.

She got around the objects without hitting any of them, despite nearly losing her balance because of her tied wrists. Equipment hung on the mud-splattered wall above her, and she grabbed what looked like a long hook before pushing herself into a corner where the hay was higher.

"Elora?" Richard called out. He sounded furious, his footsteps stomping across the ground.

She held her breath, holding her weapon tight against her chest, the rope tightening on her wrists. She had to find a way out. But where would she even run to? She was in the middle of nowhere.

*I just need to get away from him.*

"I understand you're scared," he said, switching to the gentle tone he used whenever he'd apologized for hurting her. "If you come out now, I promise not to discipline you for running off."

She did her best to breathe through her mouth. Glancing around, she noticed a small hole that looked like it led into one of the stalls. Her pulse sped, trying to lift herself a bit to see if the stall door was closed or opened, but she couldn't tell.

The sound of metal hit the ground, and she froze, listening.

"The Savior is forgiving, Elora, but I'm not like him. When he found out what I'd done to Sophie, he had members get rid of the evidence for me. He was understandably angry. After all, I'd betrayed his trust." He chuckled. "His mercy will allow both of us to join him, though. I repent by giving him the gift of an infant, while you show your loyalty by bearing that child for the future of our flock."

The scraping of iron dragged across the floor as he approached where she hid. Elora pressed her hand against her mouth, trembling violently. He'd wanted a baby with her to give to these monsters? Bile burned the back of her throat, her pulse pounding in her ears as the sound got closer.

She crawled forward and started sliding inside. The rough boards scrapped along her skin, but she wiggled, doing her best to ignore the discomfort. Her neck prickled as footsteps came closer and closer.

Something slammed against her calf, and it took a second for the anguish to register. She screamed, pushing her forehead on the prickly straw as her fingernails dug into her palms. Her leg felt like he'd ripped it off, every beat of her heart sending renewed waves of nausea.

She couldn't breathe through her sobs, but she gritted her teeth and pushed forward using her upper body. Her feet dragged behind her, and she didn't dare look back as warm liquid streamed down her skin. She took in gulps of painful breaths, clinging to survival.

The squeak of the gate opening happened as though in slow motion, and she looked up as Richard stepped inside the stall holding a pitchfork. Her eyes widened as she glanced at the pointed ends covered in crimson.

He smiled sadistically and threw the tool aside before moving on to her. She lifted the hook and swung, but he caught it midair.

"I warned you," he hissed through his teeth as he wrenched the weapon out of her hand.

He punched her in the face, her nose crunching as blinding pain blurred her vision. She gasped, blood pouring into her mouth as he pushed her on the floor, then pressed his knee against her back. She squirmed, coughing with every breath.

He untied the rope, then stretched her arm to the side, holding her wrist down. "Your disobedience can't be tolerated."

Her eyes widened as he swung the handle part of the hook against her arm, and a gurgled scream ripped through her throat as her bones shattered.

The world faded in and out as anguish pulsed through her. He walked away from her, then crouched near the stall gate, and picked up his knife.

She whimpered in tiny gasps. "Please, Richard. You... don't have to do this. Just let me... go. Please."

"You believe you can leave me?" he shouted. "No. It's 'til death do us part."

He kicked her in the side, forcing her to roll onto her back, and she cried out as agony shot through her body.

"Stop. Richard, no!"

"Shh," he leaned forward and pressed the knife on her abdomen. "As your last duty as my wife, you'll open yourself to me, then I'll release you from your vows."

Her heart throbbed inside her ears, and she choked on bile.

*No. No. No!*

He kissed her, and she bit hard. Fresh blood filled her mouth, and she spit it out, coughing and gagging.

"You stupid bitch."

He backhanded her across the face, over and over. She tried getting up to escape, but he punched her, and her skull hit the ground as pressure built behind her eyes. She couldn't see. Couldn't think.

She lifted her good arm, but he grabbed both her wrists and pinned them above her head. She shrieked, feeling as though it shattered.

Darkness took hold, but only partially. She faded in, the sounds of his grunts churning her stomach.

After what seemed like forever, he let go of her, and plunged the knife into her abdomen, groaning when she cried out, the pain burning so badly, she was sure her heart would stop. Every second felt like the slicing agony deepened, a burning throb sending bile to the back of her throat. Her fingers clawed along the ground, desperate to find anything to escape. She gasped when her fingernails broke as she dug them into a crack. Blood streamed from the ends as fast as her pulse. With a few final useless kicks, she closed her eyes as Richard muttered a curse and pulled away.

"You didn't beg for my forgiveness," he said, panting. "You truly are lost to Satan. I can't save you."

Relief flooded her mind for a split second before he pressed something cold and sharp between her thighs. The world turned black with the sound of her shrill screams.

# 48

# VINCENT

Sunlight filtered through Vincent's eyelids, and he groaned as he turned to his other side. He'd gotten home early in the morning after the ethics board grilled him for hours, demanding answers and contacts' information. And after all that, he was under review, which meant leave without pay until they made their final decision.

Needing to get away from the bullshit, he crashed in his bed, fully dressed, and passed out.

He scrubbed his hand against his face as he trudged to the bathroom. Still in a bit of a daze, he slowly got ready for the day, wondering what he'd do. He didn't have any construction jobs, and with his leave from the police, there wasn't much for him to do.

As he slipped on a black t-shirt, he thought of Elora. Was she alone today? He wanted to bring her to a park where they could have a picnic together. Then later, they could watch *Doctor Who*. It sounded like such a perfect day that his mood lightened, and his energy buzzed with excitement. If she wasn't free, maybe he could see her for a few minutes somewhere.

He grabbed his phone, and his heart seemed to stop.

Missed calls from Elora and Liana.

Several. All since early this morning.

His breath caught in his chest as he noticed the time; it was past one in the afternoon. He tapped on Elora's contact, and waited. Every ring sent more bile into his mouth, and he did his best to keep breathing.

Liana picked up, and his heart tightened. "Vincent? Oh god, Vincent. Elora is gone. Someone took her while we were at the grocery store together. I think it's Richard. She left him yesterday and…" She burst into tears, unable to continue.

Vincent leaned on the wall, trying to find something to hold on to. He couldn't breathe. Nothing seemed to make sense except one thing; someone took Elora.

There was background noise for a few seconds, then Brad spoke on the other line.

"Are you there?" Brad asked.

"Yeah," Vincent breathed, his mind slowly catching up to the information Liana had told him. His old instincts filled him, and he focused. "I need as many details as possible."

He stalked to the door and opened the fake book, pulling out his pistol.

"Elora left Richard yesterday. From what I understood, he tried to force her to go somewhere with him, and almost killed her. She ran, then told him she was filing for divorce." Brad murmured something that sounded like he spoke to Liana as she continued crying. "Liana picked Elora up, and when she got to our place, she passed out from exhaustion, and slept through the rest of the day and night."

Vincent's heart hammered in his chest. Elora had left Richard. She'd taken the steps herself to leave, and he couldn't put into words how proud he was of her.

"Liana had to get groceries and new clothes for the kids, and Elora asked to go so she could help." Brad's voice turned somber. "While Elora took a call from the nursing home where her father is, Liana finished loading up. They were supposed to meet in the parking lot, but when she never showed up, Liana drove to the side of the building."

Vincent slipped on his shoes and snatched his keys, walking out of his condo. "And?"

"Liana found Elora's cellphone on the ground. It was smashed up." Brad let out a breath. "This was around nine this morning. I called the police and explained the situation. They won't file her as missing until it's been forty-eight hours. Especially since there's nothing on Elora being a domestic abuse victim."

Vincent got to the bottom of the stairwell and pushed up the door with such force it nearly cracked the hinges. Red seemed to blur his vision, tunneling it to one focus.

Find Elora. That's all that mattered to him.

Liana's sobs echoed. "I shouldn't have left her alone. It's my fault. I'm so sorry."

Vincent got into his car and started the engine, "I'll bring her back."

"Let me know if you need anything," Brad added, his voice thick.

"I will, and you'll be the first I call when I find her."

Vincent hung up and drove out from his building's private parking lot, unsure where he headed in that moment. Taking deep breaths, he connected the wireless feature for his phone, and called Daniel.

"Hey," Daniel said on the other line, "that was one hell of a meeting——"

"Elora was taken." The words spilled out, unable to think of anything else but her. "She left her husband yesterday, and today, someone kidnapped her from outside a grocery store."

"Have you called it in?" Daniel asked, his tone serious.

"Her friends tried, but you know how it works. Forty-eight hours before they'll file a missing person's report." He clenched his jaw, driving toward one end of the city. If he got onto the Perimeter Highway, at least, once he'd figure out where to go, it would be faster than traveling through downtown.

"I'll open it now." The sound of typing, and Daniel returned to the phone. "Let us do our jobs. We'll find her. Do you need someone to stay with you in the meantime so you don't do anything stupid?"

"No, it's fine. I'll wait alone." His hands tightened on his steering wheel. "Thanks, Daniel."

He pushed the button for Benjamin's business number, and Vincent recognized Martin's voice—a man who used to work under him.

"Vince, how's it going?"

"I need you to put Benjamin on the line. And if he says to call back, tell him I'm calling in that favor from when he showed up at the police station years ago." Vincent's voice sounded cruel to his own ears, but he didn't care. He'd do whatever it took to find Elora.

Martin said nothing before transferring him, and a few seconds later, Benjamin picked up.

"I don't see the point—"

"Elora left her husband yesterday, and someone kidnapped her this morning," Vincent said through gritted teeth. "I need to know if this is part of your plan, or if Richard is the one who took her."

"Wait, are you telling me you let her go back home after I told you I was investigating something about Richard?" Benjamin's tone was dark.

"If you'd fucking informed me what you planned, then I could've convinced Elora to stay with me. But she needed to continue pretending everything was okay until she was sure she could leave him safely."

"And how did that work out?" Benjamin spat.

"Are you going to help me or not?" Vincent asked as he pulled onto the highway.

Benjamin sighed. "Look, I thought she'd be with you for a few days, so I didn't bother taking those types of precautions. Richard left when he caught Krystal trying to place a tracking device in his wallet."

"You better start making sense, or I'm coming after you after I find Richard," he said, meaning every word. "If he took her because of you... if anything happens to her, I'll—"

"You'll what, Vince?" Benjamin's tone was icy. "Kill me? You should've let dad beat me to death if that's the case. Makes those beatings you took a bit useless, don't you think?" He scoffed. "Now spare me your dramatics. You can't make this personal, and you know that. So step the fuck back from your pussy meltdown and focus."

Vincent turned at the next exit out, heading out of Winnipeg, needing to stop the car before he'd cause an accident. As the gravel dust rose, and he put his vehicle in park, he leaned his head back and closed his eyes.

"You're… right. I'm sorry," he muttered.

"Wait, what was that?" Benjamin asked in an amused tone. "I didn't hear you correctly."

"I said you're right and that I'm sorry. Now shut up about it or I'll take it back."

Benjamin chuckled. "While you had your whiny princess moment, I sent a message to my IT guy. I've got Elora's location."

Vincent straightened so fast, he thought an iron rod had replaced his spinal cord. As his brother gave him the coordinates, Vincent inputted them into his GPS, then drove toward the highway.

"She doesn't have her cellphone, so how the hell do you or your IT guy know her location?" he asked with a frown.

"Is that an important explanation now?"

"Don't try avoiding the question. I've got time while I drive out there, so explain."

"Fine. Remember when I visited Elora's house?"

Vincent let out a scoff. "Yeah. Visit."

"I had one of the guys plant a tracking device in her purse and phone just in case something like this ever happened."

Vincent couldn't find the words to thank his brother for thinking of that, and taking steps to make sure they could track her. "Thank you," he said quietly.

"Just don't…" Benjamin said, his voice wavering. Vincent frowned; it wasn't like his brother to hesitate. "You remember what you always told me as a life motto?"

Vincent chest squeezed, his stomach churning violently. "She's fine. I just need to get to her and—"

"Richard is one of the murderers from the women's shelter case you're working on. He killed the latest victim, Sophie Wilson."

Hot and cold chills ran through Vincent as he pushed harder on the gas pedal. He recalled what her body looked like, lying in the morgue, and he forced himself to swallow the bile rising into his mouth. "How—?"

"I'll explain later." His voice gentled. "I already had Martin dispatch 911 to Elora's location, and they'll probably be there before you."

"Why did you call them?" he asked quietly.

"Because she'll likely need paramedics." There was a knock, and Benjamin muttered something before returning. "I'll keep in touch, but Vince, live by the motto you held us both to for our whole lives. If you don't… it'll break you."

Benjamin hung up, and Vincent wasn't sure he was even alive; his heart seemed to have stopped, air wasn't reaching his lungs anymore. All he felt was numbness spreading over him.

*Hope for the best, but expect the worst.*

# 49

# VINCENT

*R*ed and blue lights flashed ahead, but Vincent didn't slow as his car rolled onto the private road leading to an abandoned barn. He put the vehicle in park, and jumped out, not bothering to turn off the engine. It didn't matter. Nothing mattered except reaching Elora.

Two police cars and an ambulance were parked out front near the opened doors of the building. Light flooded from inside, and Vincent picked up his pace, rushing forward.

An officer blocked his way, raising his hand. "Whoa. You can't go through here. This is a crime scene."

Vincent's stomach clenched, and he stiffened to keep from shaking. "I'm a consultant with——"

"We didn't get any information about an expert being sent here, so I'm going to need you to back up, okay?" He took a few steps forward, but Vincent didn't move an inch.

Vincent couldn't see inside the barn, but people spoke in urgent voices, every word like arrows plunging into his heart.

"I'm losing the pulse," a man called out loudly. "More pressure on the abdominal wound, now."

Vincent gritted his teeth. "Let me through."

"Can't follow directions? Let's go. I'm placing you under arrest." The cop took out a pair of handcuffs, but Vincent wrenched out of his grip and backed away.

He pulled out his wallet and opened it so he'd see the consultant ID. "I know her." His voice was tight, and he could barely form words.

"Like I told you, we didn't get any mention of you being sent here, so you're going to need to contact your boss, so he can let—"

"I vouch for him, it's fine," a woman said. Kimberly walked out of the barn and gave Vincent a curt nod before turning to her partner. "If there are any issues, I take full responsibility."

The cop glanced from Kimberly to Vincent, but put away the cuffs. "Got it."

Vincent took a few steps forward, but Kimberly grabbed his arm. "Listen, Vince. It's... they're not sure she's going to make it." She let out a shuddering breath. "We can't even tell if it's Elora because... her face is..." Her grip tightened. "If it is her, and she doesn't survive, do you really want to remember her like this?" She shook her head. "Don't do that to yourself."

"I... need to see her," he said, his voice cracking. "I want to be here with her. It doesn't matter what she looks like. I just want... I need her to know I'm here."

She held his gaze. "Okay, but don't get in the paramedics' way. If you do, I will remove you by force if I have to. Understand?"

He nodded, and she stepped aside. Vincent rushed inside and continued up ahead to the stalls. A paramedic was crouched, their feet sticking out near the gate as they worked on their patient. With each step Vincent took, he was sure he lost a few pieces of his heart as it shattered.

They'd deposited lights on a few of the shelves, pointing at a woman lying on a sheet placed beneath her. Vincent could only see her lower body with the first responders hovering near her torso.

Although the clothing was smeared in dirt and crimson, he recognized it at once; the navy blue dress with white flowers he'd bought for Elora. Her underwear hung around her ankle, and one of her legs was swollen and covered in blood. Vincent's vision darkened on the edges as he took a shaky step forward.

They'd placed an oxygen mask over her mouth and nose, while the rest hid behind bruises, cuts, and blood. He wasn't sure he was looking at someone's face for a second. A paramedic grabbed a thick cloth from the bag next to her and pushed it into a hemorrhaging wound in Elora's abdomen.

There was so much blood. This couldn't be Elora. Where was her smile? The passion in her gaze?

*I failed her.*

"I've got a pulse, but it's weak," the paramedic said. "Is the bleeding controlled?"

The woman nodded. "Wounds are packed." She took out a brace, then placed the chin section before carefully wrapping it around Elora's neck. "Stable."

"Okay, transferring her to the stretcher." He caught sight of Vincent. "Do you know the victim?" he asked, as both paramedics grabbed one end of the sheet, and transferred Elora to the gurney.

Vincent nodded, his mouth dry. His mind still refused to accept this was Elora. It was impossible. They'd danced recently. She'd told him how she wanted to be a kindergarten teacher when she left her husband. There was faith in her eyes.

*Hope for the best, but expect the worst.*

They raised the stretcher, and the paramedic hung the IV bag to a small bar attached to it. The cuts covering her skin sliced from her shoulder to her wrist, and he stared at her hand, unable to look away at the fingers bent at odd angles.

How would she draw? His chest tightened so hard, he thought it would crush his heart. But he didn't care; it would hurt less than the agony filling him like hot lead.

"Do you know her blood type?" the paramedic asked.

Vincent shook his head. "No... I..."

"Are you with the police?"

Kimberly approached. "He's a consultant under Sergeant Williams. And he's also the victim's boyfriend."

The word seemed so strange to his ears. Was that what he was?

But this wasn't Elora, so it didn't make sense. She was still at home, pretending everything was all right. Waiting for Vincent to let her know it was safe. That she'd be okay. He promised her.

"All set," the paramedic called out, taking Vincent out of his thoughts.

The man looked at Vincent. "Are you riding with us in the ambulance?"

"Yes," he mumbled, following them as they rushed out of the barn.

The air was warm on his clammy skin as he waited for them to get the stretcher into the vehicle. He stared ahead at nothing, barely noticing when Kimberly stood in front of him.

"Do you really want to go with them?" she asked. "You're in shock."

"I'm fine," he muttered.

"Then you need to snap out of it," she said in a sharp tone that shifted his attention to her. "Think of her. When she wakes up, she'll need you to be there for her. Whole and ready to be strong for the two of you. Can you do that for Elora?"

*Elora.*

It was her in the ambulance. Her life faded away as he stewed inside his own mind. His hands turned into fists as his head seemed to clear of a thick fog.

"Got it," he said with a nod.

Kimberly smiled, but it was strained. "Now go be with her."

The paramedic called out to Vincent as the other one rushed to the driver's door and jumped in. Vincent grabbed the handlebar to the side, and stepped in, sitting on the padded bench as the ambulance roared to life.

For the first few minutes of the ride, items shook in storage cupboards above as the vehicle drove over the gravel and dirt road, almost covering the sound of the sirens overhead. Vincent held onto the stretcher, terrified it would roll away from him. That Elora would vanish from in front of him.

The paramedic in the back with Vincent put a device on the end of Elora's finger—one of the few not twisted—and a monitor bleeped, showing her heart rate.

Vincent stared at the number going up and down. That was her heart. Elora's beautiful and kind heart. It was still beating.

His hand hovered above her head, but he pulled away quickly, too scared to touch her. She looked so… fragile. Torn apart and barely holding on.

*She's strong.*

He'd confided his secret to someone for the first time. She had stared into his eyes without recoiling and told him it wasn't his fault. Elora accepted him for his faults and mistakes; something he never thought would be possible.

"My name is Roger," the paramedic said with a quick smile.

"I'm Vincent," he replied, glancing from Elora to the man.

Roger opened a small door to a compartment across from him, and pulled out a blanket, then placed it gently on her. The bright overhead lighting showed the extent of her wounds, and Vincent let out a sigh. But it quickly turned into a sob, and he pressed his lips together as he gripped the stretcher tighter.

"She's not out of the woods, but she's holding on," Roger said in a calm voice. "Talk to her." He grabbed a blood pressure cuff and wrapped it around Elora's calf on the leg that wasn't wounded.

The diagnostic equipment started up, then let out a hiss of pressurized air. Vincent wasn't an expert in first aid or medicine, but he knew her pressure was low. Too low.

Her heart rate dropped, the machine beeping quickly, and Vincent's pulse seemed to sync at the same rhythm. He slipped his fingers along her opened hand, careful not to touch any wounds or broken bones.

"Elora, I'm here," he said, his voice thick as he desperately tried not to choke on the lump squeezing his throat. "Hold on, okay? I need you to hold on for me. I'm here."

Roger tapped on the plastic window to the front of the ambulance, then opened it. "We need to hurry. Which hospital has a surgeon who can take her asap?"

"St. Boniface," she called out.

The engine rumbled, and they picked up speed faster than Vincent had ever felt while inside a vehicle. The sirens continued wailing, the horn blasting a few times as they slowed a few seconds. Roger pulled out a syringe and filled it with a clear liquid before attaching it to the needless connector in the IV line. He injected the medication as they took a few turns, and the siren's noises changed.

The hospital came into view as they drove up into the emergency entrance, and Vincent looked back at Elora as his vision blurred.

"Elora, please… I need you. You're so strong. I know you can fight." When her fingers twitched, he held his breath. "I love you, Elora. So much. You'll be all right."

# 50

# VINCENT

*V*incent sat on a waiting chair, his elbows resting on his knees as he pressed his knuckles against his mouth to keep from screaming. Or crying. He wasn't certain what he felt anymore. His emotions were in a whirl of turmoil, and until he received news of Elora's condition, he couldn't seem to feel anything specific.

She'd gone into surgery, and with no word from anyone, he was sure he'd go insane soon. As his mind slowly seemed to wrap around everything else, he pulled out his cellphone, and called Liana.

"Vincent! What's going on? Did they find Elora—?"

"She's in critical condition," he said, not hearing himself as he focused on an empty wheelchair left out in a hallway nearby.

Liana sniffed loudly. "We're on our way. Are you there now? Which hospital?"

"St. Boniface."

"I know they won't let us visit her soon, but we'll support each other. You don't have to be there alone," she said in a trembling voice.

He nodded, despite knowing Liana couldn't see him. "Thanks."

Hanging up, Vincent slipped the phone into his pocket, rolling his neck to loosen a kink. The whir of the elevator caught Vincent's attention, and he turned as the motorized whoosh of the doors opened for Benjamin striding inside. Seven of his men followed behind, and a few of the people in the waiting room shifted nervously on the creaking chairs.

Without a word, the men dispersed in different directions as Benjamin approached Vincent.

"I take it she's alive since you're in the waiting area." He spoke like it was nothing. Like Vincent hadn't spent the last hours of his life having his heart crushed to death.

"If you're here to cheer me up, it's not fucking working," he said through his teeth.

Benjamin raised an eyebrow. "Hostility gets you nowhere." He glanced over his shoulder toward the information desk. "Let's go find a place to speak in private."

"I'm not moving until I get an update on Elora."

Benjamin rolled his eyes. "They won't tell you anything. You're not her common-law partner, nor are you married, and you're not family, either."

Vincent curled his hands into fists, knowing his brother was right. The only people the doctors would report to at this point would be the police.

"What's with the protection brigade?" Vincent asked, needing to change the subject.

"That's what I need to talk to you about. I don't trust the cops to keep Elora secure because we both know organizations tend to have a few law enforcements in their pockets." Benjamin motioned his head. "Let's go find a quiet place."

Vincent's mind slowly detached from what was happening to Elora, focusing instead on what Benjamin needed to tell him. There was nothing Vincent could do for her while she was in surgery, but what he could do was get Richard.

Benjamin swept the crumbs from the table before taking a seat in the corner of the cafeteria. It was closed, but that suited them fine since they wouldn't be overheard.

"The MOW organization is active, but under a new front and name," Benjamin said in a rough tone. "It's called *Followers of Old*. They're registered under a religious group, but they opened an investigation into whether they fall under a cult. Their leader is known as the Savior, and word is out it's Jack Cross, but no interviewer has seen or met him."

Vincent's jaw clenched as he stared at the menu board listing items and prices, his memories bringing him back to when they'd found the boss's headquarters and the warehouse below. "I'd hoped when the organization fell, it would be the last we saw of that piece of shit and his right-hand man."

The night they raided the mansion above, they discovered one of Jack Cross' captains butchered like the pig he'd been in life, but no sign of who had murdered him. The rest had escaped, though, and no one had heard of them since.

"I told you back then not going after them was a mistake," Benjamin said, glowering at Vincent. "The only way to destroy an organization for good is by killing the main serpent."

"I was preoccupied about getting the survivors out and locating the families of the deceased." He let out a breath. "But I should've given the order to try. After seeing that freezer room in the warehouse with all those bodies…"

Benjamin reached into his jacket and pulled out folded sheets, then placed them in front of Vincent. "Those ear tags they had were the same as the ones used for farm animals. You mentioned the latest victims in your case had holes in their ears, and they match the same type. But they changed their methods of selling," he pointed at the papers.

Vincent unfolded a few, staring at a screenshot of a website. "The numbers on the tag are how you buy the women." His stomach churned. "No photos or anything, so it's hard to prove what those figures mean." He stared up at his brother. "Hasn't this site been flagged yet?"

"It was coded to be active during certain times of the week, at a specified hour, and for a predetermined amount of time. Unless you're in the loop to know when, you'd likely not stumble on the website since the name and search terms are vague." Benjamin grabbed a paper and placed it at the forefront of the rest. "When I looked into Richard to see if there was any dirt on him we could threaten him with, I found a few interesting things."

Vincent read along the printed information. Richard had quit his job, but the amount of money he made was over what he used to earn, yet his social insurance number wasn't registered for any other work. Vincent searched his mind, trying to recall what the bastard said when they were at the charity event, and his back stiffened. "He mentioned he worked in code development."

"He was likely recruited by the new **MOW** organization, and being the scumbag he is, bought into the whole 'men are superior' bullshit." Benjamin pulled another and pointed at a number. "This is how many orders they made on the website."

Vincent wanted to throw up. Seventy-six human beings, and all with ear tag numbers. That meant they were already dead. He gritted his teeth. "The coding and job loss isn't enough to pin any of these murders to Richard, and since you don't do things half-assed, you've got more proof."

"I sent Krystal to get information out of Mr. Reverie. She recorded everything. From her saying how she misses the days when men were in charge to him talking about the Followers of Old, and how they provided services to the members by being able to purchase meat." Benjamin leaned back, looking like he'd love nothing better than to wipe the knowledge from his memory. "They're selling women. He called it a way to vent." His hand gripped the side of the table, his knuckles turning white.

Vincent shifted on the hard bench, needing to punch the living shit out of something before he'd explode. "So Richard admitted to killing one of them?"

"Yes, and then he complained about how long he had to wait between orders. That's when I knew for sure he also murdered your latest victim, Sophie Wilson. When I left with Elora, the first time I *met* her," he scoffed when Vincent shot him a glare, "I had my men look into Richard's home computer. They brought it to my IT guy, and he found a reserved motel room that is the same as where Sophie was killed. It was rented out for several months, but paid with cash and a fake name. The owner of the establishment is likely with the organization."

"If it was so clear Richard killed Sophie, why not tell me?" Vincent said through his teeth. "Why wait?"

"Because if they arrested Richard before I could gather information about the new Followers of Old, it would've meant several more lives lost. I had to make sure I could get the most out of him before throwing him to the wolves."

Vincent slowly got to his feet, looking at his brother with a boiling hatred. "You were willing to sacrifice Elora to save others. Is that it?"

He shook his head, his expression pained. It was the first time Vincent saw his brother react like that since he was a child.

"I thought she was with you. If I'd known, I would've done things differently." He stood and pointed at the printouts. "Bring these to your boss. They already put a warrant out on Richard, so this will push them to hurry."

Vincent grabbed them and handed them to his brother. "I don't plan on letting the cops arrest Richard."

"We talked about this. You—"

"I'm hiring you and your organization to recover him for me. I'll pay, so it means I won't need any favors from you, nor do I have to join. If I go to prison, so be it. But I will be the one to end Richard."

Benjamin observed Vincent in silence for a few seconds, and a slow icy smile curled his lips. "Do you trust me to do the right thing here?"

"As long as you're clear about who gets the son of a bitch."

"It's clear."

"Then yes."

Benjamin slipped the papers into his jacket pocket. "I'll be in touch real soon."

51

# VINCENT

*B*y the time Vincent returned to the waiting room, Kimberly had arrived.

She approached him. "Daniel called in a favor with the staff, so they'll be giving you the information about Elora once she's out of surgery. But the condition is that an officer remains with you to make sure you don't get... excessive."

"Remind me to thank him later," Vincent muttered with a grin as he leaned against the wall, the smell of cleaning supplies sending a wave of nausea through him.

She straightened and held his gaze. "I need to apologize for what happened when I was at your place. You were right. I was jealous when I realized what was happening, and I took it out on Elora and you. It was unprofessional, and... a bitch move on my part." She clenched her jaw. "I'm sorry. And I want you to know I've told HR to drop the complaint. They were still making a final decision about it, but I insisted it gets expunged from your file."

Vincent gave her a pat on the arm and smiled. "Thanks, I appreciate it. And no worries. We all make mistakes. If people held everything I've ever done over my head... Well, let's just say there'd be several lifetimes to repent for."

Kimberly leaned forward, staring down the hallway. "I think they know you."

Vincent turned. Liana and Brad strode toward them, her eyes bright red and swollen. Before he had the time to do anything, she hugged him tight, knocking the wind out of him.

Brad gave Vincent a friendly pat on the arm as Liana withdrew, then stared at Kimberly.

The officer smiled. "I'll give you a chance to speak in private," she said, then walked away.

"Any news?" Liana asked, her voice cracking. It sounded painful.

"Not yet."

Brad pulled Liana in his arms as she burst into tears. "Breathe, honey."

"She's... tough," she said through sobs.

"Yes she is." Brad rubbed her back. "Right now, she's fighting hard, and she'll need you to be strong, too."

Vincent stared toward the posters warning patients about the dangers of the flu. "They're going to let me see her once she's transferred to a room."

Liana beamed. "That's good. It'll help her feel safer if she wakes up to you being there."

They sat in the waiting room, and Vincent couldn't seem to stay still. Part of him wanted to be by Elora's side throughout every single procedure, while another part needed to hunt Richard.

As time ticked away, doubts and fears slithered into his mind. What if it was taking so long because something went wrong? What if she woke up, and the shock stopped her heart? He took a deep breath, wiping the sweat from his forehead.

Liana placed her hand on his shoulder, and he turned toward her. "She'll be okay."

Vincent's name was called on the intercom, and he glanced at his friends before rushing to the doors leading to the corridor.

A nurse strode forward. "This way please," he said.

Vincent wanted to shake the nurse until he told him what was going on, but he breathed in deep, and followed in silence.

They entered a small waiting room separated from the rest, and

Vincent's chest squeezed. Were they giving him privacy to receive news because it was bad?

Kimberly joined and took a seat. "How are your friends holding up?"

"They're... hopeful."

He couldn't sit, so he paced, his mind flooding with memories of Elora doing the same when she was frightened.

He stopped. "She must've been... so scared," he mumbled, his throat closing.

Kimberly opened her mouth as though to say something, but before she could, a doctor walked in. "I'm Dr. Cyr."

She stuck out her hand, and Vincent shook it on instinct alone. "Please, is Elora okay?"

The surgeon motioned to a chair, then took a seat as she looked at her chart. "Elora is in recovery now. She had a lacerated spleen and required twelve units of blood, but the internal bleeding has been controlled. Her prognosis is still guarded, but we are cautiously optimistic. The orthopedist is overlooking Elora's x-rays and she'll be recommending necessary procedures that'll be undertaken for her broken bones."

Vincent slumped in the chair, rubbing his hand across his face. She had survived the surgery. He took a few deep breaths, calming himself.

The doctor continued, "Her injuries were likely inflicted when she was conscious. That kind of trauma is hard on the mind. She'll need physical therapy for several aspects, including her hands, fingers, arms, neck, abdomen, back, leg, and..." She paused, and looked up at Vincent. "You're her boyfriend, correct?"

"I am."

"Are you the person who'll take care of her during recovery?"

"Yes." He didn't hesitate for a second.

"In that case, I'll give you a full report so you know what she'll require. Specialists will contact you to make appointments." She drew out a page from underneath the top and handed it to Vincent. "She'll need time. A lot of patience."

He took the paper from her. "Thank you, Dr. Cyr."

"You'll be able to see her soon. Once she's placed in a room, someone will call you." She got to her feet and left.

"She's alive, Vince." Kimberly gave him an encouraging smile.

He read across the notes and diagnostics on the report. When he found the list for the therapies and reached the end, he stopped reading, and put the sheet down so he couldn't see the words anymore. Tears blurred his vision, and he pressed his lips together, not trusting himself not to scream or vomit.

Richard had done one of the worst things imaginable to her.

*I'll make him suffer twice as much.*

❦

When Vincent's name was announced on the intercom for a second time, he strode to the room number they'd announced. A nurse waited for him and Kimberly, and as Vincent followed, sweat soaked through his clothes as though he'd run for hours.

"I'll be out here if you need anything," Kimberly said in a quiet voice.

Vincent stepped into the dimly lit room and held his breath. Although it didn't matter, since the air was sucked out of his lungs the moment he laid eyes on Elora.

She lay in the hospital bed, half her face covered in bandages while the other was swollen and bruised. Series of stitches were visible along her skin, IVs and tubes running through her and into machines. They'd wrapped her leg in gauzes, and one arm had a cast, while both her hands were heavily bandaged.

He rushed forward, kneeling beside the bed as he placed his hand on her wrist. "Elora... I'm here. You did so well. Keep holding on." His voice cracked.

Her breathing was shallow, and she twitched in her sleep a few times as though running from something.

"I'm sorry I wasn't there to protect you," he said through his tears. "I shouldn't have let you go. I'm so, so sorry, Elora." He kissed her wrist. "Please come back to me so I can tell you every day how much I love you."

His cell buzzed, and he inhaled deeply as he straightened, then slipped it out of his pocket.

*Benjamin: It's set up. If you're still determined to do this, then I'll pick you up in ten minutes.*

Vincent frowned. Had Benjamin already found Richard? At the thought of getting his hands on that monster, a strange calm washed over Vincent; he knew what he'd do and didn't feel any guilt about it.

A nurse stepped into the room and gave a gentle smile to Vincent before checking a few machines.

"Will…" Vincent cleared his throat, trying to get it to work. "How long will it be before she wakes up?"

"She'll be sedated for a while longer, but the numbers for her blood pressure and heart rate are positive." She grabbed Elora's chart and scribbled a few things before withdrawing.

He stared at his phone and typed his response.

*Vincent: I'll be out front.*

He hated leaving her alone, but the threat to her was out there. And he'd hunt it and permanently rip it out of the world to keep her safe.

# 52

# ELORA

*E*lora faded in and out, unsure whether she was half-awake or stuck in a dream. Or dead. Her body ached in a slow throb, but from time to time, a pang of agony shot through her, and she gasped. Shapes and colors flitted across her vision, and she closed her eyelids tight.

Fog filled her head, and all she saw were glimpses of horrific images.

Blood.

A knife.

Her mind gave the order to call out, but nothing happened. Was there anyone with her? Was she alone? Her breathing sped as she struggled to think. To recall something—anything.

*Vincent.*

They danced. He held her, but someone ripped her away from him. Who? She reached for him, but her hand and arm twisted, curling against her as though her bones bent on themselves. A scream caught in her throat as Vincent vanished, and blood poured in front of her. Pain radiated through her, and no matter what she did, she couldn't escape. She tried to run, but her legs wouldn't move.

*Why?*

She stared down at herself, and her eyes widened. Holes covered them. She pressed her hands on the wounds, trying to keep the bones and muscles inside, but there were too many. Blood streamed out, and she sobbed. She needed someone to help her stop the bleeding.

A figure appeared in front of her, and she looked up, her heart beating so fast it seemed to break.

*It stopped?*

The silver of a blade swiped down on her, and she stared as it stabbed her in the abdomen. Anguish burned through her like fire, and she shrieked. But the weapon continued plunging inside her.

Richard loomed over her, and she opened her mouth, but no sound came out. No one would help her, and that was why her voice didn't work. It didn't matter. She was worthless. She was nothing.

Darkness enveloped her as she crawled away from the misery. It followed her everywhere; entering her like a slithering shadow so the hurt would never end.

Silence hung heavy, but she frowned when she heard her name whispered. Was… someone there? A voice whispered gently, and she pushed through the torment, trying to find who spoke.

Arms wrapped around her, and she leaned her head against his chest. Vincent. She felt his heartbeat and smiled.

*That's right. I'm not alone.*

Elora opened her eye, her vision blurry as though she hadn't used them in a long time. There was only darkness for the other eyes, and she trembled. Why couldn't she see? Sweat plastered her hair onto her face, but she couldn't push it away. Her limbs were heavy, and so tired.

She tried to move; the bed creaked as she shifted an inch, but when pain shot through her body, she froze. Her vision blurred as fragments of nightmares repeated inside her mind.

She licked her chapped lips, and nausea hit her hard at the smell of disinfectant. Was she at home and had forgotten to close one of the cleaning products?

Blinking a few times, her gaze swept the room. Her pulse sped.

Where was Richard? Was he here? She tried to move, and her eye widened when she noticed her arm and hands were in casts and bandages. Her abdomen throbbed, and the memory of Richard stabbing her flashed inside her mind.

Her stomach churned violently, and she turned her head to the side, throwing up. She screamed at the agony burning throughout her body as machines blared out warnings.

People rushed in, and she fought to escape despite the pain. Were these the ones Richard spoke about? The ones he called members of the flock? Were they here to take her to him?

A woman leaned close, and Elora stopped, dizziness making it impossible to move anymore. "I'm Dr. Cyr," she said in a gentle voice. "You're in the hospital."

Her words seemed to float in Elora's head for a few seconds before they made sense. "Ri... chard?"

"There are police officers outside your room. You're safe. But I need you to calm down. We don't want you hurting yourself." She smiled. "I worked hard on fixing you up, so let's keep you nice and relaxed, okay?"

Elora nodded slowly.

Another woman approached and passed a wet washcloth against Elora's mouth. "I'm the nurse responsible for you. My name is Pauline."

*Nurse. My father had a nurse. Richard murdered him.*

Tears ran down Elora's cheeks. She frowned. No. Just one cheek. Why couldn't she see with her other eye?

"I'm going to check your abdomen to make sure no stitches tore. Is that okay?" Dr. Cyr asked. There was something so gentle and calming about her. Vincent was like that, too.

Where was he?

Elora's fingers twitched, and she gasped at the pain, trembling at the sight of them. What happened to them? Were her hands gone? She couldn't breathe. Her pulse raced faster and faster, spots filling her vision.

People spoke in urgent tones, and the world faded to black.

❧

Nothing plagued Elora's sleep this time. She opened an eye, taking deep breaths to try staying calm, but every little noise sent her heart racing.

Elora turned her head a bit, and tears stung her eyes as she met with Liana's gaze. Her best friend sat on the chair next to Elora's bed, her cheeks stained with mascara.

"Elora?" Liana's voice cracked.

Elora forced a smile. "Hi."

Liana burst into sobs. "Thank god you're alive." She scooted closer. "The staff let me sit with you. They said it might help you stay calm if you had a friendly face to see."

"It... helps." Every word hurt, but she took a few deep breaths, trying her best not to wince. "Is... Richard?"

Liana shook her head. "They haven't found him yet, but the police are looking high and low for the fucker."

Elora's stomach churned. He was out there. Could get to her. Her pulse sped, and the machine beeped louder. Elora closed her eye, taking deep breaths.

"I'm... okay..." she whispered.

When she opened her eye, Pauline hovered at the foot of the hospital bed. "Do you want something to help you sleep?" she asked.

"Not... right now. Thank you," Elora said, trying her best to smile, but every movement of her muscles sent pain through her body.

"Don't worry about anything. Just focus on mending."

Elora stared at her hand. "Yeah... I must... look like... shit."

"You're alive. And a survivor. Don't put a value on physical looks. Vincent won't." She pushed Elora's hair from her face. "Scars heal and fade with time. But your life? That's so much more important. And who you are. I know you're going to have to learn to cope with... what happened. We're here for you, okay? You're not alone."

"Thanks." She smiled, and this time, it didn't feel as forced. "Is... Vincent—?"

"He said he had to leave, but asked me to tell you he'd be back soon."

Elora's chest tightened. Richard was out there, and Vincent had ties to the criminal organization. After what Richard had done, Benjamin might not be opposed to helping his brother go after him.

"I need... to call him..."

Liana frowned. "He'll be—"

"It's important. I have to stop... him." Elora held her best friend's gaze. "Please."

Liana dialed her phone and helped Elora hold it to her ear. Every ring tone echoed within Elora's mind, and she closed her eye tightly.

"He's... not answering." Elora panted. Where was he? Had she forced him to return to his old life? Was he going to kill again?

Elora tried moving her legs. She needed to find him.

"What are you doing?" Liana placed her hands on Elora's shoulders, but barely put any force.

A nurse Elora didn't recognize strode into the room, frowning. "You're in no condition to move. Please lie down and stay still, Mrs. Reverie."

Elora's body convulsed at the last name, and she closed her eye to get rid of the dizziness. Pain shot through her, and she cried out in agony as though every stab wound had sliced through her again.

"Help! She needs help!" Liana screamed.

Footsteps sounded inside the room, Elora's vision blurring at the edges as she fought for air. There was a sudden decrease in anguish, and she watched as Brad held a crying Liana in his arms. Machines beeped until the line suddenly continued in one long wail as Elora closed her eye.

*Please, Vincent. Come back to me.*

# 53

## VINCENT

*V*incent's pulse steadied as the driver switched off the headlights. They approached an abandoned factory; boarded windows, spray paint covering the walls. It was as decrepit as they came.

Benjamin took out his phone. "Plate number."

Gary recited it, and Benjamin tapped the screen a few times. His cell buzzed, and a second after, a garage door opened to their left. The driver reversed the SUV a bit, then drove into the building. Once they parked, it closed, leaving them in the flickering fluorescent lights overhead.

"Wait here," Benjamin said, giving a friendly tap on Gary's arm before stepping out of the vehicle.

Vincent followed. How long had he been away from Elora's side? Was she all right? Had she woken up and wondered where he was? He pushed the thoughts from his mind. This was beyond important; it was life or death. He had to eliminate the threat against her once and for all.

The garage had seen better days. The cement walls had turned an orangey brown color from rust and water damage, and the smell of mold was impossible to ignore.

A metal door at the end was the only way forward, but Benjamin didn't move.

Vincent stood next to his brother and arched an eyebrow. "Any reason we're standing here?"

"Where are your manners?" he asked with a grin. "You don't just barge into someone's workplace without being invited in first."

"What are you talking about?" He spun on Benjamin. "No more riddles. Start explaining."

"What's the number one rule you taught me?" Benjamin cocked his head.

Vincent frowned.

*Never get your hands dirty as boss.*

That meant…

"Fuck," Vincent said in a groan. "You didn't hire *him*, did you?" Vincent asked, running his hand across his face.

The door swung open, and a man stepped out. On the rare occasions Vincent was near him, he seemed able to quiet his environment, and this time was no different.

The man, known only by the name Nox, was not someone to fuck with. His hair was jet black; one side hanging past his ears while the other was shaven. He looked dangerous. People quickly found out it wasn't only looks. He was a monster in his own right.

"Mr. Karson, always a pleasure doing business," Nox said with a wintry smile. His gaze focused on Vincent for a few seconds. "Mr. Voden, long time no see."

Nox moved to the side, holding the door open. "Please come in."

Benjamin took a step forward, but Vincent grabbed his arm. "Care to explain why I paid you for a contract, and Nox is the one who gets it?"

Benjamin rolled his eyes. "This way, there's no actual connection between you and my organization. It's a third party, and it keeps it a little less biased. I need information from Richard before you kill him."

"So what does he do in this?" Vincent asked, keeping an eye on Nox as he leaned on the open door with a smile.

"He helps persuade Mr. Reverie to answer questions." Benjamin pulled away from Vincent's grip. "And he provides tools you can use on him if you so desire."

With a sigh, Vincent followed his brother, keenly aware that Nox walked behind them down the narrow hallway. He wasn't someone to turn his back on, no matter who paid his contract.

They stopped at another metal door, and Nox strode ahead. He pressed a few buttons on a keypad, and the door unlocked with a loud click.

A mixture of several unpleasant smells reached Vincent instantly, and he stiffened. He couldn't tell exactly what they were, but there was definitely blood, sweat and urine in the mix.

They stepped inside, and the door closed behind them. The room could easily have been a replica of a medieval dungeon. Weapons and tools hung from the low ceiling, and Vincent did his best to hide the chill running down his spine. Nox had everything from brands to knives, hooks to hammers. An old salmon-pink oven sat against a moldy wall, the elements glowing red like the blades leaning on them. The man was a psychopath, but it was also why he was the most hired contract killer in the underground.

They followed past an archway, the stone walls cracked like they were a few days away from crumbling. Vincent stopped as his gaze focused on the scene in front of him.

Richard Reverie.

The man's eyes darted from Vincent to Benjamin, then widened when he seemed to recognize them. The bloody piece of cloth in his mouth muffled his begging, and Vincent couldn't help smiling at the sight. Nox had even tied the monster to a chair with rusty nails sticking up in the armrests. One minor hit would puncture his skin.

Nox pulled two regular chairs from a corner and placed them in front of his victim. As Vincent and Benjamin sat, Nox pulled the gag out of Richard's mouth. He coughed, his breaths labored as though he was in pain.

Vincent focused on the monster sitting across from him, but couldn't form any words to tell him off.

Benjamin smiled. "Hello Mr. Reverie."

"Please. Get me out of here. I did nothing——"

Nox backhanded Richard in the face. "Don't interrupt people. It's rude."

Richard blinked several times, but he pressed his lips together. Once Nox looked sure his victim would listen, he leaned against the side of a wooden table, waiting in silence.

"As I was saying," Benjamin continued pleasantly as though they weren't in a dungeon that looked like something out of King Henry the Eighth's torture chamber. "I have questions I'll ask you, and I need you to answer them without lying." He motioned at Nox. "When you lie... Well, you can see everything in this place can be used for painful inflictions on the human body."

Richard burst into tears. "Please. I'll tell you anything. Just let me go."

Vincent curled his hands into fists. How dare he cry like that? After what he'd done to Elora—throughout her life and then trying to kill her—he had no right.

Benjamin chuckled. "I'm glad you'll comply. This will make our business quicker." He glanced at Nox. "No offense, but I'd rather not stay here longer than I have to."

Nox waved his hand dismissively. "None taken. It's the point of the room."

"None of us were talking about the room," Vincent muttered.

Nox's smile widened, his light blue irises contrasting against the area, making them look synthetic.

Benjamin laughed, keeping his good humor as he turned to Richard. "First, before you even try lying, I want you to be aware of what we already know. Someone in the MOW organization approached you. They don't go by that name anymore, though. You know them as a religious group called Followers of Old."

Nox straightened, his smile vanishing. It gave him an even deadlier look. "The MOW organization?"

Benjamin nodded. "Unfortunately so."

Nox fell silent, but something in his gaze changed, as though he was excited and furious.

Benjamin returned his attention to Richard, who looked like

he'd paled more in the last few seconds. "These Followers of Old wanted you to build them a website with particular requirements. For example, being accessible during certain days, hours, and amounts of time." He leaned forward. "How am I doing so far?"

Richard opened and closed his mouth, then glanced at Nox. "Yes."

Benjamin clapped his hands, and Richard jumped. "Good. We're already on the right track. How do members receive this information?"

"Texts through burner phones. I don't know how they choose members, though."

Benjamin nodded. "You eventually found out this website would serve one purpose. To sell women. The numbers corresponding to the ear tag of each victim displayed on the orders. These human beings were also known as meat by monsters like you." Benjamin pulled out his cellphone, his thumbs hovering over the screen. "Approximately how many were for sale every week?"

Richard licked his lips nervously. "I'm… not exactly sure. Maybe twenty or so? It depended if there were any in the flock who they determined to be lost causes."

Benjamin tapped his screen a few times. "So that's how they chose victims? Because they don't follow cult rules?"

"It's not a cult," Richard spat. "We're following the word of God. You're——"

Nox leaned forward and grabbed Richard's face, squeezing until all he could do was sputter. "Now, now." He pressed his finger against Richard's lips. "*For the time is coming when people will not endure sound teaching, but having itching ears, they will accumulate for themselves teachers to suit their own passions.*" When Richard gawked, Nox grinned. "Don't speak on subjects you have no knowledge of."

Vincent's eyebrows shot up; Nox was the last person he expected to be religious or even know quotes from the bible by heart. Although, he realized he knew nothing about the man.

Benjamin finished typing. "The victims from the women's shelters. Why were they chosen, and why were their bodies used as messages afterward?"

Richard averted his gaze. "I know nothing about that. I noticed they were for sale, but I wasn't told why they put them on display in front of the shelters."

Benjamin cocked his head. "I never mentioned where they displayed the victims," he said with a cruel smile. "Strike one for lies."

"No. Please," Richard begged. "I heard it on the news!"

Vincent's jaw clenched. "Nowhere was it reported where they were located. The police kept it under wraps because it was an ongoing case."

Benjamin cringed exaggeratedly. "Oof, make that strike two for lies."

Nox grabbed a pair of bolt cutters and without a second of hesitation, placed Richard's index finger between the jaws, and tightened his grip on the handles.

Richard screamed as his finger fell to the floor, blood streaming out of the stump. Not waiting a second for the man to recover, he placed a second of Richard's fingers between the tool, and cut off another.

Nox walked to the oven, and grabbed one of the knives leaning on the element. He hummed a tune, partially drowned out by Richard's continued screams as he pressed the glowing blade against the bleeding. The smell of roasting flesh filled the room as Richard's cries grew higher pitched.

Vincent could barely hear Richard's shrieks anymore. That the monster was alive grated on his nerves. He needed to get back to Elora, but not before making certain the bastard was dead.

Benjamin let out a sigh. "Let's try again, Mr. Reverie. Why were the victims of the women's shelter displayed like they were?"

Richard sobbed, shaking his head. "They... just said... they wanted to... make sure... if anyone escaped... they would have... nowhere to go."

"And you're the one who murdered Sophie Wilson, correct?"

Richard nodded, snot mixing in with his tears. "Yes. I... couldn't wait for... another order anymore."

He continued babbling on, but Vincent tuned out, sick and tired of watching the pathetic insect beg.

Until Richard mentioned impregnating his wife.

Vincent gritted his teeth. "Are you saying you tried to get Elora pregnant and planned to... what exactly?" He could barely keep his rage in check, wanting nothing better than to rip Richard piece by piece himself.

"I swear I don't know. All they told me was the Savior would forgive me if I provided them with an infant from a holy marriage. It had to be a baby born of my wife and me."

"Did you tell your spouse about this?" Benjamin asked, his voice quiet.

"I did, and she ran away from me. I was bringing her to our new home within the community of the Followers of Old, but she wouldn't listen," he said, his jaw clenched as sweat drenched his face. "That's when I realized," he muttered.

Vincent's hands curled into fists. "Realized what?"

"That no one could save her. Satan had already warped her mind. She was a lost cause. So I had her repent for her sins by performing her duties to me as a wife, and then I purged the demons from her with a knife." He smiled, letting out a breath as though relieved. "I never felt like that before... When I stabbed her and her muscles spasmed; it was magnificent."

Vincent bolted to his feet, ready to punch Richard, but Nox grabbed his wrist.

"If you show up with bloody knuckles, you can blame it on punching a wall out of anger, but the minute they swab it and find this pest's DNA on you? You're done." His eyes seemed to see through to Vincent's soul, and Vincent yanked away from him.

Nox opened a drawer and handed him a pair of black leather gloves. "There. Now have fun."

Vincent slipped them on, then rounded on Richard. "I've been seeing Elora for months. We met at the book fair when she won an award. Then I was on the construction team for the sunroom at your house. We spent many hours of... quality time together." Vincent's lips curled as Richard's face turned bright red. "I've shown her being touched doesn't have to hurt, and after being intimate with her several times at my place, our feelings deepened. I love her, and she loves me. And you'll never lay a finger on her again, you fucking piece of shit."

Vincent punched Richard in the jaw. He barely felt the blow, but the monster did as he coughed and gasped.

"You're... a sinner. Fuck you and your... kind," Richard shouted through his raspy breaths. "I knew she was a... whore, spreading her legs for——"

Vincent slammed his fist against Richard's nose even harder, the sound of cracking bones resonating in the room. Blood sputtered out of Richard's nose as he wheezed, his eyes shut tight. The bridge of his nose was swollen and gashed.

But it wasn't enough. Not after what he'd done to Elora.

Vincent glanced around the room, his gaze settling on a device he recognized all too well. He marched over to the wooden counter, and grabbed a gas torch.

"Any full canisters?" Vincent asked, ignoring Richard's cries for help.

Nox opened a cupboard, a few wooden chips cracking at the hinges. "Do you want basic butane, or the one mixed with propane?"

"I'm not planning on just warming up the son of a bitch." Vincent's hold on the torch grew tighter, the image of Elora lying in the hospital bed burned into his mind.

Nox scoffed, and grabbed the mixture of butane and propane canister. "Need an extra four-hundred degree for that little extra warmth?"

Without a word, Vincent grabbed the can, and installed the gas torch onto it. He'd used this type of tool a few times back when he'd been in charge of Crimson; often, the sight of the thing was enough to get people to talk. But with Richard, he wanted to use it. No matter how much the monster begged and screamed.

"No," Richard sobbed, "Mr. Karson, please. I can get you in with the Followers of Old."

Vincent clenched his jaw as he turned. Benjamin arched an eyebrow, giving a side glance at his brother.

"You barely had any information to share in the first place. They certainly know the two of us," Benjamin said as he motioned from himself to Vincent. "Care to explain how you'd manage this little magic trick?"

He opened and closed his mouth, his breathing hollow. "I know how to get in contact with them. If you manage to buy meat, they'll bring you to the location where they're taking care of. If you swear you won't hurt me, and that you'll let me go, I promise I'll tell you."

Nox's smile widened. "Does that count as a lie?"

Richard's hand with the missing fingers twitched as he stared toward him. "No! I didn't lie. No one asked if I knew how to get in touch with them."

Vincent took a step forward. "You fucking——"

Benjamin raised his hand. "Wait a minute," he said calmly. "Mr. Reverie makes a good point. It's not a question I asked." Something in Benjamin's smile turned to something dangerous. "Although, I should have." He leaned his forearms against his knees, staring at Richard intently. "However, in your position, you can't bargain for anything, so why not just tell me? Do one decent thing before you die."

Richard burst into tears. "I swear, I'll tell you. Just please let me go. I'll leave and never come back." His body trembled violently. "Please don't kill me. I don't want to die."

Benjamin motioned to Vincent as he leaned back into his chair. "If you insist on suffering first, I certainly won't argue."

Vincent approached, anger rushing through him as he still clearly saw Elora lying in the barn stall. He turned the gas flow knob and a small hiss released from the fire nozzle. Richard shook his head, mumbling for help, but Vincent wasn't listening anymore; he didn't care. Part of him wanted to say something clever to the monster. Something that would sound dark and morbid. But he couldn't find the words to describe his fury. To express his devastation that Elora had been hurt.

He pushed on the one click starter. A whooshing sound filled the room as a blue flame ignited, and Richard's eyes widened. Vincent leaned the fire near Richard's arm, and the skin reddened.

"I'll tell you! Please don't!" he screamed, squirming to try getting away from the heat.

*It never takes too long.*

Vincent grabbed the strap holding Richard's wrist to the chair, slowly undoing it. Richard leaned back, letting out a breath as he babbled about kindness, thanking Vincent for stopping and releasing him.

Vincent had to stop himself from scoffing. With one quick yank, he tightened the strap so hard that Richard's arm pushed down on the armrests, the rusty nails impaling through his skin.

A half-cry, half-strangled noise left Richard's mouth. Vincent punched him in the face, then grabbed him by the chin. "Shut. Up."

Richard pressed his lips together, more snot and blood streaming down his nose. Vincent clicked the blowtorch off, but pressed it against Richard's wounded arm. The tip was still hot, and Richard screamed, but quickly grimaced as his jaw tightened.

Benjamin leaned forward. "Now then. Start talking."

"In my... cell's documents. A code to... unlock a program... file on..." he took a shallow breath, and tried clearing his throat. "It's... in my home... computer. Those numbers will... give you the... date and hour."

Vincent rested his finger on the blowtorch's trigger. "Date and hour for what?"

Richard let out a few whimpers. "For the next... three times... the website will be... available to buy... meat from." He sniffed deeply, but choked as he coughed blood and saliva. "Each time... you go on... the website, you have... to note the..." He trailed off, staring down at his legs as though lost in a daze.

Vincent grabbed Richard's hair, and wrenched his head back. "Keep going."

Richard blinked a few times, the swelling around one eye turning a deeper shade of red. "What's the... point? You're just... going to... kill me."

Vincent pushed the bastard back, and clicked on the trigger of the blowtorch. This time, he ignored Richard's shrieks as he burned a line from his wrist to the crook of his arm. The wound glistened as Richard turned his head to the side and threw up all over the floor.

It was such a tiny injury compared to what the monster had done to Elora.

"Okay," he panted, still sobbing. "I... Please..." He took a few deep breaths, glancing toward the wound, and turning away quickly.

Benjamin rolled his eyes. "You were saying how, when we go on the website, we have to note something."

"Two numbers... bottom right... page. Those... are part... of the code... for the... next days."

Benjamin leaned back in his chair. "So you're saying we need to buy one of these women? And then what?"

Richard's chin trembled as he nodded. "Put in... the numbers... Burner phone... only. Text will.... be sent." He shook harder, and no matter how many times he swallowed, it didn't seem to be enough. "Coordinates for... same day. Always... at 10:15... evening."

"That's helpful information, Mr. Reverie," Benjamin said as he got to his feet. "I can't say it was nice to meet you, but I'm glad to know there will be one less scumbag out there after tonight."

Nox straightened as Vincent handed him the blowtorch. Part of Vincent was glad this would finally be over.

"Please... no," Richard said through more crying. "Please... have... mercy on.... me."

Vincent stiffened as he stared at Richard, his teeth clenching so hard he was sure they'd shatter. "Mercy?" he repeated. His voice had turned to something beyond cruel; he barely recognized it himself.

Vincent swung his fist across Richard's face. "Mercy?" he shouted. "Like how you showed Elora mercy, you fucking piece of shit?"

Another punch, this time higher. He wanted to hit every inch of this monster's head. He needed Richard to feel more pain.

"After everything you did to her," he screamed, punching over and over. He couldn't even feel the impacts anymore. His arm didn't feel tired; almost like it wasn't attached anymore. "How could you do that to her?"

Tears blurred his vision, but he didn't care. It didn't matter. Elora had suffered, and part of her likely would for the rest of her life. All because of the man tied to a chair in front of Vincent.

Because of the person who was vulnerable and under Vincent's power.

Vincent was the only one who could grant the monster mercy. But Vincent couldn't stop hitting him. Sounds muffled around him. His arm grew heavy, and he switched to the other. Back and forth. Richard's bones barely felt solid anymore. All Vincent could see was Elora lying in the hospital bed.

The fear in her eyes the moment he'd met her.

Every time she cried because of the terror she'd experienced.

Vincent barely heard his brother calling his name, but finally, with a final huff, he backed away. Richard coughed, and a few teeth fell to the floor as blood streamed from his mouth. One eye was swollen shut, his lips torn in several places. He couldn't even seem to cry anymore.

"Did you bring an extra gun like I asked?" Vincent panted, trying to catch his breath. He wanted to see the despair in his eyes before murdering him.

Benjamin let out a sigh. "I didn't."

Vincent ripped the gloves and threw them in Richard's face. "He's not your responsibility. You saw what he did to her—"

"Yes, and I also heard what he said." Benjamin shook his head. "You've done more than enough here tonight. I get that this was personal, but it ends here. You can't return to this world. It was tearing you apart."

Vincent took a few steps toward his brother. "I need to kill him myself."

Benjamin rolled his shoulders. "This is my organization now. You left it to me, and I'd say, I'm pretty fucking good at it." His expression gentled. "Go back to her whole. Be the man she needs you to be."

Vincent let out a breath, but nodded, turning to Richard.

Benjamin motioned his head, and Nox pulled out a gun from behind his back.

Richard muttered something, but it just sounded like gibberish.

Nox reached behind his back, and pulled out a gun, then pointed it at Richard's face, his lips curling into an icy smirk. He cocked the hammer, and Richard's one opened eye widened as Nox fired.

A flash sparked.

The bullet tore through Richard's forehead leaving a bloodied black hole behind.

Richard seemed lost in a daze for a second and with a final shudder, his head dropped forward, his chin resting on his chest.

It was the end of Richard Reverie.

Relief flooded Vincent as he stared at the corpse of the monster who'd hurt the woman he loved. Blood dripped from his head, pooling on his lap.

The bastard was dead.

"It's done." Nox put away his gun. "As agreed, I'll dispose of the body. I expect the rest of the payment by tomorrow morning."

Vincent glanced once more at Richard before walking out without another word. It seemed to take a long time returning to the SUV. As he slid into the backseat, he leaned against the headrest. Gary remained silent as he peered at Vincent in the rearview mirror.

Benjamin joined them, and the vehicle drove away from Hell.

"I have an alibi for you," Benjamin said, staring out of the window. "I'll give you the details when we get to your drop off location." He glanced at Vincent's bloodied knuckles. "Remember. You punched a wall."

Vincent grabbed a first aid kit from under the seat; they regularly kept a few in these vehicles. "I always hated hiring that man."

"Yeah, but he gets the job done each time without fail," he said with a shrug. "Wish he'd be exclusive to the organization. I don't like that he takes contracts from just anyone."

Vincent pulled out a disinfectant wipe. "I should've been the one to murder him."

"You know, I told Elora to open up about her situation to you so it would keep you out of this. The look in her eyes when she realized you wanted to kill her husband... It wasn't grief for his death, but for what you'd do."

"Still—"

"I owed you a favor. Consider it repaid in full. Now. Let's get you back to her. She's probably awake and worried about you."

Vincent stared at his brother and smiled. "Thank you."

"I'd say anytime, but that wouldn't be true," he said with a chuckle.

# 54

# VINCENT

*A*s Vincent approached Elora's hospital room, two officers blocked his path.

"There's a psychiatrist and psychologist with the patient at the moment. We were told not to let anyone in while they meet."

His chest squeezed, but he nodded. She needed to talk to professionals, and he hoped she'd open up to them and allow them to help.

He returned to the waiting room and slumped into a chair. Running his fingers through his hair, he shifted to get comfortable on the thin-padded seat, and sighed.

Kimberly strode forward. "Where have you been?" She eyed his wounded knuckles and arched an eyebrow.

"Wall took a beating," he said with a laugh that didn't sound real. "I needed to clear my head while Elora was sedated. Can barely think in here." He pointed at the people sitting in the waiting room. Most were on the cellphones, noises sounding every few seconds. "It's been... hard. I knew what was going on at home for her, and... Well, I should've pushed harder to get her out of there. Whether or not she wanted to."

"What matters is she's alive."

He nodded. "With everything that happened to her, I'm... I'll stay in the city as long as she needs me to, but once she's healthy, I'm asking her to move in with me at my house." He curled and uncurled his hands, staring at a coffee table covered with newspapers and books. He hadn't felt this uncertain since he was a teen. "I know it might be too soon, and I won't push—"

Kimberly chuckled. "Don't over think it. You both care about each other, and yeah, it might be fast, but you need her, and she needs you." She shrugged. "Life isn't easy; doesn't come with a manual, but we do the best we can. Put the offer on the table and go from there."

"Thanks, Kimberly."

They waited in silence, his mind on thoughts of Elora. Would she want to move to Ottawa with him, or would she prefer staying in this city? Here, she had Liana and Brad, and the last thing he wanted to do was separate her from the important people in her life. And her father was here. Would they transfer the guardianship back to Elora now that Richard was gone?

"I'm going for a walk," he said, getting to his feet.

Kimberly nodded and gave him an encouraging smile as he walked away.

He wandered through a few corridors and eventually headed toward Elora's room. As he approached, two women stepped out, talking to one another in low voices.

Vincent stared at the officers, leaving his unasked question lingering in the air. One nodded and cleared the door so he could go inside.

A shudder slammed into him as he strode into the area and locked gazes with Elora. Only one eye was opened, but it shimmered as she looked at him. He rushed forward and sat on the chair, placing his hand on her arm.

He swallowed hard, trying to rid the burning in his throat. "I'm here, Elora. Right here."

She smiled. "I... came back... to you... see?"

Tears flooded his eyes, and he nodded. He rested his forehead on the side of the mattress, his shoulders shaking as he cried.

"I'm… I don't know what I would've done if I'd lost you." He stared at her.

It was her turn to cry. "I'm sorry… I didn't leave… him sooner."

He shook his head. "You're so strong and brave, darling. I'm so proud of you." He glided his knuckles gently along her arm. "He won't ever bother you again. And I understand you'll want time to adjust. I won't push, but I'm here for you. Liana and Brad, too. Anything you need."

"I… Will you stay with me… when I press charges… and go to trial?"

"Of course." He took a deep breath, knowing she'd guess what he'd done as soon as Richard's disappearance became public. They'd never find the remains, but in time, he'd tell her that Richard was dead and gone. "We'll get through this together. And once it's finished… Do you intend on staying in this city?"

"I don't… know. There are… so many bad… memories here. But Liana is here. And you." She took a shuddering breath and winced.

He ran his fingers through her hair as gently as he could, his hand trembling. "The house I have in Ontario is a few minutes outside Ottawa. It's a four-season cottage."

A small smile touched her lips. "Is there… a forest?"

"Yes, but it's not too secluded. There are other homes, and even a convenience store, and restaurant that's family-owned." He leaned forward a bit. "You'd love it there. It's quiet. And in the autumn, the maples turn bright red. They mix with the oranges and yellows; it's breathtaking."

"Maybe… I could get a teaching position in Ottawa. At a kindergarten."

Something in her gaze fell.

"Elora?"

Tears filled her eyes as she touched the bandaged side of her face. "I must look… like a monster… Who would ever hire me?"

His heart hammered at her pain. "You'll have scars, but it won't stop you from getting your dream job. And you're still beautiful no matter what." He kissed her wrist. "Let's focus on one thing at a time."

"Okay."

"It's fast, and there's a lot going on, but when everything is over, I'd like it if you moved in with me. Living with you, holding you every night as we fall asleep... I can't think of any other way I want to live my life anymore." He smiled. "But if you prefer having your own place, I'll understand. Remember, you always have a choice when you're with me. And even if..." He swallowed hard. "Even if you need space, your life is your own now. You control what happens."

She let out a small breath. "I should... take the time to be on my own but... being with you... It feels right, you know? But..."

"But what?"

"Are you sure... you even want to be... with me?" Her chin trembled. "You could... have anyone. Why would you settle... for Frankenstein's... monster?" she finished, bursting into sobs.

"Stop talking like that. I already said you're beautiful to me." He leaned forward. "Do you think I'm shallow?"

"No, but——"

"No more buts." He brushed his lips over hers, careful not to hurt her. "You make me so, so happy, darling. Can't you see that?"

When she smiled, he knew for sure, he'd never let her go.

# 55

# VINCENT

With the white walls, and beige-colored wooden floor, the room seemed to glow too brightly. Especially with the natural lighting coming from the skylight. Vincent squinted for the first few seconds, keeping his arm around Elora's shoulders. A few tremors passed through her body—they still happened from time to time since she was released from the hospital a few weeks ago, but she was getting better.

While she'd been staying in the hospital, he continuously wondered if she was healing physically. Yet, once released into his care, all he thought about was her mental wellbeing. He'd been terrified she'd shut him out, but if anything, she opened up more to him than before.

He'd held her hand before she had to stand in front of a judge and answer questions, and he watched with pride as she told her story. Richard's disappearance opened an investigation, but Elora, being hospitalized, had a solid alibi.

Vincent, on the other hand, was more than suspicious. But with friends in a crime organization and crooked judges, the monster's murder didn't come back to him. Not even to Benjamin. It also hadn't helped Richard's case that his body wasn't found.

Catherine, the photographer, busied herself with her equipment, but when she spotted them, she stopped. "You're finally here." She beamed, striding to them quickly.

He pulled her in a quick hug, then beamed at his girlfriend. "This is Elora Letan."

Catherine took Elora's hand, her brown eyes softening. "It's so good to finally meet you."

"I'm sorry Vincent insisted on doing the photoshoot with the way... I look." She crossed her arms as she averted her gaze from them, and he pressed his lips tight to stop from growling. She thought she looked horrifying when she looked as beautiful as ever, a survivor. Strong.

A few scars remained along the left side of her face, starting from her jawline to her ear, and one near her eye. On her right cheek, a smaller one was left behind—the one she hated the most since her hair couldn't cover it. Vincent had spent days holding her as she broke down into tears after looking at herself in the mirror. He wished more than anything that she'd see herself the same way he did. Her arms and legs had crisscrossed scars that were beginning to fade. Slowly, she started wearing sleeveless tops and even dresses. But it would take time, and he was more than willing to help along the way.

Catherine took a step closer. "Oh honey, you look beautiful. And you know what? We need models who have scars to show what they've survived. There are so many books about survivors breaking through the odds, finding their own ways through life. We need to show you on those covers."

A tiny sob escaped Elora, and Catherine pulled her in a hug. "You are beautiful. Don't ever think otherwise."

A smile curled his lips as Elora nodded at Catherine's words. The woman was a goddess for helping Elora feel better. She'd been working photography for several years, and had a way with people.

When Catherine pulled away, Elora leaned against Vincent, and his heart sped. He loved it when she approached him on her own terms, showing she wasn't afraid. That she knew he'd never hurt her.

Catherine clapped her hands and walked to a chest at the foot of the wall. "Here's what you ordered."

When she pulled out a navy-blue and black corset with a lace back flowing to the floor, Elora gasped.

She stared at Vincent. "You ordered this for me for the photoshoot?"

"Navy-blue suits you," he said with a grin.

Her cheeks flushed when Catherine pulled out panties made of lace, shaped as tiny shorts.

"I can't… wear that." She pointed at it with a shaky hand.

Catherine scoffed as she handed them to Elora. "Oh, you can honey, and you'll look sexy as hell. Now, go get changed behind the curtains, and come out when you're ready."

Elora turned a glare on Vincent. "And what about you? Are you wearing little lacy panties for this shoot?"

"I'll either have my black jeans or nothing a bit later." He winked as her blush deepened. Before he added anything else, she marched behind the curtain, and he smiled at her fiery attitude. It was like she was slowly coming back to life. And he loved it.

Catherine hadn't taken her gaze off Elora. "She's been through a lot, hasn't she?"

"Yes."

Her expression turned into a sort of haunted gaze. "She's tough. Tougher than she thinks or knows, but she'll see in time." She turned to Vincent and grinned. "And I'm sure you'll help her too."

"I'll do everything I can for her."

Elora stepped out from behind the curtain, wearing the corset and panties. Her hair fell loosely down her back, the brown color of her hair bringing out the dark blue. Catherine clapped her hands several times as she moved to Elora, staring at her from head to toe in the new outfit.

"Oh you look even more beautiful wearing that." Catherine took Elora's hand and pulled her to the small stage she had set up for the shoot. It was decorated in a Gothic style, matching Elora's look perfectly.

Vincent pulled his t-shirt off, and Elora swallowed hard as she watched him. Her skin turned pink, starting above her breasts, and climbing to her ears and cheeks.

Elora averted her gaze when she realized she'd been caught and wrapped her arms around her waist. "So... how does this work?"

Catherine moved to her camera and angled it. "We'll start by candid shots. Just get comfortable together, chat, do whatever you'd like." Her smile widened. "And then we'll try for specific poses."

Vincent hopped on the small stage with Elora and smiled. "How are you holding up?"

"I think I'm okay. I know I shouldn't be so nervous, but I guess I have some issues to work on." She half-shrugged, but the pain in her gaze was obvious.

Wrapping his arms around her waist, he brought her close. "It'll take time, but you don't have to do anything alone. I'm here for you whenever you need me."

The smile lit her face, and his pulse sped. "Thank you. You're *fantastic*."

He chuckled. "So are you. And one day, I hope you can see yourself the same way I do; perfect."

A few clicks resonated across the room, and Elora smiled. Leaning forward, he brushed his lips over hers, kissing her gently as a small whimper escaped her. He loved the noises she made.

This would be a fun photoshoot.

# EPILOGUE

## ELORA

*Dear dad,*

*I'm sorry I wasn't there for you like I should have been. My entire life you did everything to make sure I was healthy and happy, and when it was your turn to need help, I ignored you. Words will never describe the regret I feel, but I hope you knew I love you.*

*I left Richard. I'm sorry I ever gave him the power to hurt me, and you, Dad. The police declared Richard as missing, but I have the feeling he's gone forever. It changes nothing, but there's a weight lifted from my shoulders knowing I'm truly free. He'll never harm me again.*

*When Vincent came into my life, I changed. I wish you could have met him, Dad; you would have liked him. He's a good man, and although he doesn't think so, I know he is. I never thought I'd be as treasured by someone as I am with him. I don't know if I believe in an afterlife, but I hope you're somewhere now and you can hear me.*

*I promise I'll live to the fullest and follow my dreams. And I'll always keep you in my heart.*

*I love you very much, Dad.*
*Elora.*

❧

*E*lora folded the paper she wrote to her dad and slipped it into a small box next to her father's ashes. Vincent, along with Liana and Brad, had returned to Elora's house to pack her personal effects. With the help of Benjamin's connections, they sold the place quickly, and it was a relief for Elora not having to deal with returning there.

Writing a letter to her father was a recommended exercise by her new psychologist, and it helped Elora practice using her hand. Thankfully, the right one had taken less damage than the left, but simple tasks took effort.

The sun lowered behind the mountains in the distance, and she smiled. Vincent wasn't joking when he'd said how beautiful autumn was at his place in Ottawa. Most of the leaves turned a vivid red, orange, or yellow, creating an effect of flames engulfing the forest.

The part he hadn't mentioned was how charming his home was. No wonder he missed living here. He had built a back porch, wooden beams and framings, giving it a real cottage feel. A cool breeze fluttered through the windows, and she glanced at the matching furniture; it was a great place to sit and relax. Couches nestled next to the shelves anchored on the walls, and lights hung from the ceiling.

Vincent's arms wrapped around her waist, and she leaned into his chest.

"I'm nervous for Monday," she said with a laugh.

She'd landed her first ever job, and as a kindergarten teacher. She couldn't help the excitement and fear coursing through her mind.

He nuzzled her neck. "You'll do great. I know you will."

Her fingers found the one scar she couldn't hide. "You don't think they'll…" Her voice barely came out in a whisper as tears burned her eyes. She let out another small laugh. "Never mind, it's fine."

She pulled away, but he turned her, grasping her shoulders. "Do you want to talk about it?"

"What if the kids are scared of me because of the way I look? I don't want to frighten them…"

"Children can be cruel, but it's also the age when it's important for them to learn people come in all shapes, sizes, and scars. Teach them survivors sometimes have them, and it doesn't make you any less of a person." He traced his finger along her cheek and smiled. "You're still the most beautiful woman, darling. And I want you more than ever."

Her stomach clenched, and she took a step back, turning toward the scenery outside. Her eyes filled with tears, the screened windows blurring.

Once they settled things in Winnipeg, Vincent had brought Elora to his house for a visit. Throughout that time, he hadn't pushed once for intimacy. But she wasn't blind; he'd taken more cold showers than she could count since being here the last few months.

"Are you sure you still want me?" She rubbed her arms. "I mean, I wouldn't blame you if you'd break up with me, being damaged—"

"Don't finish that sentence." His voice was hard, almost a growl, and she jumped. When she faced him, he took a step closer. "I'm the one who received your medical report, remember?"

Her body grew stiff. "Exactly. You know what happened. Who wants to have sex with someone maimed? You need a stable person. You should find—"

She yelped when he drew her up in his arms and walked to the sofa. Once seated, she tried squirming off, but he tightened his grip. "I knew you'd need time to heal. Not only physically, but mentally and emotionally. I committed to you knowing this, and I don't intend on changing my mind."

"But… aren't you getting frustrated?" she asked quietly.

"Having blue balls is a small price to make sure when we are intimate, it's pleasurable for you. No matter how long it takes."

"But—"

"Once you get the doctor's approval, then we'll talk about it, okay?"

She bit her lower lip, but nodded.

He pulled her closer, and she rested her head on his chest. "I never want you to feel guilty about it."

She let out a breath, staying quiet as he stroked her back. The idea she'd had the past few weeks crossed her mind. She was nervous about going through with it, but for Vincent, she wanted to do something for them both. With a hidden smile, she closed her eyes, determined to break out of her shell with him.

❦

Rain poured onto the roof, and Elora approached the floor to ceiling window in the master bedroom. Lightning ripped through the sky, thunder pounding harder than her heart against her ribs. Storms didn't terrify her as much anymore, but they shook her a bit.

She glanced at the bed for the hundredth time and took a deep breath. Not that she didn't want to go through with her idea—she really did—she was just nervous she wouldn't pull it off. Her whole life, she was never comfortable with her body, and she certainly didn't find herself confident enough to do anything like this.

Vincent would return from work any minute. He'd gotten a job at a construction company in the tiny village, and when it rained, he usually stayed at the office later to help organize projects. It would be another few minutes before he arrived, but she was ready two hours ago in her eagerness to do this. She lusted like crazy with each passing day, but she was so nervous about starting anything that would end up with sex.

Elora and her psychologist worked on her fears, and as she progressed, Elora was ready to move past one of her issues. And she knew that with Vincent, not only would she be safe, but she'd enjoy it, too.

The door closed downstairs, and her breath caught in her throat. She stood in front of the mirror checking to make sure she was perfect... or as perfect as she could be.

Before leaving Winnipeg, Liana had taken Elora on a shopping spree, and Elora had bought a bunch of kinky items, including lingerie.

She wore a black bra with matching panties, but these were special. They had an opening at her backside, but were closed the rest of the way. She swallowed hard, wondering if the garter belt and thigh-high pantyhose were too much, but she scoffed. No, she was sure Vincent would love the entire outfit.

She slipped on her bathrobe, grinning at how strange she looked with makeup and clothing that looked like it could belong to her grandmother.

"Elora?" Vincent called from downstairs, and her chest tightened with excitement.

"I'm upstairs."

She patted the pocket of her robe, satisfied to feel the keys to the handcuffs hanging on the chair's armrests, and then grabbed the liquor she poured him. Rye, hold the ice. It was a good thing, since she prepared it an hour ago.

Vincent stepped inside the room, staring from her face to the drink with an arched eyebrow. "Should I ask?"

She grinned, pushing the glass in his hand. "I want to... do something, but I need it to go my way... at first."

"Now I'm more than curious. Continue," he said, his voice husky.

She pointed at the chair near their bed. "Please sit down."

He opened his mouth, then closed it, shaking his head as he did as she asked. Apparently, his curiosity won over his urge to take control.

She leaned forward and kissed him, his lips warm on hers as she grabbed the handcuffs hanging on the side. Before he had time to react, she cuffed his wrist and backed away.

His eyes widened for a second as he tugged at the restraints, then his gaze darkened, fixating on her.

"Oh darling, you're about to regret this."

Her pulse throbbed in all the right places as she giggled. "It doesn't end here."

She slipped off the robe slowly, and his jaw clenched, the corners of his mouth curling into a lecherous smile. He moved the glass, the liquid inside swirling. "A chair won't keep me in place."

"True, but the thing is heavy, and I trust you'll honor my request that I need this to start with me in control."

She turned and bent to retrieve the key from her discarded robe. Her face heated as she took her time, knowing he could see how her panties were designed and what she had in mind.

"Fuck…" he groaned, inhaling deeply.

She placed the key on the side of the table where he couldn't reach unless he dragged the chair, then met his gaze.

"I left one hand loose so you can touch yourself."

He gaped at her, but desire pooled in his eyes, mixing with something that looked like anger. She took a deep breath, reminding herself what he often told her; communication was key.

"Do you want me to stop this?"

He shook his head, leaning into the chair. "Definitely not, but I promise I'll make you scream in pleasure once you give me permission to unlock myself."

Her panties soaked at the thought, and she pushed her legs together. His gaze lowered, catching the movement, and he grinned. Thunder crashed from the sky as she moved to the small bag she left on the bedside table. She pulled out a butt plug and lube, then proceeded to the bed.

She turned her back to him, but the way she angled the mirror, it allowed her to see him. He took a drink from his glass, then set it beside him, leaning forward. He caught her gaze and lifted his restrained hand, reminding her of what he'd do once he was free.

Opening the lube, she dribbled a generous amount onto the plug. Her ass clenched as though knowing what came next, but she exhaled, relaxing her muscles. She'd practiced with several sizes for a while, wanting to grow accustomed to one day surprise Vincent, and tonight was finally the time. She wanted him inside her so badly, she almost felt shameful.

Almost.

She grabbed an extra pillow and slid it under her hips, then lowered herself forward so her backside stuck out in the air. In front of him. If she was ever going to die of embarrassment, it would be at that moment.

The growl resonating from him made her smile, knowing she was desirable for him to sound so animalistic. She reached behind, rubbing the end of the butt plug between her cheeks, pushing in and out slow. Her toes curled, and she moaned as her muscles clenched around the toy, holding it in tight.

She lifted herself on her hands and knees, her breath catching as she caught his gaze in the mirror. With his free hand grasping his cock, he moved up and down slowly, his expression dark.

"Do you like it?" she whispered, spreading her cheeks, so he'd see she picked a plug with the end shaped in a heart with a blue jewel.

"I swear if you don't give me the go ahead to unlock these, I'll break them off." His voice was raw with lust.

She took the bottle of lube and gave him a small smile. "I'm using bigger and bigger plugs, but they don't fill me enough. Could you pull this one out and put your cock inside my ass instead? Please?"

A mixture of a snarl and a groan escaped him as he bolted to his feet, dragging the chair to the table as though it weighed nothing. Her eyes widened as he unlocked the handcuff and stalked toward the bed slowly.

"Turn and face me, darling." His voice snapped her into motion, and she spun, kneeling at the edge.

She shifted, the plug inside her sending jolts of pleasure.

His mouth curled into a dark smile. "Will you undress me?"

She got to her feet, her hands trembling as she pulled his t-shirt over his head. He grasped her wrist and kissed her palm before placing it at his belt. Her shoulders relaxed as she unbuckled it. She wanted to please him so badly; her panties grew wetter with every passing second. She kneeled at his feet, pulling his jeans to his ankles, and licked her lips as she stared at his shaft.

His scent teased her, and she needed to taste him. She grasped his erection, moving her hand up and down as he groaned. Darting out her tongue, she flicked the head, then took his cock into her mouth. She loved it. It tasted like he did, but stronger. She sucked hard as he slid his fingers through her hair, a shudder running through him.

She lifted his balls in her palm, fondling them as she sucked the pre-cum on the tip. Giving a blowjob wasn't something she usually enjoyed, but with Vincent, it was as pleasurable to give as to receive. Her nipples tightened as she swirled her tongue around his shaft, breathing in his scent.

Gently, he pulled her away, staring down with hunger in his eyes. He grasped her shoulders and helped her to her feet. Before she had time to say anything, he kissed her, hard. His hands slid to her back, unclipping her bra, then moved lower to the garter belt.

He withdrew, his breathing uneven. "Turn."

She did, and heat engulfed her body as he crouched behind her, lowering her stockings. He pressed on the end of the plug, and she gasped.

"I love this color on you," he said in a husky voice.

When he pushed the panties down, she stiffened. "I never wanted to do anything intimate because I'm scared it would end with… vaginal sex. I bought these to make sure it couldn't happen."

He lifted her feet, so the underwear came off, then stood and grasped her breasts from behind. "I won't touch you there. You're not healed, so it's out of the question." He spun her and grinned. "But I want access to your clit so I can make you come hard while I fuck your tight little hole."

Her face heated at the words she wanted to say; they felt too vulgar. Yet, she couldn't help herself. "Well, are you going to fuck me or talk about it?"

The laughter that left him was borderline evil, and she backed away until she fell onto the bed. He smirked as he spun her, and she crawled forward to place herself on the pillow.

He moved the plug, pulling it out a bit, then pushed it inside. She moaned, burying her face into the mattress. He pulled it out, and she gasped at the sudden loss of pressure.

She glanced over her shoulder, swallowing hard as he squeezed the lube bottle between her cheeks. He spread them, and shudders of pleasure ran through her as he rubbed it along her sensitive spot. Positioning the tip of his cock against it, he pushed in slowly, taking his time. She winced, panting as his shaft slid into her.

Hell, he was big.

"Ah… Vincent…" She wanted to beg him to stop, but took another deep breath instead. "Wait…"

He stopped moving, and she slumped onto the mattress, relaxing as her muscles adjusted to his girth. His hand moved between her body and the pillow, his finger circling her clit.

"That's it, darling… relax. You can take all of me." His voice sent her into renewed lust.

He pushed in, adding cool lube to his cock as he drove farther inside. With one last push, his thighs hit the back of her legs, and she let out a moan. She'd never felt so full in her life. The pressure built to a burn while his attention on her clit brought her closer to the edge.

"Fuck me. Please. I need you."

He slid out, then thrust in, slow. He leaned close to her ear, and she gasped as his cock pushed in even deeper. "You make me so hard," he said in a rough tone.

She gasped as he straightened, lifting her ass higher as his movements sped, pumping inside her like a burning desire.

She clutched at the sheets, tightening her grip as she cried out his name. The sound of their skin slapping filled the room, his groaning and panting turning her on more than she thought possible.

"Come for me. I want to hear you scream."

He rubbed his finger over her clit, and a wave of pleasure

crashed over her as her muscles clenched. She screamed, her own desire rolling along her inner thighs as she shook.

"Ah… Fuck yes." He growled as he jerked faster and faster until his cock spasmed, and he flooded himself into her.

He pulled out slowly, and she trembled at the intensity of her orgasm.

"Wow," she said, panting.

He chuckled as he got to his feet, and she smiled as he returned with moist towelettes. Once done with cleaning up, he lay next to her, and they faced each other in silence.

The thunderstorm continued outside, the rain hitting the windows in sheets of water. He pulled her closer, his thumb tracing along her jaw.

"What did I do to deserve someone as magnificent as you?"

Her heart swelled. "I ask myself the same question about me deserving you. I love you."

"And I love you, darling."

He sat up and grinned. "I forgot I had something to show you. Arrived in the mail today." He shot her a playful look. "Someone distracted me, though."

Arching an eyebrow, she watched as he left the bedroom, and a few seconds later, Vincent returned holding a photo, and she kneeled on the bed as he sat next to her.

Her eyes widened. It was a photo from their photoshoot together; the only one showing their faces. Their gazes were fixed on one another like they were each other's lifelines. In a way, it was exactly that.

"It's… perfect." Her heart swelled. "We look so… natural."

He kissed her cheek. "Well, a picture is worth a thousand words."

She giggled, shaking her head. "Puns, now?"

He put the photo on the armchair. "Actually, it's a proverb," he said with a grin as he traced his fingers along her thigh. "But I prefer the real thing."

"So do I," she breathed, grasping his hand.

Slowly, he grasped her wrist, and pulled her onto his lap, holding her close.

She smiled, the sound of his heartbeat comforting. "I don't need a thousand words," she said as she stared at him. "Just three."

A gentle expression softened his gaze. "I love you."

"And I love you."

# AUTHOR NOTES

Well, it's finally done. I won't lie; this wasn't an easy story to write, but it had been filling my mind for a long time. It was originally ready around two years ago, but I lost my nerve to continue working on it. I'm glad I waited because I ended up adding more to the story and changing a few details that, in my opinion, make it stronger. I also want to say thank you to Wendy; she had beta read my manuscript when I thought it was ready, and this year, edited it despite the craziness going on – with her usual honest critiques and *[much needed]* humour, she made writing this a little easier. Thank you so, so much Wendy.

# ABOUT THE AUTHOR

M. A. Fréchette writes the darker side of romance.

Being an extremist, she loves both the dark aspects of life and everything sweet. All her stories are either set in Canada where she lives or in alternate worlds she made up while living within her imagination. When not writing, she thinks of the next scene or plot while enjoying her work as a cover designer. Although she has a fascination for monsters, with a bachelor degree in criminology, she understands there's no need to create the paranormal; humans are capable of inflicting nightmares of their own.

*Please feel free to reach out through any social media. I truly love hearing from readers!*

facebook.com/AuthorMAF

twitter.com/authormaf

instagram.com/authormaf

amazon.com/author/authormaf

bookbub.com/authors/m-a-frechette

goodreads.com/authormaf

# ALSO BY M. A. FRÉCHETTE

**A Demon's Love series**

MY SOUL TO GIVE (book #1)

MY LIFE TO TAKE (book #2)

CPSIA information can be obtained
at www.ICGtesting.com
Printed in the USA
LVHW090348260121
677402LV00005B/156

9 781777 069858